FALLING FOR THE UNDERDOG

FALLING FOR THE UNDERDOG

A Rescue Dog Romance

CASEY GRIFFIN

CHARMING FROG
PUBLISHING

ISBN: 978-1-990470-10-3

2nd Edition Large Print Paperback: September 2021

Published by Charming Frog Publishing

www.CharmingFrogPublishing.com

For Devin
Finally

JOIN CASEY'S PACK

Casey Griffin's newsletter followers get access to exclusive content such as free stories, fun gifts, and random shenanigans (who doesn't love those?). They're also the first to hear about her new books.

SIGN UP AT CASEYGRIFFIN.COM

1

DOGGY STYLE

Fur flew under Addison Turner's skilled touch as though she were Edward Scissorhands, sculpting purebred pooches into masterpieces. Her current muse came in the form of a fluffy bichon frise named Elvis. Unfortunately, his hair clippings stuck to the glittering details of her black sequined dress—not exactly the come-hither look she was going for.

Frowning, she assessed the state of her cocktail dress, picking at the tufts of fur that clung to it. It wasn't the most sensible uniform for grooming dogs, but tonight was special. It was a cocktail mixer that kicked off the two-week-long parade of events leading up to the Western Dog Show—and Addison had a VIP backstage pass to promote her dog-styling business.

However, a good PR campaign wasn't the only

1

reason she'd been looking forward to the dog show. She also wanted to build a few "personal relations" of her own. Tonight was the night she was going to meet her Prince Charming.

Addison's assistant, Melody, finished cutting the last of Elvis's nails and noticed the wardrobe mishap. "Oh, no. Your dress. How are you going to hook your man now?"

"It's okay." Addison winked. "I can make anything look good. Even dog hair."

Melody grabbed a brush and worked the excess hair out of Elvis's coat. "You keep talking about this perfect guy, but I don't think you've told me his name."

"That's because I don't know it … yet," Addison replied. But he was out there; she could feel it. If only she could get a free moment to go meet him.

The mixer was being held in the grand ballroom of the historic Regency Center on Sutter Street. The neoclassical surroundings created the perfect romantic ambiance for the elite dog-lovers of San Francisco to rub elbows, not to mention size up the competition before the dog show in two weeks' time.

Addison sighed just thinking about it. The glitz, the glamor, the extravagance, the beauty. Nobody showered their four-legged friends with more affection and luxury than hopeful winners of the coveted Best in Show award. Now *that* was a client list she wanted to tap into. She was going to be the Coco Chanel of the four-legged world, and the next two weeks were going to make her or break her.

Unfortunately, she was stuck behind the scenes. Literally. She'd been allotted the ballroom's built-in stage to set up her portable grooming station and pamper the party's furry guests. While that should have allowed her the best view of the event, the stage curtains had been closed. Apparently, a guest had complained. Maybe they didn't enjoy witnessing all the hard work being done while they enjoyed their escargot and champagne.

As Addison trimmed around the dog's face, her normally steady hand shook. Not with nerves, but irritation. Elvis's owner, Kitty Carlisle, hovered nearby. She twitched with each clip of the scissors, as though Addison was going to accidentally slip and cut a jugular vein.

Kitty paced across the stage behind the curtain. Twelve pairs of canine eyes watched the woman's anxious movements with interest. Addison already had a full array of clients lounging on colorful embroidered pillows, all in various stages of her patented Pampered Puppies Program. She'd given them puppy pawdicures, Shih-Tzu shiatsus, bowwow baths and brushes, and hound hydrotherapy, all free of charge to create buzz.

Kitty flinched again and tensed. She looked ready to lunge for Elvis.

"Mrs. Carlisle," Addison addressed the nervous woman. "Are you certain you wouldn't feel more comfortable out in the ballroom, enjoying the cocktail mixer?"

The older woman stiffly shook her head. Not a single lacquered white hair stirred. "I'm perfectly fine here with Elvis." She cringed as though Melody's brush was going to grow teeth and bite her dog. "You just never know who you can trust during competition season." Her pug-like eyes bulged conspiratorially.

Addison bristled at the comment. Surely Kitty wasn't suggesting that Addison would do anything to risk a show dog's chances. That would mean the death of her business before it even had the opportunity to take off. She was only just beginning to break into the niche show dog market.

One last snip of the scissors and Elvis's traditional show cut was complete. His head looked like what Addison could only describe as a ball of white cotton candy. Two black eyes blinked out from the sphere of fur. It mirrored Kitty's '60s beehive hairstyle almost perfectly. Or perhaps Kitty modeled herself after her dog.

For the pièce de résistance, Addison fastened a formal bow tie and tuxedo collar with a hidden metal leashing ring—one of her own creations—

around Elvis's neck. *Fashion, meet function*, Addison thought.

Wiping away the mounds of white, feathery fur, Addison unclipped Elvis from the grooming arm above the table. She stood back and held out her arms, Vanna White style, to display Kitty's dog. "What do you think?"

Kitty reached out and straightened the bow tie. "How charming."

Was that an actual smile? Addison felt giddy, like she was on an ice cream high.

"It's part of my premier fashion line for four-legged fashionistas. It's called Fido Fashion." Addison whipped out a sparkly pink flyer and held it up. "I'm launching the line on the same weekend as the dog show. You and Elvis should come check it out. In fact, I'm still looking for volunteers to model the designs. Maybe Elvis would like to be involved." She gave Kitty a hopeful smile, trying her best not to come off as a desperate salesperson.

Kitty clung to Elvis like a mother on her kid's first day of school. "I don't know …"

"He'll get to keep any outfits he models," Addison offered.

Biting her lip, Kitty took the flyer. "I'll think about it."

She cradled Elvis to her chest and whisked him across the stage. His black eyes bored into Addison over Kitty's shoulder like something out

5

of a horror flick. Addison shivered as they ducked through the heavy stage curtains to the main ballroom.

When the thick drapes parted, classic jazz music punctuated by the clink of glasses and the murmur of voices drifted into Addison's workspace. She peeked through a gap. Men in tuxes and women in beautiful cocktail dresses danced across the blond hardwood floor, flirted on opulent camelback sofas, and showed off their sure-to-win purebreds near the cocktail bar.

It was all so perfect, just like Addison's life. Her business was doing well enough that she could afford to hire an assistant, and she was about to launch her new fashion line. Everything was unfolding like a Hollywood blockbuster movie, except for one thing: her leading man had yet to be cast.

Okay, so she was more like the makeup artist than the leading lady, but after the fashion show turned out to be a hit and her business reached a whole new level of success, that would all change. It was time for her Cinderella story to begin.

Addison could feel the clock run down as she hid behind the scenes. She'd been so busy that she hadn't had a chance to enjoy the evening herself.

Maybe I could slip away for a little while, she thought.

She glanced back at the work left to be done. Equipment awaited dismantling, furry floors required sweeping, restless dogs needed arranging for the big reveal at ten o'clock. That's when she noticed her own object of affection saunter across the stage: a beautiful, long-haired cream dachshund.

Like a movie star, the doxie strode imperiously down the length of red carpet rolled across the stage to join the lineup of other stars. Her beaded flapper-girl dress glittered beneath the lights.

As the doxie passed each dog show contender, she eyed up the competition. Her ample chest swelled with confidence—which said much about her belief in her own beauty, as these pups were the crème de la crème of the western United States.

Finding her adversaries wanting, the beautiful blonde huffed. With a flick of her long, wavy locks, she returned to her pink velvet pillow that had been embroidered with her name in gold: *Princess.*

Addison walked over and scratched Princess behind the ears. "What do you think of our customers? Do they pass your rigid beauty inspection?"

Princess yawned, unimpressed.

"Of course, they don't even come close to your caliber, your highness." Addison gave her a little bow. "You don't need to compete in the dog show. We already know you're the best."

"Woof," Princess agreed, then bestowed a lick upon Addison's hand. *You have pleased us.*

Addison didn't mention the real reason she wouldn't enter Princess in the show. Despite deserving every award there was, she would sadly lose.

An angular limb deformity had left Princess with one leg shorter than the rest. It had devastated her previous owner to discover his precious Princess would never be able to compete in a conformation show. Devastated him so much it seemed he couldn't even look at her. Instead, he'd dropped off Princess at a shelter.

Addison recalled the day she'd met Princess at the San Francisco Dachshund Rescue Center, where she volunteered regularly. Maybe the limb that made the doxie a little different was why she'd felt an instant connection with the abandoned show dog. It meant they had something in common. Only, Addison's so-called imperfection couldn't be seen by the naked eye. No one could guess what hid beneath all that perfect makeup, hair, and stylish outfits.

But beauty was only skin deep. It was what was on the inside that mattered. While Princess would never reach the pinnacle of pooch perfection sought after by dog show enthusiasts, she was number one in Addison's heart.

Now, if only Addison could find that special

someone who saw her the same way. Preferably one with two legs.

Addison scanned the collection of aspiring champions lined up on the stage, all pampered and ready to show off. She gave a nod of approval. "I think they look pretty good."

"Good?" Melody asked. "They look amazing! Everything's perfect." She gave Addison a reassuring smile. "You've outdone yourself tonight. Once the curtains open at ten o'clock and everyone sees your talents, they'll be scrambling to come to your fashion show."

"You think so?"

"I know so."

A Pekingese named King Winky Von Rainbow Valley, or Kingy for short, was wandering around Addison's supply bag. He'd obviously sniffed out her treat stash. Plucking him up into her arms, she carried him back to his pillow and snuck him a treat.

"Don't tell the others, okay?" she told him.

She fluffed the ascot around his neck. The orange koi embroidered onto the silk accented his royal blue velvet smoking jacket perfectly.

Addison picked up a half-inch barrel curling iron, ready to get started on a silky terrier's bangs.

Melody stopped her with a look. "Back away from the curling iron. Everything is ready for the reveal. Just go out there already and advertise a little, promote, rub elbows, and enjoy yourself."

Addison looked around at all the equipment again. "But there's still so much to clean up."

"I'll get the stage ready for ten o'clock. Don't worry." Melody waved Addison away. "You need people to put a face to your infamous name and your work. Now go."

Addison sighed and put down the iron. "You're right. Thanks."

After checking on a Maltese whose Rainbow Frenzy nail polish was drying, Addison brushed the dog hair from her dress. She grabbed the leash belonging to a pinscher named Rosie and clipped it to the new collar fastened around the dog's neck.

The piece was designed to look like a gold and ruby necklace. Addison had created it for the pricier end of her line; each item was made with quality gemstones and even had a GPS tracking chip hidden within. More importantly, the collar was a showstopper piece that she knew would blow Rosie's hot owner away.

As Addison prepared to make her debut, Princess pranced over, ready to shake her tail on the dance floor.

"Don't worry, I wouldn't leave you behind," Addison told the doxie. "Are you ready to go make some friends?"

In response, Princess spun in a circle, already getting her groove on. *Let's get jiggy with it.*

Addison fastened Princess's lead to her Art

Deco pearl collar and waved to Melody. "I'm going to return Rosie to her owner."

"Good luck. I hope he likes it." Melody gave Addison a wink that told her she didn't mean the grooming they'd done on his pinscher.

"Who wouldn't?" Addison threw her friend a flirtatious smile. She checked her hair in one of the mirrors placed around their makeshift salon, ensuring it was perfect, then whipped the thick curtains aside.

The moment Addison emerged, expensive perfume replaced the smell of wet dog. The sounds of barking faded beneath the calming clarity of classic jazz floating over from the band in the far corner. From high above, teardrop chandeliers cast a warm glow on the guests circulating around the ballroom.

She felt like Alice passing through the looking glass. It was an entirely different world. Sure, it wasn't a singles mixer, but it was still a social event —something she hadn't seen much of since opening up shop two years earlier. Finally, a chance to find her Prince Charming, a part of the happily ever after she'd been dreaming about since she was a little girl.

She descended the stage stairs like Cinderella at the ball, escorting Rosie and Princess. The dogs strutted with confidence, owning the room. Only, Princess's stride had the slightest hiccup, a little limp that you'd notice only if you were really paying attention. Addison liked to think of it as a swagger.

With the lights dimmed, hundreds of candles around the room set the mood. Their flickering glow reflected off the gilded wall décor, champagne glasses, diamonds caressing throats, gold Rolexes, and her own dazzling sequined dress. The ambiance, the energy, the allure. It was all so romantic, a real fairy tale. The perfect place to meet her Prince Charming.

Addison's eyes cast over show dog owners and event supporters sipping their martinis and pinot grigio in search of Rex Harrison, Rosie's owner. She spotted him at the bar in the center of the room.

Hair fashionably coiffed, body svelte in his three-piece suit, Rex leaned against the bar. He watched the room with a confident ease as he sipped his drink. Whiskey, maybe. No. A martini. Just like James Bond. Yes, he looked exactly like the secret agent—Pierce Brosnan style.

Ooh, Addison liked that. *Two thumbs up.*

When Rex spotted her slinking toward him, his eyes drifted down the length of her curvy body with appreciation. Well … she thought so until his eyes didn't roam back up. They remained fixed on Rosie.

Ouch.

Second-guessing herself, Addison glanced down at her dress with its sleek black lines and revealing—though, not too revealing—neckline. There was a fine line between saying, "I'm your *one*" and "I'm your *one-night stand*." But when she noticed the tall, dark, and sexy bartender flash her a lingering look over the bottles of top-shelf liquor, she knew it wasn't the dress's fault.

She flashed the bartender a smile. *Definitely an option*, she thought. Maybe she'd stick around for a drink. Then he returned the smile—or ten. Drawing herself up, she headed over to meet her new prince.

2

BEWARE OF DOG

"Rex Harrison." Addison smiled as she approached the bar. "Rosie is all ready for you. What do you think?"

To let him know she didn't mean his pinscher's grooming, she leaned against the bar to give him a better view of that low neckline—even Prince Charming probably needed baiting.

She toyed with Rosie's leash, wrapping it teasingly around her finger. But Rex's loving gaze was still glued to his pedigree pooch. Oblivious to her efforts, he bent down and gave Rosie a pet.

Addison thought she heard a soft snort from behind the bar. When she turned to the bartender, he was studiously wiping down the glass counter, but she could have sworn that was a smirk on his full lips.

"Wow," Rex said, drawing her attention back

to him. "Rosie's fur has never looked so shiny. How did you manage that?"

Addison beamed. "That's the yogurt and oatmeal rub."

"Yogurt?" He glanced up and seemed to notice her for the first time.

If she'd had a tail, it would have wagged. "The yogurt strips away the dirt and adds moisture, while the oatmeal treats the skin and softens the fur. It also makes for an excellent breakfast," she joked.

He smiled, standing up to take in the full view of her body. "I can think of better breakfasts to make."

"You like to cook?"

"Only when it's for someone special." Rex swirled his drink before taking a sip, eyeing her above the rim. "Maybe I could cook for you sometime."

That would make Addison "someone special." "That sounds nice."

He reached into his suit coat. "Here's my card. Why don't you call me sometime?"

"Maybe I will." She took the card and traded it for Rosie's leash.

"Thanks again," he said. "Come on, Rosie. Shall we go for a walk?"

The pinscher's nubby black tail wiggled in response.

Rex gave Addison a wink and turned to head

across the ballroom, holding the leash aloft in true show form. Rosie trotted alongside him, already showing off for the judges attending the cocktail mixer.

Addison was watching him stroll away when a small wastebasket was thrust in front of her, obscuring her view. She flinched and turned to find the sexy bartender holding it out. His dark eyebrows quirked up as he shook the basket expectantly.

She frowned at it. "What's that for?"

"For that card," he said.

"For Rex's card? Why?" She bit her lip, wondering if he wanted to give her his number instead. "He told me to call him."

"You and about ten other women at this party tonight." He shrugged and put the wastebasket under the bar again. "But it's your call."

Her face fell. "Ten?"

The bartender tilted his mop of dark curls across the ballroom where Rex was slipping another card from his pocket. He flashed it at a young brunette server.

"Oh ..."

"Don't feel bad," the bartender said. "I've got eyes like an Afghan hound. I see all. I know all. Most of all when it comes to slimeballs like him."

Addison gave the tall bartender the once-over. He had a certain tilt to his square jaw that spoke of confidence or cockiness—she wasn't sure which. However, she was sure that, as a bartender, he'd had plenty of conversations across a bar with a pretty woman to make it the latter.

She threw him a wicked grin. "Is that right? Or does it just take one to know one?"

She'd been that woman across the bar before, had heard every cheesy pickup line there was— she'd certainly fallen for enough of them. And she was dangerously close to falling for his.

He flashed a good-humored smile. "No. It's because I'm in an ideal position to people-watch, to observe the human species and understand what makes them tick. I've had years of practice."

"I bet you have," she teased. "And I'm sure it has nothing to do with the fact that if you ply anyone with enough alcohol, they'll spill their guts."

"What can I say? People open up to a bartender. I've seen and heard it all. Nothing surprises me anymore."

He held her cornflower blue eyes with his own dark gaze, and she got the impression he could sell a Jägerbomb to a nun. Maybe he had. She wondered what kinds of things he'd seen and heard.

"But there's more to it than that," he continued, rearranging the liquor bottles so that all the labels faced out. "There's a difference between what people are telling you and what they're saying. You just have to know how to read between the lines. It can be how someone enters the room, in the way they dress, what drink they order, how fast they drink it. Body language, you know?"

"Is that so?"

"Take you, for example." His eyes roved over her.

Addison leaned in, excited to see where this was going. "What about me?"

"You walk in here like you own the place, yet you're practically the help—"

"I'm not the help." Her chin rose indignantly. "I'm an artist."

"And your canvas … dogs?" He gestured to Princess.

"Well, I am an artist. Business is booming," she told him defensively. "Before long, everyone in the doggy couture world will know who I am. I'll be a household name."

"What kind of house?" he asked with a sly grin. "A dog house?"

He was making fun of her. This was so not where she thought this was going.

"Look …" She glanced down at his nametag. "Felix. Canine fashion is very popular, I'll have you know." She ran a critical eye over him. "But what would you know about fashion?"

He wasn't even clean-shaven for the stylish event. And his loose curls flopping around unchecked told her he'd probably never heard of styling gel. However, she had to admit he had a nice head of hair. Just long enough that the soft waves curled around his handsome face.

As though he noticed her scrutiny, he tucked a curl behind his ear. "Okay, okay. I've been working the dog show scene long enough to know people get really into trendy dog stuff."

"Good. See? You don't know what you're talking about. And you don't know the first thing about me."

"Don't I, *Addison Turner?*"

Her mouth popped open. She was about to ask how he knew her name when he held up one of her business cards. "I assume this belongs to you. I've been finding them left all over the bar." He bit the inside of his cheek, clearly trying not to laugh. "I'm running out of garbage bags from cleaning them up."

Ugh! Okay, he was so *not* her Prince Charming.

Addison didn't need this kind of negativity. "Excuse me. But I have to look for someone." Her shoulders kicked back as she walked away with Princess.

Felix called out to her. "Wait! Wait. You didn't let me finish."

Addison hesitated. As hard as she tried, she couldn't seem to leave, especially once she saw the sheepish look he gave her. Cautiously, she returned to the bar.

"You're right. I don't know everything about you," he began. "But I do know that your posture is strong and proud, like you're six feet tall, not five-foot-nothing."

She scowled. "Five-foot-two." Why was she even bothering to argue with him?

"Five-two. Okay." He held up his hands. "You're clearly confident, gorgeous, intelligent …"

She smiled.

"But desperate."

She gasped. "Desperate?!" Her voice rose, then she noticed an elderly couple with a Tibetan terrier shoot a look her way. She lowered her voice and hissed across the bar. "What do you mean 'desperate'?"

"Your eyes scan this room like laser beams. Your target? Any single man."

Her mouth dropped open, and a sound of complete and utter indignation came out. When she couldn't find an argument, she snapped it shut and looked at Princess like "Can you believe this guy?" But she couldn't ignore Princess's piercing stare. The pup knew Addison too well. Okay, so maybe she was coming on a little strong.

She gave her dog a look that said "traitor" and placed Princess on a stool. "I'm not desperate. I'm just determined. I happen to be looking for Mr. Perfect."

"Then it's your lucky day. You've found him." Felix spread his arms, presenting himself. "Right here."

Addison snorted and rolled her eyes. "We must be talking about a different guy."

He chuckled, not deterred in the slightest. "Oh, you mean a different perfect guy. Sorry about that." He went back to wiping the counter with his cloth. "I'll let you in on a little secret. There's no guy who's perfect."

"Sure there is," she said. "I just haven't found him yet."

As hard as she tried to ignore the guy, Felix had piqued her curiosity. He was a smooth talker, engaging, with an undeniably charming smile that bordered on devilish, the kind of smile that probably earned him a mint in tips.

"Look, I'm not saying your determination is a bad thing. You know what you want. But you're like a woman on the prowl. I can feel the anxiety oozing off you."

Addison rolled her eyes. "You cannot."

"In fact, you're getting it all over my counter." To prove his point, he picked up his cloth and shooed her away before wiping down the spotless glass.

"And I'm not anxious."

"Really?" His eyes dropped pointedly.

She followed his gaze and froze as she noticed the confetti in her hands. She'd shredded Rex Harrison's card into a million pieces. Okay, so maybe she was a bit on edge. It didn't mean she was desperate.

Felix reached under the bar and brought out the wastepaper basket again. He held it up while Addison threw away the evidence.

He leaned against the bar, resting on his elbows like he was at home and not in a room full of San Francisco's high society. "Maybe you're not desperate, but you're coming off that way. You're a pretty woman. Let the guys come to you. Besides, what are you in such a rush for? You can't be more than twenty-four."

"I'm twenty-eight. And thank you." She liked how sincere he sounded. It curbed a tiny bit of her annoyance with him. "But if I've learned anything from running my own business, it's that you can't wait around for things to happen. You have to make them happen, take chances, put yourself out there."

"Well, just don't put yourself *so* out there." He gestured with his hands like "out there" was an actual place to avoid.

But where that place was, Addison couldn't be sure. "What do you mean?"

He leaned in until they were close enough that she could smell his cologne. The kind of cologne she'd follow a man around a store just to inhale. Princess must have smelled it too, because she placed her front paws on the counter to get closer. Felix gave her a soft rub under her chin.

"You have to be logical about it. Choosy," he said. "You've got to hedge your bets and make a wise investment of your time. Think of it like a numbers game."

"Love isn't logical." Addison laughed, wondering what cave this guy crawled out of. "Love is a dream come true. It's destiny. You can't explain it with numbers and odds. It's a feeling." She sighed. "Like when Meg Ryan hears her computer tell her 'You've got mail' and it's from Tom Hanks. Love is Julie Andrews spinning on a grassy knoll, singing 'The Hills Are Alive.' It's the wind beneath Rose's arms as Jack holds her at the front of the *Titanic*, and the orchestra builds to a climax and—"

"And don't forget lollipops, rainbows, and unicorns." There was a condescending smile on his full, way-too-luscious lips.

She cocked a perfectly penciled eyebrow. "Clearly, someone like you wouldn't understand. You're obviously not my Mr. Perfect."

Felix's eyebrows shot up, but he shrugged it off. "Fair enough."

He moved to the other side of the bar and began stacking clean glasses into a delicate pyramid. After a minute, a pretty server sauntered up to place a few orders.

Princess watched her chin-scratcher leave with a whine. *I didn't dismiss you.*

Addison turned her back on the bar and continued her search. She was done wasting time on a guy who made fun of her career, insulted her, called her desperate, and thought love was about hedging her bets. She hadn't pulled out her best dress that night for nothing. Prince Charming was somewhere in that room. She could feel it. And it most certainly wasn't Felix.

Princess followed her cue and turned around on her stool to face the dance floor. She jutted her chest out, acting all *I'm too good for you anyway.*

Addison's eyes scanned the room, totally not like lasers, checking for wedding bands on fingers. But there were hundreds of people there that night. Finding Prince Charming was going to be like trying to find a dachshund in a hot dog factory.

After a few moments, she picked up Princess and circled to the other side of the bar where Felix was talking with the server—shamelessly flirting, more like it. Addison wondered if she was one of his "numbers." Not that she blamed him. The server was pretty, if a little obvious; she wore a bright red bra under a thin, white button-up shirt.

Setting Princess down on another stool, Addison took out a stack of business cards from her clutch. She arranged them neatly on the countertop while she waited. Finally, Red Bra left with a tray of champagne glasses.

Addison leaned closer to the bar to get Felix's attention. "If I were to hedge my bets," she began hesitantly, "you know, filter out some rainbows and unicorns, where exactly would I start?"

Felix's eyes slid over to her. He seemed to think twice about helping her before finally relenting. Throwing the white cloth over his shoulder, he leaned in and dropped his voice.

"You have to look for subtle clues. Don't be too hasty. Just sit back and watch."

She pursed her lips. "What am I watching for?"

"General behavior. For example, if they're eyeing up every skirt that walks by, then you'll just be a number to them. Another skirt."

"Like Rex."

"Like Rex," he agreed.

While she was watching for clues, a customer strolled up to the bar with his English bulldog in tow. He was maybe ten years older than Addison with salt and pepper flecking his hair. His smile showed all his brilliant white teeth, and when he turned it on her, she found herself glancing at his ring finger. Finding it conveniently naked, she smiled back.

Addison waited off to the side while he ordered a whiskey on the rocks and left. Once he was out of earshot, she leaned across the counter. "How about that guy?"

"Married," Felix said.

She frowned. "But he wasn't wearing a ring."

"He took it off." He tucked away the bottle of whiskey. "There was a faint white line around his ring finger where the sun couldn't tan it."

"Maybe he's recently divorced," she said.

"Or separated. And if it's that fresh, do you want to risk being a rebound?"

"Okay, let's try someone younger then. How about that guy over there?" She pointed across the room to the man tapping his foot to the jazz music.

Felix's eyes flitted around until he spotted the guy. He shook his head. "You're barking up the wrong tree. He's gay."

"Really?" She appraised the man in question. "I usually have pretty decent gaydar. How can you tell?"

He smirked. "Because he gave me his number."

Her head snapped toward him. "Are you …?" She eyed him, searching for the clues he saw in others, reading between his lines.

Felix shook his head. "Considering what the sight of you in that dress does to me, I'd say I'm straight."

Addison opened her mouth, but no sound came out. Before she could find something to say, another man came up to the bar. This time, she ignored the newcomer. Instead, she gave Felix another look as he fixed a Bloody Mary.

The bartender held himself like he was the biggest, baddest dog in the neighborhood and he knew it. And *big* he was. Broad-shouldered and muscular, he stood a good foot and a half above her—which wasn't tough, since she was so short. But he wasn't the hard, ripped kind of muscular that meant his favorite topic would be how many grams of protein he'd eaten that day or how many reps he'd done. It was a comfortable kind of muscular. The kind made for working rather than looks and was perfect for snuggling. Not that Addison was imagining what it would be like to snuggle with him. Okay, who was she kidding? She totally was.

While Felix cleaned up his station, she nodded toward the customer leaving with his Bloody Mary. "How about him?"

"No."

Addison blew out a breath, her blonde bangs fanning out. "Okay."

Felix wasn't wrong; the bar seemed the prime place for watching people. If they weren't wandering up to it for a drink, they were congregating around it. She pointed out several more men, but each time she found a potential Prince Charming, Felix shot them down for one reason or another: too rich, too flirty, too awkward, too good-looking.

"Too good-looking?" Addison asked. "Is there such a thing?"

"Do you want the man on your arm drawing attention away from your good looks?" Felix grinned.

She flashed one right back. "No one could draw attention away from me."

"Touché."

"And besides that, what's wrong with being too rich?"

He shrugged. "I suppose if that's what you're looking for."

"No. I'm not out for someone rich. You don't choose who you fall in love with. But if it turns out that way, it doesn't hurt to never have to worry about money." Financial problems were something she knew about all too well.

He relented with a tilt of his head. "I'll second that."

"There has to be someone you approve of," Addison said to Felix. "Do you always see the worst in everyone?"

"Occupational hazard," he conceded. "But your faith in people makes you an easy target for men. You need to be more discerning."

"At least I'm open to the possibility of love."

"Or an unrealistic ideal of some Mr. Perfect fantasy. It's delusional," he said, but not unkindly.

Her chin rose a fraction. "I like to think of it as optimism. You, on the other hand, have rejected practically everyone at the party."

"Well…" His eyes dropped to the counter. "Not everyone."

Addison blinked at him, realizing he meant himself.

The bartender was right up her alley, both physically and when it came to his sharp wit and brash charm. He was the kind of guy she'd snatch up like a cashmere sweater from a Boxing Day bargain bin. But that was just the problem. She'd dated enough Felixes to know he didn't fit into her fairytale dream. She wasn't looking to be just another "number."

Ignoring Felix's hint, she turned her attention back to the rest of the room. That's when she spotted Thor. Okay, well, he probably wasn't the Norse god, but he sure looked like him—very Chris Hemsworth. To add to his dignified appearance, he stood next to his English mastiff. He was the perfect picture of godliness. The kind of guy who should pose for canvas paintings.

Thor was tall and broad, his frame filling out his designer suit like it was an extension of his body. It was as though the chandelier's light had been created just to shine down on his close-cropped golden hair, to highlight his strong features. It was heaven's light sending her a sign.

"What about him?" Addison's voice was hushed, matching the reverence of that fated moment.

Felix followed her gaze and huffed. "Well, if you like that obviously rich and handsome act."

"You can't act rich or handsome," she said.

"I mean, what is he trying to prove with that chiseled jaw and those perfectly straight teeth?"

"So, what you're saying is you can't find anything wrong with him."

Addison stood there, breathing in the moment, committing it to memory so she could reflect on it for years to come. She wanted to recall everything about it when, on their wedding day, she retold the story of how they met.

She sighed, maybe a little too loudly.

Princess seemed to give her a nod, as if to say, *This is it.*

Addison set the doxie on the hardwood floor and blew a kiss at Felix. "Wish me luck."

He scowled. "I thought it was destiny, not luck."

"What can I say? You've made a big impression on me."

He stood a little straighter, a grin spreading across his face. "I have?"

"Yeah. I think you're right. I need to be more logical about love and hedge my bets. And I bet *he's* my Mr. Perfect."

The smile slipped from Felix's face as Addison turned and headed toward the owner of the English mastiff.

She felt as though she was walking in slow motion. This really was *it.* Her search for the perfect man had been building up to this one romantic moment in time. It was the climax of her movie.

As she made her way across the room, the crowd moved like it was parting for her, for them, making way for destiny. The red-bra'd server passed by, the movement raising a breeze that blew Addison's golden hair like a wind machine.

As though he sensed her, Thor looked her way. His eyes were drawn to hers like it was scripted. Or, better yet, predestined.

The jazz band in the corner drowned out the clinking glasses, the occasional bark, the murmur of voices. It all faded away. It was just the two of them, hurtling through time and space, overcoming all odds to meet at this exact point. Like it was meant to be.

Addison moved faster and faster, and Thor rushed toward her. Some unseen force drew them together. Then she realized it was their dogs tugging on their leashes to close the distance between them.

The heels made it difficult for Addison to hold back Princess. They skidded and clicked on the polished floor. Since her soul mate's dog probably weighed two hundred pounds, she imagined Thor had a harder time. But it didn't look like he was putting up much of a fight. Not with that dazed grin on his face—probably the same one she had on hers.

Addison's attention was so fixed on him that she'd forgotten there were other people in the ballroom. So, when she bumped into a passing server handing out champagne glasses, it came as a complete surprise to her—and him.

The silver tray went flying. Glasses smashed

around their feet. Addison stumbled forward. The server tried to catch her, but Princess had stopped to lap up the champagne, and they both got caught in her leash.

Addison pitched forward. Her hands flew out. The hardwood floor flew up to meet her.

But she never reached it. Instead, she landed in cashmere-clad arms, staring into eyes as blue as the heavens from which he fell: Thor.

3

DOGGONE IT

Addison gazed up at the man of her dreams, conscious of his muscular arms around her waist. "My hero."

Thor's face lit up. Felix had been correct: he really did have perfect teeth.

"My pleasure," Thor said. "Are you all right?"

She did a quick mental check. There was light-headedness, heart palpitations, and stars blinking across her vision. In other words, she was as twitterpated as Bambi. Addison reminded herself to breathe.

"I'm much better now, thank you."

Thor steadied her as she untangled her legs from Princess's leash. His firm hands burned hot against her arms, and the sensation coursed through her. When she looked up, his gaze locked on her eyes, not her low neckline. But of course;

she wouldn't have expected anything less from her soulmate.

He held out his hand. "My name is Philip Montgomery the third."

"Addison Turner." She put her hand in his and felt the sparks fly, just like in the movies.

Instead of shaking her hand, he kissed it lightly. Not many men could pull off the gesture. She would have rolled her eyes if it had been anyone else—especially a guy like Felix. But this wasn't just anyone. It was Philip Montgomery III.

"It's a pleasure to meet you, Addison."

"Likewise." She tried to sound posh. Posh enough to date a guy who had a number after his name.

Addison could have stared into those beautiful blue eyes all night long if someone nearby hadn't cleared their throat. Reluctantly, she pulled her attention away from Philip. The small group he'd been standing with stared expectantly as though waiting for introductions. Princess bumped into her ankle, reminding her she was there too.

Philip gestured to the round man on his left. "Addison, this is Walter Boyd. He's a judge for this year's Western Dog Show."

"Actually, I've been a judge every year for the past fifteen years." His chest puffed up. "I'm the longest-running judge on the panel."

"Judge Boyd has a very keen sense of perfection," Philip told her. "Like a sixth sense. It's uncanny, really."

"Hopefully that keen eye spots my Lily this year," said a short, balding man with a cane. "Not that I'm worried. She hasn't let me down yet."

Philip laughed good-naturedly. "She'll have a tough time stealing the attention away from my Baxter." He patted his English mastiff's wide head. "Addison, this is Alistair Yates." He gestured to the balding man. "He's been competing in conformation shows for ... What is it now? Forty years?"

"Careful now." He teasingly shook his cane at Philip. "You're aging me."

"Alistair has hired a handler this year to prepare his beagle for conformation," Philip said.

"The old hip isn't quite what it used to be. But my Lily is in expert hands this year." Alistair gestured to the tall, thin woman standing next to him. "This here is—"

"Penny Peacock," Addison breathed. She gaped at the woman's familiar face, one she'd seen in magazines, on dog food tins, etched into dry treats, and on pooper-scoopers. "I've read all about you in *Doggy Digest.* You're the best handler there is," she gushed, feeling the rush of meeting a Dogdom star.

Princess barked, maybe recognizing Ms. Peacock from the aisle in the pet store dedicated to her products. And to think, Addison was actually meeting her in person. If only she could get Penny to notice her designs that night. One word from her on social media and Addison would have no trouble filling the seats at her fashion show.

"Penny is the best of the best," Philip agreed.

Penny's hooked nose rose an inch. "Well, I wouldn't go that far." But she looked pleased.

Alistair leaned forward on his wooden cane. "She has never lost a competition. That's why my Lily's a sure win."

"We'll see about that," Walter said. "That's for the judges to decide."

"I'm only as good as the dogs I handle," Penny replied.

Addison thought it would have sounded humble if she were a better actress. But she supposed the handler deserved to be a little smug with a resume boasting a qualification like "I'm the best." Besides, when your face is on dog food, you don't have to apologize for anything.

Philip gestured to Princess. "You have a beautiful dachshund."

Princess's floppy ears perked up, relieved the conversation had finally moved on to a more interesting topic: her.

"Thank you." Addison picked up Princess to involve her in the discussion.

Penny's eyes narrowed, homing in on the competition. "She's quite the specimen. Are you planning to enter her this year?"

"No. Unfortunately, she wouldn't get very far," Addison whispered so Princess wouldn't hear.

Judge Boyd barked a laugh. "She would have been a fine specimen. Of course, I could see the bitch was flawed from a mile away."

Addison cringed at the word. She didn't think she'd ever get used to the b-word used so flippantly in the dog show circuit—especially when it came to her Princess.

"She's not flawed," she said, a little sharper than she'd meant to. "She's perfect."

"I'm sorry to hear you won't be entering," Penny said, shoulders relaxing. "But she's lovely. Who is your stylist?"

"I style her myself," Addison said. "I own a business called Pampered Puppies."

Alistair leaned forward. "So, you're the dog stylist everyone is talking about tonight. I'm looking forward to seeing what you've done for my Lily."

Addison went through a mental list of all the dogs she'd styled that evening. Melody must have checked in Alistair's dog. "Lily ... Lily. Is she the tri-colored beagle?"

"That's her." His expression was that of a proud father's.

Penny grabbed a glass of champagne off a passing server's tray. "Best of Breed and Best in Show three years running, you know. I thought since it was still two weeks away from the show, I would allow her a little TLC. It is a special occasion after all." She eyed Addison sharply. "As long as you don't use products that are not one hundred percent natural-based."

"Of course not," Addison said. "My assistant is just putting the finishing touches on her pawdicure. Don't worry. She's in excellent hands."

Penny's mouth pursed. "I hope you're not trimming her nails this close to the competition."

"No, definitely not," she assured the handler. "But if you like the results of today, I'd be happy to be her stylist for the show." She automatically drew out a card from her clutch.

Penny held up a hand. "No one touches my dogs but *me*. Tonight was a special occasion."

"I understand," Addison said, a little miffed. To be fair, Penny hadn't even seen her work yet, so how could she judge? Famous or not, there was smug and there was pompous. "I suppose a marathon runner wouldn't trade in his old, worn-out running shoes for new ones before the big race."

Addison regretted the comment immediately. She was trying to get on Penny's good side—if she had one.

Philip snorted but covered it with a cough.

Penny didn't seem to notice she'd been compared to a pair of stinky, old running shoes. If she did, she was too serious about show dogs to comment. "I not only train them, but I also groom them, exercise them, and make their dog food from scratch."

"From scratch?" Addison said. "That sounds like a lot of work."

"Only the best for my dogs."

Addison returned the card to her clutch. "I have other services available if you're interested," she suggested, altering her sales pitch. "And there's always my upcoming fashion show."

Alistair looked up from his glass of port with an expression of mild interest. "A fashion show, you say?"

"I'm launching my new fashion line for dogs the weekend of the show. I still need volunteers to help model the designs if you're interested in involving Lily."

Alistair smiled. "That sounds—"

"Tasteless," Penny cut in. "My dogs don't wear clothing."

Addison frowned. Penny might have been the best handler in the world, but she seemed to forget Lily wasn't her dog. Lily was Alistair's.

Philip ruffled the fur on his dog's head. "Well, you can count Baxter in."

"Really? That's great." Addison clapped her hands. "I have the perfect letterman jacket in mind."

"It will suit him," he said. "I was never on the football team, myself. I'm more of a tennis man."

The others sank into a heated debate about

the historical purpose of the ankle fur on a traditional poodle cut. While they were distracted, Philip drew Addison away.

"So," he began. "Is your schedule fully booked tonight?"

"Why? Does Baxter need grooming? I'm sure I could fit him in."

Philip's ears turned pink, and he ducked his head. "I was asking more for myself."

Addison blinked, her one-track mind focused on work. "You need grooming?"

He laughed, and it sounded clear and musical. Oh, how she could listen to it all day long, maybe even record it and set it as her ringtone.

"No," he said. "I was wondering if I might steal you for a dance."

"Oh." Addison wanted to slap herself. Sometimes she opened her mouth before her brain caught up. Batting her eyelashes, she tried to hide the blunder with her best flirty look. "I'm sure I could spare a little more time."

"Good." He took her hand. "Because they happen to be playing our song."

Philip led her to the other side of the historic ballroom, where couples circled the dance floor to the classic jazz music. Although Felix was busy behind his bar, Addison could sense his eyes on them as they passed. She kept her gaze forward, fighting the urge to stick her tongue out at him like a two-year-old. He'd called her "delusional." *Well*, she thought, *how was that for "delusional"?*

At the edge of the dance floor, two dog-watchers approached them. They wore suits with red cummerbunds and bow ties. The watchers took Baxter and Princess while Philip swept Addison away.

And boy, could the man dance. *But of course he can*, she thought. *He's Mr. Perfect.*

Addison had learned how to ballroom dance from online videos as a teenager. Because what kind of princess wouldn't be able to dance with her Prince Charming? While she'd realized a long time ago that she wasn't, in fact, an undiscovered Disney princess, she'd obviously been preparing for this night. For Philip.

"How long have you been competing in dog shows?" she asked him.

"A few years now," he said. "It's something special Baxter and I can do together. It's a shame your doxie can't enter. She looks well-bred. Were you upset when you found out you couldn't show her?"

She shook her head. "Not at all. I knew she had a deformity when I brought her home."

"You did?"

"I adopted Princess from the San Francisco Dachshund Rescue Center, where I volunteer. Her owner dropped her off after she realized there would be no blue ribbons in her future. Princess came from the breeder as a puppy," she explained, "so there was no way to know. It surfaced as she grew older."

Philip nodded and spun her in a circle. "Even if I couldn't show Baxter, I would never give him up. He's like family to me."

Addison felt her heart swell until it left her lungs no room to breathe. Could Philip get any more perfect?

"I enter him into competitions because I want to see him win," he said. "But many breeders and owners see it as their own win. It doesn't matter what dog they use to get there."

"We see a lot of purebreds come through the rescue center," Addison said. "People buy them because they're so beautiful, but they don't realize the work or cost that goes into them if they have health problems. And a lot of them do. Especially when they come from a puppy mill looking to make a quick buck."

"I'm surprised you're supporting the dog show lifestyle after your experiences with Princess and your rescue center." Philip's dancing became a little stiffer as he watched her expression. "Some people in your circumstance might look down upon dog shows."

It was a touchy topic for any show dog owner: the rescue-versus-breeder debate. Those passionate about dog shows were sensitive to the accusations from the public and the local group,

San Franciscans Against Animal Cruelty (SFAAC).

Addison's expression barely wavered. "I'm neither against nor in support of dog shows. I just support dogs in general. Purebreds and mutts alike. The only thing I'm against is disreputable breeders and puppy mills."

Philip seemed to relax, and he spun her once again. "You must really love animals. I do a fair bit of fundraising myself for SFAAC. In fact, I'm hosting an event to raise money next weekend. Would you like to attend?"

She beamed up at him. "I'd love to."

"Good. I thought you might be interested. You follow the dog show circuit, you volunteer, you're a dog groomer—"

"I prefer the term 'dog stylist,'" she corrected him. "My services encompass so much more than simple shampoos and trims."

"Excuse me." He flashed her a teasing smile. "Dog stylist. And by the looks of the dogs around here tonight, I'd say you're pretty good."

"I like to add my own special flair. Part of the Addison Turner experience. Hopefully, after tonight, everyone in the San Francisco dog show world will remember my name."

Philip's hold around her tightened a fraction. "I know I certainly will."

She smiled coyly and let him spin her around the dance floor a couple more times, while inside she was screaming *We-e-e-e-e-e!* like she was on the Tilt-A-Whirl. It was the perfect moment. She thought she could get lost in it forever—that is until she caught sight of his Bulgari watch.

Addison gasped, her waltz faltering. "Is that the time?" She stepped away from him. "I'm late."

"For what?"

"A sneak peek at my fashion line. I'm supposed to reveal a few dogs wearing the designs." She backed away to the edge of the dance floor, dodging the oncoming dancers.

"When?" He tried to follow, but a couple bumped into him.

"In less than five minutes."

"Wait! I haven't gotten your number yet!" He gave chase, weaving in and out of dancers twirling under the chandeliers.

"I'm sorry. I'm late." Finding Princess's dog-watcher, Addison swept the doxie off the floor and into her arms. She waved at Philip over her shoulder. "I'll find you after."

Addison scurried across the ballroom as fast as her heels would allow. She'd been so distracted by Philip that she'd almost forgotten the entire reason she was even there that night. She wasn't about to waste all her time and hard work, even for Prince Charming.

Rounding the bar, she saw Felix eye her curiously. Perhaps curious about how things went with

Mr. Perfect. She took on the cocktail tables and settees like a slalom course. The event organizer, Darcy, approached her, slinking out of the shadows.

"Excuse me, Miss Turner," he said. "Are you almost ready on stage?"

"Absolutely." She tried to catch her breath; her push-up bra was too tight—but so worth it. "Give me sixty seconds."

Melody would have prepped the dogs and positioned them all on pillows. However, this was Addison's moment to shine, to make a name for herself. She wanted to ensure everything was perfect—every dog on its pillow, every hair in place, every bow fluffed.

She carried Princess up the stage steps and ducked behind the curtain, ready to make some last-minute changes. But when her eyes landed on the pillows arranged neatly in a semicircle, her steps slowed. Almost all of the dogs were gone.

Only three dogs out of the original ten remained: a bull terrier in a black leather jacket with sunglasses on his head, the Maltese with the Rainbow Frenzy nail polish and pink tutu, and a miniature schnauzer wearing a bowler hat and monocle.

Addison dropped Princess by her pillow. She raced from one side of the stage to the other, as though the rest must have been hiding around there somewhere. But Melody had already cleaned up the stage. There was no place for them to hide. Not all seven dogs. And where on Earth was Melody, anyway?

Addison checked her phone just as the clock struck ten. Her eyes widened. She stood frozen at center stage as the curtains began to part.

"No. Stop!" she cried out. "I'm not ready. I'm not ready!"

She darted to the front of the stage and grabbed both curtains, gripping them shut. She had to prevent anyone from seeing before she could figure out what happened.

There had to be some mistake. Maybe they all needed to go for a walk at the same time, or all the owners took them back, or … she didn't know what. Alien abductions?

The motorized track whirred above her, dragging the curtains apart. She dug her heels in, not ready to give up yet. She'd worked too hard.

Addison's hands cramped. Her muscles screamed. She gritted her teeth and pulled back in a game of tug of war.

The entire room full of guests turned toward her, watching with curiosity and anticipation. The owners of the models gathered the closest, eager to see their stars shine. Alistair and Penny stood at the front.

Oh God, she thought. *Not Penny Peacock's dog.*

Addison held the drapes for as long as she could, arms outstretched, heels slipping on the stage. The crowd began to chatter, laughing at her antics, but she wasn't kidding around.

Finally, when the curtains threatened to tear her in two, they ripped out of her desperate grip. She was left standing alone in the middle of the nearly empty stage. The floodlights poured down on her glimmering sequined dress, lighting her up like a disco ball.

The gathered dog-lovers grew still, tense with anticipation. It seemed they held one collective breath, like this was some kind of magic show and she could go "Alakazam," and the missing dogs would suddenly appear.

But she was not the Wizard of Oz. She was the fraud hiding behind the curtain, and she'd just been exposed.

After a few hushed moments, the murmurs began, followed by the vicious snarling and growling —not from the dogs, but from the human guests.

"Where are they?" Judge Boyd demanded.

"My dog was supposed to be up there," a voice said, but Addison couldn't pinpoint who with the lights glaring down at her.

"What's happening!?" a woman cried. "Where did they all go!?"

Addison spotted Kitty Carlisle in the crowd, cradling her dog protectively.

Darcy appeared at the bottom of the stage. "What's going on?" he hissed up at Addison. "Where are they?"

"I … I don't know. Th–they're gone." Her answer was barely a shocked whisper, but a man nearby must have heard her because he gasped.

"They're gone!" he yelled. "The dogs are missing!"

Addison squinted against the spotlights, peering at the crowd, but she instantly regretted it. Enraged expressions glared up at her. Eyes narrowed. Fists clenched. She wanted to close her eyes, to make it all go away. It couldn't be real.

From the sides of the room, large men in dark suits closed in on the stage with placid expressions and purposeful movements. Security, she realized, getting ready to control the crowd if necessary. Or were they coming for her?

A man with red hair rushed the stage, maybe to come look for the dogs himself or maybe to strangle Addison. She backpedaled, but the security guards took action before the irate man could get his hands on her.

The redhead shrugged off the guards and jabbed a finger in Addison's direction. "You'll be hearing from my lawyer."

"Give me my dog," someone else was saying. "I just want my dog."

Addison searched for the voice. A man with a cul-de-sac of hair on his shiny head was arguing with security at the base of the stairs. She remembered his last name was Jackson.

He climbed onto the stage. Security shadowed

him to make sure he didn't try anything funny. But he completely ignored Addison. The Maltese consumed his focus. The dog trotted up to him, Rainbow Frenzy nails clicking on the stage floor. Jackson picked her up and held her close, clearly grateful to still have his dog.

The other two owners followed his lead, coming up to claim their pets. As they passed Addison, they glared at her and threw insults her way. She winced.

"Someone call the police!" Rex Harrison called out.

Addison wanted to find his ripped-up business card and jam it down his throat. They didn't need the police. Because the dogs weren't missing. They just couldn't be. She adored dogs too much to let anything happen to them. She wanted to pamper them, love them, and show them that they mattered. Melody could vouch for that.

Addison scanned the stage desperately. Where was Melody, anyway? Why would she leave the dogs so close to curtain call?

She couldn't breathe. The spotlights roasted her like an oven, but not quite as badly as the angry, laserlike glares shooting at her.

Alistair Yates pointed his cane at Addison. "What have you done with my Lily?" His lip curled and spittle flew from his mouth.

"Nothing," Addison panted, feeling faint. "I didn't do anything."

"No-o-o-o!" a woman screamed. It drew out like someone was falling from a tall building.

When Addison searched for the source, she saw Penny Peacock burying her hooked nose in her hands. "My Best in Show. My blue ribbon. My perfect streak. Gone. All because of you, Addison Turner!"

Addison's legs felt like bendy Twizzlers. She sank onto a pillow, tugging her dress down so the entire room wouldn't see her underwear, and stared at her empty stage.

When she'd hoped to make a name for herself, this wasn't exactly what she'd had in mind.

4

THROWN TO THE DOGS

"Addison ... Addison ... Miss Turner?"

Addison's trance broke, and she tore her gaze away from the stage to refocus on Officer Simpson. "Sorry. I just ... I can't believe they're gone."

She held Princess closer to her chest, hesitant to put her down, as if the ballroom were some kind of Bermuda Triangle. No one could explain what had happened to the dogs. However, there had certainly been enough theories screamed at her before the police had arrived.

Princess grumbled, probably annoyed that she hadn't been able to touch the ground in the last forty minutes. She shifted in Addison's hold and nestled in.

"I understand, ma'am," the officer said. "I just have a few more questions for you."

Addison nodded numbly, glancing at the middle of the stage floor where the dogs should have been. If she stared hard enough, maybe she would see a glimmer in the air like there was a magic door the dogs had accidentally passed through.

Once the police had arrived and the truth sank in, Addison could no longer deny reality. She'd lost the dogs. They were out there in the city somewhere, maybe wandering the streets. Or, worse, in the hands of someone who wanted to use them for money or even illegal dog fights.

Officer Simpson scanned his notepad. "You said you were dancing when the dogs went missing?"

Addison cringed. It sounded so unprofessional when he said it. Why had she allowed herself to get so distracted on such a critical night?

"Yes, I was dancing with Philip Montgomery the third."

The officer wrote down the name. "You didn't see anything before you left? No one hanging around the stage?"

"No. Everything was normal. It was perfect, in fact. Melody was just finishing up the last of the grooming, and …" Addison stiffened, suddenly remembering. "Actually, there was one person who hung around way longer than any of the other dog owners. Kitty Carlisle." She recalled the way the older woman had nervously stalked backstage. Maybe she'd been casing the place, making her evil dog-stealing plans.

"Was her dog stolen as well?" he asked.

"No. In fact, she seemed overly protective of her bichon frise, hovering, making sure she got him back. I didn't see her again until the dogs were long gone."

Officer Simpson made another note. "Can you think of anyone else acting unusual? Maybe someone might have said something alluding to the dogs going missing."

"Not that I can remember."

Through the thick stage curtains, Addison could hear the few remaining guests—or witnesses, she supposed—talking to other police officers in the ballroom. Most of it was muffled murmurs to her ears, but every once in a while, her name rang clear. Probably because they said it with such ferociousness that it cut through the curtain, and her, like a freshly sharpened pair of trimming scissors. She closed her eyes and rubbed a hand over them.

"How long has Melody Butters been working for you?" the officer asked.

Addison's eyes flicked open, and her voice rose an octave in surprise. "Melody? About six months now. Part time."

She hadn't suspected her assistant for even a

second. But, of course, she would be a suspect since she was directly responsible for the dogs when they went missing. The police were probably drilling her at that very moment.

His pen scratched across the notepad. "Do you know much about her personally? Like who she hangs out with, or if she has any criminal connections."

Addison huffed. "The only thing criminal about that woman is her addiction to ABBA. But I suppose I don't know her extremely well outside of work." Then she quickly added, "We talk a lot at the spa, though, and I can't see her doing anything to these dogs. Not on purpose, anyway."

She thought back to the curtain call. Melody had been nowhere to be found. Had she run to the bathroom? Maybe Addison had taken too long to come back, and she couldn't hold it any longer.

Addison peered at the officer's notes. "Do you think someone might have stolen the dogs?"

"We're considering all possibilities at this point. Not all of the dogs disappeared, so it may just be a case of them wandering off. It's too soon to tell."

"Is anyone out there looking for them? Has anyone called animal control or any rescue centers?"

"We're taking steps to look for them."

Addison's mouth turned down. That didn't

exactly sound like they were scouring the city. It sounded like a generic police-y type answer to her. "Seven dogs have vanished. If you think they might have run away, shouldn't someone be out there searching the streets, just in case?"

She sounded harsher than she'd meant to. No. Actually, she meant to sound harsh. It wasn't exactly hard to drive around a few blocks. The police were out there patrolling as part of their job anyway.

Officer Simpson glanced up from his notepad, keeping his tone level but firm. "We're doing what we can."

It looked like that "someone" was going to be her. She wanted to wrap things up, to get out on the streets and search the neighborhood herself. She needed to help find those poor dogs.

Addison squished Princess against her chest, thinking of how she would feel if her doxie were out there lost and alone. Her stomach flipped with nausea. Now there were seven dogs out there somewhere and seven owners with flipping stomachs. And she was responsible for it. It suddenly occurred to Addison that she could be sued by seven powerful and expensive lawyers.

Show dogs were pricey breeds to begin with, even before the cost of their training, grooming, and only the best products and food. Over the lifetime of a show dog, owners sometimes invested hundreds of thousands of dollars. Plus, those deemed the best of the best were often used for their superior genetics. A stud fee could be a thousand dollars or more. The owners might claim a loss of that income.

Addison swallowed hard. She didn't exactly have that kind of coin lying around. But that could be the least of her worries. Forget losing her business—Addison could be held criminally liable.

"Miss Turner? Are you all right?" Officer Simpson eyed her closely.

Her breaths came faster than a panting dog's on a sunny day. She felt dizzy; the room looked a little crooked.

Officer Simpson laid a hand on her shoulder as if preparing to catch her. "I think you should sit down."

She nodded and collapsed onto one of the pooch pillows. Princess curled up on her lap and promptly fell asleep as though everything were perfectly normal.

"Am I going to jail?" Addison asked between panicked breaths.

Officer Simpson squatted down to her level. "Right now, we're just investigating. You're free to go. However, we'll need you to come down to the station tomorrow morning to answer more questions."

His response didn't make her feel any better. It wasn't exactly a "no."

"You're looking a little pale, Miss Turner."

"I'm okay. I'm okay." She held a hand to her forehead as though she could feel if she were pale. All she felt was cold, damp beads of sweat. "I just need a little sugar is all. I'll be fine."

The officer seemed reluctant to leave, but he eventually took a card out of his pocket and handed it to her. "If you have any questions, here's my contact info. Please stop by the precinct in the morning."

Addison took it, staring at Officer Simpson's name as he left the stage, his big boots clomping on the wood. He'd been nice, even concerned for her, but all she could wonder was if he would be the one to clamp a pair of cuffs on her if the dogs weren't found.

She suddenly had a whole new reason for searching the neighborhood that night: to stay out of jail. And then there was Princess. Who would take her in when Addison was behind bars? And orange was so not Addison's color …

Her thoughts flipped around erratically. She had to do something, but first she needed to find Melody and question her assistant personally.

Since she could still hear guests and police officers lingering outside the closed curtains, she chose the back door to the alley where they'd unloaded her car at the start of the night. It seemed so long ago now.

Juggling both Princess and her clutch, she

headed for the exit. An empty storage bin propped the heavy metal door open. When she slipped through, she found Melody absently picking at her lip in the alley, a smoke in her hand.

Addison watched her suck on the cigarette like a scuba diver would oxygen. "I didn't know you smoked."

"I don't," Melody said. "Well, I didn't." She took another drag, her hand shaking. "I quit a couple of years ago, but I started up again this week."

She didn't bother to flick away the long length of ash drooping at the end before she took another desperate drag. The ash escaped on its own and fluttered down the front of her work apron.

Addison nodded. She couldn't blame Melody. She'd already gone through four pints of her ice cream stash leading up to this event. When she'd zipped up her dress that night, she'd been surprised it had even fit.

Princess squirmed and whined desperately in her arms. Reluctantly, Addison set her down but didn't let the leash out far.

Melody tossed the butt aside and turned to Addison. Even in the poorly lit alley, she could see her assistant's red-rimmed eyes were swollen. Pale tear tracks smeared the blush on her cheeks.

"I'm so sorry." Melody's voice broke. "I only stepped outside for two minutes to have a smoke. I felt fine until a customer showed up and started screaming at me. Afterward, my nerves were shot. I just needed to relax before the reveal. I gave all the dogs treats before I left. They were all happy, and healthy, and … *there* when I left. I don't know what happened."

Addison felt bad for her. She'd obviously had a rough night, too. "Are you sure the dogs didn't follow you when you went out the backstage door? Maybe they snuck out here when you weren't looking." She glanced both ways down the dark alley, half hoping they were hanging around the dumpsters. But there was only Princess, relieving herself after Addison's long Q and A session with the cop.

"That's what the cops wondered too, because I stuck a storage container in the door to hold it open. But when I tried to get back inside for ten o'clock, the door had closed and locked. I had to go around. That's why I was late." Melody teared up again, and her voice wavered. "But I'm sure I would have seen the dogs sneak out. I'm sure of it. I only planned to be a minute."

Tapping out another cigarette from the pack, she stuck it in her mouth and lit up. In the flare from the lighter, Addison could see fresh tears roll down Melody's cheeks.

"I'm so sorry," her assistant said again.

Addison shook her head, but she couldn't

quite look her in the eye yet. "It's not your fault. We don't even know what happened. The police aren't exactly saying, but I can't see all those dogs running away. They're too well trained."

Melody sniffed. "You entrusted them to me. They were my responsibility. I let you down." She waved the cigarette around while she talked, the glowing end creating swirls in the dark before Addison's tired eyes.

"You didn't let me down. It wasn't a normal setup. You're not to blame. Maybe if I'd been around—"

"Don't do that," Melody told her. "You deserved a break. I told you to go."

Addison had replayed the evening's events over and over a hundred times. She could recite every moment, every word spoken, just like she could *The Princess Bride*, her favorite movie. She'd considered all the if-onlys: if only she'd stuck around, if only she'd been watching the dogs and not dancing with Philip Montgomery III, if only she hadn't bothered arguing with that nosy bartender, Felix. But dwelling on what might have been wouldn't change what was. The dogs were gone.

She shook her head to snap herself out of the never-ending self-blame cycle. "Look, Melody. Why don't you just go home and get some rest? I have to go down to the police station tomorrow and answer more questions. Let's call it a night."

"You're right. Thanks." Melody sucked back the rest of her cigarette. "I'll talk to you tomorrow?"

"Sure thing."

As Melody passed the dumpster, she tossed her near-full pack of smokes inside, along with her lighter, as though it were the cigarettes' fault the dogs disappeared. Addison thought it was likely she'd probably stop on the way home and pick up another pack. Heck, Addison already planned to stop for some Chunky Monkey ice cream herself.

Instead of taking her own advice and going home, Addison scooped up Princess and wandered back inside. Crossing the stage, she peeked through a tiny gap in the curtains. Most of the people had cleared out of the ballroom, except for a few stragglers. Slipping through to the other side, she went to the bar. Felix wasn't around, but she took a seat on a stool anyway, setting Princess down at her feet. The doxie spun twice before curling up for a nap on the floor.

Addison banged her head on the bar's sticky countertop, hoping it might knock her senseless. If it did, at least she wouldn't have to answer any more of the cops' questions the next day. Questions that she wouldn't know the answers to. And the only explanation the owners of the missing dogs were interested in involved pointing their fingers at Addison. No matter how it happened or why, it was her fault. Now what was she going to do about it?

Addison banged her head again, but a pair of hands held either side of it, gently raising it up. It was Felix.

He gave her a sympathetic smile. "You look like you could use that drink now."

"Then I must look better than I feel, because I feel like I could use the entire bottle." She sighed, playing with the clasp on her clutch. "My career is over."

"It can't be that bad." He took his cloth and dabbed away the grenadine syrup smeared on her forehead.

"I lost my clients. Whole clients." She threw her arms in the air. "These poor dogs might end up in some back alley dog-fighting ring, getting torn to shreds, and it's all my fault." She imagined Kingy walking into the ring, dressed in the designer smoking jacket.

"Look," he said. "I love dogs too, so I understand your concern for these little guys, but I think you need to consider your long-term plan. Have you thought about lawyering up? Protecting yourself, just in case?"

Addison dropped her head into her hands. "I'm going to jail."

Felix snorted. "You won't go to jail. Look, maybe they got loose and ran away. They're dogs, after all." He tried to sound offhand about it. "They might turn up. No harm done."

"No harm?" Addison sputtered. "Except when it comes to my reputation. Even if the dogs turn up perfectly unharmed, God willing, who is going to bring their dog to me for styling if they can't be sure they'll get them back?"

She knew he was only trying to cheer her up. He was being pretty nice, actually. But there was no cheer to be had. This was bad. Very bad.

Addison grimaced in self-loathing. She hated throwing herself a pity party, hated worrying about anything but the dogs.

"There are other dog owners all over this city who will never even hear about this," he said. "This was just one event."

"A big event." She widened her eyes to show just how big.

"And it wasn't even your fault."

"That makes little difference to the owners," she said, refusing to be cheered. "The dogs were under my care."

He held up a finger. "Correction: they were under your assistant's care."

"My assistant who works for me."

Felix let out a breath, giving up the argument. "Chin up." He set a glass of orange liquid down in front of her. "It's just orange juice. I'm not allowed to serve alcohol anymore tonight."

As Addison reached for the glass with a

shaking hand, she realized she could use a bit of sugar. She downed it gratefully.

"Look," Felix said. "It's not over yet. They could still find the dogs. Besides, you don't strike me as the glass-half-empty type."

"Oh?" she inquired. "What type do you think I am?"

"I'm not going down that road again." He raised his hands and backed away. "I have the right to remain silent."

She eyeballed him. "Har har."

"What? Too soon for the cop jokes?"

"Considering I might hear those words repeated to me any time now, I'd say yes. And you're wrong. It is over. These next two weeks were my chance to make a name for myself, to build up interest in my fashion show. But the dog show community is tight. Talk will get around."

"Then it's a good thing dogs don't talk," he joked. "I'm just saying, so a few of these over-priced-dog owners know. So what? These aren't the only people with dogs in town. San Francisco is a big city with lots of potential customers."

"Except it may not stop with local gossip. If it hits social media, we're talking national news. Global, even."

Penny Peacock had enough followers online to force Addison into hiding for the rest of her life. She wouldn't be able to start another business ever again. Maybe she wouldn't even be able to leave the house. She'd have to dye her hair and move to Canada.

"I guess I could always change my spa name," she said, attempting the glass-half-full thing. "Starting over from scratch might be easier than trying to repair the damage to my reputation."

"Exactly," he said. "Maybe you can even switch species."

"Species?"

"Yeah." He thought as he cleaned up for the day. "You could be a cat groomer."

"Maybe hamsters." She spread her hands in front of her like she could see the billboard already. "San Francisco's premier hamster hair stylist."

"That's the spirit. See? Your business will be fine. Besides, this was an isolated incident at a single event. Who really follows the dog shows? Chances are, no one will even hear about this." He poured another two glasses of orange juice and handed her one.

"You think?" she asked.

He clinked his glass against hers in cheers. "Absolutely."

They drank in silence. Addison already felt a tiny bit better. Maybe things weren't so doom and gloom. But when the smile on Felix's face dropped and his thick eyebrows furrowed, that doomy feeling returned.

"Uh-oh." His gaze zeroed in on something behind her.

"What?" She turned around and wished she'd already left to look for the dogs.

The press had arrived in the form of a thin, platinum-blonde reporter. Clad in a bubblegum pink pantsuit, she checked her hair in one of the silver serving platters near the cocktail tables. Behind her, the cameraman scrambled to set up his equipment. The reporter watched him, only lifting a finger to snap them while she snarled demands.

Felix was watching in fascination. "Is that *the* Holly Hart from Channel Five News?"

Addison groaned. "Yes, that's her."

"Do you know her?" He sounded awestruck, like she was an A-list actress.

"Yes. And I have a bad feeling about this."

"Why?"

"Because I know her."

The reporter saw someone from across the ballroom and waved them over. Addison's orange juice turned sour in her stomach when she saw who it was: Penny Peacock and Alistair Yates. Holly was going to interview them on the news.

The group spoke in hushed tones while the cameraman hoisted his burden onto his shoulder. Dread filled Addison as Holly took up her microphone and moved her mouth in some vocal exercises. She hoped they were simply making a plea to the community. The more people out there looking for the dogs, the better. If only they would keep Addison's name out of it.

The cameraman counted down on his fingers. Three, two, one. Then Holly began.

"I'm standing in San Francisco's historic Regency Ballroom on Sutter Street, the location of the premier event for this year's Western Dog Show, and boy, have things gone to the dogs. I'm with Alistair Yates, longtime dog show enthusiast, and Penny Peacock, the top dog of the dog handling profession." She gestured to both of them. "Mr. Yates, can you please explain to us what happened here tonight?"

He leaned on his cane and spoke into the mic. "My precious Lily is gone. She's a tri-colored beagle. She won the title of Best of Breed and Best in Show the last three years running. And she was stolen from me."

Holly gasped. "You think she was dognapped? Why would someone want to take her?"

"Isn't it obvious? It's because she's utterly perfect." He stared at the camera, a desperate plea on his face. "I'll do anything to get her back. I'm offering a fifty-thousand-dollar reward for anyone who returns my Lily to me unharmed."

"I understand that more than just your dog went missing tonight," Holly said. "Is that correct?"

Penny leaned toward the microphone. "Yes, six other dogs were stolen. Thieves often target purebred dogs because they're worth a lot of money when resold as pets or used to breed. Tonight, some of the best and brightest in the country disappeared."

Holly sighed and tilted her head like the tragic heroine on the front cover of a cheesy romance novel. "I have an adorable Chinese crested, myself. I couldn't imagine what I would do if I ever lost her."

Addison rolled her eyes at the fake drama. She'd seen Holly's aversion to dogs. Plus, the reporter had severe allergies to them. She'd probably made up the dog to gain viewer sympathy. Holly wasn't concerned for the dogs, just her ratings.

"How could this tragic incident have happened?" Holly turned the mic on Alistair.

"Oh no," Addison breathed. Her heart pounded beneath her dress. She felt sick to her stomach. "Don't say my name. Don't say my name. Don't say my name." She grabbed Princess and took a step closer to the group to hear what came next.

"I don't know, exactly." Alistair told Holly. "Lily was in the care of a dog groomer at the time."

"Dog stylist," Addison muttered.

Felix reached over the bar and latched onto her arm, as though sensing she was teetering over the edge. "It's best to stay out of this," he told her.

68

"Keep a low profile, and don't add fuel to the fire."

Penny grabbed the microphone right out of Holly's hand. "It was Addison Turner of Pampered Puppies. She took Lily under the pretense of grooming her."

Addison inhaled sharply. "Pretense?"

She wrenched out of Felix's grip. Before she knew it, she was across the room with Princess at her heels, seizing the microphone.

She scowled at Penny. "I took great care of Lily."

Holly tried to wrestle the microphone back. "But the beagle disappeared under your care, did she not, Miss Turner?"

"Well, yes, technically." Addison frowned. "But that doesn't mean I stole her or had anything to do with the dogs going missing."

Holly ripped the microphone away, clutching it possessively. "It's the perfect crime. Lure unsuspecting pups into your lair and snatch them up to make a quick buck."

Princess growled at Holly, defending Addison's reputation. If only everyone could translate dog; however, they'd probably have to bleep out a few words.

"My lair?" Addison cried. "Who am I? Cruella de Vil? And why would I want to give my business a bad name?"

Holly sneered, her bleached teeth flashing

69

with the excitement of a hot story. "Make enough money from a few valuable show dogs, and you can move on to the next town and start the scam all over again."

Addison's mouth dropped open. Holly was making her Enemy Number One on television.

Reaching out, Addison covered the microphone with her hand. "Whose side are you on, anyway?" she hissed at Holly. "Think about it. Why would I work my butt off for two years to build a reputation, just to steal a few dogs?"

Holly's shoulders raised in a heartless shrug. "I can't play favorites, Addison. A good reporter is always impartial. I'm just looking for answers."

Addison flinched, startled by Holly's indifference.

She'd witnessed the reporter target one of her best friends, Piper, the year before, and knew just how dirty she could play. Now, Holly's sights had zeroed in on Addison.

She glared at the hack reporter. "Why would you do this? After you helped me promote my business when I first launched? After you helped us gain community support for the rescue center last year?"

"Hey You." Holly snapped at the cameraman, whose name Addison still hadn't heard after everything that had gone down with Piper. "Cut that part. I don't want to remind the viewers I have any association with this."

Addison gave a throaty noise of disgust. "Nice."

Holly smoothed out her blazer for take two. "I have a reputation to maintain, you know."

"Yeah, so do I," Addison shot back. "And you're ruining it."

"Maybe you should have thought about that before you dognapped six dogs."

"Seven," Penny said.

"Seven dogs," Holly corrected herself.

Addison stomped her heel on the hardwood floor. "I did not dognap them."

"Tell that to the cops." Holly waved a dismissive hand.

"I did," Addison growled. "And if you knew how to investigate, you'd know that there's no conclusive evidence that this was a theft." At least she hoped not, because that meant they might still be out there on the streets, waiting to be found.

Holly clicked her fingers at Hey You. "Cut that too." She straightened her back with an air of trustworthy authority and stared into the camera.

"Well, there you have it, San Franciscans. It's dog show week, and there's a puppy pincher on the loose. Have they acquired their target among the missing, or is this just the beginning? With such stiff competition, no one can be trusted in this dog-eat-dog event. This is Holly Hart for Channel Five News, signing out."

Hey You gave a thumbs-up, and Holly

slouched in relief. She turned to leave, but Addison was right in her face.

"What was that?" Addison demanded. "You can't air that. It will destroy me."

"It's nothing personal. But when I got the call, I couldn't ignore it." She tossed her microphone to Hey You, who was packing away all the equipment.

"The whole dog scene is kind of my thing now. My M.O. My calling card," she told Addison, all smiles now. "My ratings have gone through the roof since I started reporting on all this fluffy, happy dog crap. The viewers lap up this stuff, no pun intended. Oh, wait. I think I'll write that one down for later." She drew out her phone and tapped the screen a few times.

"But you don't even have the full story," Addison argued. "This wasn't my fault."

Holly stopped her with a warning finger. "Don't even bother complaining to my producer. It's not like I said anything that wasn't true. Not exactly, anyway. You're still the lead suspect."

"I am?" Addison started. "The lead? Really?"

"Rumor has it."

"But—"

"Look, kid." Holly patted her on the head, even though she was probably less than three years older than Addison. "It's the kind of juicy story that the people want to hear. It's ripe with drama, drama, drama." She shuddered like the word turned her on.

Princess growled and snapped her jaws at Holly's hand. She barely snatched it away in time.

Addison glared at Holly. "How is this drama supposed to help find the dogs? You didn't even make a plea to the community for help."

Holly waved a manicured hand. "It was implied." She snapped her fingers. "Hey You. Let's go, while the night is still young." Like nothing mattered but her ratings, she turned on her Manolo Blahniks and left.

Fuming, Addison held Princess close and stormed after the reporter. She reached out for that platinum-blonde hair. But her fingers had barely brushed the over-processed locks before her feet left the ground, and she was swept away.

She kicked at the air, struggling against the firm hold around her waist. "Let me go! Let me go! I'm going to kill her."

When she finally stopped struggling—mostly because her dress was creeping up—the person released her. She elbowed them, shoving them away, and turned to find Felix grinning down at her.

Wincing, he rubbed his stomach. "You're a feisty one, aren't you?"

"I'll show you feisty," she said, stomping past him.

But it was pointless. With a sweep of his arm,

she and Princess were right back in front of him again.

He shook his finger at her as if chastising a five-year-old. "Now, don't do anything you're going to regret."

"I won't regret it," she said calmly.

"It will only add fuel to her story, and you know it. Come on. Why don't we go find you a drink? My treat."

Addison frowned at the escaping news reporter. Because she couldn't take it out on her, she turned her glare on the bartender. "No one will know, huh?"

"Yeah, well …" He pulled a sheepish expression. "I didn't exactly see that one coming."

"People rarely get forewarned about the end of the world." She gripped her hair. "We're talking zombie apocalypse kind of stuff."

"It's not the end of the world. I bet if you just go home and get some rest, this will all blow over before you know it." He reached into his pocket and pulled out a business card. It flashed a metallic gold in the dim chandelier light. "If you ever need anything or you change your mind about that drink, give me a call."

Without looking at it, she shoved the card into the depths of her clutch, that special place reserved for old receipts, gum wrappers, and those bobby pins she always lost.

There was only one number she'd wanted that

night, and it wasn't a player's like Felix. It was Philip Montgomery III's digits. But after everything that had happened that night, she'd be lucky if she even got to wash his dog.

Turning her back on Felix, Addison headed for her car to scour the city for the missing dogs.

5

BONE TO PICK

Addison sat in her Mini Convertible, psyching herself up to get out. Even though it was a bright and sunny Sunday morning, the weather did nothing to improve her self-hating mood. She stared up at the pineapple yellow historic home she'd parked in front of. The engraved sign out front loomed over her with reproach: *San Francisco Dachshund Rescue Center.*

She glanced at the passenger seat. Princess sat with an entitled thrust to her barrel chest, waiting for her door to open. Her blonde head swung toward Addison impatiently. It was like driving Miss Daisy. But to Addison, she was worth the extra effort.

"Home sweet home," Addison said.

Princess barked and wagged her tail, the decorative pink ribbons Addison had tied to it fluttering with each swipe. The doxie pawed at the passenger door, eager to greet her subjects inside the building.

The center had been Addison's home ever since she'd graduated from pet-grooming school five years earlier. She'd been offering her services pro bono to different shelters around the city, both to hone her skills and to give a little TLC to those dogs that needed it the most. But the day she'd met Princess, she'd known the dachshund rescue center was her home for good. She'd fallen in love with it and its inhabitants—both the two-legged and four-legged kind. After that, she'd continued to return every week.

But this morning, it didn't feel like a welcome sight to Addison. Even with a pancake breakfast waiting inside. Today, it was a reminder of her failed attempt at combining her two favorite things: dogs and beauty. She was supposed to help lost dogs, not be the one to lose them.

There was also the matter of a broken promise to a friend: Aiden Caldwell, Piper's boyfriend. He was CEO of Caldwell and Son Investments, and, more to the point, a key investor in Addison's business.

How was she going to tell him she'd lost seven dogs at the cocktail mixer? That her reputation was being slandered far and wide throughout the local doggydom—if it hadn't gone national yet, that is. Most importantly, how would she explain that she'd taken the money he'd invested in her Fido Fashion line to help her get it off the ground and threw it all into one basket: the two weeks leading up to her fashion show?

Addison's phone rang. Pulling it out of her purse, she checked the caller ID. Hitting the icon, she accepted the call. "Hi, Dad."

"Hi, sweetheart. How are you?" Just the sound of his voice was comforting, but it was tinted with concern. "I saw you on the news. What in the world happened?"

Great, even her dad had heard. "Oh, that? Er, yeah, some dogs were stolen at the event I was working last night."

"Is everything okay? Have they found them yet? And why were those people blaming you for it?" He was asking questions faster than she could answer. Not that she had many answers.

She usually told her dad everything, but if they ended up finding the dogs, then she didn't want to worry him for nothing. And if she were honest with herself, she didn't want to tell him how bad things were because she didn't want to disappoint him.

"It was a misunderstanding," she said, finally. "It's the dogs I'm really worried about. They haven't found any trace of them yet."

"That's too bad," he said. "You're doing okay though, right?"

"Yeah, of course. You know me." She tried to

muster some enthusiasm, but it sounded weak even to her.

"That's my girl. Nothing can get you down."

Addison rolled her eyes at herself. "You bet." She hated lying to her dad, but she just needed a little time to figure out how bad things really were.

There was a pause on the other end before her dad finally said, "I also called to give you some news."

"What is it?" She sat up straighter, glad the focus was shifting off her.

"Well, you know things haven't been going great at the store," he began. "Dora and I have decided that it's time to sell. Or rather, the bank has decided for us. It's either sell fast or we'll be facing bankruptcy."

Addison blinked as she let the news wash over her. The little family corner store in Linda Mar had been her second home growing up. "Dad, I had no idea things were that bad."

His laugh sounded strained over the line. "Me neither. I'd hoped we could turn things around."

Addison suddenly felt guilty. Her father was admitting his own dire situation to her while she was hiding her bad news. But she knew it was the right decision. He had enough on his plate to worry about; she didn't need to add her own side dish.

"That's terrible, Dad. I wish there was something I could do to help."

"Don't worry about us. I just wanted to let you know what was going on," he said. "I'd better get going. Dora's keeping an eye on the store by herself. Lots to do. Anyway, I'll talk to you soon."

"Okay, Dad. Love you."

"Love you too, muffin."

After she hung up, Addison stared at the phone. How was she not supposed to worry? Bankruptcy? She'd grown up watching her parents' marriage fall apart because of money problems. She recalled the struggling, the bills, the bickering over finances. It had all ended with a nasty divorce when Addison was seven years old that had left her father raising her alone.

Her dad had always been there for her. He'd raised her by himself, sacrificed for her. He'd even put her through dog-grooming school, although she'd always planned to pay him back. Now he was in trouble, and there was nothing she could do to help him and his new wife, Dora. If only there were a way to turn things around for her business, she might be able to do something.

A gentle breeze kicked up, and Addison caught the faint whiff of mouthwatering pancakes. Obviously, so did Princess, because she whined and fidgeted on the seat.

Addison sighed. She knew she couldn't hide in her car forever. It was Pancake Sunday, after all. And she was craving the comforting carbs after the lengthy chat she'd had with the cops that morning.

"Well, Princess? Shall I go explain to Aiden how I lost his money?"

Princess didn't seem to care. She waved her nose in the air, searching for the source of that delicious smell.

Addison rounded her car to open the passenger door, as if she were Princess's chauffeur. The doxie dropped delicately to the pavement next to Addison's shoes and trotted up to the old two-story farmhouse. The flagstone steps took a little extra effort as Princess awkwardly hopped up each one.

Following the doxie through the open French doors, Addison glanced around the reception area. No one was manning the desk or sitting on the antique furniture by the hearth. The place was empty except for the exotic fish swimming around an aquarium that took up the entire back wall. A little sign on the desk read "If you need help, you can find us around back."

Addison heard laughter mingled with a few distant barks filter through the cozy house from outside. Princess strutted toward the sounds, her Persian Pink toenails tapping the high-quality vinyl floor.

The back door was propped open. Addison was about to walk onto the wraparound porch when she heard footsteps shuffle behind her. She turned to find Marilyn, the center's manager, balancing a steaming plate of fresh pancakes. They jiggled with delicious moistness upon each step she took.

"Addison, would you be a dear and grab the syrup for me?"

The glass dispenser dangled from Marilyn's pinky finger. It threatened to drop its gooey contents on the woman's heels. Cheetah print, Addison noted.

"Sure thing." Addison grabbed it. "Nice shoes, by the way. You dressed up for anyone in particular?" She gave Marilyn a sly wink.

"What? These old things?" She waved away the comment. "Just a silly way to make an old lady feel young."

"If you're old, then I'm a hundred and ten."

The spry sixty-two-year-old British woman had more energy and spirit than Addison had at twenty-eight most days. The recent love glow that Marilyn wore only added to her youthful disposition.

Grinning to herself, Addison followed Marilyn out onto the porch where the older woman's dog, Picasso, waited patiently. He followed Marilyn everywhere, despite the fact that getting around was harder for him than for most dogs. He was in a wheelchair.

Picasso was a blue dachshund that Marilyn had rescued from a kill shelter. When she'd brought him back and had him checked over, it turned out that he'd developed a severe case of intervertebral disc disease, which was not unheard of for doxies.

After the center had paid for Picasso's surgery, Marilyn took him home and cared for him over the next several months of his rehabilitation. Of course, once he'd healed, she couldn't give him up to another home. She'd grown too attached and so had he.

Unfortunately for Picasso, his spine worsened over time. Addison remembered when Marilyn bought him a little doggy wheelchair to help him get around. It broke Addison's heart when she first saw him in it. But once he started rolling around the center on his own set of wheels rather than being carried, he seemed like a puppy again. He could even frolic through the grassy field with the other dogs, playing fetch without pain.

Remembering not to use stairs was something Picasso was still working on, so as Marilyn carried the pancakes to the gazebo, she used the wheelchair ramp. Picasso followed her, as he always did. You didn't often see Marilyn without hearing the rolling of wheels on the floor.

Everyone was hanging out beneath the huge gazebo for their usual Sunday brunch. Bob, Marilyn's sweetheart, stood at the grill. He brandished a pair of barbecue tongs, flipping sausages.

They'd first met Bob when he was the inspector assigned to investigate a series of attacks against Piper and the rescue center's old location. However, once the case had been closed, he kept finding excuse after excuse to come around the new center. Eventually, he'd stopped coming up with reasons, and no one bothered asking, since it was obvious that he was there to see Marilyn.

Addison's two besties in the whole world, Piper and Zoe, sat at the picnic table. Zoe looked caught up in a story she was telling, eyes shining with a glint of juicy gossip. But Piper's attention wandered to where a fenced enclosure dominated the back of the property.

Addison followed her gaze and saw a handsome man in a polo shirt and cargo pants tossing a ball for some of the rescue dogs. Aiden. As though they were so in tune with each other, he glanced back to lock eyes with Piper. She waved him over, and he threw the ball one more time before joining them under the gazebo.

As he approached, Addison's mouth went dry. What would she say to him? Could he read the failure all over her face? She climbed the steps as if to the gallows.

"Hey everyone," she said. "Sorry I'm late."

Bob waved his tongs at her. "Perfect timing. The sausages are just about done."

"Good, because here are the pancakes," Marilyn sang.

Addison dropped her purse under a chair and

sat down across from Piper and Zoe. Or at least, they looked like her two besties. Only, they wore the strangest expressions. It was like a couple of aliens had body-snatched them, but they'd put their faces on all wrong. Their smiles were strained, their expressions stiff.

"Hi," Piper said.

Zoe waved. "How are you?"

"Good …" Addison eyed them. Now that she really looked around, everyone was acting strangely except for Bob.

The detective placed a piping-hot plate of sausages in the middle of the table and took a seat next to Addison. "So, how's business?" he asked her.

Zoe groaned, Piper cringed, and Marilyn swatted him with her napkin. Aiden averted his gaze, reaching to straighten a tie that he seemed surprised wasn't there.

Addison suddenly realized what had everyone so on edge. They must have watched Holly Hart's segment.

"What?" Bob asked. "What did I say?"

"Nothing," Addison said. "It's fine. Business is, er, swell." She studiously avoided eye contact with Aiden.

The truth was, she'd closed the spa for the day since every one of her customers had canceled their appointments. She'd also given Melody the week off because she didn't need anyone to watch the shop when no one was going to come in anyway. And as much as she didn't like to admit it, she still worried that maybe Melody had more to do with the missing dogs than she was letting on. Addison couldn't risk her being around more dogs until she was certain of her innocence.

"Swell?" Bob studied her. "Where's the usual enthusiasm? Don't you normally use words like 'fantabulous' or 'awesomeness'?"

"Maybe not 'swell,'" Addison said. "But it's fine. It's okay. Good, I suppose."

Zoe set her fork down. "Let's not sugarcoat it. We all saw the news. Things are terrible."

"Zoe, come on," Piper said. "It wasn't that bad. Besides, who really watches Holly Hart's Hounds anyway?" By the look on Piper's face, she did.

Addison leveled her with a look. "Besides every dog lover in San Francisco? The segment's a hit. Holly's popularity has skyrocketed ever since she started it."

"All thanks to us," Zoe said. "If it hadn't been for our drama last year, Holly'd be back working at that cheap rag, *The San Francisco Gate*, by now."

"Yeah, and she couldn't wait to use my drama last night for another breaking story." Addison pushed her pancake around her plate.

"Do they have any leads?" Aiden asked.

Addison shrugged. "If they do, they're not saying."

Marilyn clicked her tongue. "All those dogs. They must be so scared. Right after I saw it on the news, I called all my contacts at the other shelters in town," she told Addison. "You should give me a list of the dogs that went missing. I'll call around regularly to see if any of them get picked up."

"That's a great idea, Marilyn. Thank you."

Marilyn poured Bob some coffee. "Dear, have you heard anything around the station?"

"Sorry. It's not my case, nor my place to say anything," he said in his no-nonsense cop voice. As though realizing he wasn't on the record, his mouth softened beneath his salt-and-pepper mustache. "But what I can tell you is that a few missing dogs aren't going to rate high on their list of priorities, especially if they're not certain an actual crime was committed. No one knows for sure that these dogs haven't run away on their own."

Addison frowned, once again doubting that it was possible for them to have snuck out entirely of their own volition, either past Melody while she was outside smoking or through an entire room full of guests.

She'd driven around the hilly streets of San Francisco until three in the morning, working her way from the Regency Center out, down back alleys and through dark parking lots, shining her headlights into driveways. She hadn't spotted a stray. Not even so much as a cat.

Maybe the cops just didn't want to say one way or the other until they had more evidence. But what would it take to make them see?

"The precinct has been strapped for staff lately," Bob said between bites. "On top of a few early retirements and the recent rash of murders in the city, let's just say we got caught with our pants down."

Zoe grinned. "I hate when that happens."

"Zoe," Piper chastised. "This is serious. Nobody wants to see Bob with his pants down." She cracked a smile, and Zoe snickered.

"Cheeky." Marilyn threw them a look as though they were a couple of silly teenagers. "So many murders lately. Those poor people." She shook her head. "I've been following it on the news for weeks."

"I hear they suspect it's a serial killer," Zoe said. "They've been calling him the San Fran Slayer."

Bob dabbed a napkin across his mustache, neither confirming nor denying the rumor. "So, you can see that with everything going on, a few missing dogs don't justify pulling people off murder cases."

Addison frowned. She was obviously not the only one around the table doing so, because Bob held up his hands in defense.

"I'm not saying these missing dogs aren't important," he added quickly, "but the city is up in arms over these murders. The entire country is watching, demanding the cases be solved. Unless they can find evidence that it was dog theft, or unless it happens again, I don't think this case will be a top priority. The police force only has so many resources to go around."

Addison turned to Bob. "So, what you're saying is you don't think my name will be cleared anytime soon, if at all?"

Bob's mustache twitched, and he took a moment too long to answer, which worried Addison. In his forty-plus years of service, he'd probably seen it all, the worst of it. Maybe Addison didn't want him to answer after all.

Aiden cut in before the silence continued for too long. "At least there's one benefit to Holly sticking her big nose into the disappearances last night."

"What's that?" Piper asked.

"The case might get a little more public attention, meaning it will get solved faster."

Addison hoped Aiden was right. While her first concern was the dogs getting home safely, she had a lot of money riding on the next two weeks. As in, all of it. The faster the dogs were found, the better.

"Things will die down," Aiden told her. "I remember the heat I faced last year when my company came under scrutiny over the old rescue center. As a business, you lie low, pivot strategies if you need to, and you'll weather the storm. Caldwell and Son Investments pulled through just fine. In fact, ever since the case closed, business has been better than ever."

Addison knew it wouldn't be that easy. She was in too deep financially. If she continued to lose customers, there would be no weathering the storm in that boat. It was going to sink like the *Titanic*.

But even as she opened her mouth to tell Aiden just how bad things were, she realized she couldn't face the music yet. She'd tell him. Eventually. *Maybe after pancakes,* she told herself.

For the moment, she put on her best I-can-do-it face. "You're right. I'm sure it will all blow over soon. Maybe I'll just hold off on the marketing for a while, then rebrand and make a comeback when things die down."

"That's the spirit. Smart business is not always about investing in a good product. It's about investing in people." Aiden gave her a sincere look. "And you are a good investment."

Addison felt the heart-warming compliment like a blow to her gut. She imagined her makeup cracking as she tried her best not to let her smile waver. "Thanks."

Turning to Zoe, she changed the subject. "How is the planning for the dog show gala coming along?"

"Excellent." Zoe's eyes lit up. "I just have to

confirm the band, meet with the caterer, send out the tickets, and pick out an outfit." Her gaze focused on nothing in particular, as though she was consulting the to-do list in her mind. "Are you still coming?"

"Wouldn't miss it," Addison said. "Where is it being held again?"

"Actually, I've decided to change the venue, considering recent events. It will be held on the *San Francisco Belle*."

"The old paddle wheeler?" Bob asked. "That's some venue."

"I wanted to make sure the guests were comfortable bringing their pets. Once we've cast off, there will be no way on or off, for humans or dogs."

Addison winced slightly. The extra planning her friend had to do somehow felt like her fault too, but she gave a thumbs-up. "That's a fantabulous idea."

Bob waved a sausage in the air. "There's our girl."

Addison's phone buzzed in her purse. Pulling it out, she checked the new text message. It was another cancellation. This time for a fashion show model. The last one. A fashion show wouldn't be effective without dogs to wear her designs. It wasn't like she could wear them herself.

While she'd been planning on borrowing some of her furry friends from the rescue center as models, she'd been relying on the support of the dog show world. The core value she wanted to promote was that every dog was beautiful, mixed breed and purebred alike. Her statement would lose its impact, not to mention a huge source of potential customers, without the latter.

And who could blame them? *Those poor missing dogs*, thought Addison.

She only wished she knew how to find them. If her life were a movie, now would be the moment where the plot should twist, giving the main character hope. An invitation from Hogwarts, a fairy godmother's appearance. Addison would have settled for a yellow brick road.

As she stared at her plate, something nudged her leg. She glanced down to find Princess dragging her purse out from under her chair. She was licking the zippers and nosing her way through the pockets in search of dog treats.

Addison shook her head but bent down to give the doxie a treat. That's when she saw something sticking out of the main compartment. A ray of sun hit it like a sign from above, casting her in its golden reflection. Felix's business card.

Curiously, she pulled it out. She'd been running late for the cop shop that morning, so she'd dumped the contents of her clutch from the cocktail mixer into her usual purse. Felix's card, which had been at the bottom, ended up on top.

She read the card. *Felix Vaughn, bartender.*

Addison remembered how well Felix had known the crowd at the mixer, how he could read his customers. Heck, he'd downright bragged about it. "I'm in an ideal position to people-watch, to observe the human species and understand what makes them tick," he'd proclaimed.

If anyone could help her save those dogs, it would be him. It might not be too late, after all.

It wasn't a fairy godmother giving Addison an easy way out, but maybe it was a chance to find a solution for herself.

6

DON'T HAVE A DOG IN THIS FIGHT

Addison stood on a gum-speckled sidewalk on the edge of the Mission District, double-checking her golden ticket one more time. She held Felix's card under a flickering streetlight to read the address. It was far from the glorious chocolate factory, but she was in the right place.

When she crossed the street, she could read the faded sign at the top of the building that assured her she was at Joe's Dive. She approached the heavy oak door and peered through the cracked stained-glass window next to it.

It was only nine at night, but the lights inside the bar were dim. She wondered if it had already closed and someone just forgot to turn off the flickering open sign in the window. However, when she tried the grimy brass door handle and stepped inside, the room was sparsely populated with Sunday night faithfuls. And one quick scan of her surroundings told Addison that Joe couldn't have chosen a better name for the place. It was a dive.

She hesitated in the entrance to let her eyes adjust to the weak glow from the filthy pendant lights dangling from the exposed ceiling. Dark leather booths hid lone drinkers and a young couple canoodling in the far corner. The theme could have passed for a chic industrial with very little effort, but she doubted Joe had had a particular décor in mind when he'd chosen the mismatched wooden chairs and metal tables.

Addison's shifting eyes found the bar at the back of the room. Felix stood behind it like a king in his castle. As he leaned across the bar to talk to a brunette in painted-on jeans, his black button-up shirt collar gaped open to reveal a Rolling Stones T-shirt. His thick black curls shone beneath the pendant lights, and his white teeth flashed with a flirty smile.

The woman shifted beneath the light, and her red bra peeked out of her low-backed top. It was the server he'd been flirting with the night before at the cocktail mixer.

Felix hadn't seen Addison come in yet. She was tempted to watch him for a while and observe him in his own element, to study the man who supposedly "sees all." To discover what made him tick. But as he laughed again at something Red Bra said, Addison marched up to the bar.

She dropped her purse on the counter with a thud to catch his attention and instantly regretted it—the thick oak slab was sticky from years of marinating in spilled drinks.

Felix pulled away from Red Bra and sauntered over to Addison. He did a double take when he recognized her. Or maybe it was the low cut, hot pink halter top she'd slipped on that night—and not by accident. She needed all the help she could get to convince Felix to join her cause. It was an inelegant tactic, but Felix didn't strike her as the elegant type. Besides, desperate times called for desperate measures.

He ran a hungry tongue across his bottom lip like an animal on the hunt. Halter top one, Felix zero.

"Just couldn't resist me, could you?" he asked her.

I might be desperate, but I'm not that desperate, Addison thought. "You're not as charming as you like to think."

"You're here, aren't you?"

"Okay, you caught me." She batted her eyelashes, just in case the halter top wasn't enough. "Actually, there is something you've got that I want."

"There is? Well, I aim to please." Felix pushed up his sleeves and leaned his elbows on the bar. "Tell me, what can I do for you?" He laced each word with meaning, or maybe a promise.

The deep hum of his voice washed over Addison, settling low in her belly like a warm massage stone. She cleared her throat, ignoring the effect he had on her.

"I want information."

"Well, I'm thirty-one. I like sports—the Forty-Niners are my favorite team—and I love music. The classics, mostly. You know, Rolling Stones, Zeppelin, Journey. Oh, and don't forget banana pancakes with caramel chocolate chips after a sleep-in on Sundays."

"Caramel chocolate chips?"

"I have a sweet tooth. Not that I'm not sweet enough already." He flashed that charismatic smile at her, and Addison took it back: he *was* as charming as he thought he was—not that she'd ever tell him that.

She felt the surge rush over her again, this time specifically beneath her miniskirt. His gaze drew her in like a storewide sale on the most recent ticketed price.

Men like Felix—men who knew the power they had over women—were dangerous. At the cocktail mixer, Felix had told her she was a target for men to take advantage of. Well, if anyone knew how to read her and play her, it was going to be him. And when men knew how to use their power, it was usually because they exerted it often. Felix was bad news.

She shook her head, hoping to bring some of that blood flow north of her waistline. "Not that kind of information."

"We can get a little more personal if you like. But you'll have to buy me dinner first."

Bad news, bad news, bad news. She crossed her legs, clamping them tightly together. "No. I mean information about the other night at the cocktail mixer. You said you work the dog show circuit often."

The sudden change in direction put a furrow between his eyebrows. "Every year for the last five," he said, after a moment.

"You know the contestants, the owners, the judges, the ins and outs of the competition."

"It's like having a backstage pass." Felix smiled, clearly happy she'd taken an interest in what he'd said the night before.

"So you know the owners of the missing dogs?"

He shrugged. "Sure, I know of them."

"And their dogs?"

His eyes narrowed in suspicion. "Mostly."

Addison leaned in closer. "Even potential suspects?"

Understanding dawned on his face. He held up a hand, pulling away from the bar. "Now, hold on a minute."

Addison leaned even closer. "You would know who was there last night, both contestants and the staff."

"Yes, but—"

"And anyone else with a vendetta against the dog show. Maybe someone with a grudge or who runs an underground show dog puppy mill. Or maybe someone who has a debt to the mob and their only way to pay it off is by selling show dogs on the canine black market."

Felix's expression screwed up with the tumult of ideas. "Canine black market? You've been watching too many mobster movies."

Addison ignored the jibe. She was onto something. She could feel it. "Or maybe it's someone who hates what dog shows stand for, and they wanted to set them all free as a statement."

Felix reached across the sticky bar and shook Addison's shoulders to get her attention. "Whoa, Nancy Drew. You're getting a little ahead of yourself, aren't you?"

Her starry eyes focused again, and she returned to reality. "You're right. Sorry." She waved off the excitement. "You're the expert here. Where do you think we should begin?"

"How about with a cocktail?"

"Like as in the cocktail server? You think it was one of the staff who took the dogs?" Her eyes shifted around the room. Secretly, she hoped Red Bra was the criminal, or that might have been a little jealousy talking. At the very least, her fashion sense should have been considered a crime.

"No." Felix slammed a glass down in front of Addison, making her jump. "Cocktail. As in alcohol. This is a bar, sweetheart, and if you haven't noticed, I'm a bartender. Last time I checked, that means I serve drinks. I don't solve crimes."

He turned his back on her and picked out a few bottles of alcohol and mixers seemingly at random. As he sloshed them into a battered old cocktail shaker, Addison reached into her purse and drew out his card.

She slapped it down on the bar, pointing at it like an accusation. "But you said if I ever needed anything—"

"Yeah, like a drink." He poured the mystery contents into her glass. It came out in a shock of pink, like a glass of blended flamingos.

She narrowed her eyes at it. "What's this?"

"A consolation prize." He pushed it toward her.

"So, you won't help me?"

"I am helping," he said. "I'm a helpful guy. But I've got other customers I need to help right now." Reaching under the bar, he produced a pink umbrella and plunked it in her glass. "Enjoy."

Addison's shoulders slumped as Felix turned to a middle-aged man wearing a plaid shirt. However, Addison wasn't giving up that easily. It wasn't like he'd given her a firm no. Not exactly. There was still room for argument. Besides, without Felix and his intel, her next best strategy was to hang posters around the city that said "Have you seen this dog?" Not exactly an investigation worthy of Sherlock Holmes.

Settling back onto the bar stool, she eyed the drink in front of her suspiciously, wondering if he'd poison her just to get rid of her. *Not likely,* she finally decided. She took a sip. Her taste buds sang with pleasure. It was like a liquefied tropical island, flamingos and all.

Addison took another sip as she waited for Felix to finish serving the lumberjack, but then another customer ordered a round of shots. But man, was her drink ever good. *There can't be much alcohol in it, if any,* she told herself. It tasted practically like juice.

After the minutes ticked by and more orders rolled in, she figured one more drink couldn't hurt, right? She'd had a rough week, after all. She waved down Felix, and he slid another toward her.

At the cocktail mixer, he'd looked civilized, polished, a man who could serve gentlemen with numbers at the end of their names—that is, until he'd opened his mouth. But he also seemed to fit in this rough dive. The man was like Ewan McGregor, a chameleon of roles. Here in a little hole in the wall, he was at ease. In fact, he seemed to thrive, a prince among thieves.

Finally, Felix finished serving an elderly

woman her brandy and grabbed a cloth. With practiced hands, he wiped down the counter even though he'd barely let a drop hit the surface.

Addison stared at those hands, wondering what else they were practiced at—not that she cared. She shook the thought right out of her head. She was still hoping to receive a call from Philip Montgomery III. Okay, who was she kidding? After what had happened at the cocktail mixer, she'd probably never see him again.

When Felix continued to ignore her, Addison switched bar stools to sit closer to where he was pretending to look busy. He removed her empty glass and replaced it with a full one.

"Look, Felix. You said it yourself. You're in the perfect position to people-watch, to understand what makes them click."

"Tick," he corrected her with a smirk.

"Tick," she agreed, chasing her straw around with her tongue before catching it to take a drink.

"There's a reason people trust me," Felix said. "It's because I can keep my mouth shut. And I definitely don't investigate them."

"No, no, no." She wagged her finger. "Not investigate. This is just a friendly chat between two professionals." She indicated him and herself, nearly knocking her glass over. "This is business."

"And why would I want to talk to you?"

Addison flinched. *Why wouldn't he want to talk to me? And why do I want him to want to talk to me?*

Now she wasn't even making sense to herself. She pushed the drink away, focusing her thoughts.

"Because it's about one professional helping another professional. You know, helping? Caring? Because these poor dogs need us. What have you got to lose?"

"My job," he said flatly.

"What do you mean?"

"I mean these rich, snooty types live some interesting lives—lives they want to keep secret." He widened his eyes. "If people suspect I'm sneaking around and spying on them at functions, I won't get any more private gigs. And my boss, Joe, won't be too happy about the complaints. He's not exactly the forgiving type."

"Okay, fine. Mum's the word. I get it." Addison pretended to zip her lips. "How about I just talk, and you listen? If I get close to guessing the truth, all you have to do is wink. Like this." She gave a slow wink, as though he needed a demonstration.

His stare remained even. "The answer is no."

"Good, good. Play along. That's perfect." She gave him a thumbs-up. "Okay, here we go. Do the missing dogs have something to do with the mob?"

Addison watched his eyes carefully. His left eye moved. For a second, she thought it was a wink, but maybe it was more of an annoyed twitch.

She waved it away. "Okay, that's not it. On to the next question."

He sighed and yelled out, "Last call!" making her jump.

Felix turned away from her. She opened her mouth to argue, but a sharp clink of a glass on the counter interrupted her. She looked down to find another tropical island sitting before her like a mirage.

Well, she wasn't leaving until she got the answers she was looking for, so one more couldn't hurt.

Imbibing the nectar of the gods, Addison watched Felix tidy up the bar. Every time he got a break between customers or cleaning, she tried once again to convince him. But every time she did, she found a fresh drink in front of her. Probably because she couldn't argue if her mouth was busy. *Little does he know,* she thought.

Addison was sticking another umbrella into her updo when the pendant lights shut off. She glanced around to discover she was the last customer in the bar. In fact, she and Felix were the last two people in the whole place.

There were noises coming from the adjacent room where she could see pool tables through the doorway. Sliding off her stool, she followed the sharp sounds of billiard balls cracking together and found Felix tidying up.

Startled, he glanced up to see her standing in the doorway. "You're still here."

"You can't get rid of me that easily." Addison leaned against a table. "I haven't gotten what I wanted yet."

"You're a persistent little thing, aren't you?" He organized the pool cues into their wall holders before shutting off the lights.

Darkness swallowed the bar. The only light filtered in through the dirty windows and cracked stained-glass accents. Streetlights glowed green and purple through images of grapes on vines, coloring Felix's tanned skin.

She followed his movements as he walked across the pool hall, slinking with that same animal allure she'd seen in him earlier. A predator looking for the kill. She shivered slightly. No prey had ever been so eager to be caught.

Felix stopped in front of her and reached up. She thought he was going to touch her face, but then he plucked an umbrella out of her hair with a smirk. When a disappointed sigh escaped her, she realized how badly she'd wanted him to touch her.

"What about me?" he asked. "If I'm putting my job on the line, what do I get out of this deal?"

"The satisfaction of knowing you helped save seven poor, defenseless dogs?"

"Not quite what I was thinking." His bright teeth flashed like a panther baring its fangs.

Addison couldn't help the pant that escaped her. Her body tensed, her senses heightened, as though waiting for him to pounce. Heat radiated off him, or maybe she imagined it. *When did he get so near?*

She cleared her throat. "What did you have in mind?"

"I'll help you," he said. "I'll give you some leads … in exchange."

"Exchange for what?"

"A date with you."

Addison inhaled sharply, wondering if the drinks were making her foggy, or if it was Felix's nearness, the spice of his cologne, the way his eyes were holding hers. "What makes you think I'd go on a date with you?"

"You're here, aren't you?" he said, with a cocky tilt to his head.

"Only because I need your help."

"You know what I think?" he asked, closing the last few inches between them. "I think it's more than that. I think it's an excuse to come around and see me. I think you're interested and just won't admit it." The umbrella twirled between his fingers, and he brushed the crepe paper against her skin, down the low neckline of her halter top.

Addison snorted, backing away. Her butt hit the pool table. "You're obviously delusional."

"And you're obviously curious," he retorted, moving closer.

"What would I be curious about?"

"What it would be like to kiss me."

His voice sang with confidence, making Addison second-guess herself. Was she sure Felix wasn't the Prince Charming she was looking for? She scoffed, but her eyes automatically dropped to his lips.

Felix placed his hands on the pool table on either side of her, trapping his prey. "You want to feel my lips against yours."

"Ha."

She turned her face away from him but couldn't find the words to deny it as he brought his face close to her neck. His wavy hair brushed her face. Warm breath tickled her skin as his lips hovered over her, not yet touching.

"You're curious to feel what it's like to run your fingers through my hair, to press your body against mine." His lips finally grazed her neck, as light as a flicker of eyelashes.

Her breath left her in a moan that startled her. "Too close," she said. "Too close."

Felix drew back slightly but not too far. Although she couldn't see his face, she could sense him smile.

"Then push me away."

Addison brought her hands up. But instead of

shoving him away, those curious fingers of hers wove into his thick locks, dragging his face to hers.

Like that panther pouncing, he finally made his move. He met her hungry need to taste him with his own animal hunger, his tongue finding hers over and over again.

His hot hands ran down her halter top and then her skirt to cup her butt. He lifted her as easily as he'd lifted the stools onto the bar, and he set her on the edge of the pool table. He pushed his hips between her legs, parting her thighs, hiking up her skirt.

Now that they were at an even height, Felix could kiss along her neck, down her plunging neckline. Addison's toes curled as his lips found that perfect spot beneath her ear. She couldn't take it anymore. Gripping his shirt, she yanked him closer. Felix didn't need any more encouragement. He hopped onto the pool table.

As he laid her down against the green cloth, hard balls dug into her back. She quickly rolled them aside before dragging him down on top of her. Then he settled between her legs, and she could feel something else just as hard press against her. But it wasn't the pool balls.

Her moan was cut off as his mouth found hers again. This time their hands ran over each other with a new purpose, greedily, over clothes and under them, tugging impatiently at fabric.

Addison's head swam from the storm of sensations surging through her body. She'd never felt such a pull toward anyone. Maybe it was because she'd told herself she couldn't have Felix, that he'd be a mistake. Felix was off limits.

She thought she was done choosing the wrong guy. She was supposed to be ignoring her heart, her instincts, and using logic for once. Just like Felix had suggested.

Think of it like a numbers game.

The only "number" she wanted to be was somebody's number one. It would mean finding someone who would be there for her through anything, for better or worse. They wouldn't run out on her after three years when they'd found something that wasn't perfect about her. She'd had enough people walk out on her for one lifetime.

Then there was Felix, Mr. Numbers himself, with his midnight bartending job that he probably used to hook up with stragglers at the end of the night. The women who were desperate for attention, who confused the bartender's glances and free drinks with affection. Women who stayed after last call, hoping there was something more. Women, she realized belatedly, just like her.

Addison shoved Felix as hard as she could, wriggling away from him. "Get off. Get off."

Felix backed off, his hands in the air. "What? What's wrong? Did I hurt you?"

"Not yet, you haven't. And you're never going to."

Felix flinched like she'd just slapped him. "What is that supposed to mean?"

She scrambled off the pool table, landing awkwardly. She gripped her head, suddenly feeling the full effects of those deadly pink drinks. Why did she have to be such a lightweight?

"Look," she said. "I didn't come here for a make-out session. I came here for help." She jabbed a finger in the middle of his chest, unsure if she was angrier with him or herself. "Now, are you going to help me or not?"

He glanced down at the finger poking him. "Not with that attitude, I'm not."

"I won't go on a date with you just because I'm desperate for information. It's coercion. It's extortion. It's—"

"Is it a deal?" He grabbed her finger, dragging her closer to him.

But Addison wasn't playing. As she pushed him away again, the look on his face showed that he finally got the hint.

"So you won't help me unless there's something in it for you?"

Felix shrugged, but the flirtatious smile had left his face. He was serious too. "A guy's got to try, right? Besides, I have my own livelihood to look out for. I can't lose my job."

"And what about mine? What about the dogs?"

He pointed a thumb at his chest. "I've got to look out for number one."

"You're looking out for something, all right." Her eyes dipped down to the crotch of his well-worn jeans, which she couldn't help notice were a little tight at the moment. "You're exactly who I thought you were. Forget it. I'll figure it out on my own. Thanks for nothing."

"What about the free drinks, the company, and the hot make-out session? You call that nothing?"

Storming over to the bar, Addison reached into her purse and grabbed all the bills she had. She slammed the money down on the counter. It was only twenty-four dollars. It definitely wouldn't cover the bill, or a tip for that matter—not that he deserved one. But it would have to do.

"There. Now all I owe you is a bad memory."

"Keep your damned money," Felix said, thrusting it back at her.

"Is that how you get women to go out with you? You liquor them up, take advantage of their situation? That doesn't surprise me!" she yelled, because if she didn't yell, she thought she might cry.

Why did she always fall for the wrong guy? Why was she so gullible? She wanted a good guy like Philip Montgomery III. A man with manners and sophistication. She didn't want to want a guy like Felix. A guy who wouldn't inconvenience himself to help somebody unless something was in it for him.

But she wanted Felix. Oh boy, she wanted him. The pool table could attest to that, and she felt all the worse for it. She was hopeless.

"Excuse me?" Felix wasn't yelling, but his voice held a certain power. It was kind of hot but almost worse than if he did yell.

Addison was so used to his cool, cocksure attitude that the little vein popping out on his forehead had her backing up.

"I'm not trying to take advantage of you," he said. "You came here looking for me tonight, remember? And I'll have you know that I've got a lot going for me. I'm a catch."

Addison didn't need the reminder. She scoffed. "A catch? Yeah, as in I might catch something from you."

He crossed his arms. "Why don't you tell me how you really feel?"

"Why bother?" She slung her purse over her shoulder. "I don't want to waste my breath."

He huffed. "You weren't able to catch your breath just a minute ago."

Addison sneered and turned on her heel, but he grabbed her arm.

"Why the sudden change of heart? What's going on in that head of yours?"

"I just wasn't into it. I was faking it." She

flicked her hair in his face and marched toward the door.

"So that's a 'no' to the date, I suppose?" However, by the sarcasm coating his voice, it didn't sound like he wanted one anymore.

Grasping the door handle, she glanced over her shoulder. "You've got about a dog's chance."

"That's good," he threw back at her, "because I hear you have bad luck keeping track of dogs anyway."

Addison's mouth dropped open. She stood there sputtering for a moment, caught between fury, humiliation, and outright insult. When all the insults and swearwords she wanted to spit back at him balled into one, the only thing that came out was something between a grunt and a scream.

Wrenching on the heavy door, she flung it open and stormed out onto the sidewalk. The door slammed behind her. She heard the deadbolt snap home.

Addison was in no shape to drive, so she abandoned her car and stomped down the street in search of a cab. Her car would have to sit until she came back for it in the morning.

The walk did Addison good, the cool night air like a splash of water in her face. All the things she didn't say to Felix, the responses that wouldn't come to her, suddenly formed clearly in her head. Boy, were there some zingers. She was tempted to turn right around and throw them in his face, but at that moment a cab appeared. With a shaking hand, she hailed it and got in.

The taxi drove down the rolling San Francisco streets to her tiny apartment. The eclectic mix of row houses and colorful shops and bars passed outside her window. Looking for a distraction from her anger and her sudden self-loathing—because she was beginning to think she'd taken out her anger on the wrong person—she pulled out her phone to scroll through her contacts.

She didn't know many of the people at the cocktail mixer the other night. It's not like she'd been on the scene as long as Felix had. The only relevant person she had a connection with was Holly Hart. However, she was the reason the entire incident had escalated in the first place.

Addison just couldn't bring herself to suck it up and call her. Besides, Holly wouldn't help her prove her innocence. That would only take the wind out of Holly's own story, not to mention make her look like a sloppy reporter—which would be entirely true.

She was about to chuck her phone into her purse when a new text message caught her eye. It was from an unknown number. Dreading yet another appointment cancellation, she opened it.

Hello, Addison. This is Philip Montgomery III. I hope it's all right that I tracked down your number through a client of yours. It was a pleasure meeting you at the cocktail mixer. I'm sorry events prevented us from getting to know one another better. I'd like to see you again. I'm still holding the fundraiser this week, if you're interested in attending.

—Regards, Philip.

Addison clutched the phone, reading it over again. Philip had tracked her number down. After losing seven dogs, her embarrassing debut on stage, the media blowup, and everyone blaming her, he still wanted to see her.

She automatically touched her locks to see if there was a hair out of place—which, after her run-in with Felix, there were probably a lot. The giddiness she'd felt when she'd met Philip at the cocktail mixer returned like a refreshing rain. It cleared her mind of any fog remaining from the heated pool table session.

Who cared if Felix saw her as a last-call hookup when she was destined to be Mrs. Philip Montgomery III?

7

FIGHT LIKE CATS AND DOGS

Cinderella arrived at the prince's castle just a little late. Unlike the real Cinderella, Addison didn't have a fairy godmother to magic her a gown and a classy hairstyle. But if she knew how to do anything, it was how to doll herself up. Besides, she preferred her Mini to a pumpkin anyway.

However, as Addison pulled up to a small circular drive in front of an Italian Renaissance-influenced mansion, it appeared as though her prince really did have a castle. Well, it was close enough. The fact that he had a driveway at all in San Francisco was impressive enough, but the three-story home was like something from a fairy tale.

After rearranging Princess's feather fascinator on her head, Addison picked her up and got out of the car. She handed the keys to the valet driver and set Princess down so she didn't wrinkle the doxie's delicate lace sundress. Suppressing a giddy squeal, she headed for the mansion's arched doorway.

It may not have been a ball, but at least it was a date. Well, sort of. She was going to count it as one, anyway. If she didn't see it that way, it was going to be one awkward afternoon with dog show hotshots, judges, and highbrow dog-lovers who still associated her with the missing show dogs.

Raising her head high, Addison climbed the stone stairs. She was Philip's guest; she deserved to be there. Besides, no amount of criticism was going to keep her from her dreams. No matter what anyone said, she knew what was in her own heart. She was just as worried about those dogs as everyone else, and she planned to find out what happened ... somehow.

Addison was just about to enter through the doors when two men in suits converged on her. By their dark sunglasses and the wires coiling into their ears, she assumed they were on security detail.

"Good afternoon, ma'am," one said. "We've been asked to greet all guests as they arrive today. Name, please?"

"Addison Turner."

The other guard took out a tablet, jotting

down a few notes. Addison kinked her neck to see what he was writing. He frowned and tilted the screen away.

"Is this the only dog you have accompanying you today?" Guard Two asked.

"Yes," she said. "This is Princess."

He typed the name into his tablet. The first guard held up a small silver tag and a matching bracelet. "This tag is for your dog's collar. And you're welcome to wear the bracelet. They're a gift from the host. May I?"

Addison raised her wrist while he fastened it for her. The delicate bling glistened in the sunlight. When she looked closer, she realized it was actually white gold. Her eyes widened, thinking it was a bit much for a first date.

She noticed a little charm dangling from it and held it up to the sun to read it. There was a number engraved on it that matched the one on Princess's tag. Okay, so not exactly a gift specifically for her, she realized. Every guest would probably get one. At least, the ladies would. The men would receive something different.

Most of the guests would probably see it as a fun memento from the fundraiser. However, the bracelet was of finer quality than any of the jewelry Addison had at home.

Guard One slipped the tag onto Princess's crystal collar. "Simply show the bracelet to the guard upon your exit to ensure you have the correct pet."

"Thank you." Addison was pretty sure she wouldn't forget Princess. Then it dawned on her that it wasn't to make sure the guests left with their own dog. It was to ensure they couldn't leave with anyone else's.

She climbed the stairs to make her grand entrance. When she walked through the double front doors, Philip was waiting to greet her. He spotted her across the cavernous foyer, and his perfect smile spread across his face like a commercial for teeth-whitening strips.

Excusing himself from a conversation, he walked over and took her hands in his. "Addison. I'm so happy you came."

"Thank you for inviting us," she said.

He turned to his other guest and greeted her with a bow. "Hello, Princess. It's a pleasure to see you again."

Princess sat down on the marble floor and stuck out her chest. *Of course it is.*

"Please, come in," he told Addison. "Most of the guests are on the veranda."

He led Addison and Princess back, *way* back, toward a set of open doors that led outside onto a stone patio. Behind it, a sizable backyard stretched into the distance, the grass so manicured it looked almost fake. It was the same size as the small park she often took Princess to. But she supposed that was what craploads of money got you in San Francisco.

Dotted around the backyard, guests nibbling on caviar leaned against pillars and sipped champagne among marble statues. The furry guests drank bottled water from gold-embossed bowls. The sun glinted off expensive jewelry and watches, almost blinding Addison.

She noticed a couple of faces turn her way, a frozen smile, a double take. They recognized her. Ignoring them, she kept a pleasant look on her face and followed her date.

Philip didn't make it far before a guest stopped him. When he turned to greet them, Addison relaxed at the sight of a friendly face. It was Julia Edwards, one of her best customers. She wore a sapphire blue dress that complemented her willowy figure. With her hair pinned back, her diamond earrings caught the afternoon sun like disco balls. They'd probably cost more than Addison made in a year.

"Fabulous party, Philip," she said. "Good turnout."

"Thank you." He turned to Addison for an introduction. "Addison, I'd like you to meet Julia Edwards. Her cocker spaniel was the Best of Breed last year."

"Of course," Addison said. "We already know each other. Nice to see you, Julia."

The woman held her martini aloft while she leaned in to kiss the air next to Addison's cheek. "What a surprise to see you."

Philip watched Julia's cocker spaniel and Princess sniff each other with familiarity. "How do you two know each other?"

"Addison here is the reason Precious won his title last year. Wasn't she, Precious?" Julia asked the dog sitting at her feet.

Precious stared back passively, turning politely to Addison as though in greeting. His long fur fanned out on the stones like an elegant cream gown.

Addison waved away the compliment. "I wouldn't go that far. Julia is a regular customer of mine," she told Philip.

"Don't be so modest," Julia said. "You're very talented at what you do."

"It's a lucky thing I found her then." Philip gave Addison a look that made her feel like *she* was the lucky one.

"She might be a whiz with a dog brush," a harsh, nasal voice cut in, "if you want to risk never seeing your pet again." Penny Peacock approached their group, swishing her appletini around her glass. She leaned down to whisper to Princess conspiratorially. "I'd be careful if I were you."

Sensing Penny's hostility, Princess growled, and her lace collar bunched up over her hackles.

Julia rolled her eyes. "Addison isn't responsible for the missing dogs. She's not capable of something like that. Precious and I have been going to her faithfully every Saturday for two years now. Haven't we, Precious?" She bent down to her cocker spaniel and kissed him on the snout. "And that won't change now." She leveled Penny with an icy look. "Sensationalism. That's all that media nonsense was."

"'Nonsense'?" Penny looked aghast. "Her carelessness cost me this year's Best in Show title."

"You know *you're* not competing, right?" Julia asked her. "I know it's confusing when they refer to the *bitch* category, but they are referring to the dogs, not you."

Penny's mouth dropped open with a squawk not unlike a parrot's. Addison had to smother a burst of laughter behind her hand. Even Philip's cheeks were quivering as he tried to control himself.

He cleared his throat. "Ladies. Ladies. Let's not allow a little healthy competition to ruin the afternoon."

"What competition?" Julia asked innocently. "Penny doesn't even have a dog to handle anymore. There is no competition."

Penny's grip on her martini glass tightened with a squeak. "Maybe it was *you* who stole Lily. You just couldn't stand to see me beat you again, could you?"

Julia yawned. "I'm not as obsessed with winning as you are. I have a life." As though bored with the conversation, she turned to Philip. "I'm going to get more of that quiche before it's gone."

"Of course. Enjoy yourself."

"See you on Saturday, Addison?" Julia gave her a wink.

Addison waved. "Four o'clock, as usual. See you then."

She felt a little ray of hope shine inside her. At least not everyone believed the rumors. When she turned around again, Penny had already stormed off. Her day was getting better and better.

Philip shook his head at Penny's retreating back. "Ignore her," he told Addison. "She's just angry about what happened, and for good reason. But it wasn't your fault."

She placed a hand on her chest. "Thank you for saying so."

It felt good to have his faith in her innocence. Of course, he wouldn't have invited her to his party if he didn't believe her, but it was still nice to hear it while surrounded by so many people who would disagree.

"Besides," he said, lowering his voice, "Alistair couldn't have won for a fourth time in a row. Everyone knows that Lily is past her prime. She was lucky to win last year. So don't let anyone here ruin your day."

Nothing could ruin her day when she got to

spend the afternoon with Philip. Letting it roll off her back, she beamed up at him. "I don't intend to."

At that moment, one of the security guards approached him and murmured something in his ear, too low for Addison to hear.

Philip nodded briefly and turned back to her. "I'm so sorry, Addison. This is Carson, my head of security. I have to deal with something. Why don't you order a drink from the bar? I'll be right back."

"Of course," she said. "Take your time. You're the host."

He reached out and squeezed her hand. A pulse of energy coursed through her like he'd just transferred all his feelings into her with that one touch. He was totally into her. She just knew it.

With a grin on her face, she and Princess drifted over to the bar set up at the edge of the grass. It sat in the shade of a huge umbrella. The doxie trotted next to her with the same tilt of her chin as Addison's, the one that said she belonged there. Even among the potential Best of Breeds and Best in Shows, Princess knew she was just as good as they were.

Addison looped Princess's leash onto one of the dog-minding hooks on the side of the counter and waited for the bartender to finish organizing his bottles. When he turned around, she scowled. It was Felix.

"What are you doing here?" she demanded.

Felix flashed a winning smile, as if he were actually happy to see her—unlike how she felt about him at the moment.

"Well, hello to you, too. Can I get you a drink, madam? Might I suggest a Dog's Lunch or perhaps a Hair of the Dog? Or maybe you'd like a replay of the other night?" He waggled his dark eyebrows at her.

She made a repulsed, throaty sound. "No, thank you. I'd rather forget about that."

"I meant the drink. What were you thinking about?" He clicked his tongue teasingly. "You should feel flattered. I've named it after you. I called it the Head Turner. It certainly seemed to turn *your* head."

Her scowl faded slightly. He'd named it after her? Not that it mattered. He probably did that kind of thing all the time to impress women.

"You mean that pink drink you probably drugged?"

Felix was already grabbing bottles and mixing them into a cocktail shaker. "Drugged?"

"That's the only way I can explain why I lost all my marbles," she said with the most aloof air she could manage.

"Or maybe," he said, "it was because you'd been dying to kiss me ever since the cocktail mixer."

Some guys just can't take a hint, she thought.

"Yeah, right. I plead temporary insanity. Besides, I'm interested in someone else."

Addison glanced around the veranda, hoping Philip would come back soon. More and more of the guests were throwing her sharp glances. She could feel the daggers. Surely no one would cause a scene if he were there.

The clinking ice in Felix's cocktail mixer fell silent as he froze. "Who? Not Philip Montgomery?"

"The third," she added airily.

He pulled a face. "Is he your Mr. Perfect?"

"Yes. We're practically dating now." Well, that wasn't entirely true, but he didn't need to know that.

Felix shook his head, pouring the familiar bright pink liquid into a glass. "Not that guy."

"Yes, *that guy*," she said. "He is perfect. He's a gentleman, he's got looks, manners, a good job—"

Felix glanced around, lowering his voice. "Being a rich man's son isn't a job. It's lucky genetics. It's not like he worked hard for it."

Addison frowned. Come to think of it, she didn't know exactly what Philip did for work … or much about him at all, really. But those were all just details. They would come in time. After all, Sleeping Beauty had known nothing about the prince when he'd kissed her. They got to know each other during their happily ever after.

"Well, he fundraises for good causes." She

swept her arm, indicating the party. "Which is even more remarkable. It means he's selfless."

"When you have nothing else to occupy your time, you have to do something." Felix set the drink in front of her.

She grinned over the bar. "You're just jealous."

"And you're just desperate."

Her grin vanished. "What is that supposed to mean?"

"I called it the moment I met you. I knew you were desperate enough to jump at any guy who looked your way."

"Obviously not any guy. I didn't jump at you."

"I know a pool table that would disagree." The way his eyes roamed over her made her knees shake.

A flash of memory from her visit to Joe's Dive and Felix's touch came to her. She could practically feel the billiard cloth rubbing against her skin.

While Felix set a gold bowl of Evian down for Princess, Addison slid onto a stool to hide her sudden weakness. She took a big gulp of her drink. She was just tired. Or nervous. Yes. She was nervous about seeing Philip, not Felix. How could the two possibly compare? Felix was rude, brash, insensitive, like the antagonist in her love story. The villain to Philip's hero.

"He's not the one for you," Felix told Addison flatly. "You just want him to be."

Addison gaped at him like he'd just said he hadn't seen any of the *Lord of the Rings* movies. "What are you talking about? Philip's utterly perfect. I'd be crazy not to want him."

"Are you trying to convince me or yourself?"

There was that cocky, all-knowing look again, as if Felix saw right through her. It was an uncomfortable feeling. Like someone seeing her first thing in the morning, with a rat's nest for hair, no makeup protecting her, and dragon breath. It unnerved her.

She shifted uncomfortably and took another sip. "You don't even know me. You only think you know it all. But you won't even help me find the show dogs, so maybe you're just all talk."

Picking up his cloth, Felix wiped down the counter. "I can't get dragged into that. It's your problem. Not mine."

She hopped to her feet, glaring across the counter. "You arrogant—"

"Addison." Philip's voice brought her up short.

She quickly rearranged her expression into an innocent smile and turned around. "Philip."

"Sorry about that," he said. "I'm all yours now. Would you like the grand tour of the house?"

"That would be lovely." She leaned to grab Princess's leash and whispered over the counter.

"He's going to give me the grand tour." She threw Felix her best eyebrow waggle.

Philip offered her his arm, and Addison slid hers into place, feeling like a puzzle piece had just found its home. A subtle squeeze of his firm bicep told her it was an impressive home.

She tossed Felix a dazzling smile over her shoulder, batting her eyelashes. "Thank you for the drink."

"You're welcome, madam," he said with a surprising amount of professionalism.

She suddenly felt more than a little childish.

The chatter of the guests died down as Philip led Addison and Princess inside his mansion. Hidden from all the piercing stares, she realized just how on edge she'd been. But now she was all alone with her prince.

"Where's Baxter today?" she asked.

"Oh, probably sleeping somewhere. We went for a big run this morning before the fundraiser started."

"You like to run?"

"I like to join at least one triathlon a year."

And it showed. She supposed that's how he occupied his time. When was the last time Felix had entered a triathlon?

Although Philip's home was well over a hundred years old, he had modern tastes in furniture and style. Addison's expression might have displayed serene interest—at least, that's what she was going for—but her internal jaw was hanging as they went from room to room, each grander than the last.

Princess took it all in with an air of *Been there, done that.* Addison wondered if she was faking it, too, since she was used to running around a tiny one-bedroom apartment.

Floral aromas tickled Addison's nose when they entered the sitting room. She inhaled deeply, recognizing the light scent in the air. She found a giant crystal vase of white and pink lilies on the table.

She paused to smell them. "Mmm. My favorite."

When she turned back, she caught Philip gazing at her. She blushed and looked away, feigning interest in a sculpture. They wandered through halls lined with gold-framed artwork, past rooms filled with high-end furniture and a grand piano or two.

"Do you play?" she asked Philip, lightly tinkling the keys on one piano.

"No. I just enjoy the sound. Sometimes my guests play when they're here."

"You have a beautiful home."

"Thank you." He seemed less interested in his surroundings than he was in her. "I'm happy to open it to people for such a good cause. Besides, it's an excuse to throw a party. I enjoy entertaining."

She noticed another security guard stationed at the end of the long hall, his posture rigid, as though he was ready to tackle someone. "Are your parties usually this … safe?"

"You mean the security? It's just a precaution." Philip barely noted the guard when they passed him. He might as well have been a houseplant.

"You mean because of the missing dogs from the cocktail mixer?"

"Yes." He eyed her expression. "Don't pay any attention to the media and people like Penny Peacock. They just want someone to blame."

"So does the rest of the city, it seems." Addison laughed humorlessly. "But it's good that you're taking precautions to protect the dogs here today. I just hope the missing show dogs are okay."

"The police are on the case, so it's only a matter of time before the dogs turn up."

She didn't exactly want to explain that a serial killer was taking up all of the police department's time and resources. That life wasn't all grand pianos and crystal vases, and there was no reason to believe they'd simply "turn up." But the fact that Philip was trying to comfort her made her cheeks flush again. She sighed, giving his bicep another squeeze.

"I'm sure you're right," she said. "It's not easy to keep a pack of dogs hidden without someone noticing."

"I'm sure it will turn out all right and everyone will stop searching for a scapegoat. Your name will be cleared soon enough. And if there's anything I can do to help in the meantime, don't hesitate to ask."

"Thank you." She smiled gratefully, but she couldn't stop thinking about the poor missing dogs and worrying about their fate.

He gestured to a staircase that curved up to the second and third floors. "The third-story terrace has a magnificent view of Pacific Heights. Shall we?"

"Lead the way."

They ascended the marble staircase and cut through a drawing room. They had the terrace all to themselves. Princess found a spot in the sun and plopped down for a nap, sprawling out on her back like she was working on her tan.

The view really was amazing. The grounds spread out before them, the grass mowed in a perfect grid, like it was a chessboard and Philip's guests the chess pieces. People walked their dogs while attendants followed behind, ready to clean up after them. Manicured trees stood at attention down either side of the enclosed property, giving the opulent estate a sense of privacy and distance from the busy city.

It was all so different from the life she'd grown up knowing. Her mother wouldn't have left if her dad had had all this. What would anyone have to complain about? To worry about?

Addison had been ecstatic for her father when he'd married Dora five years earlier. She was the sweetest woman, and her dad deserved no less. But as sweet as she was, Addison knew firsthand how finances could destroy a relationship. She'd watched it happen to her mom and dad.

Addison's father had been through enough the first time around. She just didn't want to see it happen to him again. Would the strain be too much for him and Dora? What if he didn't sell the corner store in time and they went bankrupt? Would their marriage survive?

She considered her surroundings again with an appreciation of what it was like to go without. *What a life*, she thought. And the guy who owned all of it was interested in her.

It wasn't like she'd been looking for someone with money. After all, nothing was more important than love. She believed in the promise "for richer or poorer," maybe more so because of her mother.

"It's beautiful," Addison breathed.

"Not as beautiful as you," Philip said.

She turned to find him gazing into her eyes, as if all their surroundings, the opulence, the luxury was nothing compared to her. Reaching up, he

133

held her chin as he dipped his face to hers. However, just before their lips touched, there was a change in the surrounding atmosphere. A buzzing of agitated voices reached Addison's ears.

The veranda was too far down for them to pick out specific words, but a woman's shriek echoed across the yard. There was the soft rustle of quality fabric as though the entire party was moving as one. Oxfords and heels clicked on stones.

Philip and Addison exchanged a look before leaning over the banister to peer down at the party below. She was too short to see, but whatever Philip saw made his jaw clench.

"What's going on?" she asked.

"I'm not sure. I should check it out."

Addison tugged on Princess's leash, but she resisted, enjoying her sunny nap. Bending down, Addison scooped up her pet and rushed to keep up with Philip. They found the head of security at the base of the sweeping staircase to the foyer. Carson had removed his secret agent glasses, so things must have been serious.

"Carson, what's happening out there?" Philip called down as he descended.

"It's the dogs, sir."

Philip came to a stop at the bottom of the stairs, his chest moving evenly. Addison's rush through the house, on the other hand, left her gasping for air. But then, she was no triathlete.

"What about them?" Philip asked.

"Some of them, well ..." Carson swallowed. "They vanished."

8

PACK MENTALITY

"The dogs vanished?" Philip repeated, cool and calm. But his stare was so intense, he might as well have been yelling at Carson. "As in disappeared from my property? How many?"

The tone of voice and the way he held himself, chest puffed up, looking down his nose at Carson, spoke of a quiet fury. If it had been someone else, someone not used to stress and pressure like a security guard would be, Addison thought they might have melted beneath Philip's steady gaze.

"Three, sir."

Philip's nose rose an inch. "How could you let that happen?"

Without waiting for an answer, he pushed his way past Carson and headed through the house to the backyard. Addison held Princess close and rushed to keep up. Her heels clicked on the marble floors, echoing around the absurdly cavernous hall. Princess grumbled as the jostling slowly dislodged the fascinator from her head.

Once Addison crossed the threshold to the veranda, exclamations and excited chatter accosted her ears like a swarm of angry bees. The guests huddled around the tall wrought-iron fence at the edge of the property.

The wall of bodies slowed Carson and Philip down. Addison caught up, following in their wake, as the guests made way for them. She couldn't let herself fall behind. She needed to find out what had happened.

More dogs had gone missing. Twice in one week couldn't be a coincidence. It had to be connected to the cocktail mixer somehow. Addison held Princess tighter, like the doxie might disappear right out of her arms.

Philip pressed his way to the front of the crowd as Carson gave him an update. Addison strained to listen.

"I'm not sure how it happened, sir. We're still looking into it. We have guards posted at every entrance. No one has left with any other dog but their own."

Philip wheeled on the head of security, coming nose to nose with him. "Obviously, someone has. Now what are you doing about it?"

"We have the place on lockdown. No one in or out. The police are on their way."

"Good," he said, turning away. "Keep me posted. And find my dog, Baxter."

Carson nodded and turned around. He reached up to his earpiece and murmured something, but Addison missed what he said. The gathering crowd quickly swallowed him. She decided to stick with Philip.

When she broke through the thick mass of people, she stumbled into a semicircle of open space. At the center of the commotion, three guests argued with the security guards who had checked her in at the door.

"Just calm down. The police are on their way," Guard One was saying.

A man wearing a toupee wagged a finger in his face. "The police? The police? Then what are *you* here for? What were you doing when they disappeared?"

"Yeah, what are you doing to find them?" another man asked. He had his back to Addison, but she'd recognize that coiffed hair anywhere. Rex Harrison.

A young woman with tears sparkling in her eyes ran over. "Oh, Philip." She grabbed the front of his sports jacket. "He's gone. Someone took my Lionel. You said it was safe here."

"Don't worry, Kayleigh." He patted her hands

and gently dislodged them from his lapels. "I'm taking care of it."

He handed her his pocket square, and she dabbed at her eyes.

"You'll be lucky if I don't sue," said the man in the toupee.

"This is a disaster," Philip muttered under his breath so only Addison could hear. "How could this have happened? I don't understand. I had safeguards in place."

He looked distraught. In fact, he looked as upset as she had felt at the cocktail mixer. His body tensed like he wanted to take action, but it seemed there was nothing to do but wait for the police. He began to pace.

Addison laid a comforting hand on his arm. "It's not your fault. You did everything you could. Maybe they got out of the yard somehow? Found a gap in the fence or dug a hole."

Now she sounded like Felix. She recalled the way he'd comforted her at the cocktail party, tried to convince her it was going to be okay when all the facts pointed to the worst-case scenario. But now she understood why he'd done it, because she wanted to do the same for Philip.

"My Rosie would never run away," Rex said to her. "She's too well-behaved. Someone stole her. I know it."

"My property was secure," Philip said. "I took every precaution I could for this party."

"If it was secure, then how did the dogs get off the premises without anyone noticing?" Rex practically shook with anger, his hair falling down in strands across his tall forehead.

Addison saw a finger rise from among the crowd to point straight at her. It was Penny.

"It was Addison Turner!" the famed handler called out. "It's the cocktail mixer all over again."

"What?" Addison sputtered, practically laughing at the absurdity of it. "Me?"

Philip stepped forward. "Absolutely not. She was with me the entire time. She had nothing to do with it."

But Penny's comment sent a surge of whispers and sidelong glances through the crowd. Those who hadn't recognized Addison before now put a face to the name.

"Funny that she was present during both incidents," Penny noted coolly.

"So were you," Philip said. "So were all of us."

"You can't blame me for this one," Addison told her. "I'm just a guest here."

"Maybe you had help," she said. "A partner in crime."

Noises of affirmation rippled among the guests. Heads nodded up and down.

Addison threw up her hands. "Like who?"

A honking horn interrupted her. Through the vines covering the wrought-iron fence, Addison could see a vehicle pull up to the mansion's back access.

Curious, the crowd surged forward, bulldozing Addison closer to the gates. She cradled Princess close to protect her from bumps and elbows. For a moment, she worried they'd be trampled.

The van crawled forward. The driver impatiently honked the horn again, but the security guards kept the gates firmly shut.

Guards One and Two rushed ahead of everyone. They waved their hands in the air to signal the van to stop. Guard Two moved a hand across his throat in a "kill the engine" motion.

The van shut off, and the door popped open. The impatient driver jumped down onto the flagstone driveway. It was Red Bra.

She took in the crowd from the other side of the iron bars. "What's going on?"

Carson pushed his way through the mob with Baxter on a leash. Philip rushed over, bending down to his English mastiff as if he had to touch him to believe he was safe.

Carson stalked up to the gate. "Where have you been?" he asked Red Bra.

"The bar." She eyed the crowd with confusion. "Making a supply run."

Guard One turned to his boss. "This was the only vehicle to leave the premises."

"Did anyone search this van when it left?" Philip demanded.

The security guards glanced at each other. Eventually one said, "Yeah, but it was just full of empty barrels and boxes."

"How do you know they were empty?" Carson asked them. "Did you look inside them?"

They silently conferred with each other again before shaking their heads.

Carson swore. "Who was in charge of this vehicle!?" he called out, as though it was the guests' job to know and not his.

"I'm the supervisor." A deep voice carried over the crowd.

Addison turned, along with everyone else, to see Felix walking down the drive. He came to a stop next to her and crossed his arms.

"How can I help you?" But with the scowl on his face and his head cocked like he was ready for a fight, he didn't come off as helpful.

Carson faced him, calling his tough-guy bluff. "Were you aware that your employee left the premises?"

"Of course. I'm the one who sent her. We ran out of supplies, so she went to the bar to stock up on a few items." Felix was close enough to Addison that she heard him mutter, "The Head Turner was more popular than I expected."

Out of the corner of her eye, she saw Penny note the exchange. The look on her pinched face made Addison's toes curl with annoyance in her pink heels.

Red Bra grabbed the iron bars and stared helplessly through them as though already condemned. "What have I done wrong?"

"How long ago did you leave?" Carson asked her.

Felix stepped in and answered before she could, keeping the focus on him. "About an hour ago."

"That was when I last saw Gumball," the man with the toupee said.

"This guy was at the cocktail mixer last weekend too." Rex indicated Felix as "this guy." "Maybe he stole those dogs."

Penny turned to Addison, almost gleefully. "Looks like we've found your partner in crime," she said, eliciting a sudden uproar from those around her. It sounded like calls for blood to Addison's ears.

"She had nothing to do with this!" Philip yelled over them all. "She's my guest here."

"I saw them talking together earlier, at the bar," Kayleigh said between shuddering sobs.

"Probably conspiring," Rex added.

Addison shot daggers across the stone driveway at Rex, sorry she'd considered him attractive for even a second. "I was ordering a drink."

"They must be working together," toupee man agreed.

Penny never said another word. She didn't have to—her nasty theory had taken root and was growing all on its own, fed by everyone's fear and anxiety.

Addison threw up her hands, ready to argue. Felix sidled close to her and shut her down with a look.

"You're dealing with a mob mentality here," he advised under his breath. "You're going to lose. Stop before they pull out their torches and pitchforks and you have a real problem on your hands."

She glared at him as if this were somehow his fault. Heck, maybe it was. Maybe he did steal the dogs. After all, he was so determined not to help her find the guilty party. Maybe that was because *he* was the guilty party. But by the looks on everyone's faces, he was probably right about keeping quiet, so she took his advice.

She held Princess close to her chest, like someone might want to get revenge through her own dog. An eye for an eye. "Well, it looks like it's not just my problem anymore," she informed Felix coolly. "Now, it's yours too."

9

END OF THE TETHER

No matter where Addison tried to hide in Philip's mansion, angry whispers followed her, accusing, blaming, condemning. The estate had seemed so large two hours before, but now that no one could leave, the place felt stifling. It was packed with shifting eyes, pointing fingers, subtle head nods, and those whispers.

She'd hoped the gossiping would have stopped now that there was a new suspect: Felix. But it hadn't. The speculations had merely changed.

Addison heard the people murmur with their backs turned in exclusive clusters in the foyer, in the halls, on the terrace. Their voices grew louder as the police took statements and the alcohol had time to sink in. Apparently, Addison and Felix were in league with each other in black market dog trading. No, an illegal dog-fighting business.

No, they were criminal breeders out for a monopoly on the best litters in the country.

Some guests eyed Princess as though Addison should feel guilty that she still had her dog. Or maybe it was because they were considering stealing the doxie to get revenge. Addison rarely let Princess down except to drink water or stretch her legs on the grass. Even then, she was always on a leash wrapped securely around Addison's wrist.

As they wandered the property, Addison attempted to overhear the gossip without being too obvious about it. The last thing she wanted was to draw more attention to herself, but even more dogs were missing now. She needed to look for clues, to find the dogs and get them home safe, and hopefully clear her name. With or without Felix's help.

As she passed the drawing room, she overheard Philip talking to the head of security, or rather, at him. His shoes clacked on the floor as he paced back and forth.

"How could you let this happen?" he demanded.

"Well, sir. We—"

"What am I paying you for?" he interrupted. "I thought you secured the place."

"We did everything—"

"Your company was supposed to be the best in town."

Addison didn't blame Philip for being upset. Those three dogs had disappeared right from under his nose, in his own home. She imagined he felt like she had the night of the cocktail mixer.

Pretending to appreciate a painting in the hallway, she peeked into the drawing room to see Philip rub a hand over his clean-shaven jaw. The sight of him so frazzled filled her with guilt. He was the last person she wanted to spy on. Besides, she already knew Philip couldn't be culpable. She just knew it. Someone whose eyes sparkled like diamonds couldn't be evil. Philip practically glowed with angelic innocence.

Addison tiptoed past the doors to sneak away, but then she heard him call out.

"Addison!"

Totally busted. She waited in the hallway, trying to think of some excuse. However, when he caught up to her, he was the one who looked guilty.

"There you are," he said. "I apologize. I don't mean to ignore you. I've just been pulled in so many directions."

She laid a hand on his arm. "I completely understand. There's so much that you have to deal with."

He blew out a weary breath. "This wasn't exactly the fundraising event I had planned."

"It seems someone else had their own plans for your party."

His handsome face twisted. "I'm sorry that you got caught up in all this."

She laid a hand on his arm. "It's not your fault. They just need someone to blame." *I just wish it weren't me*, she thought.

The tightness around his eyes and perfectly sculpted lips relaxed. He slowly reached out to her, and she thought he might try to kiss her again. But then frantic barking and yelling carried down the hall, echoing throughout the expansive home.

Philip's hand froze in midair, and he gave a small, frustrated groan. "I'd better go check that out."

The tension was getting to the humans and canines alike. After being cooped up for so long, it wasn't the first dogfight to break out. It was only a matter of time before the humans snapped and threw the first punch. Addison just hoped she wouldn't be on the receiving end.

She sighed in disappointment as Philip walked away. But that disappointment quickly turned to annoyance. Annoyance at the situation and the unknown surrounding the poor lost dogs, at her own vulnerability and public disgrace.

Not only had the new round of missing dogs convinced people that Addison was somehow involved, but her sort-of date with Philip had been ruined. And for some reason, the only person she could think of to blame was Felix. Not that it was his fault, exactly. It wasn't like he'd taken the dogs himself. Or had he?

Felix was the one in charge of that van, after all. He'd sent it back to the bar. Maybe he and Red Bra were in on it together. If that was the case, then Addison needed to find him.

Spinning on her heel, she stormed outside to find Felix so she could ... well, she didn't know what yet. Rub it in his face now that he was accused? To spy on him, maybe interrogate him until he snapped like a brittle nail?

The first place Addison searched was the temporary bar by the veranda. When she didn't find him there, she wandered around to the private drive where the van was parked. Felix was MIA, but his van was still there. For now. She watched as a tow truck backed up to it before the driver jumped out to speak with the police.

Making her way around the other side of the house, she froze when she heard Felix's voice nearby.

"I'm sorry," he said. "It's not like I planned for this to happen. I was bartending the whole time."

Addison and Princess peered around the corner of the mansion. Felix had his back to her. His fist clenched at his side as he talked on the phone.

He kicked a stone in frustration. "I know this is a big deal, but there's got to be a way to fix it."

Felix was talking about the missing dogs. She

wondered who was on the other end. There was only one way to find out.

Glancing over her shoulder, Addison checked to see if anyone was watching. Once she was sure the coast was clear, she snuck into a gap in the pruned hedges he was pacing in front of.

"Who cares what a bunch of uptight customers say?" he growled into the phone.

Uptight? Who was he calling uptight? Well, okay, some of the guests fit the bill, but that didn't include her, did it?

She crept closer, but dense bushes blocked her view. Setting Princess down on the ground, she shuffled even closer and swept some leaves out of the way to see him better.

Felix paced, his posture stiff. He was actually a little intimidating when he was angry. Addison was sure he could hold his own in a fight. He might have cleaned up as well as the gentlemen at the party, but looks could be deceiving. Felix was definitely no gentleman.

"I had nothing to do with it," Felix said. "Come on, you've known me for four years." He ran a rough hand through his hair, gripping it in frustration as he listened. "But this is *my* livelihood too."

Livelihood? Addison wondered if he was talking to his boss. Maybe he was getting fired.

"But I've been banking on the extra side work.

I've got bills to pay … Yeah. Fine. I understand … Goodbye."

Felix hung up and jammed the phone into his pocket. He closed his eyes and slowly exhaled.

Addison shrank back from her viewpoint. Felix might have deserved a taste of his own medicine, to be accused after he refused to help her. But that didn't mean he deserved to get fired.

Guilt for listening in tickled at her insides. She tried to sneak away before he discovered her hiding in the bushes, prying into his personal affairs. But that's what private eyes like Dick Tracy did, right? Surely they never felt guilty while on a stakeout or squeezing information out of informants. Some spy she made.

Addison took another step backward. Her foot came down. *Snap.* A twig broke under her shoe. She froze.

"Who's there?" Felix demanded.

She winced. "Oops." Now it was definitely time to scram.

Addison spun around, intending to bolt before Felix discovered her, but when she turned, she came face to face with a half-naked woman.

A yelp escaped from her lungs before she realized it was only a moss-covered statue. She clamped a hand over her mouth, but it was too late.

The grass outside her shelter swished as Felix approached. "All right. Come on out."

Addison searched for an escape route, but she'd trapped herself in an alcove of sorts. Like a romantic little nook, nestled into a horseshoe of vegetation long since overgrown and forgotten.

She glanced at Princess for help, but the doxie was too busy sniffing the ground. Giving up, Addison tried to act natural. She slung an arm around the statue like she was just hanging out there by complete coincidence.

Felix brushed aside the hedge, and his eyes landed on her. His scowl eased slightly. "Oh, it's you."

"Hello." She gave him a look like "Fancy meeting you here."

"Eavesdropping, are we?"

She wrinkled her nose at him. "Don't be paranoid. The world doesn't revolve around you, you know. Princess had to pee." She waved at her dog as evidence.

Thankfully, Princess corroborated her story and squatted near the base of the statue.

Felix tilted his head. "In here?"

"Princess has a shy bladder," Addison said. "She's a lady."

He shrugged it off, either believing her weak story or because he didn't really care. "Well, in case you didn't catch every word, Joe laid me off."

"I'm sorry."

His head snapped to her. His eyes narrowed like he thought maybe she was being sarcastic.

"No, really. That sucks." She gave him a small, earnest frown. "Trust me. I know what you're going through. I'm losing my own income." Not just her income but her business, her passion, her dream.

"It's not indefinitely," he said. "It's just until things calm down with this damn dognapping business. Joe doesn't want to lose me, but he also has to appease the customers who are calling for blood. He does a lot of private gigs for these rich types." He waved a tired hand in the general direction of the house. "As long as I'm working for him, people are threatening to cancel their private bookings." He sank onto the curved marble bench in the center of the alcove.

Addison sat down next to him. "That's not fair."

"I'm associated with this whole dognapping crime, fair or not." Felix raised a shoulder. "Isn't that exactly what happened to you? Was it fair then?"

She was surprised by his sincerity, at the temporary truce between them. When he was the one who admitted it, it took the satisfying "Aha! In your face" feeling out of it. Now Addison just felt bad for him. Maybe for both of them.

"No. You're right," she said. "I just didn't think you cared."

He huffed. "That's fair. But trust me, I felt bad for you. I just couldn't risk getting involved."

"Why? Is this job really so great?"

"It's not the job, really. It's ..." As he considered her for a moment, his eyes softened. She could see a vulnerability in them that she'd never seen before.

He rubbed the back of his neck and looked away. "Never mind."

There was something important Felix wasn't telling her. It nagged at her curiosity, but she let it go. For now.

"So, are you going to look for a new job now?"

"No way." He shook his head. "This gig pays great. Besides, that will take too long. I'm on a tight deadline."

Addison smirked. "Loan shark got a hit out on you?"

He gave her a withering look. "Ha ha. Very funny."

"Then what are you going to do?"

He sat up straight and seemed to consider the question for a moment. "I'm going to clear my name. Prove that I had nothing to do with the stolen dogs."

"What?" She laughed, for what seemed like the first time in days. "*Now* you're interested in helping me find the real dog snatcher?"

"I didn't say anything about helping *you*." He flashed a wolfish smile. "I just have to prove it wasn't *me*."

She groaned. So much for the truce. "You're a

real prince, you know that? Ever hear of a damsel in distress?"

"It's the twenty-first century, sweetheart. Damsels help themselves now. Gender equality and all that. Get with the times."

Addison stood up. "Well, good luck then. Things don't look good for you either, you know. After today, the evidence is stacked against you." She grabbed Princess's leash, marching out of the hidden alcove.

"Okay, okay." Felix tugged on Addison's arm and pulled her back inside. "You're right. Things don't look good. How are we going to fix this?"

She snorted. "So, now you want my help? Why should I help you? You weren't exactly leaping to my rescue." She remembered his ultimatum. Shoving her fists on her hips, she stared him down. "What's in it for me?"

"One"—he held up a finger—"we're their two lead suspects. At least, as far as the public is concerned, we are, and sometimes rumors are all that matter in the service industry. Even if they can't send us to jail, we'll both be searching the help wanted ads within a few weeks."

Felix took a step closer. His cologne overpowered the smell of roses in the garden. It smelled good, distracting, actually. But she stood her ground.

He held up a second finger. "Two, I know I

seem tough and rugged, but I'm far too sensitive to go to jail. I wouldn't last a week."

Addison snorted. He'd be running the place within a week, more like it.

"And three." He closed the gap between them so that she was staring straight at the lips she'd sucked on just a few days before. "They're saying we're in cahoots, that we've somehow set this all up like we're a pair of criminal canine masterminds." Felix reached up and held her chin. "So, like it or not, damsel, we're in this together."

She groaned, swatting his hand away. "Fine. I guess two heads are better than one anyway."

"Great." He rubbed his hands together. "And I'll do it for only ninety percent of Lily's reward money Alistair Yates offered on the news."

"What?" She balked. "How do you figure that?"

He crossed his arms with a giant grin on his face. "It's my expertise and knowledge that's going to solve the case."

"I don't think so," she said. "Fifty-fifty."

"Sixty-forty, and that's my final offer."

Addison gritted her teeth. "Fine. I was going to be nice and offer you a ride, but I'm sure with all your expertise and knowledge, you can find your own way home."

He wrinkled his nose. "What makes you think I'd ride in that thing?"

"Because your ride is being towed as we

speak," she informed him with a satisfied grin. "Probably for evidence."

"What?" Felix's snide grin faltered. He shoved past her, out of the alcove, and circled around to the private driveway.

Addison sauntered after him, feeling a bit smug. Even Princess held her tail a little higher. When the empty driveway came into view, Felix slowed his steps. He ran a hand through his thick waves, gripping them like he wanted to pull them right out.

He swore under his breath. "My car is in the shop. Joe was letting me use the company van for the week."

"Then I guess we'll need my car to solve the crime." Addison patted him on the back, giving him her sweetest smile. "Don't worry. I'll let you have forty percent."

10

BONE OF CONTENTION

Addison hit the brakes as she and Felix approached Joe's Dive, which was even divier in the light of day. She whipped into a free space along the street like they were shooting a scene from *Tokyo Drift*.

It took a moment for Felix to release his death grip on the seat. He gave her a look but said nothing. It's not like he had a choice in transportation. The cops were still dusting the company van for prints after towing it from the fundraiser the day before.

Addison tipped up her fedora and studied the joint, watching her mirrors to make sure no one had tailed them. She felt like a regular gumshoe, ready to crack the canine case. She'd even worn quiet shoes—or gumshoes, if you will—in case she needed to do some sneaking around. The fedora was just a fun accessory, but she'd thought the trench coat might be over the top, so she'd skipped it. Besides, she was wearing her sexy fifties-style dress, and it would have been a shame to cover it up.

Addison grabbed a notebook from her purse and ran down a list that already included Kitty Carlisle, Melody, Julia Edwards, and—at Felix's insistence—Philip Montgomery III.

At least it gave her a reason to see Philip again, to remind him of what he was missing out on. She'd probably never hear from him again after what had happened at his fundraiser. Not with all of his guests still blaming her for the missing dogs.

But the first name on her list was Red Bra, which is why they'd come to the bar. She clicked her pen, holding it at the ready.

"Do you think we've missed anyone on our list?" she asked Felix.

"Oh, probably about a hundred names."

She glared at him. "I'm serious."

"So am I. But we can only do so much." He shifted in his seat to face her. "We're assuming the dogs were stolen for one of two reasons: money or competition."

"So, who else can we list with competition as their motive?"

"Anyone who's had their dog stolen is automatically off the list. They can't exactly show a dog that's supposed to be missing. No competition there."

Addison tapped her pen on the steering wheel. "That still leaves a lot of dogs that have the potential for Best in Show and the potential for thieving owners. The Western Dog Show is a big competition."

"We have to start somewhere. That's why we've got your customer, Julia Edwards."

Addison had been reluctant to put Julia on the list, but she'd recalled how Ms. Edwards had baited Penny Peacock at Philip's party. There was more than a healthy dose of competition between them.

Felix pointed to the list. "Why Kitty Carlisle? She hasn't competed in years. I thought her dog was too old."

"Yeah, but she got major creep factor points."

"Creep factor?" He raised a skeptical eyebrow. "So we're basing our investigation on your heebie-jeebies now?"

"If that was the case, *you'd* still be on there." She smiled sweetly. "But Kitty was the only one hanging around the stage area when her dog was getting groomed. She could have been casing the joint."

Addison ran through the list of names under the financial gain category. "The breeders, handlers, and owners wouldn't steal a dog to sell it for gain," she said. "They compete because they love animals. They wouldn't want anything bad to happen to them. It would have to be someone outside of the competition. One of the staff at the parties."

"Or someone on the outside using them as an inside man. Someone who overlapped both the cocktail mixer and Philip's fundraiser. That leaves our list of staff to investigate pretty small since there weren't many who worked both."

"Except for you," she said, with a suggestive tone to her voice.

"And you," he shot back.

She stuck her tongue out at him. "Don't forget Red Bra. She was at both events too."

His forehead wrinkled. "Who's Red Bra?"

"The server we're here to talk to. The one you were flirting with at the cocktail mixer."

"You mean Charlotte?" He laughed. "Are you jealous?"

She felt her cheeks warm. "You wish."

Gripping the wheel, Addison psyched herself up for her first interrogation. She could sense Felix eyeing her from the passenger seat.

"Are you okay?" he asked her.

"Yeah. You know, just going over the plan in my head. So, how are we going to do this? Are we going to drill her? Good cop/bad cop kind of thing?" She punched her palm in case it wasn't clear who the bad cop was.

"No. We're going to sit down with Charlotte

and have a chat thing. Maybe a snack, if you're good."

"And if she doesn't spill?" Addison punched her palm again.

"Stop with the gumshoe talk. And what's with the fedora?" Plucking it off her head, he tossed it into the backseat of her convertible. "Charlotte is a friend."

"But she was the one who drove the van away from Philip's house. And that's the only way those dogs could have been taken off the property."

"We don't know that for sure yet. The police are still searching the van and Philip's property for clues. Besides, I know Charlotte wouldn't do something like that."

"How do you know?"

"Because I trust her," he said, in an "end-of-story" kind of way.

But Addison wasn't about to take his word for it. She'd be the judge of that.

"We're just going to see if she knows anything," Felix said. "Maybe she's heard something from the other staff. She hangs out with some of them outside of work."

"And you don't?"

"No. I go home. I keep my work life and personal life separate." He reached for the door handle. "Come on. I've already texted her. She's expecting us."

Addison looked at him in surprise. She

thought he'd be more the party type. But she kept the thought to herself as they got out of the car and headed to Joe's Dive.

The afternoon sun hit the dirt on the bar's windows. It looked like they hadn't been cleaned in years. Addison skirted around a suspicious stain on the sidewalk that she thought could use a good hosing off. Beneath the grime and the neglect, she imagined the bar could be a pretty cute place if Joe took a little pride in it.

Felix held the door open for her, and they stepped into the dim interior. The dirt-caked windows didn't allow much light to filter in, but she figured those already drinking at one in the afternoon probably wanted to hide in dark corners anyway.

Addison scanned the room and spotted Red Bra, or Charlotte, right away. She was picking up an order of drinks at the bar.

Felix waved, and she smiled back, nodding to the side of the room. Heading for the corner, Felix slid into a booth. Addison sat across from him. She watched as Charlotte finished serving a table their sandwiches and beer.

"So, when are we going to go talk to your assistant Melody?" Felix punched his own palm, making fun of her earlier good cop/bad cop routine.

"Not yet," she said. "I can't just roll up and ask her, 'Steal any dogs lately?' We've got to be crafty about it. If she's hiding something, then she's hiding it well. Otherwise, the police would have arrested her by now."

Besides, Addison really liked Melody. She didn't feel comfortable even suspecting her, but facts were facts. However, if it turned out Melody really was innocent, Addison didn't want to lose her assistant because she'd wrongly accused her.

Charlotte finished up with her table and went to talk to an older guy with a shaved head behind the bar. The guy nodded and held up a hand, showing five fingers. Taking off her apron, Charlotte joined Felix and Addison in their booth.

"Hey, Felix." She gave him a smile Addison thought was too cheerful and friendly to be real.

"Hi," he said. "Thanks for talking to us."

"No problem. Joe says I've got only five minutes. We're working short-staffed today. Jayden never showed up for his shift. Apparently, he came down with food poisoning or something." She dropped her voice. "Between you and me, I think he helped himself to some of that leftover quiche after it had been out in the sun too long."

Addison took the pen and notebook out of her purse and wrote *Jayden*. When she looked up, both Felix and Charlotte were staring at her.

"Don't worry about her," Felix told his friend. "How have you been?"

"Okay. It could have been worse. I didn't get much backlash from the Montgomery fundraiser. I just got pulled from the high-profile events for the week. But what about you?" She laid her hand on Felix's arm. "Joe said you're done."

Felix shrugged. "I'm only laid off for the time being. I'll be fine. I have some savings set aside."

"But what about your down payment?" Charlotte asked. "You won't save up enough by the deadline."

Addison frowned. *Down payment?* She resisted the urge to jot down questions she needed to ask Felix too.

"That's exactly why we need your help, Charlotte."

"Anything for you." She beamed at him. "What did you have in mind?"

It was like Addison wasn't even in the room. Okay, well, she hadn't really said anything, so that might be why. She pretended to jot a note down just to feel useful.

Felix lowered his voice. "If we can figure out whodunit, then I can clear my name."

"Our names," Addison cut in.

"Our names," Felix corrected. "And I can pick up extra gigs to make up for the lost wages. Plus, if we find the dogs, there's a reward. I can still make the deadline."

Deadline? Addison wrote.

"I'll help if I can," Charlotte said. "What did you need to know?" She sat up straighter, finally pulling away from Felix. Not that Addison noticed or anything.

"When you were at the Montgomery event, getting ready to head back to the bar, did you see anyone hanging around? One of the guests? Did anyone help you load up the empty kegs or crates? Maybe someone followed you out of the gates."

"Not that I can remember." She glanced back at Joe behind the bar.

He gave her a pointed look, tapping his watch.

"I can't say for sure," she added quickly. "It was a busy event. I was in and out, making kitchen runs around that time."

"How about any of the other staff from either that event or the cocktail mixer? Have you heard any talk going around?"

"No. Nothing much, just—"

"Charlotte!" Joe barked from behind the bar. "Orders are backing up. Break's over."

"Coming!" she called, slipping out of the booth.

Addison leaned forward, not ready to let her go. "Just what? What were you going to say?"

Charlotte raised a red bra–strapped shoulder. "Just the usual gossip, but nothing that would be of any help to you."

Addison wanted to ask her more, but Joe dinged the bell sitting on the counter and threw Charlotte a sour look.

Charlotte rolled her eyes.

"Thanks for talking to us," Felix said.

"No problem. Sorry I can't be of more help." She gave him an apologetic wave over her shoulder as she ran back for her apron. "Good luck!"

The moment they were out of the bar, Addison returned to her bubbly self. "Okay, where to next?"

Felix gave her a weird look.

"What?" she asked.

"What was that?"

"What was what?" She unconsciously reached for her hair to check that every curl was in place.

"You could have been a little nicer."

Addison began walking back to the car, not meeting his gaze. "There's something off about her. I just don't trust Red Bra."

He opened his mouth to speak, but she held up a hand. "It's not jealousy."

"What's the big deal about wearing a red bra, anyway? Is it a fashion faux pas?"

"Nothing's wrong with it. I have plenty of colored bras. Red ones, pink ones, blue ones, animal print ones ..." She tapered off as his eyes drifted down to her dress's neckline, as though he were wondering what color she was wearing today. "But I don't show everyone. That's reserved for VIP eyes only."

"Really? How does one get on this VIP list?"

His lips curled into that hungry, wolfish smile she recalled from the night at the bar.

As they passed a tailor shop, she glanced into the window. "Sorry. It's a black-tie event."

Addison gazed at the storefront display. The three mannequins lined up behind the window wore quality suits, handmade from the finest fabrics.

"There's just something about a man in a suit, you know?"

"Can't say I do," he said.

"A well-tailored suit is to a woman what lingerie is to a man."

"I assure you that's not true," he said, eyeing her neckline again like he had Superman's X-ray vision.

"Oh, but it is," she argued. "It's romantic. It's mysterious. It takes a man's game to a whole new level. Heck, it could even clean *you* up a little."

Addison eyed the tux in the middle, practically drooling as she imagined Felix filling it out to perfection. "*Men in Black* wouldn't be the same if Will Smith ran around in sweatpants. James Bond would otherwise be just a ruffian, but the suit transforms him into a gentleman. A tuxedo on Bruce Wayne is as powerful as the batsuit is on Batman."

When she finally turned away from the window, Felix was staring at her.

"What's your obsession with movies, anyway?"

The abrupt question caught her off guard. She blinked, wondering why he cared. "My parents ran a corner store that rented movies back in the day. Once they became obsolete, we had a million of them lying around. I probably watched them all a dozen times growing up."

Addison headed back for the car, mostly so she wouldn't have to talk about it anymore. She didn't have the worst of childhoods, but there were aspects she didn't exactly remember with fondness.

Felix trailed behind her, not dropping the subject. "I bet you had the perfect life growing up. Let me guess. Cheerleader? Homecoming queen?" he teased. "Life must have been so easy for you. Like one of your fairy tale movies."

Addison snorted. It was far from a fairy tale. Maybe that's why she escaped into movies growing up, so she could imagine herself in a different life, with a mom around, and a dad who didn't have to work all the time. Instead, she was raised by good old Walt Disney.

"My mom left when I was seven. My dad had to raise me on his own while trying to keep the corner store afloat. It kept him busy, so I had to entertain myself." She fidgeted with a curl, twisting it around her finger. "I watched movies in the back of the store. It was like a free babysitter."

"Sounds rough," he said. "I'm sorry. A kid needs both parents."

She glanced at him, wondering if he spoke

from experience. By the furrow on his brow, she thought he might.

Addison could still remember the night she'd woken up from a bad dream and stumbled into her parents' bedroom to find her mother packing. When she asked her mom why she was leaving, she'd said it was because they didn't have enough money for all three of them to survive on. Like she was being selfless.

For years, Addison wondered about that. How could one less income earner in the household make things any better? But what her mother had really meant was that there wasn't enough money for *her*.

The almighty dollar had ripped their family apart. It had left her father working sixteen-hour days to keep the convenience store they owned afloat, had left Addison in her cousin's hand-me-downs. It had left her without a mother.

But she was an adult now. Her life could be whatever she wanted it to be. A Choose Your Own Adventure story. She wouldn't settle for anything less than her happily ever after, something she'd been imagining since she was a kid watching those movies in the back room of the store.

She waved the heavy mood away. "I don't have any regrets. If my mom didn't want to be a part of my life, then no big loss. My dad did the best he could. He worked hard to take care of me and keep a roof over our heads. And I hope to return the favor one day. As in *soon* since he's about to lose his roof. And his wife."

"His wife?"

"Well, maybe I'm overreacting," she said. "But money problems can tear relationships apart, you know?"

"Not if your relationship is strong enough." Felix spoke with such certainty that, again, she wondered about his past.

She made a noncommittal noise. It wasn't like she'd been old enough to understand the dynamics between her parents. "I just worry. Dad's been through a lot. He deserves to be happy, and Dora makes him happy. I just don't want to see them struggle."

Felix gave her an amused look. "So you're going to save them."

"Well, I can help, at least. But first things first." She gave a peppy go-get-'em fist pump as she rounded the car. "We have a mystery to solve."

Felix stood on the other side of the car, regarding her with a curious look. Not giving him the opportunity to throw her a pity party, she hopped behind the wheel and whipped out her notebook.

"Okay, so who's this Jayden character Charlotte mentioned?"

He slid into the passenger seat. "He's the new

kid. I don't know him very well. We'll put him on the list to check out."

Addison flipped back through her notebook and added Jayden's name to the list. Then she returned to her questions. "Charlotte mentioned a down payment, that you had a deadline. What was she talking about?"

"Is that part of your investigation?"

"Maybe," she said vaguely. "I have to consider all angles."

He sighed, but his mouth quirked into a smile. "I am going to buy a bar. Or at least, I'm hoping to."

"Really? A bar?" she practically blurted. "You want to start your own business?"

"You don't have to say it like that." He pouted.

"No. That's great. It … It just surprised me, is all. I had no idea."

Felix stared at her for a moment, and she felt the weight of his next words. "There's a lot you don't know about me."

Addison was beginning to see that.

"I've got goals," he said. "What do you think? I want to work for minimum wage for the rest of my life?"

Addison shrugged. In fact, she hadn't given it much thought. "No. Of course not."

"A buddy of mine is going to sell his Irish pub in the South of Market area. He knew I was interested, so he's letting me have first crack at it before putting it on the market. But I have to come up with the down payment by the end of this month. I've been working my ass off." His hand clenched into a fist on his knee. "I almost had it, too."

Addison could see how much this meant to him. It looked like they both had dreams to protect.

"And you still will. It's not over yet," she said with conviction. "Let's see, who's next on our list today? Ah, yes. William Jackson. Do you have an address for him?"

"You bet I do."

"Great. I just want to make a quick stop at the Regency Center first."

Felix was reading the list over her shoulder with curiosity. He reached over and pointed at *Red Bra* written in the notebook. "You can cross Charlotte off the list."

Addison's pen hovered over the page uncertainly. "Did you notice how cagey she got when we started asking her questions?"

"She wasn't cagey." Felix leaned back and put his seatbelt on. "Joe was rushing her. He can be a total dick sometimes."

Addison pretended to scratch the name off the list. She closed it before Felix could see that she'd actually put a star next to it.

11

PLAY FETCH

Felix and Addison stared up at the imposing white facade of the Regency Center as they waited to cross the street. Addison never wanted to show her face there again, but it was the best way to wrap her head around the events of the cocktail mixer.

That night had left her too rattled to ask the important questions at the time. Now, she wanted to know how the dogs disappeared. If they could figure out the how, maybe it would lead to the who.

"What are we doing here?" Felix asked. "Want to relive your big moment on stage?"

She glared at him over her sunglasses. "Not funny. We're here to do a little crime scene investigation. It might give us more insight before we start pointing fingers."

He hit the crosswalk button. "What do you expect to find that the police didn't?"

"Nothing," she said. "I just hope to figure out whatever they did. They probably uncovered everything they could find, but it's not like they're going to tell us about it, are they?"

"So you just hope to find something to help our own investigation." Felix gave her an astonished look, like he'd just seen a miracle performed. "That actually makes a lot of sense."

Addison swatted him on the arm. "You don't have to say it like that."

The light turned, and their pedestrian symbol lit up. They crossed the street, heading up the stairs to the Regency Center entrance. Felix held the door open for her, but she paused just outside to remove one of her crystal earrings.

"What are you doing?" he asked. "The earrings don't match your shoes?"

Addison gave him a smug look. "You'll see."

Placing the earring in her dress pocket, she slipped inside. The doors closed behind them, muffling the traffic noises. It was like stepping back in time to 1909 when the center was built and the loudest things out on the street were the clip-clop of horses and buggies or the clang of the odd trolley car rolling by.

Men and women dressed in suits and sensible pencil skirts lingered in the lobby. A few heads turned their way, but after giving Addison and

Felix the once-over and realizing the pair wasn't part of their event, they returned to their conversations.

Addison scanned the room, searching for someone in charge. It didn't take long before the center's event organizer from the night of the cocktail mixer approached them.

Darcy's warm customer-service smile faltered when he spotted Addison. "Good afternoon," he said, a dubious squint to his eye. "How can I help you?"

Felix turned expectantly to Addison for a cue, but she was already prepared.

"Hi. I'm so sorry to bother you. I'm not sure if you remember me, but—"

"I remember you." His face tightened as he battled to keep the smile in place.

She wondered if he'd ever had an event go so wrong.

"I think I lost an earring while working on the stage that night," she told him. "I was wondering if I could look for it." It was a simple enough fib. Which was a good thing since Addison was a terrible liar.

Darcy glanced back at the guests in the lobby. They were filtering through a set of doors, and he looked ready to follow.

"Please," Addison begged. "It will only take a few minutes. They were my grandmother's earrings, and she was special to me." She tilted her head to the side to show the one lone earring left in her lobe.

Darcy considered the now-empty lobby one more time before giving her a brief nod. "Okay. But it will have to be quick. They are about to start a presentation that I need to be there for." He curled an impatient finger. "This way, please."

He led Addison and Felix through the lobby and into the ballroom. Without the candles, dimmed lights, and, of course, Philip, it was less romantic than she remembered. However, with the lights turned up and the room cleared of guests and furniture, she could appreciate just how rich and detailed a setting it truly was, from the intricate ceiling moldings to the pattern in the hardwood floor.

"I'm sure our cleaning staff would have found it," Darcy said as he climbed the stage stairs. "Or else it went out with the trash."

Addison gasped, as though afraid she'd lost her heirloom forever. It couldn't possibly be replaced at any cheap jewelry store—which was exactly where she'd bought the earrings.

Darcy may not have been pleased with her, but he at least looked slightly embarrassed. "Don't worry," he added quickly. "I'm sure we'll find it."

Felix assessed her with a shrewd look. Either he judged her for being such a schemer or she'd impressed him. She suspected it was the latter.

Strolling to the center of the stage, Darcy spun

on his oxford heel. "Here we are," he said, as if Addison might have missed it.

"Thank you so much."

Darcy nodded but remained fixed to the spot, waiting for her to begin her search. She suddenly realized he wasn't going to leave them alone.

Crap. That was as far as her plan went.

Awkwardly, she bent over and began scouring the stage. She hemmed and hawed. "I remember being over here ..."

Felix began looking for the nonexistent earring too while Darcy scrutinized them. He didn't help them look. He just stood there watching like he didn't trust them. *For good reason*, Addison thought, but it still annoyed her. They couldn't inspect the place with him standing right there.

Addison continued to mumble things while throwing covert looks around the stage. However, she was too nervous with him around. After a few minutes of fake searching and Darcy clicking his tongue impatiently every so often, a young red-head interrupted them.

"Excuse me, Darcy." She hovered at the base of the stage. "The Covington party says they can't get the projector to work."

"What?" Darcy leaped to attention. He descended the steps two at a time, waving over his shoulder as he walk-sprinted. "I'll be right back." It almost sounded like a threat.

Once the redhead left, Addison searched in earnest. But for what, she wasn't sure.

Felix crossed over to her. "Nicely done on the earring story. What are we looking for?"

"I don't know," she said.

"What do you mean? This was your idea."

Addison positioned herself in the middle of the stage, staring out to an invisible audience. But when the cocktail mixer came rushing back to her and an image of the angry crowd flashed through her mind, it didn't feel so invisible.

The room swelled around her, the floor beneath her feet shaking—or maybe that was her legs. She closed her eyes and took a deep breath, clearing the memory. After a moment, she opened them again to find Felix staring at her curiously.

She ignored the look. "We know the dogs couldn't have left the stage through the curtains. There were hundreds of people here that night. Someone would have seen them." Turning, she faced the glowing exit sign off to the side of the stage, hanging above the door to the back alley. "And we know they didn't leave through the alley because Melody would have seen them."

"That's if she wasn't the one who took them," he reminded her.

"Let's just say she didn't. How else could they have gotten out of here?"

Felix grew quiet as he considered this. He rubbed the scruff of his five-o'clock shadow, and it scraped beneath his hands. It brought back Addison's memories of the night at Joe's Dive. She could almost feel the rough hair brushing against her neck.

She shivered, in a good way—which was bad, very bad—and then mentally slapped herself. Philip was going to call any time now to ask her out again. *Think positive*, she told herself.

Addison tried to put herself in the shoes of a criminal mastermind. She tilted her head back to glance at the rafters above, the spotlights, and the curtain tracks. Could the dogs have been hoisted up in a cage somehow? Which might have been slid out of a window using a complicated system of pulleys and cables and then deposited in a garbage truck making a late-night run. Then she remembered this wasn't *Ocean's Eleven* and continued to brainstorm.

Felix skirted the open area, running his hands over walls, flipping back curtains, and opening and closing the alley door.

The backstage was simplistic, bare bones. No place to hide, no mysterious doors, no windows, no props, no equipment. Addison could feel the clock ticking. Darcy would be back any minute, and they were no further ahead. She wanted to prove Melody's innocence. Or at least have a reason not to suspect her anymore.

"Ugh. I'd hoped there'd be something here." She stomped her foot like a five-year-old.

Felix spun to face her, giving her the strangest look.

She blushed at her childishness. "Sorry."

Then he stomped his foot.

For a second, Addison thought he was making fun of her. But then he did it again, and she heard the difference. The wooden thump beneath his feet sounded hollow. Like an echo in an empty room beneath them.

Their eyes dropped to the floor at the same time, searching for something, anything, that stood out among the black paint. Addison spotted it. A notch cut out between the wooden floor panels, just large enough to slip her fingers into.

Checking over her shoulder for Darcy, she reached down and pulled on the panel. The entire thing lifted right up, revealing a trap room below.

Felix helped her set the panel aside, and she squatted by the hole in the floor. Squinting down into the darkness, Addison had a fleeting vision of all the things that might be lurking down there.

Taking out his phone, Felix shone the light inside. He moved it around, highlighting the framework beneath. It was a five-foot drop into the black pit.

Addison bit her lip. "I suppose one of us should go down."

"I'll go." Felix held his phone out to her. "Here, hold this."

Addison fought her instincts that told her there

were all sorts of scary things down there. *Too many horror movies*, she told herself.

"No. I'll go," she finally said. "I'm smaller and lighter, so you can help me back up."

Dropping her purse on the stage, she sat down and dangled her legs over the edge. The cold stage made her bare legs tighten with goose bumps beneath her fifties-style dress. She wiggled her way forward, wondering what the best way to land was, when Felix grabbed her hands. He extended her arms above her head.

"Hold on," he told her. Bracing himself on either side of the hole, he lowered her into the black pit beneath the stage.

Even when her feet were firmly on the ground, she didn't want to let go of Felix. But as his hands slipped from hers, she felt the darkness envelop her and could sense all the zombies and vampires.

She took a step back, and something brushed against her. She spun around. A scream built inside her lungs. Then Felix's phone shone on her mysterious attacker.

It wasn't Freddy Krueger. It was just a wooden post. Addison grunted, clutching her chest in relief.

"See anything?" Felix asked, passing her his phone so she could see better.

"Not yet." She couldn't mask the shake in her voice.

Addison knew she didn't have much time. She

needed to do this. For the sake of the missing dogs, for her dad, for her passion, and, maybe, a little for Felix. Swallowing her fear, she took the phone and shone it around the space.

A series of crisscrossed beams and posts held up the stage. Enough space lay between them for performers to move freely. She assumed it was so they could pass things up through the trapdoors or pop up during a certain moment in a play or concert.

Shining the light at her feet, she weaved in and out of the wooden framework. All she could see was a thick layer of dust coating the floor. Overhead, cracks of light shone down on her face from more trapdoors. Felix's footsteps shifted above her head, echoing through the space around her.

Addison took another hesitant step forward and felt a crunch beneath her shoe. She pulled her foot back and held the phone over the spot, half expecting to see human bones. It glistened as the light hit it, sparkling brightly amidst the thick, gray dust. Whatever it was, it hadn't been there long.

Her fear momentarily forgotten, she bent down and picked it up. She recognized it right away: the handcrafted details, the careful color choices. It was the tiara she'd outfitted a Chow Chow with at the cocktail mixer.

She glanced up. The accessory wouldn't have fallen through the cracks around the hidden trapdoors. They were too small. So small that she hadn't even noticed the doors were there in the first place. And by the lack of footprints in the settled dust, neither had the cops. Paw prints, however, were a different story.

Addison hadn't noticed the prints before, but now she saw them everywhere. Big ones, little ones, scattered haphazardly around the floor. Or at least they appeared that way until she followed them with the light and saw that they all headed in the same general direction. She fought the temptation to track them; if the cops hadn't been down there to investigate, then they'd want to see all the evidence intact.

She put the tiara back on the ground where she'd found it and carefully retraced her steps. She didn't want to disrupt the crime scene any more than she already had.

As she made her way back, her fears crept up again, tickling her scalp like a thousand bugs crawling over her skin. By the time she stood beneath the opening in the stage floor and Felix's face hovered above her, she'd never thought she could be so happy to see him.

Darcy's face appeared next to Felix's. He, on the other hand, didn't look particularly happy to see her. However, she didn't care at the moment. The monsters were converging again, the dusty floor pulling her under. With shaking hands, she reached up to Felix.

His strong hands gripped hers. Grunting, he hoisted her out of the pit of doom. She stumbled against him. Her fingers automatically curled into his shirt. His solid presence soothed her frantic heartbeat, grounding her from the inexplicable terror that had consumed her down below.

"Are you all right?" Felix asked, his eyes scanning her face.

Addison wasn't sure what expression she wore, but it made a crease form between his brows.

She nodded but still didn't let go of his shirt. "Yeah. I found it."

Felix inhaled sharply; he understood more than she was saying. Handing back his phone, she reached into her pocket and pulled out the "missing" earring.

Darcy clapped his hands. "Good. You found it. So you'll be on your way now." He waved toward the stage stairs in a polite "get the heck out" manner.

Addison didn't move an inch, mostly because her legs still wobbled. "Is there any way out from under that stage? Does it go anywhere?"

Darcy frowned. "It leads to a side entrance. Why?"

Addison let out the breath she was holding. "Bingo."

When Felix gave her a strange look, she made a mental note to come up with a better "aha" word.

"Call the police," she said. "They'll want to see what's down there."

Darcy snorted. "I've had just about enough police for one week. They've already completed their investigation."

"What's going on?" Felix asked Addison.

"That's how the dogs got out of the building. From underneath the stage." Addison managed to pry her hand free of him to replace her earring. "I found evidence down there."

The pinched look on Darcy's face faltered. He blinked. "Oh … It's been so long since we've used the trapdoors that it didn't occur to me to mention it to the police."

Felix pulled out his phone again. "I'm on it."

Darcy glanced at his watch. "I have an event booked in this room in four hours. This was the last thing I needed today."

Addison scowled. "I'm sure losing their pets was the last thing the cocktail mixer guests needed too. This might help them get their dogs back. So suck it up."

Felix was half listening to their conversation. His eyebrows rose at her lecture. She shrugged at him, and he stifled a chuckle.

Darcy shut his trap, thankfully. Now that he looked a bit sheepish, Addison took advantage, hoping he'd be more cooperative.

"Are there any cameras in this room?" She scanned the ceiling.

"Only at the exits," he said. "And before you ask, there isn't one at the exit for beneath the stage. Just ones that guests would normally use."

But Addison wasn't thinking only about the dogs. She was thinking about her assistant. "Do you have access to the video footage from the cocktail mixer? Specifically, the alley exit?"

"Yes. But the police have that now." He stiffened a little with self-importance. "Not that I could show anyone if we did have them."

Addison figured he'd say something like that.

"I can tell you that if it hadn't been for your assistant neglecting the dogs for a cigarette, this wouldn't have happened."

"She didn't neglect the dogs. She took a break." She crossed her arms. "Maybe your facilities are to blame." Then it dawned on her what he'd said. "How did you know she went out for a smoke?"

"Because the camera caught her heading outside holding a lighter and a pack of cigarettes. Doesn't take a genius to figure out what she was doing."

Felix covered his phone with a hand. "The police are on their way."

Addison nodded in response. It surprised her how well their investigation was going already, considering the only experience she had solving crimes was watching *Sherlock Holmes*. Even then, the context was a bit outdated.

The new evidence was both good and bad. She was happy it supported Melody's innocence. It didn't completely absolve her, though, since she could have had a smoke while helping load up the dogs into a truck or something. But it looked a lot better for her. However, with the discovery of the real escape route for the dogs, it opened up all new possibilities for who the dognapper could be.

Addison suddenly realized how much work they had ahead of them.

12

SNIFF OUT

Addison sped through the streets of San Francisco until they arrived at Laurel Heights for another undercover operation. This time, they planned to engage a suspect. Impatient for answers, she took the next corner without slowing down.

Felix white-knuckled the doorframe. "Where did you learn to drive?"

Addison thought for a moment. *"The Fast and the Furious, Days of Thunder, The Love Bug."*

"That explains it," he said.

"I'm making up for lost time, okay? Talking to the police really set us back." She pulled up to a stop sign. "Do you think they believed my earring story?"

Felix gave her a look from the passenger seat. "I don't think you're as good of an actress as you think you are."

"But I don't think I'm a good actress at all."

"Exactly."

She stuck out her tongue at him and whipped into traffic. "Just for that, you can talk to William Jackson. I think I remember this guy from the cocktail mixer. Kind of balding on the top, right?"

Felix ran a hand through his hair. "Not everyone can have ridiculously luscious locks like mine."

Addison snorted, but she had to admit it was true. His hair was so full and wavy, it was unfair. He probably just rolled out of bed that way too. She couldn't see Felix waking up a few minutes early to style it. But she didn't know many guys who could pull off a cut any longer than your usual man-clip. With hair as exceptional as Felix's, it would have been a crime against humanity to cut it.

"I think he had a Maltese, right?" she asked. "What do you know about him?"

"Just that he's been competing in dog shows for years and has never won anything," Felix said. "Last year, his dog actually made it to the podium. Just as the judge went to congratulate them, the dog shook out his coat like it was a living powder puff, covering the judge in talcum."

"I remember reading something about that in *Doggy Digest*," Addison said. "They disqualified him for using unnatural products to enhance his dog. Serves the selfish jerk right. Powder can be terrible for a dog's respiratory system." She made a mental note to jot that down in her notebook when they pulled over.

Addison would never have thought of a suspect like William Jackson without Felix, not that she'd admit she needed him. "I take it he falls under the revenge category of motives?"

Felix pulled an "oh yeah" face. "I was working the dog show last year. I served him at the bar after his disqualification, and he spilled his guts to me. Let's just say I wouldn't put it past him to go to extremes."

She thought back to the cocktail mixer. "I think he's the one who ordered the pawdicure. I remember he liked the Rainbow Frenzy nail polish. I brought a sample with me."

Felix glanced back at the multitude of pink gift bags in the backseat. "You hand out a lot of free stuff. You know you'll never get anywhere if you keep giving it away."

Addison snorted. "You're one to talk."

He glowered at her from the passenger seat. "What does that mean?"

"Oh, please. I'm sure you *give it away* all the time." She layered her voice with a suggestive tone. "You and Red Bra seem close."

"Yes," he replied evenly. "Charlotte and I are close."

Addison frowned at the response. She'd expected a smart comeback, but now she just kept recalling the image of them sitting next to each other in Joe's Dive. Not that she was jealous.

"Besides, you gave me free drinks at the bar," she said. "Think of it like promotional services. You give someone free drinks, and that person will tell their friends about your bar, which in turn will generate more business. I'm doing the same thing."

"True. That's the kind of marketing help I need when I open my bar. But I didn't give you those drinks as freebies. I was just testing out a new concoction on you."

"You used me as a guinea pig?" she teased.

"I didn't see you complaining." Felix licked his lips. "I certainly wasn't."

"You liquored me up just to get a kiss, didn't you?" She pretended to be outraged, but looking back, she knew it wasn't the liquor that had gotten her all fired up over him.

"Excuse me. You kissed me, remember?" He grinned. "Besides, if I wanted to get in your pants, I would have gotten in them."

"Yeah, right." She batted her eyelashes. "I'm a lady, I'll have you know."

"Right."

Her mouth dropped open in real offense. "Excuse me? You think I'm not? Who do you think—"

"No, *right*. Turn right." He pointed at the intersection they were driving through. "Right!"

"Hang on!"

She cranked the wheel. The tires screeched around the next corner. Angry honks sounded behind them.

Felix gripped the door, holding on for dear life. When they'd made the turn and were still alive, he said, "Maybe a little less flirting while we're driving. I don't think you need any distractions."

"Who's flirting?" she asked innocently, but she knew that she was.

Felix was fun to flirt with. It was impossible for her not to flirt with him. He had a personality that double-dog-dared her to just try to ignore him, which only made her think of him that much more. But she'd promised herself she wouldn't go down that path with guys like Felix anymore. Guys just out to use her. She was so much more than another "number."

She recalled her sort-of date with the far more appropriate Philip, smiling at how well things had gone. Now *there* was a guy she could bring home to meet her dad. Not a guy who wanted to take her home after the bar closed.

Her smile disappeared. Well, the date had been going well before all the dog stealing, police interrogations, and accusations. That was probably why she hadn't heard from him yet.

The police must have been keeping him busy. That was it. He'd probably text her any moment.

She glared at her phone in its holder, willing it to ring.

Felix pointed up the road to a peach-colored home with white trim. "Number thirty-four. I think that's Jackson's house over there, but park here across the street. We don't want anyone to see us together."

"I'll agree with that," she said, eliciting a glare from Felix.

Addison pulled over and parked behind a van to block her Mini from sight. She left the top down, just in case Felix needed to make a quick getaway.

He got out of the car, stretching as he did so. "Why am I the one doing this again?"

"Because it was your idea to give our suspects a fake survey of their experience with Pampered Puppies, remember? You said people love talking about themselves. So get him to talk about the dog-grooming services at the cocktail mixer. Then just go from there." She smiled extra sweetly. "You're good at reading people. I'm sure you'll think of something."

She reached behind the seat, producing a frilly pink bag. "Don't forget the samples and the coupons." She shook it playfully.

"Anything else?" he asked sarcastically.

"Remember, you're a representative of my company." She bared her sparkling white teeth and pointed to them. "So smile."

With an exaggerated eye roll, Felix reached over and grabbed the bag of samples. Waving it with sour enthusiasm, he crossed the street.

Addison spun in her seat to watch him climb Jackson's front steps and ring the doorbell. She couldn't help but note how nicely those faded jeans hung on his hips. Although they weren't an expensive label—in fact, they looked so old that the label had probably fallen off by now—that butt could have made any pants look like a million bucks.

While Felix waited for someone to answer the door, a white Audi drove up and parked on the street in front of the house. Addison ducked down. The last thing she wanted was for anyone to realize they were sneaking around, asking questions. Her car wasn't exactly covert with its Caribbean Aqua paint job.

William Jackson stepped out of the Audi. She recognized him by the cul-de-sac hairstyle he unwillingly sported. He moved around to the back of the car and popped the trunk. Reaching inside, he drew out armloads of shopping bags.

Felix noticed him and descended the stairs. By the gestures he made, it looked like he was offering to help carry some bags. William waved his arms, shooing Felix away. But Felix just smiled and took several of the bags up the steps anyway.

Jackson rushed to unlock the front door. The moment it swung open, he practically flung the shopping bags into the house. Squeezing in after them, he smiled and waved at Felix before shutting the door in his face.

Felix was left standing on the porch with the frilly pink bag still in his hands. After a few seconds, he shrugged and returned to the car.

"What was that about?" Addison asked.

"I'm not sure," he said. "He was edgy, though. He didn't even want the samples."

"Maybe you made him nervous. I know you scare me," she said extra sweetly.

He threw her a sour look. "Ha ha."

"What was in the bags?"

"I didn't get to see."

She sighed, turning over the engine and pulling away from the curb. "Well, that was a bust."

Felix drew out a long, crumpled slip of paper from his pocket. "Not necessarily."

She glanced at it while driving. "What's that?"

"Jackson's shopping receipt." Felix scanned it.

Addison's mouth dropped open. "You can't just take that. What if he needs to return something? You know a lot of stores won't do returns or exchanges without a receipt."

He rolled his eyes. "Did you want us to turn around and give it back?"

"No," she said. "I guess not."

Felix went quiet for a few moments as he read

each item. "How many dogs did you say this guy had?"

"Just the one. Why?" She pulled up to a stop sign and looked over to see him frowning at the paper.

"Why would a man with one dog need twelve leather dog collars and leashes?"

"What? Let me see that." She snatched the receipt and read it herself.

She scanned the itemized list. Not only were there twelve collars and leashes, but there were bones, food dishes, brushes, and chew toys.

"That's a lot of pet supplies," she finally said. "Seems like he owns more than one dog."

Felix took the receipt and waved it in the air like it was a winning lottery ticket. "Or we've just found our dognapper."

13

HORNDOGS

Addison crouched low to peer through the gap in William Jackson's fence, feeling the cool night air blow up her short dress. A shiver ran through her as the wind caressed her bare legs. She wished she'd worn something a little more practical for their clandestine operation. When she'd planned her outfit that morning, she'd never imagined she'd be crawling through creepy spaces beneath stages or sneaking onto people's property. At least her cute fifties-style dress was black, so she could blend into the night.

Unable to see anything, she got on her hands and knees to look through a hole in a wooden picket. There wasn't a single light on in William Jackson's backyard. Since his house was in the middle of the block, they'd been lucky it wasn't a row house, or they wouldn't have had access to the backyard.

"Can you see anything?" she whispered to Felix.

"Oh yeah," he said from behind her. "I've got a great view from here."

She glanced over her shoulder to find him standing back and enjoying the "view" of her backside.

Addison groaned and returned to her peep-hole. "Stop messing around and get over here. What if something happens and we miss it?"

"Oh, I think something's going to happen." He laid his hand over hers. "I feel it."

"I'm serious," she hissed, flicking him away.

Felix sighed and backed off. "All we can do is wait and watch. If the dogs are here, eventually Jackson will have to bring them outside to do their business."

He settled down on his side in the grass next to her, head resting on his fist. "We have to assume he's taking reasonable care of them if he bought all those supplies today. Leashes for walking them, dishes for feeding them, even toys for playing."

After Felix had swiped Jackson's receipt, they'd had to kill several hours before it grew dark enough to check things out. While Felix was just full of suggestions that involved her backseat—no matter how small it was—they'd settled on dinner at a nearby Mexican restaurant.

Returning after nightfall, they'd sat outside the home to case the place, picking away at leftovers as car after car rolled up and parked on William's street. So far, at least eight people had knocked on his door and entered.

"Why do you think there are so many people here?" Addison asked Felix. "Do you think they're all involved in the dognapping?"

"I don't know. Maybe he's selling them off or something. An auction to the highest bidder?"

Addison kept her focus on the hole in the fence, but she sensed Felix's eyes on her while they continued to wait.

"So, why dogs?" he asked. "Why not groom and dress people if you love fashion so much? Why the tutus, and the nails, and piercings, and dyed hair? It's torturous enough on humans. It borders on animal cruelty," he joked.

"Figures you'd say that. Looks like it's been a while since you've even had a haircut."

He snorted but didn't deny it.

"First of all," she said, "I don't condone piercing dogs' ears. That's a cruel practice just for fashion's sake. And I guess it's because everyone needs to feel beautiful, even dogs."

"Because dogs care if they're up to date on the latest fashion?"

"Maybe not, but they enjoy the pampering, the sense that they're important. And in turn, it gets them positive attention, which makes them happy and feel even more loved."

"Is that why you do it?"

"Do what?" she asked distractedly, focused on the hole again.

"The hair, the makeup, the carefully calculated outfits." He tugged on her dress. "Because it gets you attention?"

Addison finally tore her eyes away from Jackson's backyard. "No. I don't do it for anyone else. I enjoy fashion."

"That kind of beauty is only skin deep." He sneered. Not at her, but maybe at the general idea of it. "It means nothing."

"Why the face? You have something against a little hygiene and self-care? Oh, wait." She fingered a hole near the neckline of his Metallica T-shirt. "Look who I'm asking."

"Hey, this is vintage, I'll have you know." He frowned. "I guess I believe there's more to a person than what they look like on the outside."

"You think I'm superficial just because I like to dress nicely and spend time on my hair?" she asked. "I don't think there's anything wrong with wrapping a gift in paper that matches the quality of the present inside. I mean, you wouldn't buy a ring from Tiffany's and stick it in a shoebox, would you?"

His eyes drank her in. "And you're the Tiffany ring?"

She liked that his tone wasn't his usual sarcasm. It was full of excitement. Maybe at the prospect of opening that gift.

"Honey, I'm the whole store." She gave him a wink. "I like to bring the internal beauty to the outside. There's beauty in everything and everyone. Even you, Felix Vaughn. It's somewhere in there." She gave him a playful shove. "Deep down in there." She poked his chest. "Deep, deep, deep, deep ..."

He smiled, grabbing her finger playfully.

Addison really tried to see the good in Felix, but he made it difficult sometimes. There would be a ray of hope, a glimmer of a deeper man beneath the wolfish smile and the cocky attitude. But then he would go and say something that ruined the moment.

"The hair and makeup are just the finishing touches," Addison said. "A way to reflect the beauty a person has within. Not mask a flawed personality."

His finger trailed down her arm, causing goose bumps. "Well, if your wrapping is any indication of what's hidden beneath, then you must be perfect inside." His teeth flashed in the darkness, matching the white hibiscus growing next to him.

Addison's face fell. She knew he was just being his flirtatious self, but the words made her wonder. Maybe she was subconsciously hiding something. Making herself perfect on the outside, using makeup and clothes to cover up the scars on the inside.

"Did I say something wrong?" he asked.

He didn't mean anything by it. Of course not. He didn't know.

"I … I think I heard something," she lied. But as they grew silent to listen, she did hear a noise coming from inside Jackson's house.

"Bark, bark, bark."

"Is that …?" Felix began.

"Woof, woof."

Addison held her ear closer to the fence. "Someone barking like a dog?"

The answer came in the form of a long, drawn-out howl. Not canine but … human.

"Come on," Addison said. "Let's get a better look."

Unfortunately, there was no gate on that side of the house, but there was a garbage can. She lined it up to where the fence met the house.

She waved Felix over. "Come and help me up."

He steadied her as she balanced on the trash can, his hand gripping her thigh—maybe a little higher than he needed to.

"Now that's what I call getting a better look," he said, amusement in his voice.

She turned to find him purposely averting his gaze to avoid seeing up her dress. At least he could be a gentleman sometimes.

Addison swung a leg over the fence. She moved her foot around until she found the horizontal rail on the other side and then climbed over. The wood scraped her legs as she lowered herself to the ground.

Darkness enveloped her. She felt cornered in the yard, fearing that at any moment the exterior lights could flick on and Jackson would discover her and set the entire pack of stolen dogs on her. The possibility that she could go to jail for breaking and entering became very real in that moment. However, if she didn't find the missing dogs, she might go to jail anyway. Talk about being caught between a tight budget and a flash sale.

It didn't take long before Felix was standing next to Addison in the dark yard, making her feel safer, less alone. At least if she was going down, he'd be going down with her.

They made their way through the yard behind the house, and Addison felt her chest shake with each powerful beat of her frightened heart. Every step brought them closer to being discovered. It was unsettling yet thrilling. For better or for worse, she was glad Felix was by her side.

All the curtains had been drawn. The only light that escaped the house was from the sliding glass doors facing the backyard. The long drapes had caught on the carpet, allowing a small glimpse into the home.

Together, Addison and Felix crept up to the doors and got down on their hands and knees to peer inside. They pressed their heads together so they could both see the view. And what a view they saw.

The leather collars were being put to good use, only they weren't around furry necks. They were around the necks of William Jackson and several of his male friends. At the other end, women in various stages of undress held the leashes.

Addison's eyes widened. "Oh, my gosh."

Felix leaned forward to get a better look. "Why wasn't I invited to this party?"

"Something tells me they don't want anyone to see this. Even someone working as a bartender."

He gave her a wolfish smile. "I meant as a guest."

She hit him on the arm, chuckling. Then she heard a muffled gasp from inside the house. The music stopped.

"Did anyone hear that?" a female voice asked. "I think someone's out there."

Addison froze. Footsteps thumped inside, and the curtain shifted.

Felix clamped a hand around her wrist and dragged her back to the fence. He interlaced his fingers and held them low so she could step on them. Lifting herself up, Addison straddled the wooden pickets as she searched for the trash can on the other side with her foot. She found the metal lid just as she heard the sliding glass door hiss open.

Worried shouts and questions carried into the yard. Addison leaped off the garbage can. Within seconds Felix was next to her, running by her side down the street, back to the car.

"Do you think they'll call the cops?" she panted as she opened the door.

"And tell them what? We interrupted their freaky sex party?" Felix rounded the car and hopped in. "Time to go." He buckled up. "Use some of those *Fast and Furious* skills to get us out of here."

Addison didn't need to be told twice. She started the engine and stomped on the gas, peeling away.

They sped by William Jackson's house in a blur just as she saw the shine of his balding head beneath the porch lights. He squinted through the dark, probably trying to read her license plate, but then he was yanked back inside by a tug on his leash.

By the time they reached the end of the street, Addison and Felix had dissolved into relieved laughter.

14

DOG EAT DOG

The high-gloss red door swung open to Addison's ridiculously enthusiastic smile.

"Hello. I don't know if you remember me. My name is Addison Turner. I'd like to do a brief survey on your experience with Pampered Puppies. Would you be interested in participating?"

Kitty Carlisle stood inside her classic San Francisco painted-lady home with its adorable olive scalloped siding and yellow trim. She stared at Addison with a blank expression on her pinched face.

"It will only take five minutes of your time," Addison added. "And you'll receive this complementary bag of samples." She held out the frilly pink bag, practically forcing Kitty to take it.

Once the bag was in Kitty's hands, Addison cheerfully barged her way through the front door and into the foyer. Even though the older woman creeped her out, she had to get a closer look. Felix hadn't been able to get into William Jackson's house the day before—which might have been for the best. This time around, she needed to get closer, much closer, if she was going to investigate. There wasn't a lot she could uncover from the front stoop.

Kitty peered down the street with her bulgy eyes, as though looking for other people. *Or maybe witnesses*, Addison thought with a shiver, remembering the lady's intense looks at the cocktail mixer.

"All right," Kitty relented. "Come in."

But Addison was already inside, scoping out the place. Her gaze darted around the room. The entrance was full of fake flowers and framed pictures of what she assumed were the woman's kids and grandkids. Then her eyes fell on Kitty's bichon frise sitting by the door. He was so well-behaved that she hadn't noticed him.

Squatting down, she reached out to pet him, but he didn't move. When her hand touched his white fur, it felt cold and hard. She snatched her hand back in surprise. It was a carved statue.

Kitty giggled. "So lifelike, isn't it? I had that commissioned at the height of Elvis's competitive career. I wanted him to have a reminder of the glory days."

"It's, umm, beautiful." Addison suppressed a

shudder but couldn't help subtly wiping her hand on her leggings.

Kitty led Addison into the sitting room and waved an inviting hand at a floral sofa covered in a layer of protective plastic. It squeaked under Addison's butt as she sat.

For a moment, she felt a flutter of panic beneath her chest and the urge to run screaming out of there before she was ax-murdered. But then she took in the rest of the room. The original plastic film still protected the television frame, and display cases enclosed each dog show trophy. The couch cover wasn't to hide evidence. The woman was just fastidious.

Kitty sat quietly in her armchair, waiting for Addison to begin, pug eyes examining her carefully. "What did you want to ask me?"

"Umm," Addison referred to her clipboard—which she thought made her look very official. "How many dogs do you have?"

"Just the one. Elvis!" she called out. "Come here, Elvis!"

There was a light jingling and padding of paws before Kitty's dog twin floated into the room like a little white cloud on a sunny day.

Kitty picked him up and placed him on her lap. "There's my boy."

"He's a beautiful bichon frise," Addison said.

"Thank you. Elvis here was quite the success,

but he's retired now." She indicated the row of trophies on the mantel.

That's when Addison spotted the detailed painting above the fireplace. What she'd mistaken as a portrait of Kitty with her white beehive was actually a painting of Elvis. He sat nobly with his chin resting on his paw, replete in a green paisley vest and cravat. A monocle and pocket watch topped off the outfit.

Addison almost laughed, but then she caught herself. It was likely not meant to be cute and whimsical but a serious rendition of Elvis, which made it even odder. She shifted uncomfortably on the sofa. Her butt squeaked on the plastic again.

Kitty nuzzled the dog's halo of white fur. "We had a good run, didn't we, pookie?"

Addison cleared her throat and focused on her clipboard. "Do you think you'll compete in dog shows again in the future?"

"Not anytime soon. It just wouldn't be the same without Elvis," Kitty said a little sadly. "But I still attend the events each year and enjoy being part of the association. I've been on the judging panel for a few years now."

"I didn't realize that. How exciting."

Addison made a note of that. If Kitty was a judge, surely she wouldn't want to steal the dogs entering the competition.

"Upholding the standards are important to me," Kitty told Addison. "And if you ask me, they've been slipping under Judge Walter Boyd's watch."

She remembered the pompous man Philip had introduced her to at the cocktail mixer. "How have they been slipping?"

Kitty huffed. "Oh, please. His choice for Best in Show last year was Alistair's beagle. Who was Walter kidding? Everyone could see there was favoritism there. Judge Walter's own dogs are hounds, you see. Lily's reign should have ended the year before last."

The plastic squeaked as Kitty leaned close, like someone might overhear them in her own sitting room. "Between you and me, Alistair looked ridiculous continuing to show Lily. She was past her prime. He needed to move on. It was embarrassing."

"I see."

Addison remembered Philip saying something similar at his fundraiser. She mentally tucked away the tidbit to scribble down in her notebook later. It would be too obvious to do it right in front of Kitty.

For now, she moved down the list of questions on her clipboard. "In your experience with Pampered Puppies, on a scale from one to ten, what was your level of satisfaction with the results?"

"Ten. Elvis's fur hasn't been this soft in years."

Addison beamed. "That's the jojoba and coconut oil cleanser. It prevents tangles while increasing luster and flexibility. It's our most popular product," she rambled, excited to talk about business. "On a scale from one to ten, how safe did you feel leaving Elvis with Pampered Puppies?"

"Well …" Kitty's eyes dropped, considering Elvis cuddled in her arms. "You're always nervous leaving your pet. Elvis is like my child."

"I feel the same way about my Princess. I understand."

Addison could read between the lines. She saw the apprehension in Kitty's eyes. The older woman was anxious to begin with, but the dognapping probably had her on edge. It had everyone on edge.

Kitty's eyes narrowed. "Is it true? Did all those dogs really get stolen?"

"It seems that way."

"How?" She held Elvis closer, like maybe Addison would snatch him from her arms and make a run for it.

"They weren't certain it was a dognapping until it happened again this weekend at Philip Montgomery's fundraiser. The police suspect it was an inside job. One of the staff or a guest at the party."

Addison wasn't sure if any of it was true, but it was probably close enough. She observed the woman for a sign, a twitch, a tell. Maybe just as closely as Kitty was watching her.

"Well, thankfully I don't need to worry about

that." She kissed Elvis on the head. "He's twelve years old now and not coming out of retirement. He's no threat to anyone."

Addison stared at the woman. "You think it's someone who wants to win the contest by taking out the competition?"

Kitty's painted-on eyebrows rose. "Absolutely. It's not like we haven't all thought about doing something like that."

She laughed, and the titters sent shivers down Addison's spine. She didn't want to think about what Kitty might have done for all those trophies lining the mantel.

Kitty tilted onto one buttock to lean in closer. The plastic on her chair groaned, sounding like a fart. "You want to know the truth about conformation? It's rife with jealousy and bitter competition. People resort to prohibited plastic surgeries. Opponents snip out patches of fur on other dogs or scratch their pads so they can't walk properly. People will try to oust the competition in any way." She covered Elvis's ears so he wouldn't hear. "Even by nobbling."

Addison twitched, the word rubbing her the wrong way. "Nobbling?"

"Disabling the competition by drugging or poisoning. Food tainted with laxatives, sleeping pills, or even chocolate. It leaves a nasty film around the mouth, you see."

Addison had completely forgotten about her

213

list of questions. She stared at the woman in disbelief. "But you're talking about dog-lovers. How could they harm another animal?"

"They say these tactics exist only in the minds of disgruntled owners that have lost a competition, that there's no truth to them, only rumors. But I've seen enough in my day to know it exists. But *this*," she said. "These dognappings are bold. This reeks of desperation. It's disturbing." Her pug eyes bulged out of her head.

Addison suddenly felt cold, her fingertips tingling from gripping the clipboard too tightly. If Kitty Carlisle deemed it disturbing, then Addison was afraid of what she and Felix might uncover.

Elvis had been still on Kitty's lap for some time, as though he'd been replaced with the statue in her entranceway. The only indication he was alive was the occasional blink of his dark eyes. His constant stare freaked her out.

Kitty sat upright in her chair again, aloofness settling back over her. "I hope they find whoever is doing this. It makes a mockery of what the association and the shows stand for. At the heart of it, it's about discovering and preserving the best genetics of any particular breed. And because," she said simply, "we truly love our dogs."

That much was apparent. Maybe a little too much in Kitty's case.

As though Elvis could understand her, he

leaned back and gave her a kiss on the chin to let her know he felt the same way.

It was interesting to see the other side of the coin. Piper used to volunteer with a local animal activist group whose members protested dog shows because they loved animals. Meanwhile, breeders continued to support dog shows for the same reason. Addison didn't know which side she stood on yet. All she knew was that she loved every dog. Perfect genetics or not.

A click sounded on the wall, and the cuckoo clock struck four. Instead of a bird to signal the time, a dog leaped out of a miniature doghouse. Addison jumped at the mechanical barks. Elvis continued to stare at her with those bottomless black eyes.

"Was there anything else?" Kitty asked, drawing her attention back.

Addison mentally shook herself and glanced at her clipboard. "On a scale from one to ten, how likely are you to use Pampered Puppies' services again or recommend it to a friend?"

Kitty reached out to touch Elvis as though weighing the risk of someone stealing him versus the featherlike caress of his jojoba-infused fur. Now that Addison knew what people in her world were willing to do to win, she didn't blame her.

"I think I'll stick to my regular groomer for now."

Addison nodded and held back a disappointed

sigh. The fact that Kitty had even considered the question meant she was interested in the services, but the speculation surrounding the dog disappearances had everyone nervous. And if the roles were reversed, Addison wouldn't want to risk anything happening to Princess either.

But the "for now" gave her hope. It meant that maybe once Addison cleared her name, Kitty would reconsider. And others might follow. That was if her business survived that long.

Kitty showed Addison to the door. Elvis took a seat next to his younger marble rendition. They both watched steadily as Addison walked out the door.

"Well, if you reconsider," she said, "here's a ten-dollar-off coupon, along with samples of my homemade jojoba coconut cleanser."

Kitty's pug eyes widened as she peeked into the bag. "Oh, thank you." She bent down and picked up Elvis to wave his little paw at Addison. "Good luck with your survey."

Addison returned to her car with a smile on her face. Maybe things weren't so bleak. Maybe she could repair her reputation, one customer at a time. It would be hard work, but she could do it.

When she climbed into the convertible, Felix eyed her expression from the passenger seat. "So? How did it go?"

"Okay. Kitty doesn't want my services. But I'm hopeful. If I can just clear my name—"

"No, I meant is she our dognapper?"

"Oh, that. It's tough to say." Addison took out her notebook and mulled it over. "Her passion for dog shows borders on obsession. But she seems to truly love dogs, so I'm not sure if she's capable."

She reviewed everything discussed during her shakedown. As odd as Kitty seemed, Addison thought her an unlikely culprit, but she wasn't ready to scratch her off the list quite yet.

"But she did mention one name," she said.

"Who's that?" Felix asked.

"Judge Walter Boyd. She complained that he's letting the judging standards slip. I don't know if it means anything, but it isn't the first time I've heard that."

"Then I guess we know who to talk to next."

15

HOT DIGGITY DOG!

The thick trees at the edge of the Presidio drove away the sun as Addison and Felix pulled onto the dead-end street. At the end of the block, Judge Walter Boyd's Spanish-style home backed onto the dense woods that lined Lobos Creek. It made for a great view but made Addison's skin crawl after the last light had drained from the sky.

She stared out her windshield at the white columns and arches along the first-floor and second-floor balconies. They looked like the bared teeth of a guard dog, warning them away.

A cool breeze blew through the Mini, thanks to the open top. Her curls tickled her neck and made her shiver. Reaching for the controls, she closed the roof.

Felix was texting on his phone. Addison couldn't help but read the name at the top of the screen. It was a woman's name: Celia. She wondered if Celia was his sister or something, but he would probably accuse her of being jealous if she asked. And she was so not jealous.

"I've got a bad feeling about this guy," she told Felix. "Like creep factor ten."

He glanced up from his text. "Why?"

"Just a feeling, I guess." She shrugged. "He called Princess the b-word."

Felix's mouth twitched. "A bitch?"

She scowled and held a finger to her lips. "Shh."

"That's because Princess *is* one."

"I know," she said. "But I didn't like the way he said it."

They sat back and watched the place for a while, waiting for ... well, Addison wasn't sure what. Maybe for a pack of dogs to come rushing out of the gate or to hear a chorus of howls at the moon. But that would be too easy.

Her phone chimed. It was a text from her dad.

A potential buyer came to view the store today. They seemed very interested. Keep your fingers crossed.

Addison frowned. She was running out of time to help her dad. Things with the sale were moving a lot faster than she'd hoped. Or rather, their investigation was going a lot slower.

That's great news, Dad, she texted. *Is that what you want? Are you happy?*

A moment later, her phone chimed again. *It's not ideal. But it's the best scenario for our situation.*

No, she thought. The best scenario would be for her to find the dogs, return them to their worried owners, win back her customers, launch a successful fashion line, and save her dad's business. Then everyone could live happily ever after.

But it wasn't like she could make any promises, so she texted, *Then I'm happy for you. Fingers and toes are crossed.*

I'll keep you updated. Love you.

Love you too. Say hi to Dora for me. X

Frowning, Addison put her phone away and focused on her mission. After twenty minutes, headlights appeared in her rearview mirror.

"Car," she announced.

She and Felix sank down in their seats as the vehicle passed by. They watched its progress until it pulled up to Walter Boyd's house and parked outside the property's stone wall. The driver got out, ducking their head as they headed for the house. Before they went through the gate, the person glanced nervously around the street. Addison caught sight of their profile and their telltale hooked nose.

Her mouth dropped open. "No way. That's Penny Peacock. What do you think she's doing here?"

Felix leaned forward in his seat. "A handler

fraternizing with a judge? It's got to be against the show rules."

"Come on," she said. "Let's get a closer look."

They got out of the car and snuck up to the front yard. A steel gate barricaded the driveway, but they could hop over the low stone wall. Addison was happy she'd chosen a more spy-appropriate ensemble tonight: black leggings, a loose tank top in case more acrobatics were required, and a black leather jacket for nighttime camouflage. Not to mention a badass flair.

Felix wore his usual attire, which she'd dubbed ruggedly-sexy-in-a-completely-careless-way style. While he claimed not to care about fashion, she knew that wasn't totally true. She'd caught him checking out her tush more than once that night. It wouldn't have been quite the same if she were wearing baggy sweats.

Sticking to the hedges lining the drive, she and Felix crept around the side of the house. When they reached the kitchen window, Addison could see Walter's and Penny's silhouettes through the sheer curtains like a comical shadow puppet show.

"Come on," Felix said. "We're too exposed here. A neighbor might spot us."

Addison nodded and followed him around to the fenced-off back yard. Felix unlatched the gate, but as it swung open, it creaked, a siren in the night.

Felix grimaced. They both froze, straining

their ears for a hint that someone had heard them. A few painful heartbeats passed, but no one came.

He made a show of blowing out a sigh of relief and slipped into the back. Addison followed him. At the last second, she searched around for something to prop open the gate so it wouldn't squeak when they wanted to leave. She spotted a garden gnome hiding beneath an azalea bush. Snatching it up, she placed it in front of the gate.

The backyard was pitch black. The moon hung low in the night sky, mostly hidden behind the thick cover of trees hugging the property line. Addison made her way forward more by feel than sight. She shuffled her feet through the grass, bumping into Felix whenever he stopped to listen. After the third time she face-planted into his muscular back, he reached around and grabbed her hand.

Addison tried to snatch it away. He held it firmly, tugging her along. As they crept closer to the heart of the property and into the open, she found she was holding his hand in earnest.

A scent crawled its way up Addison's nose, stinging her nostrils. The caustic smell hinted at chemicals, but it was so out of place that she struggled to find a name for it. She wrinkled her nose, fighting the urge to sneeze.

As they crept closer to the back porch, a light flicked on in one of the windows. Addison winced, momentarily blinded. Felix's body tensed next to her. She squeezed his hand as though she could silently communicate, "Oh crap, oh crap, oh crap, oh crap."

Then the porch light turned on, and it lit up the two of them like a spotlight. The back door cracked open. Voices drifted out.

Felix glanced back the way they'd come, probably wondering if they should make a run for it. But Addison spotted a small shed on the other side of the yard. Maybe ten feet away.

Gripping Felix's hand, she dragged him with her as she made a dash for it. Her skin tingled as sweat formed down her back. She didn't dare look behind her in case she stumbled.

By the time they reached the shed, her lungs were aching with a suppressed scream. She fumbled for the handle with shaking fingers. Wrenching the door open, she ducked inside, Felix right behind her.

A wave of heat hit her, nearly knocking her over. The potent scent of cedar overpowered her senses. They'd barely shut the door behind them before the voices became clearer.

Addison held her breath, listening for signs they'd been seen or heard. No one called "Release the hounds!" and there were no footsteps drawing closer. She dared to peek out of the small window at the top of the shed door.

Walter and Penny stepped out onto the back porch with a pair of basset hounds at their heels.

They wore bathing suits—Walter and Penny, that is. However, Addison thought that would make a great idea for a new design: doggy swimwear.

Addison sensed Felix come up behind her. His stubbled jaw brushed against her hair as he tried to see out the window. She flushed at how close he was. His nearness prevented her heart from slowing down after their mad dash. Was it just her, or was it really hot?

"What's going on?" Felix asked.

She shivered as his breath tickled her neck. "They're in their bathing suits."

He inhaled sharply. "That means they might come in here."

"What?" She spun around to take in her surroundings for the first time.

Her eyes roved over the dark panels of wood that made up their hiding spot. The entire structure was built with cedar, which was why the air was so heavy with its musk.

She stepped away from the window to allow the light to flow into the shed. But it wasn't a shed. They'd found their refuge in a sauna. And the reason it was so unbearably warm in there was because it was heating up to be used.

Addison backed away from the door, staring at it like it could open at any moment. "What do we do?"

Felix gripped her, maybe like he was ready to

throw her over his shoulder and carry her out if it came to that. Or maybe it was so he could throw her aside and leave her behind to take the fall. "If they come in here, we'll just barrel past them. They'll be taken by surprise if we're quick enough."

She nodded. "Okay, but we can't let them see our faces."

Addison dared another look out the window, half expecting to see Penny and Walter headed that way. But she spotted them on the porch, climbing a set of stairs to a platform. No. Not a platform, she realized as Penny threw a leg over it. It was a hot tub.

"That's what that smell was," she breathed. "Chlorine. They're going in a hot tub."

Felix ducked to look out the window. "We're okay for now. But eventually they'll come in here, or Walter wouldn't be warming it up."

Addison tugged the collar of her leather jacket away from her neck. "You mean it's going to get hotter in here?"

"We'll have to make a run for it at some point," he said. "Maybe they'll have a quick soak and head inside for a bit."

Penny's moan drifted over from the porch. "Oh, yes. Yes! Mmm. Right there."

Addison tensed. "Umm, did you hear that?"

"You like that, baby?" Walter asked Penny.

"Mmm. Don't stop."

Addison's eyes widened. "Or maybe they'll be a little longer."

She couldn't believe her ears. Her gaze automatically returned to the window, and she instantly regretted it. Penny had removed her bikini top and was straddling Judge Boyd in the hot tub.

Thank goodness for jet bubbles, Addison thought, averting her eyes. But the image had already seared into her retinas.

"I wouldn't look out there if I were you."

Felix blew out a breath. "It's kind of hot."

"If you get off on watching another couple, I suppose. Whatever floats your boat." Addison tried to fan herself with her hand, but it just wafted the hot air around. She turned back to Felix, and her eyes widened. He stood there half naked, shirt peeled off to reveal a tight six-pack.

"Oh, you mean in here. Yeah. Hot." She swallowed, but her mouth had already gone dry. "Very hot."

Now that she focused on it, it was stifling. Following Felix's lead, she pulled off her jacket, but it didn't help much. She was already sweating. And the walls felt so close. The sauna was just big enough for two people.

She sank to the cedar floor, where it was cooler, and rested her head against the bench seat. She tried not to think about the walls closing in, like when Luke Skywalker and the others had been in the Death Star garbage compactor. Felix sat down across from her, making it impossible not to stare at his muscular chest.

The stove in the corner clicked and clacked as it heated the pile of stones on top of it. Addison closed her eyes, trying to imagine she was on vacation, lying on a hot beach somewhere in the Caribbean. It wasn't hard, what with a half-naked man across from her. She pictured a big, wide-open beach. Not a tiny, cramped, suffocating hotbox.

"How long do you think they'll be?" she asked Felix.

He snorted. "Are you really asking me about Judge Boyd's stamina right now?"

"It's just hot. Like really, really hot." The dry heat made it impossible to breathe. Her next breath came in a gasp. "Aren't you hot?"

He bit his lip, eyeing the neckline of her tank top. "I know a way to take your mind off things."

Addison didn't answer. Instead, she focused on inhaling slowly, counting in her mind as she did so. *One Mississippi, Two Mississippi ...*

But it wasn't long before the famous river lost a few syllables and she was panting, clawing at her chest. It was like the feeling she'd had when she was under the stage floor, only this time, there was no way out ... unless she wanted to go to jail.

Felix had been talking; although she hadn't really been paying attention. Suddenly, he went quiet.

"Addison, are you okay?" He eyed her warily. "You're not claustrophobic, are you?"

"I-I don't think so. Maybe. It's just," she breathed, "so hot." Addison lifted her hair off her neck, hoping that would help.

After a moment, Felix shifted to kneel next to her. Reaching out, he grabbed a handful of her hair. "Turn around."

Lacking the energy or witty comeback to argue, she did as he asked. He settled in behind her. After a moment, she felt soft tugs on her hair. Felix Vaughn was French braiding her hair. Addison couldn't believe it.

His fingers slid gently along her scalp, combing through her waves. As he expertly wove each lock together, Addison closed her eyes, focusing on the sensations.

Her body was on alert, feeling each tug on her hair as though it were a limb. It was different from any way he'd touched her so far, like they'd suddenly leaped to a new level of intimacy. Felix's usual behavior was rough and brusque. This new tenderness was so unexpected that Addison found herself entirely focused on each subtle movement rather than on her panic.

Curiosity about this astonishing skill of his nagged at her. Felix was the last person on earth she would have thought could braid hair, much less French braid it.

"How do you know how to do this?" she asked.

"I'm a man of many talents, Addy," was all he said. She could hear the teasing smile in his voice.

His own labored breaths caressed the back of her neck. It hit the sweat forming on her skin, sending goose bumps trickling down the length of her arms and back. Finally, he got to the end and tucked the tail in at the nape of her neck.

The relief was only temporary. The heat continued to rise, and Addison could feel herself slipping back into panic mode. She rested her back against the cedar wall. If Felix hadn't been with her, she would have stripped right there and then.

She took a deep breath through her nose and exhaled out her mouth. "Felix, say something. Talk about something. Distract me."

Addison closed her eyes again, waiting for his usual nonsense to spill out of his mouth. But a heartbeat later, she felt his soft lips against hers.

She inhaled sharply, but he didn't pull away. His lips remained pressed against hers. He held them there, still as a statue. When she made no move to push him away, he began to kiss her softly.

His mouth tasted of peppermint breath mints, his lips as soft as melting ice cream and just as satisfying. Automatically, her tongue darted out to taste them. The slow, methodical movements of his mouth against hers were reassuring.

Felix kept the tempo even, never allowing it to heat up. His breathing flowed rhythmically, hypnotizing her, and she soon found that her own chest rose and fell in time with his.

His body didn't touch hers, not an ab or a pec, not even his hands. He hovered as far away as he could, careful not to add to her own body heat or the sensation that the walls were closing in. But she could feel his comforting presence.

Their last kiss at the bar had overwhelmed her, excited her until she wanted to lose control. But now she let him control her, losing herself in the sweetness of his kisses, sweeter than she'd expected from the caveman.

Addison's eyes fluttered open. Felix had his own eyes closed as he kissed her gently. His body shook with the strain of physically supporting himself in the awkward position. Or was it because he was holding back when he wanted more? Addison couldn't tell.

It wasn't like before when she wanted him to ravage her on a pool table—wham, bam, thank you, ma'am. She thought that if they weren't under the serious medical threat of dehydration or heat stroke, she'd like to stay there with him, just like that. It felt … well, nice.

Now *that* was an effective distraction, she realized, closing her eyes again.

After what could have been a few minutes or twenty, the sound of deep barking echoed outside their hiding place. Felix's mouth froze. Addison was the first to pull away.

"Do you think his hounds sniffed us out?" she whispered.

Felix pushed himself to his feet and staggered slightly as he moved to the window. Addison had been too busy panicking before to consider how much the heat was affecting him.

He braced himself against the doorframe. Wiping away the condensation on the window, he stared out. "They're getting out of the hot tub."

Addison grabbed her leather jacket and Felix's T-shirt. "Are they coming this way?"

"No. They're running through the yard. And you're right." He chuckled. "That's not something I can unsee."

Over the hum of the stove in the corner heating the rocks, Addison could hear the barking fade into the distance. Walter and Penny yelled and whistled after it.

"Come back, Mr. Vandermutton!" Walter called. "Come back!"

Addison snickered, feeling a little delirious. "Mr. Vandermutton?"

"Did you leave the gate open?" Felix asked.

She paused and forced her foggy brain to think. "Yeah, I did."

"I think one of the dogs got out of the yard. Penny and Walter are heading toward the tree line." He shifted his position to see farther. "I think we should make a break for it."

Reaching down, he helped Addison to her feet. The tiny sauna spun, and her vision faded to black around the edges. She swooned slightly, stumbling against him, but he held her up. Wrapping an arm around her, he supported her as he reached for the door handle.

She grinned up at him, a little dopily. "What happened to not helping a damsel in distress?"

"It's in my genetic code. Besides, most damsels aren't as cute as you." He squeezed his arm tighter around her. "Ready?"

She nodded.

Felix burst through the door. The chilly air shocked her damp skin like a Brazilian wax. Together, they stumbled across the grassy lot and out through the open gate.

Addison could hear Penny and Judge Boyd yelling into the trees, huffing and shrieking at the chill of the night on their hot-tub-warmed bodies. But Addison's own overheated body basked in the relief.

She let the cool air wash over her and felt the life flow back into her legs. Energized but still slightly shaky, she let Felix guide them back to the safety of her car. Once she'd regained her focus, they drove to the nearest gas station for two bottles of Gatorade each.

16

CHASE TAIL

Addison stood back, sizing up the erect form before her. The length, the thickness, the subtle curve. A fine specimen, but still she frowned at it. It didn't look quite right.

"Maybe I should give it a few more strokes," she said to Melody.

Her assistant hovered next to her for a closer look. "Do you think that will make it look bigger?"

"If I rough it up a bit, maybe." Addison shrugged. "It might make it look thicker. Every inch counts."

She dove in, teasing, stroking, tugging furiously until its owner wriggled and squirmed under her skilled touch. When her wrist ached from the effort, she stood back to examine the results.

"I think that's the best I can do," she said.

"We're not quite done yet. Let me finish him

off." Melody drew a length of ribbon out of her supplies and wrapped it snugly around the shaft, arranging it into an artful bow. When she was done, it wagged back and forth in front of their faces.

Addison nodded in approval. *As long as my customers are happy*, she thought. And boy, was this one happy.

He jumped up, planting a wet kiss on her cheek in appreciation.

Now, if only I could get that kind of affection from a man, Addison thought. *Not Precious, Julia Edwards's cocker spaniel.*

Ever since her visit to Judge Boyd's sauna the night before, she'd been craving the affections of one man in particular: Felix Vaughn. She just couldn't get him off her mind. Everything had suddenly become an innuendo to her sex-deprived mind.

But a few good days spent with Felix couldn't erase years of bad choices with men—men just like him. He'd said it himself: she needed to be logical about it. And her brain was still telling her that Philip was the right choice. So then why hadn't she texted him yet?

"Idiot," she told herself.

Precious grumbled in offense.

"Not you, Precious. Don't worry."

Addison gave the dog a treat as an apology. She couldn't afford to offend Precious. He was her last remaining loyal customer. At least all the gossip and conjecture hadn't persuaded Julia to turn tail.

She hoped all the bonus treatments she'd given him would encourage them to keep coming back. She'd scraped, polished, buffed, combed, shined, and moisturized every square inch of the pooch. He wagged his tail like he was a new dog. He was going to be a major contender in the show next weekend.

"I think that's it for today," Addison said to Melody. "We don't have any more bookings, so why don't you take off early?"

"Are you sure? I could tidy up the back."

Addison sighed. "The back has been tidied and re-tidied a dozen times in the last week. I've had nothing else to do."

"Okay. If you're sure." Melody hung her apron in the cupboard and grabbed her purse. "I'll see you later?"

"You bet. Enjoy your afternoon."

Addison watched her leave, happy to have her company back. After the cocktail mixer, she'd given Melody a few days off to recuperate emotionally. However, since she'd been playing spies with Felix, there'd been no one to watch her shop, so she had to close it. With the evidence they'd found at the Regency Center, she felt confident enough in Melody's innocence to let her come back to help keep an eye on things. But there still wasn't enough business to keep them both busy, even with the odd walk-in.

Addison finished cleaning up and took Precious into the back where he could relax in the lounge. Being the only customer, he had free rein of the various play areas: the toy box, the puppy palace, the lapdog lounge, the pillow pit.

Once she'd settled him in the back, bribing his patronage with another treat, she had nothing to do but think, and wonder, and worry, and pace.

Curled up on her miniature velvet settee, Princess followed Addison's anxious path, curious brown eyes roving back and forth. As Addison wore a trail into the black-and-white checkered floor, she gnawed on a sunset pink nail while eyeing her phone on the counter.

"It's already been twenty minutes. I can look again, right?" she asked Princess.

The doxie made a throaty, exasperated growl and laid her head on her paws.

"Okay, maybe it's only been twelve." She glared at her phone, her annoyingly silent phone, like it had personally insulted her.

The date of her fashion show was drawing near, and the RSVP list still amounted to a big fat zero. On top of that, there'd been no calls, no emails, no texts, tweets, or chimes of any sort. Not from customers, not from Philip, not even from Felix. Not that she cared about the last. At least, that's what she was trying to convince herself.

But he'd said he was following up on a couple of leads that afternoon. Shouldn't he be giving her moment-by-moment updates? They were supposed to be in this together, whatever that meant.

Her phone rang. *Finally.*

Addison practically sprinted across the spa and flung herself over the hot pink, shabby chic desk.

She hit the accept button. "Hello? Hello?" she panted into the phone.

"Congratulations," a recorded voice said. "You've been selected to—"

Groaning, she hung up. But she clung to the bedazzled phone like it was a discounted angora sweater.

"It couldn't hurt to check," she told Princess. "Someone might have RSVP'd by now. It is the weekend. People are off work, catching up on emails," she reasoned.

She opened an app to view the reservations for her fashion show. Determined that this time there would be good news, that by the sheer strength of her positivity she could change the numbers on the screen, she held her breath and hit the icon.

She scowled.

There must have been something wrong with her positive mojo. The RSVP list hadn't changed. It was still that big, lonely, empty-looking zero. Slumping across the desk, she tossed her phone aside just as another chime rang out. This time from the front door.

She looked up at the newcomer walking into her spa. Felix.

"It's you," she said. "Thank God."

Felix beamed down at her. "Couldn't stand being without me. I totally understand."

She felt herself blush a little at the comment, unable to meet his eyes. "You wish."

Ever since the night before, she'd imagined Felix in different ways. Not as the single-minded, womanizing bartender she'd first thought he was but as a guy who maybe she'd misjudged. A guy who could actually be sweet once you got to know him.

"Why haven't you called?" she asked. "What did you find out today? Have you got any new leads? Do we need to do another stakeout?"

"Eager for a repeat of last night?"

"I'm eager to end it."

He leaned on the desk, batting his eyelashes at her. "Not all of it, I hope."

She gave him a coy smile, trying not to give anything away. "I'm talking about solving the crime."

"You know what's a crime? That we're all alone and you're still fully dressed."

His hair was messier than usual, windblown like he'd walked all the way there from the pub.

She found her fingers itching to reach up and pat it down.

"I'm serious." She pushed him playfully. "What did you discover?"

"Nothing."

Addison pouted. "Nothing?"

"Zilch, nada, zero. I checked in on Jayden, our new hire at the pub. He really had food poisoning. No way was he busy stealing a bunch of dogs while he was making sweet love to a toilet bowl." He pulled a face.

"Well, we still have to look into Julia Edwards. Her dog is here right now, actually." Addison nodded her head toward the back room. "She told me earlier that she's going to be leaving for the rest of the weekend. We could always case her house tonight."

Felix rubbed a hand over the back of his neck. "I've got plans tonight."

"Okay." His reaction seemed strangely apologetic.

She wanted to ask what those plans entailed, but she told herself it was none of her business.

He held up a finger, interrupting her jealous train of thought. "But I have a problem you can help me solve."

She rolled her eyes. "Like I need any more problems."

"Wait here. I'll be right back."

Felix ducked out of the spa, and when the

door chimed again, Addison turned to see an unkempt furball on four legs. The dog's breed was so mixed that she couldn't begin to guess its family heritage. Gray, wiry fur stuck up in tangled tufts over his body. His ears pressed back against his head as if ashamed of his appearance.

Big brown eyes turned to look up at Addison as he begged, *Help me.*

"This is Oliver," Felix said. "He's not exactly at his best today. I tried a few DIY tricks at home to groom him, but they didn't work."

Princess padded over from her settee, the little bells on her ballerina dress tinkling. She gave Oliver the once-over, sniffing in distaste at his disheveled state.

"I didn't know you had a dog," Addison said. "Why didn't you tell me?"

"There's a lot you don't know about me. All you have to do is ask." Felix flopped onto one of the bright pink Queen Anne chairs, kicking his feet up on the coffee table.

Addison rounded her desk and knelt in front of the dog. "Hello, Oliver. It's nice to meet you."

She held out a hand, and he automatically raised his paw for her to shake.

"He's quite the gentleman," she said.

"So am I." Felix locked his hands behind his head like it was a relaxing Saturday afternoon on the beach. "When I want to be."

"So, that would be never?" She gave him her

brightest smile. "Now, what seems to be the problem?"

She reached out to pet Oliver, assessing him with her practiced eye, looking for matted hair or dry skin patches. She quickly discovered the problem on his wagging tail. What could only be described as pink goo glued the long fur together in a painful clump.

"What happened here?"

"There was a bubblegum incident," Felix said.

"How did it get so matted in there?"

He cringed. "That was my attempt to get it out."

Addison stood up and headed over to her cabinet full of various oils, tinctures, potions, and lotions. The bottles clinked as she rummaged through them to find the right antidote.

"I wouldn't have taken you for a bubblegum guy," she called back.

She heard Felix come up behind her. "What kind of guy do you take me for?"

Now there was a loaded question. "Spearmint, maybe. Spicy cinnamon?"

He ran a slow finger down her back where her floral dress dipped low. "Sounds hot."

Addison shivered, but slapped his hand away and continued to search the cupboard for the cure. "I'm going to have to use the big guns."

"Big guns?"

"Peanut butter." She held the jar in the air. "Works like a charm. And makes a great snack."

"Mmm." He brought his lips down to her neck and moaned against it. "I know I could use a bite." His teeth grazed her as he playfully nibbled her skin.

"Hey!" She laughed. "I have ways of dealing with bad dogs like you." She pointed to the chairs. "Sit. Good boy."

Felix returned to his seat in the waiting area with a smirk. Addison could feel his eyes on her as she began meticulously working out the cherry pink bubblegum, one glob at a time.

"So, how long have you been in business?" he asked her.

"About two years now," she said. "Princess was actually my inspiration for finally taking the chance."

"How so? Did she loan you the money?"

Addison snorted. "Because show dog or not, I believe every dog deserves the same care and attention. They're all beautiful in their own way. I just like to help them look as beautiful on the outside as they are on the inside. And Princess is just as beautiful as any other show dog."

"Did Princess ever compete?"

"She was bred to be a show dog, but it just wasn't in the cards for her. She was born with one leg shorter than the others."

Felix was quiet for a moment. When she

242

looked over at him, his mouth pursed thoughtfully. "She hides the flaw well. You'd hardly know unless you looked closely."

His scrutiny made her uncomfortable. She got that feeling again, like he could see through her makeup, past the liquid-lined eyes, through the sun-kissed bronzer, and under the pouty pink lips, to the real her.

Addison ducked her head, focusing intently on Oliver's tail. "Just because a dog has a so-called imperfection, doesn't mean they're any less perfect or lovable than the next one. Everyone deserves to be happy."

"Dog," he said.

"What?"

"Every dog. You said every*one*." The serious expression remained on his face.

"Oh." She laughed it off. "Whatever. You understood what I meant."

His lips pursed again, and he nodded. "I think I do. For the first time, I think I finally understand you."

Addison doubled her vigorous scrubbing, ready to finish the conversation. When she'd combed out the last glob, she patted the side of her leg and called Oliver over to the shower stalls.

He loped after her, toenails clicking on the tiles. She made a mental note to cut them after a quick hair trim.

Once Oliver was in the pink mosaic stall, Addison turned on the rain shower. Water drizzled down like a warm tropical storm. For a minute, the dog tensed and danced skittishly. Then she worked the seaweed-and-jasmine cleanser into his matted fur, and he relaxed under her massaging hands. His leg vibrated with each scratch of her nails under his chin in that "oh yeah, right there" spot.

The last of the suds finally washed down the drain. Addison reached over to turn off the water. When she straightened up, she felt something press against her from behind.

She yelped in surprise and spun around. Out of instinct she clenched her fist, realizing too late that the spray nozzle was still in her hand.

The trigger activated. Water shot out. Felix yelped and jumped back but not before she'd soaked his plaid shirt.

Addison dropped the nozzle and held a hand to her mouth, mostly to smother her giggles. "I'm so sorry. I didn't even hear you sneak up."

Felix gave her a sour look. He helplessly spread out his arms. To add salt to the wound, Oliver hopped out of the shower and shook his coat. He sprayed Felix from head to toe before going to curl up next to Princess.

Pressing her lips together to hide her smile, Addison shrugged innocently. "At least I didn't ruin a nice shirt."

His expression darkened. That predatory look

had returned. Addison was already shuffling away as he took his first step toward her.

"Now, look." She held up her hands. "It was just an accident."

He took another step, forcing her back. Reaching into his pocket, he drew out his phone and laid it on the table outside the shower stall. She didn't know what that meant, but it couldn't be good.

"Let me get you a towel." She tried to go around him.

But Felix cut her off, his lowered gaze fixed on hers. The fan of thick black lashes made his eyes look darker as he glowered menacingly. There was the smallest hint of a smile, but it had a devilish tinge to it.

Addison's shoes squelched on the wet tiles as he backed her all the way into the stall.

"I just reacted. I didn't mean to spray you."

He was nose to nose with her, or rather, forehead to chin since he was that much taller. Without a word, he reached out and grasped the shower handle.

Addison gasped. "Don't you d—"

She squealed as water shot down from above, feeling not so much like a warm tropical rain as it did a chilly Dublin downpour.

Gasping and grunting between quick breaths, she scrambled to push past him and out of the stall. But Felix planted a hand on either side of her, his thick arms caging her in.

"Not so fast," he said.

Felix was in the shower with her now. Water drenched his hair, plastering the dark curls to his face and neck. His T-shirt molded to his body like Superman's spandex, revealing the contours and swells of a figure not unlike the Man of Steel's.

As though her hands had minds of their own, they reached up and crawled their way over his six-pack, which she'd gotten a sneak preview of the night before.

Water ran in a stream down the bridge of Felix's nose and hit her cheek. She imagined she could feel it connect their bodies. Could sense his body heat warm the water before it ran across her skin, down her neck, beneath her neckline to caress her breasts. It was like an extension of his own body exploring hers, a finger running lightly down her stomach, soaking into the lace of her underwear.

Addison closed the space between them. She pressed her lips against his, sucked the water from his lips as though she could drink him in. The shower rained down on her bare arms and shoulders, tickling, energizing. Her skin felt electrically charged, sensitive to every touch.

While his tongue played with hers in a teasing game, rivulets of water ran from the hem of her drenched dress, down the curves of her legs, snaking along her thighs. Her skin tightened under the cool water, her breath hitched.

Felix backed her up to the tiles and pressed himself against her. His hot hands moved like refreshing fire over the swells of her breasts. Their lips moved faster, harder and harder, his tongue filling her mouth with his hungry desire.

Addison felt the drizzle of water rushing over them as though it were the salty spray of seawater on a pirate ship in the Caribbean. She closed her eyes. Yes, they were on the *Black Pearl*. Felix was her Jack Sparrow, and she was his naughty wench. Even caught in a raging storm, they couldn't keep their hands off each other, their lust keeping them warm.

Through her dress, she felt the heat of his hands. His grip tightened over the swell of her ample hips, and he grinded against her until it was no longer just water soaking her underwear.

Eager hands searched her body and gripped her butt, assessing the size, the weight, the feel of it through the fabric. Fingers explored the hemline of her dress, pushing it up her thigh until those exploring fingers traced the edge of her panties. They tugged at them but went no further, as though knocking at her door, waiting for an invitation.

Addison answered the gentle knock by reaching down to his belt. With a flick of leather, a jingle of metal, there came the satisfying zip as she pulled out Jack Sparrow's mighty cutlass.

Ding.

It was like someone had forgotten to turn off their cell phone during a movie. The sound snapped Addison back to reality like a cold shower —aided by the fact that they actually were in a cold shower. It was the front door. Someone had entered the spa.

Breaking away from Felix, Addison pushed against his chest. Why did this keep happening? Why did she keep letting it? Not letting it, encouraging it. Jack Sparrow was the bad boy. *Bad*, she repeated in her head.

Felix was like a scary movie she knew she should shut off but kept watching through her fingers despite herself. Yet, as he leaned against the tiles across from her, dripping wet, his fly splayed open, the only thing that scared her was just how badly she wanted him.

And maybe that wasn't the worst thing. Maybe for once her instincts were right, her heart's as well as her primal instincts. Maybe she'd made so many mistakes she was lumping him in with all the rest. In reality, she might have found her prince beneath those pauper's clothes. Her Aladdin.

Addison turned off the shower, and that's when she heard the high-pitched "Hello-o-o?"

"Oh no," Addison hissed. "It's Julia. I wasn't

expecting her for another couple of hours." She glanced down at her sopping dress. How was she going to explain this? Some professional she was.

"Coming!" She tried to wring some water out of her dress, but it was futile. Sighing, she headed up front.

When Julia spotted her, she pushed her Prada sunglasses on top of her head. Her eyes bulged as she took Addison in from her tangled hair to the puddle forming under her.

"What on earth happened to you?"

"I, um …" Addison heard shuffling feet behind her and cringed. She should have told Felix to stay put. The situation was bad enough already. Gritting her teeth, she turned to glare at him.

Felix held up the wrench she usually kept under the sink. "A line burst," he told Julia, waving the tool like it was cold hard evidence. "Water everywhere. It's best you stay clear."

Julia looked as surprised as Addison felt. "Oh dear. Your poor dress."

Addison's expression froze in what she hoped was angelic innocence. Cheeks burning, she clapped her hands and changed the subject. "You must be missing Precious."

"Yes." Julia set her Coach purse down. "How is my boy?"

"He's just hanging out in the lounge. Right this way, please."

Addison did her best to block the woman's

view of the shower stalls and the water pooling on the floor. As she passed Felix, she crossed her eyes in relief and mouthed, "Thank you."

He responded with a silent salute with the wrench.

Julia followed Addison to the playroom. "Where's my Precious?" she called out as they walked down the hall. "Where's my special little boy?"

"He's waiting for you right back ..." Addison tapered off as she opened the door and saw an empty room.

With a shaking hand, she turned the dimmer switch until every light in the room was blazing. Her body was suddenly crippled with fear. She'd been wrong before; *this* was the horror movie.

Addison leaned against the wall, her breaths coming in gulps like she was drowning. Her frantic eyes scanned the space, from the toy box to the puppy palace to the lapdog lounge to the pillow pit.

But Precious was gone.

17

GIVE A DOG A BAD NAME

"No. No. No." Addison leaned against the doorframe, feeling like the lounge room was spinning. "This can't be happening. Not again."

Running past Julia and over to the pillow pit, she tossed pillows aside. She rammed her head into the plastic halls of the puppy palace. But she couldn't find head nor tail of her last remaining customer.

"Where is he?" Julia's voice shook as she collapsed onto the pillows. "Where's my Precious? Precious!"

"Addison!" Felix called. "Back here!"

She followed the sound of Felix's voice to the hall. He headed for the alley, still gripping the wrench. The back door stood ajar, daylight streaming through. Addison ran after him.

Julia followed close on her heels, repeating,

"Precious! My Precious!" like a distraught Gollum from *The Lord of the Rings*.

Felix threw his weight against the metal door and burst into the alley. Addison glimpsed a dark van parked outside.

"Hey!" Felix yelled.

By the time Addison caught up, Felix was struggling with the van's back doors. He heaved on the handles, one foot on the bumper for leverage.

Drawing the wrench back, he smashed in the rear window. It splintered, but the metal mesh on the inside prevented him from reaching in.

Addison ran to the passenger door. A person sat behind the wheel, their face hidden beneath a black balaclava. She tried the handle, but it was locked. Bringing up a fist, she banged on the window.

The driver fumbled with the keys before the engine started and revved. Addison banged and kicked the door. Suddenly, she was grabbed from behind.

Her feet left the ground, and she was whirled away. A second later, the tires squeaked, skidding over where she'd been standing. The van took off, leaving them in a cloud of exhaust.

Felix released Addison. Coughing, she blinked her vision clear in time to see him run after the dognapper. The van struggled to pick its way down the narrow alley. Garbage and parked cars created an obstacle course, forcing it to slow down.

Addison stumbled after Felix. Hindered by shorter legs, a wet dress clinging to her thighs, and flimsy ballet flats, she quickly fell behind. Not exactly a spy-worthy performance. She didn't think Dick Tracy had to deal with problems like this.

She stared after Felix as he forged on. He sprinted down the alley after the van, proving those muscles weren't just for looks.

"Get 'em, Felix!" Addison cheered with more bloodlust than she'd thought she was capable of.

The van cranked it at the end of the alley. It tilted to one side as it turned and peeled onto the main street. Fists pumping, legs surging him forward, Felix ran after it.

There was a screech of tires, a horn honk. A car narrowly missed him. Another skidded to a stop, inches from his body.

Addison gasped, cringing. But Felix leaped over the car's hood and continued down the street after the van. He disappeared from sight.

There were more distant sounds of angry traffic. Addison's heart skipped a beat with each noise. Her legs tensed, ready to run after him, to see that he was okay. But she hesitated, knowing she'd be of no help to him that way.

Going against her instincts, she dashed back into the spa. Julia hovered on the other side of the door, tugging nervously on her pearl necklace.

"But … my Precious." Her eyes bulged as she gripped Addison's arms, gel nails frantically digging into her soft skin. *My Precious.*

Addison's heart clenched for Julia's sudden loss. But the sooner she called the police, the better. She wrenched from her grip. Julia's blubbering faded as she ran for the showers where Felix's phone lay on the counter. The moment she entered the room, Oliver and Princess got to their feet, ready for action.

Addison's fingers shook as she dialed 9-1-1. In fact, her whole body was shaking. Partly from her cold, wet dress, but mostly from anger. No, fury.

She'd never felt so furious in all her life. Forget the positivity, forget the good cop/bad cop routine. She wanted blood. Someone was taking advantage of her, and she wasn't going to stand for it. Now it was personal.

When the call connected, she said, "Hello? Yes. I own a spa, and someone just stole my customer."

"You're reporting a kidnapping?" the female voice on the other end asked.

"Yes. They drove off with him in a van. We tried to run after it, but they got away." Addison tried to rearrange her scattered thoughts to give as much detail as possible. Anything to help get Precious back.

"It's important for your safety that you no

longer follow them," the operator advised. "Is anyone still in pursuit?"

"Yes. I think so, but I can't contact him." She frowned, wondering what would happen to Felix if he caught up to the dognappers.

"Did you get a license plate number from the van?"

"No license plate," Addison said. "But it was a dark van, black, with tinted windows. It looked new." She rattled off her spa's address, just in case they wanted to send all units to the area ASAP.

"Did you see your customer when they were taken? Were they still conscious?"

The answer caught in Addison's throat. She thought back and couldn't recall hearing Precious bark or growl. There were no sounds of a fight. Surely, she would have heard it. What if they'd done something to Precious, drugged or hurt him to keep him quiet?

"No, I didn't," she said, finally. "But if he were conscious, I'm sure he would have been biting and scratching."

The operator hesitated. "Biting?"

"Yes, he gives me a good nip, now and then."

"Is he combative?"

"Only when I trim his nails," Addison said, distracted. She was peeking out the window, hoping she would see Felix strolling toward her at any moment.

Julia hovered nearby, following Addison's nervous pacing around the room like a shadow.

"What is his name?" the operator asked.

"Emerald Hill's Sir Precious Vandersnout Edwards. But he goes by Precious."

"Precious? Okay ..."

Addison could hear typing on the other end of the line.

"Can you describe Mr. Edwards for me?" the operator asked.

"He's about fifteen inches tall, brown eyes, long blond hair."

"Buff," Julia corrected between sobs. "Buff hair."

"Right. Buff," Addison repeated.

"Fifteen inches?" The operator's calm voice suddenly increased in volume. "Is the victim an infant?"

"No. He's fully grown." Addison assured her. "He's the perfect specimen."

There was a pause on the other side of the line. "Specimen of what?"

"Of a cocker spaniel."

"The victim *is a dog*, ma'am?"

"Of course," Addison said, like it was obvious. "I run a dog spa." She must have said that already, hadn't she? She glanced out the window again, but there was still no sign of Felix.

"Are you sure you meant to call the police and not animal control?"

Addison scowled. "This is serious. Precious is a major contender in this year's Western Dog Show. There have been other dogs stolen before this. It's part of an ongoing police investigation." At least she hoped it was, because she wasn't doing a great job cracking the case herself.

She saw Julia nodding along with her statement, but her red eyes had glazed over as she stared at the checkered floor tiles.

"We've dispatched a unit." The operator's voice, which had always been calm, now lacked urgency too. "They should arrive there shortly."

"But I've described the van." Addison gripped the phone as if she could keep the operator on the line that way. "They might still be in the neighborhood. Maybe they can head them off."

"The officers will decide the best course of action after they speak with you," she said with no emotion. "They will be there soon. Is there anything else? Would you like me to wait on the line with you until they arrive?"

"No. I guess not. Thank you." Addison hung up the phone and frowned at it.

It wasn't like she thought they'd send out the SWAT or anything, but she'd expected a little more get-up-and-go. Maybe just a helicopter or two. Especially since it was related to the previous dognappings.

Didn't they care? Didn't they understand? These dogs were like family to their owners. Not to mention the genetic protectors of their pure-bred lines.

"What now?" Julia asked quietly.

"I suppose we wait for the police to come."

Julia sank onto the hot pink sofa, staring at her hands. Addison sat down next to her. Princess seemed to sense the seriousness of the situation and came over to paw at her leg. Addison lifted her up and held her for comfort.

The dognappers were picking off the show dogs one at a time. Now Precious had joined their numbers, like some sick list was being checked off somewhere. The longer the police took to search for the dogs, the less chance they had of ever finding them, of ever reuniting them with their owners. Addison's insides churned with dread.

Julia sniffed, dabbing at her tears with a tissue. *Poor Julia*, Addison thought. *Poor Precious.* She wondered if Julia now blamed her like all the others.

This was the worst thing that could have happened. At least during the other two abductions, people speculated and gossiped, but no one could point their finger directly at her. This time, it would be tough to convince customers, maybe even the cops, that she was innocent. She suddenly had an image of getting dragged away in handcuffs. Feeling anxious, she began to pace.

At least she had Felix as a witness—they definitely had an alibi. But maybe that was worse. They'd already been accused of being in cahoots, and now they were alone together when another show dog disappeared.

Where was Felix, anyway? Was he okay? Her emotions were flip-flopping sporadically, and she had to sit down before her shaky legs gave way.

Felix should have been back. She tried to think positively. He might have caught up to the van, grabbed the bad guys, and saved the day. But then again, what if they'd fought back or run him over?

Just days ago, she wouldn't have felt the same sense of desperate panic. Oh, how things had changed in such a short time. Now she found herself dreading the worst-case scenario. She knew these changes had nothing to do with her undeniable physical attraction to him. There was more between them.

Felix couldn't be the selfish womanizer she'd first thought he was. He was helping her find the dognapper, after all. While he'd said it was because he was under the gun too, she knew it wasn't that simple. She recalled the way he'd acted in the sauna, how he'd taken care of her when she was freaking out. Felix had genuinely been there for her when she needed him. And he had a dog too, so he must have cared about those missing animals as much as she did.

It was like he was hiding the good man he really was under that gruff exterior. Beneath it all was an attentive man, a man who did care about the damsel in distress. His indifferent attitude was all an act. It had to be.

Addison jumped to her feet, setting Princess down. "Julia, I'm going to go search for Felix."

"But I thought the police told us to wait."

"I know, but I'm worried that something has happened to him," she said over her shoulder, already headed for the back door.

The worst-case scenarios continued to play on repeat in Addison's head. Her heartrate increased with every outcome she imagined, and her ballet flats slapped the floor to match the beat until she was sprinting down the hall.

Addison burst through the back door into the alley. The phone in her hand buzzed. She hadn't even realized she was still gripping it.

She automatically glanced at the screen, and what she saw brought her to a halt. Surrounded by a multitude of kissy-face emojis and hearts was a message.

I miss you. Come home soon. Can't wait to see you tonight. XOXO

Addison read the woman's name at the top of the conversation: Celia. It was the same woman he'd been texting the night before. Another message popped up, consisting of emoji burgers, sushi rolls, and various other foods.

Felix had plans. Addison just hadn't imagined they were with another woman. Not while he had a hard-on for her. *And not just any woman*, she thought. *Clearly someone he's been seeing for a while. Someone important, if all those hearts are any indication.*

Out of some sick need, or maybe a hope that this wasn't what she thought it was, she scrolled up to view the previous text from Felix.

How's my girl?

Addison clenched the phone in her hand and looked away. All the energy that had filled her moments before drained into the gutter.

Felix suddenly appeared at the end of the alley, his tired steps scuffing the pavement. When he saw her standing there, he picked up his pace.

"They got away." He scowled. "I never got a license plate either."

He got closer and took in Addison's expression. She wasn't sure what it looked like at that moment. Shocked. Hurt, maybe. Filled with embarrassment. To think that, even for a moment, she'd reconsidered that he could be anything but the arrogant jerk she'd first imagined he was. He was only out to use her, after all.

Whatever her expression looked like, he misread it, because his scowl softened, and his arms opened wide for her. For a split second, they called to Addison, invited her in, so warm and comforting, so genuine. But then his phone vibrated in her hand, and when she looked at it, it was another message from Celia.

I love you.

And she knew it was all just an act.

Before Felix could touch her, she chucked the phone at him. He grunted as it connected with his chest, and he lunged to catch it before it hit the ground.

Turning her back on him, she marched inside to wait for the police, slamming the door in his bewildered face.

18

SICK AS A DOG

Bang. Bang. Bang. Bang.

Addison lurched up in bed. The room spun, and a wave of nausea hit her. She grabbed her head and groaned.

Princess barked, causing her brain to split in two. It felt like an army was using a battering ram to break its way out of her skull.

"Princess. Shh." But shushing a dachshund was as useless as wishing ice cream had fewer calories.

Addison blinked, wondering why she felt like a zombie from *Dawn of the Dead*. Her eyes landed on the bottle of Shiraz on her nightstand. *That would explain it.*

She flopped back onto her pillow, closing her scratchy eyes. She couldn't move. She couldn't think. That is, until Princess licked her face, and her mind sparked with connecting memories: the stolen dogs, her ruined business, dashed hopes and dreams, the shower, Felix, his hands, his mouth, his mmm …

She drifted off.

Bang. Bang. Bang.

This time she realized it wasn't the throbbing in her head. Just the thing making it worse. It was someone at the door.

"Coming!" Addison called out, feeling the word reverberate inside her head.

She clambered out of bed. In the process, she knocked over the rest of her red wine, splattering her lace curtain.

"Crap." She picked up Princess and set her on the floor. "Who bangs on someone's door at the crack of"—she glanced at her alarm clock—"ten thirty in the morning?" Okay, so it wasn't that early.

She supposed the second empty wine bottle sitting on the hallway table explained the late start. After everything that had happened with Precious at the spa the day before, she'd gone into meltdown mode. A state that could only be remedied with ice cream, red wine, and a chick flick marathon.

On her way past her tiny bathroom, she grabbed her fluffy housecoat from behind the door, banging her elbow on the doorframe. She swore under her breath, adding the injury to the list of things she'd like to yell at the unexpected visitor for. Along with her worsening headache.

She stumbled bleary-eyed across her apartment, stubbing her toe on the coffee table leg. By the time she whipped open the door, she was already feeling like the Hulk, but when she saw who was on the other side, she saw green.

"What are you doing here?" she demanded.

Felix pulled out his most charming smile. "Good morning to you too."

Groaning, she tried to slam the door closed. He stuck his foot out before it could shut in his face.

Determined that it would be a Felix-free day—no, make that life—she leaned against the door with her entire body weight. But since she was no Hulk, he managed to slip his hand inside.

It was grasping a Starbucks cup.

"Peace offering?" He jiggled it temptingly.

She glared at the green mermaid. The siren called to her, flaunting her steamy, delicious caffeineness. Unable to resist, Addison swiped the cup from the hand and pulled away from the door.

She took a sip to calm her nerves before turning around. "What do you want?"

"You know you're going to have to talk to me at some point." He hovered in the doorway. "We still have a mystery to solve."

Princess sniffed at his feet, pawing at his leg as

though asking where her treat was. When all he did was pet her and scratch her neck, she huffed and went in search of her own treat.

"What's the point?" Addison asked. "We still don't know where those poor dogs are. We've run out of lead suspects, and I've lost the last customer that actually still believed in me."

"Chin up. Don't get so down. There's still hope yet."

He was acting super nice. Too nice. Maybe he knew that she'd seen the texts, and he was there to suck up. Well, she wasn't about to fall for it.

"What is this?" she mumbled into her cup. "Role reversal?"

"You're usually so positive. What happened to that Addison?"

He took a few steps into her apartment, leaving the door cracked open. Maybe he sensed that her inner Hulk was ready to come out and play and he might need a quick getaway.

"I'm sorry. I guess it's the wine." *Why am I apologizing to him?* "Did you want something? I'd like to nurse my hangover now."

Felix wandered into her kitchen and rummaged through her cupboards as if he owned the place. Finally, he found what he was looking for and pulled out a bottle. He gave it a shake. It was music to her sensitive ears.

"It's nothing a couple of Tylenol can't cure." Felix shook out two pills and poured her a glass of water. "And as far as the investigation goes, we still have plenty of suspects. It's always the last one you check out." He handed her the glass and medication. "So get better and we can continue."

Addison dubiously studied the pills in her hand before downing them. For a moment, she considered the possibility of resuming where they'd left off—the investigation, not the shower.

There were only a few days left before they were both permanently screwed. The dog show started on Saturday, less than a week away. If she didn't clear her name soon, her fashion show and the launch of Fido Fashion would be a flop. Besides, didn't Felix have his own deadline to keep? If he didn't get forty percent of Alistair's reward money, he wouldn't have enough for his down payment in time. Goodbye bar.

"How about tonight?" she asked.

Felix pulled a face. "I can't tonight. I work late. And I have, er … plans in the morning."

"Plans?" Her eyebrows drew together. She remembered his "plans" with Celia.

"But maybe tomorrow night."

He said it like a promise, maybe a mischievous warning, as he stepped toward her. Running a finger along the collar of her housecoat, he spread it until he could see the swell of her breasts beneath her lacy tank top.

"And then …" His voice trailed off suggestively. "Who knows?"

Princess hopped onto the couch, getting comfy to watch the show unfold. But Felix's behavior erased what little patience the coffee had given Addison.

She slapped his hand away. "And then nothing. You should be ashamed of yourself."

"What?" He held his hands up.

"I don't know what kind of woman you think I am."

Heck, she didn't even know what kind of woman she was. She was trying to turn over a new leaf, to make logical choices in men. Then why did she keep getting sucked in by Felix? One thing was certain: she wasn't going to be just another number to him.

Sure, there was the pool table, the sauna, and now the shower. But that was it. No take two, no additional after credit scene, no sequel. The end.

Felix laughed incredulously. "What are you talking about? Are those Tylenol or are they something stronger?" He picked up the bottle and pretended to scan the label.

"So now I'm over the top?" she asked, maybe just a little over the top.

"You're acting OTT."

"Maybe because men like you have driven me there."

"Men like me," he repeated.

"With your lies and your 'I'm one of the good

268

ones,' 'I'd never do anything to hurt you,' and all your empty promises."

"What promises? I've never said anything like that."

Okay, she thought, *maybe that wasn't him, exactly. It was all the guys before him. But he's just like them.*

Princess's eyes flicked back and forth between them, amused by the human drama.

Addison stomped toward Felix. "It's a game to you, isn't it? To test your skills, see how good you are at pulling the wool over a woman's eyes."

"I have no wool." He laughed at the ridiculousness of it, spreading his hands to show his complete lack of wool.

But he wasn't getting off that easily. The way he was mocking her only made her anger feel completely justified. Not unreasonable or hangover-fueled at all.

She jabbed a finger against his chest. "You're … You're a bamboozler." Her voice cracked with emotion. And here she thought she'd done such a good job smothering her feelings with wine.

"You think I've bamboozled you?" he asked seriously.

"No, sir. Not me. I'm onto you, mister. But what about your girlfriend? She probably thinks you're working late or taking your dog in for grooming. Meanwhile, you're out dry-humping women on pool tables and feeling their naughty bits in the shower."

She could feel tears form, stinging her eyes. She blinked them away, using her anger to keep them at bay.

"Woman." He held up a finger. "As in singular. Just you. I just did that with *you*."

"Great. I guess that makes me the other woman." She crossed her arms. "Well, I'm not interested."

Felix threw his hands up in frustration. "What other woman?"

"How about Celia?"

"Celia." This seemed to catch him off guard. "How do you know about her?"

"When I used your phone to call the cops yesterday, she texted you." She rolled her eyes. "'I miss you. Come home soon.'" She scowled, and he backed up as she advanced on him, forcing him to the door so she could kick him out —out of her life forever. "The hearts? The kissy faces?"

Felix covered his face with his hands like he was embarrassed he'd been caught. *Good,* Addison thought. *He* should *feel embarrassed.*

"So, what is she? A girlfriend? Or just some poor woman you're stringing along like me?" What was she saying? She wasn't being strung along. She didn't care. Nope, not at all.

Beneath his hands, his face turned red. His shoulders shook. Addison hesitated. Was he crying? But the noises that came out of his mouth next weren't sobs. They were pure, gut-aching, un-controllable guffaws.

Addison stared at him, stupefied. Felix was actually laughing at her.

Her fists clenched, and she could feel her face grow hot with fury. "This is funny to you?"

Body rigid with mirth, he leaned against the wall for support. "Yes. It's hilarious," he finally managed between gasps.

"You have no scruples, do you?" Addison's nostrils flared with anger. "I've had enough. You can leave right now."

Felix wiped a tear from his eye. "I'm not dating anyone." He took a calming breath. "Yes, the text was from Celia's phone, but she was texting on behalf of someone else."

"Who?"

"My girl."

Not willing to hear another word, Addison reached for the ajar door and flung it open. When she found a little girl standing on the other side like something out of *The Shining*, she screamed and jumped back.

Princess began to bark furiously. However, she was too lazy to leave her perch on the sofa to investigate.

Addison clenched the edges of her fuzzy housecoat together. *What now?*

She didn't think any of her neighbors had a kid, and she would have recognized this one since she was pretty cute. The little girl couldn't have been more than five years old. Two cinnamon-colored braids ran down either side of her head. A stuffed rabbit dangled from one hand, its feet dragging on the hardwood floor.

Princess was still barking, making Addison's head throb again.

"Princess. Shh."

Addison rubbed her temples. Not the best start to nursing a hangover. She'd had enough of this morning already. All she wanted to do was climb back into bed.

"Hello," the little girl said.

"Are you lost, sweetheart?" Addison asked the child. It didn't look like she was there to sell Girl Scout cookies—though, Addison could have really used some chocolate right then.

"Can I come in and see my dad now?" the kid asked.

"Your dad?" Addison leaned outside the door and looked both ways down the hall, but she didn't see anyone around.

"Addison." Felix pulled the door open farther and gestured to the child. "Meet *my girl*."

The moment the kid saw Felix, she ran into Addison's apartment and into his arms. He picked her up like she was as light as her ragged stuffed bunny.

"This is my daughter. Naia."

Addison gawked at the girl cradled in his arms as if she were an alien. "You have a daughter?"

"I do." Felix was watching her reaction carefully. He wasn't laughing anymore. In fact, he looked nervous.

"I had no idea," she said, unsure of what reaction she was supposed to have. What had he expected? "I never would have thought."

"There's a lot you don't know about me." It was his usual sarcastic response, but his expression was more serious than she'd ever seen.

The battering ram inside her head finally broke through, and her head throbbed. She collapsed onto the couch.

Felix sat next to her, an awkward distance away. Or maybe it just seemed that way to her. Naia shifted in his lap to peer at Addison from the crook of his neck.

Princess crawled over Addison's lap to greet the little girl. Naia's eyes widened, and she held out her hand for Princess to lick. Forgetting her shyness, she slid off her dad's lap to pet the doxie. Addison had never seen Princess act so submissive. Normally she was the queen bee. Instead, she flopped on her side, exposing her belly for a rub.

"Look," Felix said. "I know you're still mad at me about ... Come to think of it, I'm not sure what you're mad about anymore."

Addison half laughed, half sighed. "You and me both."

"But I'm kind of in a bind. Joe's desperate for someone to cover a split shift today at the bar. He said he'd allow me back for the day, but my babysitter, Celia, has the flu."

Addison stared at him blankly, the rusty cogs in her brain struggling to turn. She needed more aspirin. Or chocolate. Suddenly she remembered her coffee and took a regenerating sip, trying to make sense of where Felix was going with all this.

"All my usual backup babysitters aren't available," he said.

She continued to stare at him, uncomprehending.

"So … I was hoping, if you weren't busy, that you might look after Naia for a few hours."

"What?" Addison sat forward, spilling coffee on herself. "Me?"

"I know it's a lot to ask, but I wouldn't unless I was desperate. With everything that's going on, I feel like Joe is just one excuse away from firing me. As it is, I'm lucky he's giving me this shift. I can't lose this job, Addison." He reached over and grabbed her hand, squeezing it. "Please."

His forehead creased with worry. With his job on the line, she didn't blame him. And with a daughter to provide for … God, a daughter. Her thoughts were still reeling from the news, especially after she'd thought it was a girlfriend he was hiding from her. And why did he hide it from her in the first place?

"I don't want you to lose your job," she said. "But me? I've never really taken care of a kid. I'm not sure I'd even know what to do."

"It's not like she's in diapers or anything. She's five years old. Just play with her, hang out. She'll let you know if she needs anything."

Addison considered the little girl for a moment. She supposed he was right. It wasn't rocket science. It might even be fun. You know, compared to the full day of wallowing she had scheduled.

"Please," he said again.

"Sure. We can hang out," she finally said, more to Naia than Felix. "What do you say?"

Naia nodded shyly.

"Awesome. Let me grab her stuff." Felix practically shot out the door. In less than ten seconds he returned with an armload of stuff. "Here's her booster seat, her favorite book, and a list of emergency numbers in case you need them." He handed her an overstuffed bag that weighed a ton. "And I've packed the two of you a picnic, so you don't have to worry about cooking."

Addison stared at all the stuff that he'd obviously stashed out in the hall. "What if I'd said no?"

"I knew you'd say yes. You're too sweet."

Before she could react, Felix leaned over and kissed her on the cheek.

Her skin warmed where his lips had touched,

and her brain finally caught up. Felix beamed at her like he always did, but this time she wore no makeup, her hair was a mess, her breath tasted like stale wine, and her unshaven leg hair prickled beneath her frumpy housecoat.

He waved as he headed for the door. "You're the best. I owe you one. Just name it."

Addison watched Felix leave with a dazed expression. She plunked down next to Naia on the couch. Naia looked at her expectantly, and all Addison could think of was that she wanted another aspirin.

19

HAIR OF THE DOG THAT DUMPED YOU

Naia released a blood-curdling scream, running for her life across the field, a pack of wild doxies hot on her tail. Her two little legs were no match for their four stumpy ones. They surrounded her, jumping up and attacking her with vicious licks and the odd slap of a happy tail wag.

Naia's scream morphed into giggles until she just couldn't take it anymore. Whipping her arm back, she tossed the ball as far away from her as she could—which was only about ten feet. The wild pack took off after it, droopy ears flapping in the wind. She let them fight over it before stealing it back and starting the process all over again.

Addison watched from the gazebo while she ate her Sunday pancakes. Apparently, it didn't take long to fill up a five-year-old tummy, but Naia had found plenty to keep her occupied around the rescue center.

Piper had abandoned her seat at the picnic table in exchange for Aiden's lap. He lounged on the grass with Princess sprawled out next to him, her pink belly exposed. He rubbed it absently while his own dog, Sophie, wrestled with Naia and the rest of the pack.

As they watched the little girl play, Piper had a distant look in her eye. Addison recognized that face. It was the baby face. She'd had that look once herself.

Addison wondered if her friend was feeling the pressure of the ticking clock yet. She was twenty-seven. Had she and Aiden discussed it? Addison figured it wouldn't be long before they got married and started popping out ridiculously beautiful babies.

It had been a long time since Addison last thought about having kids. Could think about having kids. That was one fantasy she didn't allow herself to dream about. Because it was one dream that would never come true.

"She's a cute little girl," Marilyn said, observing Addison over her teacup. She'd taken Picasso out of his tiny wheelchair, and he sat on her lap while she spoiled him with little bits of pancake.

"She sure is," Addison said.

Bob placed another plate of sausages in the

center of the picnic table. He helped himself to one before sitting down next to Marilyn. "You're good with her, you know."

"Maybe I've found my backup career," Addison said. "Professional babysitter."

She hadn't planned on showing up for their traditional pancake breakfast, considering her hangover and plans to wallow all day. But it had quickly become apparent that there was little to interest a five-year-old in her apartment other than, of course, a ton of Disney movies.

So Addison put *Frozen* on and grabbed a quick shower before heading to the center for some help entertaining Naia. But it turned out Naia was pretty good at entertaining herself. Well, the rescue dogs were entertaining her, and she seemed thrilled by so many playmates.

When Addison shifted her attention back to the table, she found Marilyn giving her a strange look. She wondered if maybe she had something on her face and wiped a napkin over her mouth. But when the look didn't disappear, she stuck her fork in another pancake to avoid Marilyn's probing eyes.

Piper hopped off Aiden's lap and slid onto the picnic table bench next to Zoe. "So, Addy. Still no news from the police, huh?"

Addison cringed. She'd been trying to avoid the topic around Aiden. She still hadn't told him just how bad business was. But she was totally going to. Just not yet.

"No. But Felix has been helping me search for information about the dognappings. He knows the people who were working both parties when the dogs went missing."

She stuffed another mouthful of pancake into her face. She didn't want to explain exactly how they were looking, since it would probably worry her friends. Besides, some of it wasn't legal. She didn't think Bob would approve, what with him being an inspector and all.

"You two have been working closely," Piper said. "Spending a lot of time together."

Her two best friends were watching her as closely as Marilyn was. She fidgeted under their scrutiny and shoveled more pancake into her mouth.

"You and Felix, huh?" Zoe asked.

Addison pretended not to notice the thick layer of suggestiveness in her voice. "Yeah, he's got his ear to the ground. He knows a lot of people in his line of work. He's got his hands in everything."

"Everything?" Zoe bit her lip. "And how are those hands?"

Addison shot her friend a look as heat crawled up her neck beneath her polka dot scarf. "It's not like that. We're only working together to figure out what's going on. We have a mutual interest in finding the dognapper. That's all." She jabbed another piece of syrupy pancake to show there was nothing more to say.

Zoe grinned back, clearly with plenty more to say. "Oh, I'm sure there's loads of mutual interest."

"We're just coworkers. Associates."

"An associate who babysits?" Piper asked.

"He was just desperate," Addison said. "He needed someone to watch Naia or he might have lost his job."

Marilyn threw her a skeptical look. "He wouldn't have trusted you with his kid if he didn't feel comfortable with you."

"I suppose," she said. "But it's no big deal. We've just gotten to know each other well, that's all."

Then again, Addison thought, *I obviously have a lot to learn about him yet*. However, he'd gotten to know her. If he already trusted her with his daughter, maybe it was a big deal after all. But what did that even mean?

Addison grabbed another pancake, ignoring that line of thinking because it didn't go anywhere, right? He wasn't that kind of guy—the one-woman, settle-down guy. However, she also wouldn't have pegged him as a dad guy, either. And yet, here Naia was.

What exactly did a guy like Felix want?

"Philip, on the other hand," Addison said. "Now there's potential."

Zoe leaned on her fist. "Do tell."

"Well, he's cultured, an animal rights activist, and a gentleman. Of course, the good looks don't hurt." She counted all the amazing things about him on her fingers.

Philip was a great catch. Ending up with a guy like him would be like having that Prada dress and wearing it too.

"Sounds exciting," Marilyn said. "You could spend your weekends flying to Paris or Milan or London."

Addison sighed wistfully. "It does sound exciting, doesn't it?"

"Will we get to meet this Philip at the gala on Friday?" Zoe asked.

"I hope so."

Marilyn poured herself another cup of Yorkshire tea. "So, after Paris and London, then what?" She added sugar to her cup and stirred.

The spoon clinked loudly in the silence. Everyone stopped whatever it was they were doing, waiting for the answer.

Addison spread her hands. "The sky's the limit."

"Come on," Piper said. "We know you better than that. I'm sure you've daydreamed your way through every romance flick ever made."

Zoe took a sip of orange juice. "Yeah, like when Bridget Jones finally notices Mark Darcy."

"Or the one where you're Audrey Hepburn and he's Humphrey Bogart," Piper added.

"Have you imagined him as a sparkly vampire yet?" Zoe asked. "Or, better yet, *Fifty Shades of Grey*." Her eyes practically rolled back into her head.

"Audrey Hepburn? Vampires?" Marilyn shook her head. "It's fine to daydream about this man, but are you thinking about *him*? About what life would be like together? That's the real test. Consider what it would be like to live with him. Does he pick up after himself? What about waking up next to him when he's got drool stuck in his mustache?"

Zoe was fighting a grin. "Speaking from experience, Marilyn?" She glanced meaningfully at Bob's thick mustache.

Bob subconsciously dabbed at it with his napkin. Marilyn turned a shade of red that Addison had never seen on the woman before. While the center's manager had an adventurous streak, she could be surprisingly modest sometimes.

Raising her chin, the proper British woman focused on stirring her already-stirred tea. "I'm just saying that it's important to be realistic. Imagine your man the way he really is. Not how you want him to be."

"Does he leave the toilet seat up?" Piper asked.

Zoe rolled her eyes. "Does he get crabby when he doesn't get his way?"

Addison remembered how Philip had treated his head of security after the dogs had disappeared at his fundraiser. She didn't blame him for being upset, but she also thought he'd been a bit harsh. Maybe even a little condescending. At the time, she'd tried to blow it off, but she realized that it bothered her even now. The fact was, she didn't really know him at all.

Piper's eyes drifted over to where Aiden sat on the grass. "Do you dream about holding hands with him when you're wrinkly and old?"

Addison pushed her half-eaten pancake around her plate, suddenly feeling deflated. Drool and toilet seats weren't quite as romantic as sparkly vampires and Paris in the spring.

She supposed she was getting a little ahead of herself. It was something she always did when she started to date someone new. Even when she'd only just handed out her number. Okay, she'd even done it when a guy gave her a wink while serving her a latte the other week—and she was pretty sure he was gay.

But the stories in her head always went so much better than real life. In them, anything could happen. She could have any life she wanted. It could be perfect.

As Addison helped clean up after breakfast, she recalled the last time she'd truly dreamed about real things with a man. Not just dreamed. She'd been living it. Buying matching comforters and sheet sets, comparing paint swatches for the nursery, and making a home in the Sunset area with her then-boyfriend. It was a home where she could imagine their children playing in the yard.

At the time, it had felt like a fairy tale, as if she'd found her happily ever after. But it must have been a fairy tale told by the Brothers Grimm, because the baby was never born.

It was a cervical pregnancy. One that led to severe hemorrhaging that threatened Addison's life. The emergency room surgeon had no choice but to perform a hysterectomy.

Addison recovered—physically, anyway. Eventually, she came to terms with her loss, both of her pregnancy and any potential to have a child. However, her boyfriend never did.

He wanted a family, and, apparently, she alone wasn't enough family for him. When she'd suggested they adopt, he said he wanted a family of "his own."

Soon the sheet sets were divided and the home rented out to a new family. No more happily ever after for Addison. Or at least she'd thought so.

Addison carried the dirty dishes back to the house. She paused on the wraparound porch to watch Naia play with the dogs. She wasn't sure how long her focus had been on the little girl, but when Marilyn laid a hand on her shoulder, she jumped in surprise.

The woman gave Addison a look that said she could read her mind. Of course, Marilyn knew about her past. They all did. The volunteers at the rescue center had become like family to her, Marilyn like a mother. However, she probably wouldn't appreciate being thought of in that way.

Marilyn wrapped an arm around Addison and watched Naia with her. She chuckled as Colin, Piper's black and tan doxie, grabbed the ball right out of her little hand, like *Mine. All mine!*

Addison sighed. "I guess I haven't thought about the *real* things with Philip. It's still new."

Since the moment she'd met him, heck, even in the moments leading up to it, she'd imagined life could be perfect with him. She supposed she didn't really know what to expect yet. She'd formed ideas about him before she'd gotten to know him. The same way she had about Felix. And look at how wrong those were turning out to be.

"Well, think about it," Marilyn said in her no-nonsense tone. "Really think about it. You might believe you know what you want. But sometimes life doesn't always give us what we want. If you're lucky, it gives you what you truly need."

Addison nodded, taking the advice to heart. So, what was it she truly needed?

20

DOGFACED

Dearest Addison,

I'm sorry I have been so busy since my fundraiser. The best thing about my week was seeing you. I would really enjoy spending time with you again soon. Would you like to have dinner at my place this Wednesday night?
—Philip

Addison clutched her phone to her chest and sighed. Naia looked up from her bubblegum ice cream that was dripping its way down her wrists and chin.

"What's wrong?" the little girl asked between licks.

Addison smiled in return and took another taste of her licorice ice cream. "Absolutely nothing. Everything is perfect."

Philip was still interested in her. A sense of victory pulsed through her muscles until she wanted to do a cartwheel. He'd probably been too busy dealing with police and outraged dog owners to text her. But her fantasy romance was back on track.

With a little squeal of delight, she hit the reply button. Her finger hovered over the keyboard, hesitating with all the things she wanted to say, like *@#$% yes!* But she struggled to find the right response, the not-too-eager, just-the-right-amount-of-interest, with-a-dash-of-flirtatiousness response.

After a few seconds, she scowled and gave up. She'd think of something eloquent to text Philip later. Besides, it wasn't a good idea to text back right away; she needed to make him sweat a little.

She tucked away her phone, then she and Naia carried on down the park path in Alamo Square, enjoying their after-lunch treats. Princess trotted ahead, greeting each dog that passed by—and there were plenty. The off-leash dog park attracted many locals and tourists, especially with all the painted-lady homes facing the green space.

Her day with Naia was actually a lot easier than Addison had expected. She wasn't sure what she'd been so worried about. Naia was easy. Great, in fact. Addison was having fun.

The picnic that Felix had packed for them had been delicious. The man could cook. Who would have thought? All along, she'd imagined he was some bachelor probably living on takeout—one of the many things she'd assumed about him. But Naia's appearance had flipped all her presumptions about him upside down. Now she didn't know what to think.

It was like getting to know him, the real him, all over again. Addison looked back over the last couple of weeks with new eyes. Each interaction seemed completely different now. Like how he said he didn't hang out and party after work. It was because he was rushing home to Naia.

It was as though Addison had created an alternate version of Felix in her mind, starting with their less-than-flattering first encounter. She'd Mr. Darcy'd him right from the start.

In reality, there was so much more to see, like a movie she'd rather buy than rent so she could watch the rest of the story: the director's cut, some extra features, and definitely the bloopers. And part of that story was right there in front of her, licking bubblegum ice cream.

"So, it's just you and your daddy, huh?" Addison asked, hoping to discover a little more.

Lick. "Yup."

"What about your mom?"

"She lives in Urup." Lick. Lick. A pink trickle ran down her forearm.

"Do you mean Europe?"

Naia tilted the cone to lick the drip on her

hand, spilling more down the other side. "Yeah, that's it."

Addison's eyes widened in shock, but she kept her voice neutral. "Europe is really far away. Do you see her much?"

"No. Daddy says it's too far for her to come to America."

"Oh," was all Addison could say.

She watched the little girl closely, but no sadness tinted her voice or crept across her adorable features. It was like she was just stating a fact. Maybe she didn't know her mother at all. Addison could relate.

"My daddy raised me all by himself too," she said.

"Really? Oh, but Celia takes care of me when Daddy's at work," Naia offered.

"Does anyone else take care of you? Other women Daddy's age?"

"No, not really."

The news made Addison strangely relieved. It was like she'd received an exclusive club card at her favorite store. Still, she couldn't help but wonder why, out of all the people he could invite into Naia's life, he'd chosen her. The woman he'd made out with a few times.

"Celia has lots of toys," Naia told her. "Sometimes we watch movies."

"That sounds fun," Addison said. "I love movies. What kind do you like to watch?"

"Make-believe stuff. I like *Cinderella,* and *Alice in Wonderland,* and *Beauty and the Beast."*

"Really? Me too. I love those." Now this she could do. Common ground, some way she could relate to a five-year-old. However, if a twenty-eight-year-old could relate to a child, maybe that wasn't such a good thing.

"Dad likes superhero movies," Naia said. "We've seen *Iron Man* like a million times."

"Really? I never would have guessed."

Addison tried to imagine this other Felix watching Disney movies on the couch with his daughter. She wanted to know more and found herself plying Naia for information. Then she wondered at what point she'd started to care so much.

"What else does your dad like, other than movies?"

"I guess dad stuff. Like making me school lunches, and taking me to preschool, and having tea parties with me." Naia used her fingers to list each one off, spreading the ice cream on her hands even more.

Addison snorted when an image of Felix in a bonnet and pearls popped into her head. "Tea parties?"

"Yeah, Dad likes peppermint tea."

"Is that so?" She swallowed her laughter. She knew these were the things he had to do, but she was certain he enjoyed them because they were for his daughter.

All this time, she'd figured he was trying to get into the pants of last-call hookups and getting together with red-bra'd servers. When Addison had imagined him tucking a girl with a teddy into bed, it hadn't been the stuffed kind.

"How's your ice cream?" Addison asked.

"Good," Naia told her between licks. "Bubblegum's my favorite."

"Is it?" Addison remembered Oliver's visit to her spa and thought it made sense now.

Naia tried to lick the pink streams before they dripped off her elbows, but the hot afternoon sun was making faster work of her ice cream than she was. She held her arms out like she'd been contaminated. "I think I'm done now."

"Okay, me too." Addison took the soggy cone and threw hers out with it.

Naia was a pink mess. Addison dug through her purse for an emergency ice cream cleanser. She scraped together makeup remover wipes and hand sanitizer. Between the two, they did the job, and Naia was clean again, albeit smelling of bubblegum.

"Princess, let's play hide-and-seek," she squealed, taking off up the grassy knoll.

Addison restrained Princess by her shiny pink collar, giving Naia a head start. Once she was hidden behind a thick cedar tree, Addison could hear soft giggles and knew Naia was ready.

"Princess, where's Naia?" Addison asked. "Where is she?"

Princess sprang into action, but since she didn't know what to do, she ran in excited circles, barking at Addison's feet.

"Go get her." Addison encouraged. "Where's Naia?"

Slowly, she led Princess to where Naia's jean dress peeked out from behind the tree trunk. When Princess came across her, Naia scream-giggled like she was on a roller coaster and ran for her next hiding spot.

"Good girl, Princess." Addison gave the doxie a treat from her purse, distracting her while Naia settled in behind a cypress.

This time, Princess found the child with little coaxing. By the fourth round of the game, Princess beelined it straight for Naia, reveling in the congratulations and treats she received each time she found her.

Addison suspected Princess was just following the soft giggling around the park, but when Naia chose a hiding spot near the playground, it tested the dachshund's sniffer and big, sensitive ears.

Princess circled the playground. She sniffed past screaming kids and ignored a golden Lab that tried to talk to her. Focused on her mission, she bypassed them all, hot on an invisible trail.

Addison followed her weaving path until Princess came to a bench. Naia was lying flat on the seat. Princess barked and stood on her hind legs, pawing at her find.

Naia leaped to her feet on the bench, screaming and laughing at the same time. Addison handed her the dog treat. Once the girl fed it to Princess, she jumped into Addison's arms.

"You must be part badger," Addison told her.

"What's a badger?"

"It's an animal." Addison set her down and brought up a picture on her phone. "Dachshunds are really good at hunting them."

Before they moved on, Addison pulled out a Pampered Puppies coupon from her purse and approached the golden Lab's owners. They were spread out on a blanket, enjoying a picnic of their own.

She handed them the slip of paper. "If you happen to be looking for a dog groomer, I have a spa nearby. If you bring in that coupon, I'll give you twenty percent off any services that day."

They thanked her, and she and Naia headed down the path.

"What did you give those people?" Naia peered into Addison's purse curiously, as though hoping it had been bubblegum.

"It was a coupon for my business. I'm looking for more customers to come get their dogs cleaned at my spa." *Or any customers, really.*

Instead of focusing her marketing efforts, she was tossing out promotional material to just about anyone now. She thought it wouldn't be long until she began begging every dog owner in the city.

"Customers?" Naia's big brown eyes scanned the park. "There's someone." She pointed like it was an accusation. "He has a dog. Is he a customer?"

Addison followed her gaze to a man wearing a panama hat. He was throwing a ball for his dog while seated on a bench beneath a shady cypress.

"He might be. Good eye." Addison smiled. "I need you on my marketing team. What do you say? Did you want to give him a coupon for me?" She held out another voucher.

Naia's eyes grew wide. "Yeah."

She reverently took the pink piece of paper with both hands and carried it over to the man as if she were holding the crown jewels. She plopped down next to him on the bench and thrust out the coupon. "Excuse me. Do you want your dog cleaned?"

All that time spent studying marketing tactics and honing sales pitches, and the simplest offer from a five-year-old was more effective than an entire marketing-and-promotions team. Addison made a mental note to add Naia to the payroll.

The man turned his attention away from his English foxhound. He jumped in surprise to find the little girl beside him. "Oh. Thank you."

Taking the coupon, he held it up to the light, tilting his head back like he needed glasses. His hat brim rose, and the sun hit his face. That's when Addison recognized him.

"Alistair Yates."

When he noticed Addison, his expression transformed from pleasant surprise to consternation. Yet, when she approached, he grabbed his cane to stand and removed his hat, perhaps out of polite habit.

"Miss Turner." He frowned. "Good day."

The English foxhound loped to Alistair's side and placed the ball next to his shoe. When it rolled away, the dog nudged it back into place and sat patiently, waiting for him to throw it again.

The hound acknowledged Princess but didn't start sniffing. She was probably too well trained. Princess pretended not to take notice of the other dog. She puffed out her chest, demonstrating her clear superiority.

"Is that your dog?" Addison blurted.

"Of course it's my dog," Alistair said. "Do I look like a dog walker to you?"

Addison blinked, staring open-mouthed at the foxhound. She supposed it was a silly question, but she just hadn't expected Alistair to move on so quickly.

"She's beautiful," she said honestly.

His deep lines relaxed a little, and his loose wrinkles fell back into place like a heavy curtain.

"Yes, she is. Not the natural show dog Lily was." A flit of emotion crossed his face, his frown lines twitching. "*Is*," he corrected himself. "The natural Lily *is*. Fancy here is lacking some of the affinity needed for the show, but she has potential if she works with Penny."

"How long have you had her?"

"Since she was a pup."

So, Alistair had a second dog waiting in the wings all along. "Are you going to show her this weekend?"

"What other dog do I have to show?" Alistair retorted.

Addison felt a twinge of pity for the man, despite everything that had passed between them. The accusations, the interview with Holly that had sent her customers running. She couldn't blame Alistair; he'd lost his beloved dog.

She'd worked with enough owners to know that, for some, the lines blurred between their dog and a human. It wasn't just time and money they poured into their pets. It was love, sometimes bordering on obsession, as in Kitty Carlisle's case. Their four-legged friends ate at their supper table, slept in their same bed, and dressed in the same outfits—something Addison knew about herself— as though they were truly family. And Alistair Yates had lost his.

Fancy finally lost her patience and nudged Alistair's hand, greedy for more play. Leaning on his cane, Alistair bent down to pick up the ball and tossed it out into the field.

"Mr. Yates," Addison began. "I'm so sorry you lost Lily. If there was something I could do …" She swallowed hard.

"There is something you can do," Alistair said.

"Of course," she answered. "Anything."

He clenched his cane, his knuckles turning white. "You can stay away from this dog."

Turning to Naia, Alistair handed her back the pink coupon. "Thank you, my dear. But I won't be needing this."

Naia took it back with a pouty lip, and he kindly patted her on the head. He whistled through his teeth, such a loud and startling noise from the quiet, mild-mannered man. Addison flinched at the sound.

"Come on, Fancy." Placing his hat back on his head, he dipped it briefly at Addison in a farewell that looked like an involuntary twitch.

As he walked away, Addison couldn't take her eyes off the English foxhound. She was no dog show judge, but she'd seen a lot of dogs come through her spa, and even a layman could see that Fancy was utterly perfect.

Naia stared at the unwanted coupon in her hands. "He didn't want a clean dog?"

Alistair might have had a backup dog already waiting to replace the old one, but Addison knew he couldn't be a suspect. By stealing his own dog,

he'd never be able to show Lily in public ever
again, certainly not at a conformation show. While
Felix was the one who knew people in general,
Addison knew dog owners. And Alistair was one
sad pup.

"No," she said, watching Alistair leave. "I
think that dog is clean."

21

A DOG'S LIFE

Princess Addison lay slumbering on her bed of flowers, waiting for her prince to wake her with a kiss. She sensed him draw near. For even though she couldn't open her eyes, she knew it was him. She felt it resound deep in her bones like the promise of destiny.

He dipped down, bringing his face close to hers. She felt his heat, his sweet breath on her face, and finally that magical kiss. The one that trumped all others. A kiss so honest and true. *The One.*

Startled, Addison's eyes flicked open, and she let out a yelp. Her arms flew out. Her palm connected with flesh in a loud thwack.

"Ouch!" the prince cried.

Heart racing, she blinked her dream away and focused on the reality around her. She wasn't lying on a bed of flowers but on a threadbare floral couch in a living room not her own. And that was most certainly not her one true love. It was Felix.

Addison struggled to sit up and look around her. She squinted through one eye, blinded by the light from the TV screen saver. She suddenly re-membered she was at Felix's house. It was strange not to find Princess curled up next to her; she'd dropped the doxie off at home.

He rubbed the bright pink spot on his cheek. "Morning, Sleeping Beauty."

Her eyes bulged. Had she been talking in her sleep, or had he just read her mind? "What did you say?"

"But right about now, I'd like to take back the beauty part."

She touched her lips. "You kissed me."

"It's not like it was the first time." He looked away and shrugged. "You looked kind of cute lying there. You know, when your mouth was closed, and you weren't annoying me."

"Annoying?" She stared at him, bewildered by the change in his usual cocky attitude. Like he was almost embarrassed or shy.

"Where's Naia?" he asked.

She yawned. "Who?"

"My daughter? About yay tall." He held his hand up to his hip. "Big brown eyes, a hell of a sharp attitude. Kind of like yours, actually."

Addison's blurry focus flicked to the heap of

blankets and pillows at the other end of the couch. They'd constructed them into a fort to watch movies in. But Naia wasn't there.

"Naia?" She tore apart the mini-fort, like maybe the little girl was smaller than she remembered. "I swear she was sleeping right here. I don't know. I just closed my eyes for a second."

"She's not in her room," he said. "I checked."

Felix sounded a lot calmer than she felt. He'd left his daughter with her for less than a day, and she'd lost her. First show dogs and now a child. Maybe she *should* go to jail.

Addison began searching the room. Naia couldn't have gone far, right?

Felix watched her quietly from the middle of the living room. When she wheeled around, her eyes wide with fear, he laughed. When she realized he was laughing at her, she scowled. It was so not funny.

"Don't worry." He held up his hands. "I think I know where she is."

Felix ducked into the kitchen. Oliver's kennel sat in the corner. As Felix got closer, Addison noticed a furry tail twitch back and forth, but the dog didn't leave the safety of his kennel to greet his master. Once she approached, she saw why; two tiny feet dangled out of the opening.

Addison peered inside. Naia had crawled into the kennel to curl up against Oliver's warm flank. Her head rested against him, a small hand curled over a clump of his belly fur. It looked rather painful for Oliver, but he didn't seem to mind.

The dog held still while Felix reached in and drew out his daughter. The jostling roused her. She clamped two little arms around Felix's neck before falling back asleep.

Addison followed them and waited at the base of the stairs while he carried Naia up to tuck her in. Before he came back down, she checked herself in the mirror on the wall and fixed her couch hair. Then she quickly tidied up the fort, folding blankets and rearranging pillows. When she turned around to switch off the TV, Felix was watching her.

Addison hit the power button on the remote. "So, you have a daughter," she said like it was just small talk.

"You've noticed," he said, just as casually.

"Why didn't you tell me?"

"Some women get kind of freaked out when you mention you're a single dad." His shoulders slumped, and he gazed at the worn carpet. "And those who do stick around swear they can handle it. That is, until they're walking out on us. Again. I guess, after a while, I just stopped letting myself get too invested, too hopeful."

Addison nodded. She couldn't blame him for keeping it a secret. "So, you started playing the numbers game."

Felix's laugh sounded more like a heavy sigh.

"Not really. When I gave you that advice, that might have been my frustration rearing its ugly head. But I was wrong. That's just not you. You have too much heart for that, and that's what I like about you. Besides, I don't have the time for numbers, and I would never put Naia through that. She's my angel. My everything."

"Your number one." Addison chuckled, remembering his words. "At the time, I thought you were saying you had to look out for yourself."

He shook his head. "Naia's my priority. When you asked me to help you investigate, I really wanted to, but I couldn't risk losing my job, my way of taking care of my daughter."

"I totally get that now, and I don't blame you at all." If anything, she admired him for it. After a second, she frowned. "Hold on a minute. You did offer to help me at first, in exchange for a date." She crossed her arms, giving him a look.

Felix grinned. "What can I say? I was interested in you. When it comes to people who are important to me, I try to help them however I can. At the time, I thought maybe ..." He glanced down at his feet.

Addison gnawed on her lip. *Maybe what?* Had he hoped she might become important to him? That she'd be worth the risk?

He shook it off. "Anyway, Naia's the reason I want to buy my buddy's bar so badly. The reason I've been working so hard."

"Owning your own business is tough," she said. "It has its perks, but it's tough."

"I'm not afraid of hard work. It's the perks I'm doing it for." He crossed the living room and flopped onto the couch. "Like being able to schedule my own hours. Once the bar is established, I can spend more time with Naia, be here to put her to bed every night, send her off to school every day next year. I don't want to pay a babysitter to raise my own kid."

He stared at his hands, and it was clear to Addison that he'd thought long and hard about his goals.

"You're a good dad," she said. "You want to be there for her. Not just for the big things, like putting a roof over her head and dinner on the table. You really want to be there." It brought to mind her own dad and how hard he'd worked to raise her and provide for her.

"Shouldn't I?" Felix asked like it was the most obvious thing in the world.

"Not all parents do," she said. "My mom never did."

Tenderness flickered in his eyes. "You're right. You and Naia share that in common. Her mom took off to chase her dreams of dancing professionally in Europe." He shook his head. "I guess I just want to be around as much as possible to make up for Naia having only one parent."

"She's a lucky girl to have you in her life. I hope you get your bar."

"I know it won't be easy, but it will be worth it," he said. "Or at least it would have been. Even if I work every day until the deadline, it won't be enough. And that reward money is looking like a pipe dream."

He rubbed a hand over his face and let it rest there until she thought he'd fallen asleep. She supposed the double shift that day might have something to do with that.

"Don't talk like that," Addison said. "It's going to happen. There's still time. For both of us."

When he didn't reply, she sat down next to him, catching a whiff of sweet alcohol on his skin and clothes.

"We'll find the dogs and clear our names," she said with certainty. "That reward money will be ours. Then you can buy your bar, and I'll have a full house for the fashion show, and everyone will want to order my fabulous designs."

When Felix still hadn't looked at her, she laid a hand on his hunched back. "Everything will work out for both of us. You'll see."

His tired head finally swiveled to take in her upbeat smile. "Okay, Miss Positivity. How are we going to accomplish this feat?"

"We're going to keep looking. We won't give up." She brought a determined fist down against her palm. "Okay, let's review. What do we know so far?"

He sat up a little straighter. "Well, we're still on the fence about Kitty Carlisle. And we can scratch Julia Edwards off the list, since Precious was stolen."

"Oh." Addison blinked, suddenly remembering her afternoon. "I ran into Alistair Yates at the dog park today."

"The dog park?" Felix cringed. "That's depressing."

"No. He had a dog with him. Turns out, he's always had this one. He still seems shaken up over Lily." She sighed, recalling his depressed demeanor in the park. "Have you heard anything about your coworkers? Any of the servers?"

"The servers had access to the dogs, but I was the supervisor. If they weren't pulling their weight or had disappeared to steal them, I would have known. Besides, on their own, they don't exactly have the resources to pull it off."

"They could have had help."

"I know." He rubbed a hand over his face. "And if that's the case, then the possibilities are endless."

"Maybe not. What about Precious?" Addison asked. "During the first two events, the dogs were taken as a group. Gathered together, they were an easy target. But Precious was the only one taken from my spa. Someone had to go out of their way for just one dog."

"You're right. That is odd." He perked up a little at this. "But what if they didn't have to go that far out of their way?"

"What do you mean?"

"You told me that Melody was there just before I showed up. What if she came back?"

Addison wanted to deny it, to stick up for Melody. But she knew it was a possibility, and lying to herself wouldn't help them figure things out.

"It's possible," she relented. "But it wouldn't explain the dogs missing from Philip's fundraiser."

"So, what's so special about Precious?"

"He won Best of Breed last year." She went quiet as she tried to piece things together. "Maybe it's someone who wants to make sure they win, so they're taking out the competition."

Felix picked at a loose thread on the couch cushion. "It would definitely shorten up our list. It may be our best bet."

"Then whoever wins Best in Show is probably the culprit because, if they've gone this far, they'll have ensured that they've taken out their major competitors."

"But the winner won't be decided until Sunday," he said. "It will be too late then. I won't get the money, and you'll have no models or audience for your fashion show."

"And the owners won't have their dogs back in time for the competition." She ran her fingers through her hair. "At least we can keep investigating other people on the list who still have dogs. I know it's scraping the bottom of the kennel, but we've got to try something."

"I'm free on Wednesday," he said. "My babysitter's available that day."

"Okay. It's a date." Addison felt a flutter of excitement in her chest. "Well ... not a *date*."

Felix's eyelids lowered seductively. "If you want a date, Addy, all you have to do is ask."

It always surprised her how he could go from all business to fun and games—oh, so fun—in a blink of her jet-black waterproof eyelashes. Not to mention how quickly her body reacted.

"Well," he said. "On second thought, maybe a little begging couldn't hurt."

She answered him with a sour look. Only the slight smirk gave away her excitement.

"Okay, no begging," he said, backtracking. "You just have to ask." When she didn't reply, he relented. "Suggest? Allude to? Hint? Okay, okay, just wink right now if you want a date."

He was nearly begging her, wearing down her resolve. It was pretty cute, making him seem like a big softie.

Suddenly, he reached out and drew her close to him on the couch. She accidentally rubbed against his jeans and retracted the idea that he was soft. He was definitely not soft.

"Hey." She held a hand up between them. "Not so fast."

"But you winked," he said innocently.

She laughed. "I blinked. It's what eyes do sometimes."

"I like to think of it as two winks at the exact same time. Even better."

He dove for her neck, but she pushed him away. "You have a daughter sleeping right upstairs, and all you can think about is getting some action?"

"She's asleep. And I'm not looking to 'get some action.'" His tone tainted the words like they were the sticky film of alcohol coating his bar top.

"Then what are you looking for?" It just flew out of her mouth. It seemed like the most natural thing to say after wondering about it for days now.

Felix's scowl slipped away. He was staring at her with that same apprehension he wore when he revealed he had a daughter.

"Something ... more."

"Daddy?" Naia's voice drifted down the stairs.

"Coming, sweetheart!" Felix called back.

The interruption seemed to snap him out of it. As he stood up, his confidence settled back in place—the confidence of a parent who had his crap together and was sure of his one true job in life.

"So, we'll continue our search on Wednesday?" he asked.

Addison felt ripped out of some kind of moment. "Fine. I'll have another look at our suspect list tonight. Maybe I can come up with a few more."

She bit her lip. They were running out of suspects, and one name kept nagging at her. There was no time left to skirt around it.

"What about your friend, Red Bra?"

Felix froze at the bottom of the stairs. "Charlotte? I thought we were running with the assumption the dognapper is a competitor. Besides, I know she didn't do it."

Addison crossed her arms. "Why? Because you say so?"

"Because I know her. I know she wouldn't do this to a bunch of pets. To me."

She didn't like the way he said it, with such familiarity. "I just want to be thorough."

Slowly, he came back into the room, a smirk creeping across his lips. "Are you … jealous?"

"Jealous? Of her? Ha!" Addison tried to laugh for real, but it sounded fake because the words stung. He was right. She was jealous.

He crossed his arms, mirroring her determination. "Well, if you want to be thorough, then the next name on our list should be Philip Montgomery the third. He was at both events. Hell, the second event was at his house. And he could have easily found out the time of Julia's appointment at your spa."

Addison twitched at that, recalling her meeting with Julia at Philip's fundraiser. They had discussed the exact time and date of her appointment right in front of him.

She shook her head. "No. It's not possible."

"Not only that," Felix continued, "but he's one of the last key competitors who still has a dog to put in the show."

"He's not going on the list."

"Why? Because you say so?" He threw the words back at her.

"Because I know him."

"You don't know him. You only know what you've created in here." He tapped the side of her head.

She swiped his hand away. "That is not true."

Then she remembered the conversation with her friends just that morning over breakfast. But as good as Felix was at reading people, he couldn't read her mind. It ticked her off that he thought he could. And even more so because he was right.

"Just because you have the hots for Philip doesn't mean he's innocent," he said. "Maybe he's just getting close to you in order to set you up. To use you as a scapegoat. You ever think of that?"

"That's ridiculous." Addison stormed over to the kitchen table and grabbed her purse to leave.

Felix gripped her arm to stop her from taking

off. "Think about it. The dogs disappeared the night of the mixer while you were dancing with him."

"Then he couldn't have done it, because he was too busy gazing longingly into my eyes." She batted her eyelashes facetiously.

"He might have had an accomplice. Philip was distracting you."

Addison tried to yank her arm away but was unsuccessful. "Philip got major heat over the dogs getting stolen from his house."

"Which is exactly why he invited you. To take the focus off him."

"So, I guess that's the only way a guy like him would be interested in me?" She was glad she'd turned off the TV or the light would be sparkling off the tears building in her eyes.

"He's just using you." Felix's grip tightened. "There's nothing there between you. Can't you see?"

She narrowed her eyes. "You're just jealous."

"Jealous? Of that pompous asshole? Ha!" But his laugh didn't sound real either.

"Daddy!" Naia yelled again.

"Coming!" he called back. To Addison, he said, "Don't go anywhere." He pointed a finger at her, as if he could be speaking to anyone else. "We're not done talking about this."

"Oh, we're done," she said, throwing her purse over her shoulder.

But after he left the room, Addison stayed behind because the more she thought about it, the more perfect comebacks she came up with.

Who does Felix think he is? She wasn't some smitten little girl who'd lost her head just because some guy was interested in her. It wasn't like she had nothing riding on this mystery. But Philip was innocent. She was sure of it. He'd even offered to help in any way he could. Now *that* was a supportive man.

Felix, on the other hand, had to be backed into a corner before he agreed to help her. Something had to be in it for him. He clearly thought that "something" might be her.

As if, she thought. *Felix wishes. What kind of fairytale ending would that be for me?*

Whipping out her phone, Addison brought up Philip's earlier text, the one she'd completely forgotten about for some reason, and hit the reply button.

I would love to come over for dinner Wednesday night.

Tapping the send button with a flourish, she grinned triumphantly to herself. That would show Felix.

She wanted to see the look on his face when she told him about her date. She'd tell him as soon as he came back down. Then she'd leave.

Just where was Felix, anyway? What was taking him so long?

Addison glanced at the clock. It had been

nearly twenty minutes already. Well, she wasn't going to wait around for him all night. She would tell him he would be on his own for the investigation on Wednesday, and then she was out of there.

Trudging up the stairs, she headed for the door with a pink sign that said *Naia* on it at the end of the hall. Addison gripped the phone in her hand, ready to shove it in Felix's face.

"Ha!" she would say. "How about that for 'he's just using you'?" Or something slightly better.

Addison poked her head through the partially open door, but Felix didn't exactly look like he was ready to continue their discussion. Or even cared about Philip anymore. He was curled up on *My Little Pony* bed sheets next to Naia, drooling on a heart pillow.

The sight brought Addison up short. She hovered uncertainly in the doorway. There'd been a time when she'd wanted that life, had dreamed of a family, before the chance had literally been ripped out of her. Then her boyfriend tossed her aside like damaged goods.

Addison hadn't thought about it much since then. She figured she'd end up with someone who didn't want kids. Or maybe, just maybe, she'd end up with someone who saw her as enough all on her own—unlike her ex.

Marilyn's words from earlier that day came back to Addison. *Sometimes life doesn't always give us what we want. If you're lucky, it gives you what you truly need.*

Addison knew what she wanted, or at least she'd thought she did. But what did she need?

She thought of Philip. She could think of a million things she wanted from him. But what would she need from him? And could a life with him provide those things? She had a hard time imagining what that life would look like.

However, as she stood there watching Felix and Naia, she could see it like a movie playing out in her head, a montage that flicked by to a cheesy, upbeat song: evenings with the three of them making dinner while dancing to music in the kitchen, Felix casually kissing her as he stirred the spaghetti sauce, the look on Naia's face on Christmas morning when she saw Santa had come, nights spent tucking Naia into bed and reading her a fairy tale, and Addison tucking Felix into bed after.

It left Addison breathless to imagine it. Not just her and Felix together but all of it. Was that what he'd meant when he said he wanted something more?

Suddenly, the argument Addison had built up in her head seemed trivial. She put her phone away. Shutting the door silently, she turned and left.

When she climbed into her car, she glanced

back at the shabby row house and considered the life she could have if she chose Felix.

It wasn't the perfect setup she'd imagined. And it definitely wasn't "logical." Felix wasn't her white knight in shining armor. It wasn't a fairy tale come true. It was … real.

But was it too real for her?

22

BARKING UP THE WRONG TREE

The date was perfect. The wine glasses sparkled in the moonlight, the gentle breeze held a hint of the fragrant roses in the garden below, and the roasted lamb melted in Addison's mouth. Philip looked perfect. The way he was staring at her in her strapless dress let her know she looked perfect too. Just perfect, perfect, perfect.

So why didn't it feel perfect?

Philip gazed across the table at her. Her smile felt stiff as she scrambled for something to say. They'd been silent for too long.

"This is wonderful." She gestured at the balcony, the candles, and the soft music in the background. "Thank you."

"You're welcome." Philip took a sip of his wine.

Silence weighed down over them again like a

wet blanket. It was never this quiet with Felix. Probably because they argued so much. No, not argued. It felt ... more fun than that. Like banter, a repartee.

Never mind about Felix, Addison told herself. She was with Philip on his terrace in his beautiful house, spending an evening under the stars. It was so romantic.

As they finished up their meal, their cutlery clinked on their plates like the silverware was having a better conversation than they were. It only highlighted the awkward silence. Addison took another sip of wine, hoping that might help.

"This wine is amazing."

"Thank you," Philip said. "I enjoy a good wine. I'm a bit of a collector. However, my wine cellar isn't as grand as Alistair Yates's is claimed to be. I've always been curious to see it."

Addison shifted uncomfortably at the mention of Alistair. Her run-in with him at the park still bothered her. Automatically, her brain switched to detective mode, mentally reviewing her list of suspects, making connections.

A hand suddenly appeared in front of her. She jumped and glanced up to see Philip smiling down at her. When did he get up? How long had she been ignoring him?

"Join me?" he asked.

She placed her hand in his, and he led her to a marble bench on the other side of the terrace.

The moment they left, his butler, Hugh, seemed to appear out of nowhere to clear the table.

Philip sat next to her on the bench, close enough that she could smell his cologne. Her nose wrinkled at the citrus tang; it reminded her a little of a toilet bowl cleanser. She tried to focus on the scent of the flowering vine that draped over the banister behind them.

"You look lovely tonight," Philip told her.

"Thank you."

"I'm so glad you said yes to dinner. I know it's been a tough couple of weeks for you. You probably have a lot keeping you busy right now."

"It's been a little hectic." *To say the least*, she thought. But it wasn't like she could babble about that on a date, about undercover ops, dog-themed sex parties, dog show intrigue, and Felix.

The only person who would understand her surreal life at the moment was Felix himself. But she wasn't exactly talking to him. Not after how they'd left things at his house on Sunday. But Addison's life had been so consumed by all of their adventures that she didn't have much else to talk about.

She gave her best peppy cheerleader smile. "But I'm sure it will all turn around soon."

"That's the spirit," Philip said, oblivious to the strain in her voice.

"I just feel so bad for all those owners who lost their dogs. I hope they find them."

"I couldn't imagine losing Baxter." He shook his head. "I'm even hesitant to bring him to the gala on Friday evening, but they assure us it's completely secure. Are you going?"

"I was planning to. My friend Zoe is the event coordinator, and I know she's been pulling out all the stops to make it safe."

Philip slid closer to her on the bench until their legs were brushing against each other. "Well, if you're going. And I'm going ..." he said suggestively. He laid a hand on her bare leg where the slit in her dress had parted. "Perhaps we should go together?"

His fingers felt stiff and clammy. A shiver ran down Addison's leg. She hoped he thought it was a shudder of excitement.

"I'd love that," she said when she'd recovered.

Felix had originally been booked to work the gala. However, Joe was still keeping him on a short leash. She'd considered taking him as her plus-one, but that was off the table now.

Refocusing, Addison mentally shook herself, annoyed that she was thinking about Felix while on a date with Philip. She looked deep into those perfect blue eyes in front of her. They weren't muddy brown like Felix's. Well, come to think of it, Felix's eyes were a bit warmer than mud; they were a rich, polished mahogany. Very much like Naia's. And Naia's sparkled when she smiled, a little like her dad's. But Addison refused to think about Felix.

She focused determinedly on Philip. That's when she noticed him glance at her lips. He brought a hand up and ran his fingers gently through her wavy blonde locks as he leaned in for a kiss.

"Ouch." She winced as his watch caught in her hair. "I think I'm stuck."

"I'm so sorry." He tried to pull away but froze as she flinched again.

"That's okay," she said. "It's just ... pulling a little."

"Here, let me help." He fiddled with his watch, tugging on her hair for a few seconds until she was free. "There. That's better."

"Thanks," she said.

He gave her a sheepish look. "Are you ready for some dessert?"

The moment between them blown, Addison didn't know what else to do but nod.

She needed something sweet to calm her nerves. Her heart pounded in her chest, while anxiety buzzed through her whole body until she couldn't sit still. Something wasn't right.

I'm just overly excited, Addison told herself. *A hot date with Philip Montgomery III? What woman wouldn't be thrown off her game?*

Philip got to his feet and headed for the French doors to the drawing room. "I'll go see what's keeping Hugh."

The moment he disappeared from sight, Addison frantically smoothed her locks back into place. She rearranged herself into a come-hither position on the bench to await Philip's return.

No, she thought, *maybe sultry is better*. She crossed one leg over the other. The slit in her dress gaped to reveal just enough thigh to be seductive but not slutty. Yes, seductive was definitely best. Then she nudged the slit open an inch wider and waited in that frozen position.

In the silence unique to an oasis like Philip's property, Addison heard a faint rustle. Breaking her pose, she glanced behind her, half expecting a wild animal. But she saw nothing in the creeping vines along the banister.

She returned to her seductive pose. A moment later, another noise had her leaping to her feet. This time the rustling was closer, more violent.

The greenery shook like there was something caught in the ivy, too big to be a bug or a bird. Maybe it *was* some kind of animal. Faint grunts and heavy breathing reached her ears. She swallowed. *An enormous animal.*

Addison backed away from the bench. She opened her mouth to cry out. Then a hand reached over the banister. It gripped the vines for dear life. A head of dark curls surfaced, followed by a pair of mahogany eyes.

"Felix?" Addison hissed.

He gave her a strained, lopsided grin. There was a snap. The vine he was gripping broke away. He grunted, disappearing from sight.

Addison gasped and ran to the edge of the terrace. Fearing the worst, she peered over the banister. She saw Felix's hand clamped desperately around a flimsy vine just on the other side. It groaned ominously under his weight.

"Oh, my God." Addison lunged forward and gripped his wrist.

She tugged and heaved as Felix grunted his way up. She probably wasn't helping much, but by the time he'd thrown his leg over the banister and landed safely on the stone terrace, she was panting from the effort.

"What are you doing here?" she whispered between gasps for air.

Felix flopped down on the bench, face flushed, arms bright with pink and red welts from climbing the vines. He glanced up at her. "What am *I* doing here? What are *you* doing here?"

"What do you think I'm doing here?"

His eyes widened as he took in her dress. He nodded with understanding. "You're spying on him, aren't you? Deep undercover stuff. That's good. That's good. You really went all out."

He ran a finger down the front of her dress. She felt it like hot candle wax running from her breast to her belly where his touch lingered.

"You look"—Felix's eyes darkened—"seductive."

His words were honey, thick and sweet. She glanced at his lips and felt the urge to suck more of those words right out of his mouth.

Addison shook her head, trying to clear her mind. "Is that what you're doing here?" she demanded. "You're here to spy on Philip?"

"Of course. We still haven't crossed him off the list yet." He clapped his hands and rubbed them together. "What have you found out so far?"

"Nothing." Addison tried to drag Felix to his feet, but it was like trying to move a mule. "You can't be here right now."

"Why not?"

A devilish smile curled his lips. His fingers found their way to the slit in her dress. He laid his palm against the inside of her thigh, caressing her smooth skin. As it rose higher and higher, her legs automatically parted ever so slightly, enough for him to run a finger along her silky underwear.

From his position on the bench, he was at the perfect height. He pressed his face against her, teasing her with kisses over her dress. She could feel the heat of his breath. His lips worked against the fabric like they were searching.

For a moment, Addison forgot where she was, forgot the risk of being discovered together. Or maybe she reveled in it. The gamble, the excitement, the rush. It heightened her need for Felix, made her want to rip off his clothes right there and see if she could have him before their time was up. Like a race against the clock, only there was no way to know when the alarm would go off.

It seemed to be a common occurrence with the two of them. Maybe it was their thing, or maybe Addison just wanted Felix anywhere, any way.

"Philip will be back soon and catch you here," she said, even as she ran her fingers through his hair. She felt like Juliet urging her Romeo away to safety. Their forbidden circumstance at war with their undeniable attraction.

But that wasn't the only thing to consider. She needed to make the smart decision, to use her head. Wasn't that what she'd set out to do with Philip in the first place? To choose the right guy?

However, that was when she'd written Felix off as just another bad choice. Then she actually got to know him. And Naia. It didn't feel so cut and dry anymore. But this date wasn't exactly the best time to weigh her options.

"Wait." Addison pushed Felix away. "You have to go."

"Why?" He stared up at her in surprise, as if to ask, *What could possibly be so wrong about the situation?* "I haven't had time to look around."

She glanced through the French doors. Philip could be back at any second. "Because this is a date."

Felix's shoulders drooped. He leaned away so he could really look at her. "You're not serious."

The ironic look on his face ignited something inside Addison. She recalled his words from the last time they spoke. How he thought Philip was just using her, like she wouldn't be able to get a guy like him otherwise. Suddenly, she was as angry as the night they'd fought at his house.

"I'm perfectly serious. Why wouldn't I be on a date?" She crossed her arms. "And it's not like it's any of your business anyway."

But she wasn't sure that was true anymore. She rubbed her temples. She had so much to think about. For now, she had to get him out of there.

Felix's face screwed up. "A date? At his house? Isn't it a little early for a sleepover?"

But Addison didn't think that was any of his business either, and her irritation spiked. "Well, when it's right, it's right," she said vaguely.

He got to his feet, a scowl on his face. "What makes him right?"

Felix was whispering, but she could hear the anger behind his words. However, she didn't think he was angry with her. Frustrated, maybe. Disappointed.

"Is it because he's rich? Because every year *The Gate* lists him as one of San Francisco's most eligible bachelors?" That little vein on his forehead pulsed. His eyes narrowed. "Because you're so desperate you'll fall for any man?"

She inhaled sharply, clenching her fists at her sides. "I'm not desperate enough to fall for you."

The moment it flew out of her mouth, she regretted it. Both because his face flinched like she'd shoved a hot curling iron against his stomach and because she felt that same pain, an answer to his own. Because she knew it wasn't true.

The anger faded from Felix's face, and his breathing slowed like the fight was leaving him. "Fine. Enjoy your date. But I'm not relying on your fantasy obsession to tell if he's innocent or not. I'm scoping the place out myself."

"Felix." Her voice wavered with building tears. "I—"

Footsteps thumped inside. They echoed down the hall, heading their way. Addison's apology caught in her throat. She shoved Felix toward the banister.

"Someone's coming," she hissed. "Go back down the wall."

Felix's eyes went wide. "I can't. The chef and butler are down there, searching the grounds for me. They backed me into a corner. That's why I came up here."

"Then hide," she urged. "Quickly."

Felix's head whipped back and forth. Racing through the French doors, he dove for the thick, floor-length curtains draped on either side. Once he was hidden, Addison rearranged them to look natural again.

"I'll distract him," she told the curtains. "You can sneak out."

Felix peeked his head out. "How are you going to—"

"I hope you like crème brûlée," Philip called out as he swept into the room with two small dishes on a silver tray.

Felix whipped the curtain back into place just as Philip entered the room.

Addison jumped away from Felix. "Sounds delicious," she said, her voice a little too high-pitched. She cleared her throat.

Philip set the tray down. "Sorry I took so long. Apparently, the maid thought she saw someone sneaking around on the grounds, so Hugh went to check into it."

"You're kidding?" Addison opened her mouth in what she hoped looked like shock. She might have loved movies, but she'd never be nominated for an Emmy, that was for sure. "Should we call the cops?"

The curtain twitched. Addison could practically feel the agitation building behind them.

"No. No." Philip was busy arranging the dishes and dessert forks on the coffee table. Clearly, he wasn't used to serving himself. "I'm sure it's just a stray animal or something. Nothing to worry about. I wouldn't want to ruin our night together."

Addison's body felt stiff and unnatural. All she

could think about was trying not to look at the curtain, so of course, that was all she wanted to do. She was paranoid, certain Philip would somehow see Felix or hear him breathing behind the drapes.

"Shall we go back out on the balcony for a while?" she asked. If she could just get Philip out of the room, Felix could make a run for it.

But Philip sat down on the leather sofa. "I was thinking we would be more comfortable in here. I wouldn't want you to get too cold."

His usual polite and mild demeanor had shifted, and his voice had become throaty with lust. Addison could see it in his half-lidded eyes as he took in the sight of her standing in the door-way. She suddenly felt self-conscious. Was she still flushed from Felix's touch?

Philip patted the seat next to him. "I'm sure I could keep you warm in here."

There was a soft snort from behind the curtain —too soft for Philip to hear across the room, Addison hoped.

"That sounds even better." Addison smiled coyly but cursed in her head.

It would appear strange if she argued, so she had no choice but to sashay across the room and cozy up next to him. Philip watched her hips move beneath her dress. She doubted it would be hard to distract him.

She took a seat close enough to Philip that her

body rubbed against his. She crossed her legs. The slit in her skirt fell open, revealing a whole lot of thigh.

Philip slipped an arm around the backrest behind her. She caught his gaze drinking in the view down her neckline.

"See?" he said. "Isn't that better?"

"Much warmer," she agreed.

He caressed her exposed knee with a shy fingertip, sliding it slowly up her thigh. "I'm feeling a little warm myself."

There was another snort, this time loud enough for the both of them to hear. Addison froze. When Philip pulled away, she knew he'd heard it too.

His focus shifted across the room. He moved to stand. She couldn't let him near those curtains.

Addison practically lunged at Philip. Grabbing his chiseled jaw in her hands, she turned his face away from Felix's hiding spot and planted her lips on his.

His kiss wasn't exactly what she'd imagined, not warm and luscious, not falling into step with hers like two professional flamenco dancers. In fact, his lips were a little cold and thin, slipping over hers like wet hands trying to grasp a slimy bar of soap in a bathtub.

Philip grabbed her bare shoulders and gently pushed her away. "Did you hear something a second ago?"

"Nu-uh." She shoved her tongue into his mouth, shutting him up. *What strange man behind the curtain?*

Thankfully, Philip closed his eyes and relaxed into the kiss. Over his shoulder, Addison saw the curtain shift a fraction, and Felix's head poked out. When his searching eyes fell on the sofa, he froze.

They locked gazes and just stared at each other as she made out with her so-called Prince Charming. Felix didn't look angry. His jaw didn't clench. His nostrils didn't flare. He didn't bat an eyelash. The cool expression he wore hit Addison harder than if he'd thrown something at them.

Suddenly, she snapped out of the fantasy she was trying to hold on to—the stars, the candles, the wine—and fell back to reality. It was like when someone munched on popcorn in the theater, pulling her from the trance of the big screen. No matter how hard she tried to ignore it, she just couldn't return to that place of ignorant bliss. That mindset she escaped to during a movie, the one that allowed her to believe that anything was possible.

Philip's tongue swirled in annoying circles in her mouth, rubbing her molars like he was giving her a dental exam. She wasn't sure how much longer she could stand it. If Felix was going to escape unnoticed, now was the time.

Finally, she waved him on as in "Go."

Darting out from behind the curtain, he dashed across the room, footsteps light as a burglar's. Addison shifted on the sofa, tilting her head the other way so Philip wouldn't spot Felix out of the corner of his eye. Maybe this was a sign to take things to the next level because Philip planted a hand on her breast and gave it a sort of "honk" like he was a teenager touching one for the first time.

Before Felix slipped through the doors, he gave her one final look. A grimace contorted his handsome face before he turned away for the last time and left. She felt her heart contract painfully. Her eyes began to sting, and a single sob escaped her.

Philip must have interpreted this as frustrated pleasure, like she just couldn't wait any longer. His fingers started to fumble with the hem of her dress. Her body automatically recoiled. It suddenly felt so wrong.

She pushed him away. Philip stared back at her in shock as she struggled to find something to say.

"What about dessert?" she asked as airily as she could.

"I've got dessert right here."

He descended on her again, but she forced him back, unable to stand another second of his touch. Philip finally took the hint and drew away, confusion flickering in his eyes. She felt just as confused.

This is what she'd wanted, wasn't it? And yet, when Philip touched her, when he kissed her, it didn't feel like it did with Felix. Her body didn't react the same way. While her brain had been telling her that Philip was the one from the start, her body couldn't lie. *Perhaps,* she thought, *it's time to let my heart have a say too.*

Addison shook her head as though waking from a really long dream. "I'm sorry. It's getting late. I should go."

She couldn't look him in the eye. Heck, she didn't even know how she'd look her own reflection in the eye when she got home.

"Of course," he said. "I'm sorry."

"Don't be sorry." She smiled warmly at him. It wasn't him; it was *her.* "I had a wonderful time tonight, but I should get going."

"I'll show you out." A crease formed between his eyebrows, but he held out a gentlemanly hand to help her to her feet.

They were silent as they headed down the sweeping staircase to the foyer. Addison was relieved when she finally pulled on her shrug, ready to leave.

"Will you still be going to the gala?" Philip asked.

"I will." Addison grinned but couldn't seem to make it reach her eyes. "I'll see you there."

He looked disappointed but covered it with a

gracious smile as he opened the front door for her. "Great. I'll see you there."

Although she'd agreed to be his date, she was so flustered at the moment. It wasn't a yes, but it wasn't a no. She needed time to think.

"Thank you for a nice evening." To make sure he knew she meant it, she stood on her tiptoes and kissed him goodnight on the cheek. "I look forward to seeing you again." Because she did. She just didn't know in what capacity anymore.

Outside, the night felt colder. She wrapped her arms around herself and headed for her car. Once inside, she sighed and looked at her phone. There was a text from Felix.

Checked the house. Your boyfriend, Prince Charming, appears to be clean. Enjoy your fantasy.

23

A DOG'S CHANCE

The princess was supposed to run to the prince and his castle, not away from it. But that's exactly what Addison was doing, speeding away in her Mini. No. Not away from Philip, not permanently, anyway. Or maybe she was. She didn't know what to think anymore.

Seeing Felix there had thrown her off, and it wasn't just because three's a crowd. She couldn't deny it anymore. She had feelings for Felix. Strong ones, and that wasn't just her hormones talking. They were genuine feelings that she'd been pushing away from the start. And why? Because he wasn't the Prince Charming she'd always imagined she'd end up with?

Although they'd had a rocky start, things seemed different now that she knew him better.

She'd pegged Felix as the court jester, but maybe he'd been the prince all along. Well, in his own way.

He might not have been the knight in shining armor she'd always dreamed of. He was a different kind of hero. One that battled the nine-to-five workweek, vanquished utility bills, and conquered the home-cooked meal.

Addison gripped the steering wheel until it hurt. How wrong she'd had it. Right from the moment she'd first met him.

Each new thing she'd learned about him opened her eyes to a different man, a change from her usual fantasy. But this wasn't a fantasy. This was reality, and Felix, as rough around the edges as he was, was a real man. One who was looking for "something more."

Addison paused at the next stop sign and considered, for about the hundredth time, what that might look like. It would mean picnics in the park with Felix and Naia, nights spent watching Disney movies in pillow forts, eating bubblegum ice cream, and more showers with Felix.

This could be life's way of offering her something she'd been denying herself because she thought it impossible. She just had to stop being so obstinate and reach out and grab it.

Addison hadn't noticed the smile spreading across her face until her cheeks hurt. But now that she was imagining a life with Felix and Naia, it wouldn't go away.

However, those big decisions would have to wait. For now, there was work to do. She'd spent the night on what she thought would be a magical date with Philip when she should have been helping Felix solve the mystery of the disappearing dogs.

She drove aimlessly through the rolling streets of San Francisco, considering what her next move should be. All signs led to more dogs being taken at the gala on Friday night. She knew Zoe had pulled out all the stops for security measures, but what if the dognapper crashed the party and got to the rest of the show dogs? Then they would have accomplished what they'd set out to do, and Addison's leads would go cold. Her chance of catching the criminal would slip through her fingers. Addison and Felix would forever be dog show pariahs.

Ever since their meeting with Felix's friend Charlotte, something had been eating away at Addison. Okay, some of that she could now admit had been jealousy, but that wasn't the only reason. Charlotte was edgy when they'd questioned her. She was hiding something; Addison was sure of it. Felix was just too close to see it.

Pulling into a 7-Eleven, Addison parked to check her trusty notebook. She still had Charlotte's address from her previous research. She punched it into her phone and found it on the map. It was on the way home.

There was no harm in driving by the place, maybe peeking in a window or two. Right?

When Addison pulled onto the Sunset-area street, it was like driving between two colorful walls. Solid row houses lined both sides of the street, not a breath between them. Even in the dark, she could see siding rotting away, paint chipping, and windows cracking.

Street parking was scarce, but she found a free spot farther down the street, far enough away that she wouldn't be spotted. The streetlight above her car had burned out, casting her in shadow as she watched the house for signs of life.

The lights inside Charlotte's plain marina-style home were off. Sporadic flashing through the angled bay windows on the second story told Addison that the TV was on. Someone was home.

She shut off the engine and killed the lights. Sitting back, she watched the flickering windows. Only a few minutes went by before she saw a female-esque figure pass in front of a window, blocking the TV's light for a second as she sat down in front of it.

Addison held off a while longer to see if Charlotte was alone. To pass the time, she checked her website for any online reservations for the spa.

When her calendar popped up on the screen, she grimaced. No bookings.

Pampered Puppies still got the odd walk-in from random passersby who hadn't heard of the place, but work had nearly trickled to a stop. If her business had been a movie, she would have sent it out of theaters and onto Netflix a week ago.

How things had changed for her. Only a few months earlier, she'd presented her business plan to Aiden as an investor. She'd shown him numbers, pie charts, customer surveys, and market comparisons. Her Fido Fashion line was going to be a tremendous success. There was a demand for it, a hole in the market that her designs were perfect to fill.

It had been on track to be a blockbuster. Instead, it was turning into a straight-to-DVD, right-to-the-bargain-bin idea. She'd never be able to help her dad and Dora now. She just hoped their love life wasn't about to become as messy as hers.

Keeping her eye on Charlotte's house, Addison checked the RSVPs for her fashion show. She held her breath as the screen refreshed. Then it whooshed out in a disappointed sigh as the message popped up.

Zero guests.

Her grip tightened around her phone, breaking off a pink rhinestone. She wasn't giving up that easily. Tucking the phone into her jacket pocket, she slipped out of her car and onto the sidewalk. The street was poorly lit, helping to conceal her, but she was still cautious.

Addison's head swiveled on the lookout for witnesses. Thankfully, it was late enough that most of the neighbors had turned in for the night. When the coast looked clear, she approached Charlotte's home.

Since the marina-style house sat above the garage, most of the windows were on the second story. Her recon mission was going to take some acrobatics.

So far, she'd been lucky enough to spy on suspects living in wealthy homes. However, in typical San Francisco fashion, Charlotte's run-down row house was crammed between two identical houses. She studied the stucco facade, searching for a way up to the second story.

A drainpipe ran down one corner of the house. She shook it to check for sturdiness and then tested her weight on the bracket, bouncing on it a couple of times.

Headlights flashed against the white stucco. A car was coming. Her throat tightened.

Addison dove behind an oversized bush bursting with trumpet-shaped flowers. She squeezed between it and the house's rough siding just as the rumbling engine drew near. She waited for it to fade into the distance, but the noise slowed to a chug. Gravel crunched as the car pulled up to the curb, the engine puttering just outside her hiding spot.

The driver shut off the engine. It clicked so loudly as it cooled down that it was like a hammer banging in the night on the quiet street. Or maybe that was Addison's heart.

Keys jingled, a door slammed, heavy footsteps approached.

Addison held as still as she could. A mere twitch would send the leaves rustling and give her away. Something tickled her arm, and she squirmed, imagining it to be the worst kind of shrub spider there was. But she gritted her teeth and hoped the person would pass by and keep on walking.

Then the footsteps changed rhythm. They were climbing Charlotte's stairs. Of all the houses on the street, why that one?

The doorbell rang inside Charlotte's home. There was shuffling from within as she came to answer the door.

It's a bit late for a visit, Addison thought. Charlotte must have known the person. Either it was a booty call or a meeting she didn't want anyone to know about—sometimes those things were synonymous.

But only two days remained until the dog show began. Something told Addison the chances were slim that it was just an average house call. Everyone knew secret bad guy dealings only happened at night. Every blockbuster thriller couldn't be wrong. If that were the case, she'd be ready with her phone to record the two evildoers explaining their dognapping plans in detail, which is what bad guys always did.

Careful not to rustle the leaves, Addison peered around the corner to Charlotte's door. The man's face was turned away from her, but she'd recognize that backside in those faded jeans any day. Felix.

Her eyes widened. Through the gaps in the bush, she could see the van parked next to the sidewalk with *Joe's Dive* written on the side.

Addison was shaking worse than ever now. Maybe because Felix would be pissed if he knew she was there spying on Charlotte. Or maybe it was because of what had passed between them at Philip's house. But she knew it was really due to jealousy. It flared inside of her at the sight of him standing at Charlotte's door.

Addison's breaths left her in panicked pants until she worried that he might hear. There was a squeak as the front door opened.

"Felix," Charlotte said. "I'm so glad you came."

There was so much longing in her voice, almost desperate with emotion—like she would have burst into tears if he'd taken any longer to arrive.

"Of course I came. I'll always come when you call." His response was thick with sincerity.

Addison closed her eyes. She'd thought this was an evil rendezvous, but she'd realized a long time ago that Felix couldn't be involved in the dognapping. He had too much on the line. So, did that mean his visit was for the other reason? Was he there for a booty call? But Felix said he and Charlotte were just friends, so it couldn't be. It just couldn't.

Her hands balled at her sides, her gel nails digging into her soft skin until she wanted to cry out. Their voices faded as Felix went inside. The door closed, and Addison was alone again.

Scrambling out of her hiding spot, she returned to the drainpipe and crammed her designer high heels onto the bracket. Thankfully, the pointed toes fit nicely into the space.

Using the drainpipe and the electrical pipe running next to it, she shimmied her way up the front of the house. She broke two nails along the way, and her shoes slipped and scraped over the metal, probably rubbing the leather raw—at least she'd bought them on a wicked online sale.

Finally, she reached the windowsill on the second floor. The rotted wood crumbled beneath her fingers, but she leaned against it to peer into the living room. The split in her dress allowed her to sprawl against the facade of the house like Spider-Man. She knew that if anyone drove by at that moment, she'd be totally busted, but she just couldn't resist.

Addison was just in time to see them climb to the top of the stairs. Charlotte flicked on a warm living room light. Felix pulled off his leather jacket, looking at ease in the home. He'd barely hung it on the coat rack before Charlotte threw herself into his arms.

Addison gasped. Her foot slipped, and she gripped the windowsill for dear life. But instead of climbing back down to safety, she leaned in closer. She had to know what was going on. She had to be sure.

Her breath fogging up the window, she waited for Felix to shove Charlotte away, to hold up a hand and say, "Sorry, but there's only one woman for me." And, of course, that one woman would be Addison.

But he didn't. Because she'd insulted him; she'd dismissed him time and time again. Just two hours before, she'd told him she didn't want him, and then he'd had to watch her make out with another man.

Felix didn't hesitate. His arms circled Charlotte, drawing her close to him as he rubbed her back. She slumped against him in relief.

Addison couldn't see what happened after that, because everything was suddenly blurry. She reached up to the window to wipe away the fog.

Then she realized it was her tears obscuring the view.

Climbing back down to ground level, Addison headed for her car. All she wanted now was to go home to Princess, eat a whole gallon of triple chocolate ice cream, and watch a marathon of chick flicks because there was nothing left for her there. That happily ever after was now a happily never after.

24

WIENERELLA

High heels and wingtips click-clacked on weathered wooden planks over the dark waters of the bay. Rocking gently on the waves that lapped at the dock posts, the *San Francisco Belle* stood like a grand river castle. Only instead of turrets and throne rooms, it boasted three enclosed decks topped with a sundeck to enjoy the clear night. Its king was its captain, and its loyal subjects were show dogs and their humans.

Addison stood at the bottom of the gangway, admiring the paddleboat. Strings of lights wrapped around every railing and post to create a magical effect, lighting up the turn-of-the-last-century riverboat, a floating lantern in the night.

Cinderella had made it to the ball. Well, Addison certainly felt like Cinderella in her pink and black tulle ball gown. Even Princess had pulled out all the stops in her morganite necklace collar and matching tiara from the high end of the Fido Fashion line.

In other words, they looked fabulous, and they were ready to attend the ball. Only it wasn't to meet Addison's prince. Her prince had turned out to be, well, someone else's prince. And Philip? She supposed it was still a possibility. That was why she'd agreed to meet him at the gala. To give it a chance.

Philip was still all those things she'd first thought him to be: handsome, magnanimous, polite. But somehow all those things had lost their appeal.

Every time she tried to conjure an image of Mr. Perfect, Felix's face would pop into her fantasy. That opened the floodgates to all sorts of funny feelings. She imagined it was how Oscar nominees felt when the drums rolled and the winner's name boomed through the speakers … and it wasn't theirs.

Addison raised her chin and mentally focused on the night ahead. She wasn't there for the prince anyway. Sure, Philip would be there, and she'd talk to him, dance with him, give him a chance—because maybe even Cinderella had doubts. But first and foremost, she was there to protect the remaining dogs and hopefully catch the criminal in the act, if they were stupid enough to try anything.

Grasping her oversized skirts, Addison hoisted them up and squeezed her way across the narrow gangway with Princess in tow on her jeweled leash. The doxie's glittering open-pawed shoes sparkled beneath the multitude of string lights as they approached the boat.

There to greet them at the other end was someone who, if the dog doo hit the hair dryer that night, Addison knew would have her back.

"Zoe!"

Her friend looked up from her tablet. She held out her arms and hugged Addison in the manner reserved for women who are all dolled up and don't want to smudge makeup or mess up over-styled hair.

"Addy, I'm so glad you came."

"I wouldn't miss it for the world." Addison re-mained in her friend's arms a few seconds longer than normal, soaking up the love.

She'd texted Piper and Zoe for some moral support late the night before, so they were up to speed. Addison definitely needed some girl time.

Zoe gave her an extra squeeze. "You look great."

"Thanks for not crossing me off the guest list," Addison said. "I'm sure there will be more than one guest not thrilled to see me tonight."

"If they've got a problem with my guest list, they can deal with me." Zoe flicked her jet-black

349

hair. "Besides, it's not a party if my best friends aren't here."

Addison pitied any soul who took on Zoe. "Are Piper and Aiden here already?"

"Yeah, I think they're at the bar on the second deck."

An older couple crossed the gangway behind Addison, holding their pugs in their arms. Zoe brought up the guest list on her tablet again. Since Addison's massive dress was blocking the entrance, she stepped onto the boat.

"Go enjoy yourself," Zoe told her. "You can leave Princess on the sundeck. She'll be safe up there."

"Thanks."

"Oh yeah," Zoe called after her. "I should warn you. Holly Hart's here." She pulled a face. "Sorry. She's someone's plus-one."

"Great." Addison rolled her eyes. Just what she needed. "Good luck tonight." She waved as she headed through the double doors into the enclosed lower deck.

The moment she stepped inside, Addison felt wrapped in luxury. It wasn't what she'd expected the interior of a boat to look like. Rich carpet softened her steps as she made her way to the central lobby staircase that doubled back on itself overhead. The chandelier dangling from the very top shed warm light on the gold banisters and swirling rail designs.

Drawn by their beauty, she ignored the elevator sign and picked up Princess. Hoisting her skirts, she climbed to the very top. A secondary staircase led her to the sundeck. As she stepped out into the open air, her heels sank into soft grass. The entire sundeck had been laid with sod for the dogs to play and roll around on.

A white picket fence wrapped around the deck rail, a cute continuation of the yard theme. It also prevented the curious teacups and minis from squeezing through the rail gaps and doing somersault dives into the water far below.

A dog-watcher wearing a postal worker costume approached Addison. She snickered but didn't think the watcher would find it funny, so she stifled it before she handed Princess over to him.

The watcher took her name and asked for ID. She gave her doxie a kiss goodbye before Princess trotted over for a drink of water from an oversized dish that looked like a toilet bowl. Addison watched Princess for a few moments, hesitant to leave her behind. As she eyed the other guests on the deck, they seemed just as nervous.

As though sensing her reluctance, the watcher said, "Don't worry. They're perfectly safe up here. There are only two entrances onto this deck." He pointed them out on each side of the grassy area. "We keep track of everyone who comes and goes from here."

She knew he was right. They were three stories high. Besides, she couldn't very well keep Princess with her while she was trying to investigate.

"Thanks," she told him.

"And if it's an evacuation you're worried about, the kennels on board are all designed to float on water."

He gestured to the boat's starboard side, where enough kennels to house every dog stood in a row. Watertight seals surrounded their clear plastic doors, and breathing holes punctured the tops to provide enough air. The oversized bases looked heavy enough to keep them upright but buoyant enough to float even a mastiff.

Addison wondered if she should remind him that dogs could actually swim. Then she remembered how far they'd be from shore and how small and delicate some of the show dogs aboard would be. Floating kennels was actually a pretty good idea, even if it was just for the owners' peace of mind. Zoe had thought of everything.

With one more glance at Princess—who'd found a stuffed cat toy to chew on—she went to look around the deck. Although there were dog-watchers to pick up after the guests, she hiked up her dress, careful not to drag it as she made her way to the rail.

She peered over the white picket fence at the view of the docks below. Zoe couldn't have picked a more perfect venue. The paddleboat must have been forty or fifty feet tall, which meant that once they'd cast off, no one—with two legs or four—was going to sneak on or off the boat. The dogs would be safe.

Maybe Addison really had nothing to worry about after all. Then again, that wasn't a good thing. If it was impossible to steal more dogs, that meant no opportunity to uncover the dognapper.

Deckhands scrambled below, their movements practiced and swift as they prepared to cast off. Addison studied them with suspicion, watching for any odd behaviors or clues. She kept her eyes peeled for grappling hooks or suction cups stuffed into their pockets, revealing them as some kind of *Mission: Impossible* agents or something.

Just as they were unraveling the thick rope that fastened the *Belle* to the dock, she noticed a few latecomers scurry toward the boat. Their shoes clacked musically on the dock, echoing across the water. The deckhands waved them on, waiting for them to board.

She saw only a flash of their faces before they boarded, but she recognized them instantly, like an image carved painfully into her heart. It was Felix, Naia, and Oliver. And he'd brought Charlotte as his date.

Addison drew back from the rail as if she'd been burned. Well, she supposed she had been. But wasn't she the one who had rejected him?

Scorned him? Insulted him? Sent him running into Charlotte's arms?

So why did it hurt to breathe? Those two pints of raspberry lemon ice cream she'd cried into last night couldn't have tightened the bodice on her dress that quickly. And it wasn't the cool night breeze that was making her eyes sting so badly …

Thunk.

The floor shook beneath her feet. A thunderous whistle released from somewhere above. Addison jumped, and her high heel stuck in the grass. The ship lurched, and she faltered.

Slowly, the *Belle* pulled away from the dock. The dogs were in a tizzy, barking because of the horn and then barking because of the barking. That's why she didn't hear anyone approach until a sharp finger tapped her bare shoulder.

Addison spun around. Her eyes narrowed when she saw who it was. "Penny."

"Haven't stolen enough dogs for your collection yet?"

Addison's teeth clenched. "I didn't take the dogs." She tried to go around the famed handler, but Penny blocked her path.

Out of the corner of her eye, Addison noticed Holly Hart lurking nearby. The reporter clung awkwardly to her phone like she was ready to record Addison and Penny if a cat fight, or rather dog fight, broke out.

Penny leered at Addison. "Even if you didn't

steal Lily, your carelessness makes you just as guilty as if you had."

"Lily wasn't even your dog."

"A handler loves their dog as much, if not more, than the owner. We train it, we shape it, mold it into the pinnacle of excellence. We become one with it. And you tore all that time, effort, and love away from me."

Over Penny's shoulder, Addison could see Kitty Carlisle. When Kitty's shifting eyes landed on Addison, she flinched. Picking up Elvis, she moved to the other side of the deck.

Groaning, Addison pushed past Penny. "I need a drink," she muttered to herself.

She descended the stairs and followed the sound of music through the double doors to the second deck. The clinking of glasses told her there was a bar nearby. *Good*, she thought. *I could use a drink.*

When she peered through the crowd, she spotted Piper and Aiden standing next to the rich mahogany and marble bar. As usual, they were unable to see anyone but each other. Even their two lovesick doxies had wound their leashes around their owners' legs to get as close as they could.

Thankfully, Aiden's attention was too focused on Piper to notice Addison. She wasn't ready to face him. Not yet. She still had hope, however small, that she could uncover the dognapper. She just had to keep her eyes peeled and be ready for anything.

A server carrying crystal dog bowls filled with amber liquid passed by. By the smell, Addison guessed it could only be Hound Hooch, liquefied chicken made to look like beer. To hide herself from the lovey-dovey couple, Addison ducked behind the server and kept pace as he swept to the other side of the room.

The server suddenly turned away, exposing her. Addison spun, hoping to find cover among eager dancers already heating up the floor to a waltz before dinner. However, she took one too many turns.

An elbow from a server, a stray hip from a dancer. Addison stumbled. Her heel caught on a piece of her tulle gown, and she skidded on the parquet floor.

Her hands flew out, reaching for the nearest thing. She grazed a cashmere jacket as she fell against a man.

Arms wrapped around her to brace her fall. When she opened her eyes, she found herself staring up at Philip.

"We've got to stop meeting like this," he said.

There was that smile that had so enamored her right from the start. He was still that smart, charming, polite man. He was a catch.

And because she'd made a promise to herself that she'd give him a chance, when he held out his hand and asked her, "May I have this dance?" she replied, "Of course."

She placed her hand in his. His hand trailed down her low-backed dress and pressed her closer to his tennis-toned body. Then he spun her around the dance floor.

Addison's rhinestones glittered beneath the chandeliers, and the tulle of her dress trailed delicately behind her as they spun over and over again. The waltz was so romantic, and the historic boat took her back to another time, another world. She became lost in the moment, the beauty, the fantasy, forgetting her doubts and her worries until she felt like a princess.

He dipped her low, and she let her head tilt back, enjoying the magic of it all. Then she saw someone enter the room: Felix.

Philip set Addison on her feet, grinning mischievously over his suave move, but she barely noticed.

On their next spin around a nearby couple, she glanced at the front doors again. Charlotte had her arm linked through Felix's, holding him tight—maybe a little possessively, Addison thought.

Felix's dark eyes scanned the room. Addison's head moved around to keep him in sight. When his gaze fell on her, she faltered and stepped on Philip's toe.

"Ouch," he hissed.

"Sorry," she mumbled, but she was too busy weaving and bobbing her head to get a better view.

Felix had shaved. He'd also trimmed his ebony waves and combed them back from his face. And was that …? Yes. He wore one of the bespoke suits they'd admired in the shop across from Joe's Dive.

He looked even better than Addison had thought he would. This new Felix was deceptive. This cleaned-up version looked civilized and blended in with the lavish surroundings. The way he carried himself, however, with that certain swagger and that piercing look, belied the capable, cunning man beneath.

He was so much more than everyone else in that room could know. Addison had only begun to learn how much more. Now, she supposed it would be Charlotte who would find out.

Addison lost the rhythm again and did a half turn instead of a quarter turn.

Philip winced. "Ouch."

"Sorry."

Philip led her around the dance floor, and the crowd swallowed Felix. Addison tugged, and dragged, and redirected their steps to get back on the other side again until she was practically leading. She moved her head this way and that to see over Philip's broad shoulders.

"Ouch," Philip said again.

His next few steps were more like limps. That's when Addison decided to ignore Felix entirely. He was there with someone else, after all. Not her. And Addison was here with Philip. *P-H-I-L-I-P*, she reminded herself sternly.

She turned her gaze upward and batted her eyelashes at him. He gave her a flirtatious wink. Or maybe it was another wince as she stomped on his foot again.

By the time they rounded the dance floor once more, she saw Felix and Charlotte cozied up in a dark, secluded corner. Charlotte leaned her face up toward Felix. He ducked his head so she could whisper sweet nothings in his ear.

Their faces were so close together, her lips almost brushing his cheek to be heard over the big band on the stage. He turned his face toward Charlotte as though about to kiss her.

Addison's eyes widened. Pressure built in her chest as she forgot to breathe.

"Oof." Philip lurched forward.

"Ouch!" Addison cried as he bumped into her.

"Sorry," they said simultaneously.

Addison belatedly realized that she'd stopped dancing altogether and had caused a traffic jam behind them on the dance floor. At that moment, thankfully, the song ended.

Addison gave a brief, bob-like curtsy. "Thank

you for the dance. Sorry. Must be the waves throwing me off-balance or something."

"No problem," Philip said, gracious enough not to point out that it wasn't really a wavy ride.

Near the edge of the parquet floor, Addison spotted Holly Hart holding her phone. She was looking down at the screen as though checking her messages. However, as Addison continued to stare at the reporter, a naughty smile creased the corners of Holly's eyes.

Was she following Addison around to record her? Maybe Holly was conducting her own investigation that night.

It was suddenly very warm in there. Too many people crowded that deck, too many people who hated Addison, who were waiting to see if she'd do something wrong. She needed to get out of there. But there was no way out, no way off that moving vessel beyond diving into the cold bay. She tucked it away as a good backup plan.

"Save another dance for me later?" she asked Philip.

He wiped her footprint off his wingtip shoe. "Maybe I'll buy you a drink instead."

She cringed sheepishly, but she was already backing away from the dance floor. "I'm going to go get some fresh air. Excuse me."

"Certainly."

She bumped Holly's shoulder as she passed, causing her to drop her phone. Addison "accidentally" kicked it across the floor somewhere. She ignored Holly's shouts at her back, just as she tried to ignore the suspicious looks from the other guests as she weaved through them.

They whispered behind their hands as she walked by. She could feel the blame in their postures and gazes. There were so many against her, rooting for her to fail. Even Felix's cool gaze swept over her blankly as she passed.

Addison's pace picked up as she headed for the exit. The room was suddenly too small, there were too many people, and was that three-hundred-foot boat really big enough for all of them? What was worse, hidden among them all could be the real bad guy, waiting for the right moment to strike again.

If Addison didn't catch them before the night was over, if they got away with it all again, those missing dogs would stay missing forever. Not to mention, her life would be ruined and this time for good. And she was already doing a fine job of accomplishing that all on her own.

25

WAGGING THE DOG

Addison burst through the doors and onto the outer deck of the *Belle*. She leaned against the rail, almost tempted to dive overboard to escape the suffocating feeling of being trapped on the paddleboat with so many people. People who hated her.

The crisp night air was like a splash of cold water on her bare shoulders. She reached back and swept the hair off her neck, but it only reminded her of the last time she'd felt claustrophobic, when Felix had braided her hair in the sauna. She let it drop again.

The dark bay water sparkled all around the boat with the reflection of thousands of string lights. They'd left the Embarcadero, behind with its busy streets and the ships coming and going from the piers. A haze had settled over San Francisco, blurring the bright cityscape as though it were one solid band of light. From a distance, the Financial District looked so magical and foreign.

The bay was dark and lonely except for the occasional boat floating by. The *Belle* leisurely chugged on, the paddle wheel churning at the back of the boat, urging the vessel beneath the Bay Bridge. Underneath the heavy sky, the bridge stood out like a thick black strip over Addison's head.

Her clutch suddenly vibrated in her hand. She popped the clasp and pulled out her phone. The display said *Dad*.

The tensed muscles in her back relaxed a little, and she answered. "Dad?"

"Hi, muffin. I thought you had your dog party tonight. I didn't expect you to answer. I was just going to leave a message."

"I'm just taking a break." *Sort of.* "What's up?"

"I just called to let you know that we got some good news tonight," he said. "We sold the corner store."

Addison's heart clenched, and she gripped the rail. "You did?"

There was silence on the other end before he said, "You don't sound as happy as I thought you would. Is everything okay?"

Addison's memories rushed back to her as she recalled all the movies she'd watched in that little corner store, how she'd do her homework behind the counter and wash windshields for a bit of pocket change to buy candy. She'd whiled away many happy childhood hours there. And then she considered all the years of hard work her dad had put into it, and for what? To sell it at a loss out of desperation?

Shaking off the emotions eating at her, Addison tried to put aside her own selfish disappointment at the news. Her dad seemed genuinely relieved.

"That's good news." She tried to put a smile on her face, as though he could see it. But it fell flat. "I just … I guess I hoped that I could help you somehow. That if my fashion line did well enough, I could pay you back for sending me to pet-grooming school, for all you've done to help me get set up here in the city."

"Sweetheart—"

"I know it wouldn't have been much, but it might have helped hold off the banks until … I don't know, until maybe business got better." Saying it out loud suddenly made her feel childish. Like she was holding on to an unrealistic fantasy —not for the first time that week, it turned out.

Her dad chuckled, but she could hear the kindness behind it. "I appreciate the thought. It's sweet. But you need to worry about yourself. Dora and I can take care of ourselves."

Addison sighed. "I guess I just worry about the

two of you. I know that things can get tough when money is tight."

"Dora and I will be just fine. We'll get through this. It's an opportunity to do something new, to have new experiences together."

He really sounded excited, and Addison knew that was probably Dora's doing. The corner store was the only thing her dad had ever known, while Dora was more of an adventurer. Whatever was about to come next would need a sense of adventure. Addison was glad that Dora was going to be the one beside him.

"So … you two are fine then?" she asked. "I mean, you and Dora are going to work through it together?"

"Of course." He laughed again, maybe in surprise. "Dora and I are partners. We'll get through anything that life throws at us. We love each other."

"But you and Mom—"

"Your mother and I were a lot of things, but we didn't have what it took to get through the bad times. We didn't have enough love. Dora and I have that. With enough love, you can make it through anything."

Addison knew that. Of course she did. But hearing it come from her father meant more than reading the adage off a bumper sticker or a coffee mug. After he'd lost so much because of money and had to work so hard for it, if he could still say that, then it must be true.

"That's good. I'm happy for the two of you." This time the smile on her face felt real.

"Don't worry about us," her dad said. "Who's the parent here, anyway? Shouldn't I be the one worrying about you?"

"I just wanted to make you proud, to show you that your sacrifices for me haven't been for nothing." And ever since the dogs had gone missing, she'd been feeling just that.

"You've made me so proud, and I'll be proud of you no matter what."

She picked at the railing's chipped paint. "No matter what?"

"Absolutely. Dora and I are looking forward to your fashion show on Sunday. We'll be the ones cheering in the front row."

Addison swallowed hard, wondering if there would even be a fashion show at this rate. However, there was still a chance. If she could uncover the dognappers, the fashion show might still be a success. It reminded her of why she'd come to the gala that night. It wasn't to dance with Philip or cry over Felix. It was her last chance to solve this mystery once and for all. Saying goodbye to her dad, she ended the call, feeling more determined than ever.

As she was tucking her phone away, the doors to the covered deck opened behind her. A bubble of laughter and the sounds of mingling drifted out.

"There's the prettiest woman at the ball."

Addison recognized Piper's voice. She turned to find her two besties coming out to join her.

"I'm sure Aiden would disagree with that statement," Addison told Piper.

"But Philip would agree," she said, with a hint of cheekiness. "I saw you two dancing. I take it the two of you are picking up where you left off on Wednesday night?"

"Maybe," Addison said. "I mean, he's a great guy."

Zoe narrowed her eyes skeptically. "Really? Is that why you were busy eyeing up that guy across the room?"

Addison wrinkled her nose, annoyed at getting caught. "I wasn't eyeing Felix."

"That was Felix?" Zoe's eyebrows shot up. Clearly, the suit was doing it for her too. "I thought I recognized Naia when they came aboard. He told me he couldn't find a babysitter. A few other guests brought older kids, so it wasn't a big deal."

Piper leaned on the rail next to Addison. "From the way you talked about him, he's not quite what I expected."

Addison laughed, but it sounded weak. "Yeah, me neither."

Piper and Zoe exchanged looks over Addison's

head, but it was Zoe, always so direct, who asked, "Want to talk about it?"

"I'm not sure." Addison stared down at the water rippling below them. "Have you ever wanted something so badly for so long that when you finally get it, you realize that it was only a nice dream? Because now that it's right in front of me, I'm not sure it's what I want anymore."

"Like a dog chasing its tail." Piper nodded. "When it finally catches it, it doesn't know what to do with it and lets it go."

"Something like that," she said. "Maybe Philip's my tail."

"So, if not Philip, then who do you want?" Zoe asked.

Addison had been thinking about it so much lately, but it was scarier to admit it out loud, especially to the two people who knew her best. "Something I didn't even realize I wanted. Something I thought I could never have."

"A tattoo?" Zoe asked.

"Zero-calorie ice cream," Piper suggested.

Addison laughed, happy she still knew how to do that. "A family."

Piper slung an arm around her. "We're your family, Addy. We always will be. You know that, right?"

"Thanks. I feel the same way." She rested her head on Piper's shoulder. "But you know what I mean. One to go home to at the end of the day."

"Are we just speaking hypothetically?" Zoe asked. "Or do you have a particular family in mind?"

"Well, I …" Addison thought she had, maybe, possibly. But after watching Felix and Charlotte board the *Belle*, she realized that boat had sailed. "I don't think so. Not anymore."

Zoe's tablet jingled, so she checked it. "Crap. It's almost time for dinner to begin."

"That's okay," Addison said. "Go ahead. You've got a busy night. We'll talk later."

Piper squeezed her a little tighter. "Are you going to be okay?"

"I will be." Maybe she'd lost her chance with Felix, but at least she was on track to figuring out what she really needed. It was time to wake up and find her happiness. Not just dream about it.

"We are long overdue for a sleepover," Zoe said. "How about later this weekend, after all your fashion show busyness is over?"

Addison smiled, putting on a brave face for her friends. "For sure. We'll catch up."

Zoe gave her a wink before fitting an earpiece into her ear—very official looking—and heading up the stairs. A few minutes later, her sensual voice carried over the *Belle*'s intercom system.

"Attention, please. Dinner is about to be served. Will everyone kindly make their way to the lower deck? We will begin in fifteen minutes."

"Are you coming?" Piper asked Addison.

"Yeah, I'll be right there."

Piper waved goodbye and headed back inside. Addison resumed her contemplative position at the deck rail, but this time, she wasn't lost in her thoughts. She was watching the guests filter downstairs.

She kept her eyes peeled for clues. But no one was wearing ski masks or creeping along with big sacks of puppies slung across their backs. In fact, almost no one had a dog with them at all. The few people who had brought their furry friends had left them on the sundeck.

Once the coast was clear, Addison hurried back inside. The parquet dance floor clicked under her heels as she scoped out the nearly empty room. It was the size of a traditional ball-room, broken up only by the ornate support columns. She weaved in and out of them, trying to act casual while she searched for potential evildoers.

Her eyes flitted to the people still in the room, mostly workers. On the small stage, band members tuned their instruments. The bartender placed fresh glasses behind the bar and restocked the liquor. Servers cleared away empty cocktail glasses. The only shifty-looking one seemed to be her.

Addison skirted around the side of the bar to head for the back staircase. As she passed by, she noticed a clipboard on the counter with a list of all the guests' names. She glanced over at the bartender. He had his back to her.

Tucking her clutch under her arm, Addison swiped the clipboard and kept on moving before he noticed. She climbed the stairs to the third enclosed deck, holding the list aloft, very official-like. But the deck, which had been set up for after-dinner cocktails, was deserted.

Tired of taking the stairs in high heels, Addison headed for the elevator inside. Once she squeezed into it, her poofy dress took up half of the enclosed space. It was like shoving an open umbrella into a car.

She hit the button for the first deck and held her dress aside until the door slid closed. At the last second, an arm shot out, stopping it from shutting. When the metal door slid open, Felix was standing on the other side.

Addison blinked. "Oh, hi."

"Hi." He hesitated in the door. "What are you doing here? Shouldn't you be down at dinner?"

"I'm casing the joint." She figured some vernacular would help her seem far more qualified to do it on her own than she felt.

He took her in from top to bottom, his gaze finally landing on the clipboard in her hand. "Are you helping your friend with the event?"

"No. I just thought the guest list might come in handy."

Felix nodded. "Good thinking."

He was still propping the door open, but then it began to alarm. He shuffled inside the elevator, somewhat reluctantly. Addison tried to hold aside her marshmallow dress to create room, but the space was so tight that he still had to press up against her.

A few moments of awkward elevator silence passed. Neither of them knew where to look. There wasn't even cheesy music to help ease the tension.

"You look pretty," Felix finally said.

When Addison glanced at him, his expression was open, earnest. He was there with Charlotte, so he just meant to be nice. But when he kept staring, Addison fidgeted uncomfortably and looked away.

"Thank you," she said. "You look good in that suit."

"I had a good fashion advisor."

Addison smiled at that but didn't know what else to say. The elevator dinged as they reached their destination. The door slid open.

She hoisted her skirt, about to step out of the elevator, but she couldn't seem to make her legs move. There was so much she wanted to say, but she didn't know where to begin or if she should say anything at all.

Felix was the first to speak. "I see you came with Philip tonight." He said it so casually, but he was hiding some emotion. Whatever it was, it seemed raw because the vein on his forehead stood out.

"I did." *Sort of.* But she wasn't getting into it. Like he was one to judge, anyway. "Where's your date?"

"Charlotte knows I need to check the place out for clues, so she's watching Naia for me on the sundeck." As the door closed, Felix stopped it and gestured for her to go first, like that was that.

Addison frowned, imagining Felix and Charlotte going on stakeouts together and making out in saunas. "I suppose she's helping you track down the dognappers now?"

"She is, actually. What? Are you jealous?"

"Yes."

The truth slipped out in a light breath, so quiet she hadn't realized it came out of her own mouth until his head whipped toward her. By the expression on his face, he clearly wondered if he'd imagined it too.

The honesty and earnestness in that one word surprised even her. It hung in the air between them, filling the silent elevator.

Felix opened his mouth to speak, but whatever he was about to say was cut off by a loud blast from the boat's horn.

Startled, Addison jumped. A high-pitched hum from the engine vibrated the floor beneath their feet. There was a sudden change in speed, like the boat had slammed on its brakes—if it even had brakes.

The lurch shook Felix and Addison in the small space. She fell against him. His arms automatically came up and wrapped around her. Being held by him, his touch, his hands—unlike Philip's—felt warm and right … like home.

The elevator door timed out and closed. Addison wanted to stay there forever, but she was dimly aware of hollering outside their little moment. Dishes clattered on the dining deck and footsteps shuffled through the lobby.

After a moment, Felix pressed the *door open* button. By the time the door slid aside, the lobby was filled to capacity.

Most of the dinner guests had pressed their way to the bow of the boat. Those who couldn't fit on the outer deck rubbernecked for a view of whatever was going on outside.

Their awkwardness forgotten, Felix and Addison shared a look. The foreboding in the air made her shiver.

Felix stepped out, and she squeezed her puffy dress through the elevator doors to follow him. They didn't get any farther, since it was elbow-to-elbow. Chatter drifted back through the crowd like a game of telephone.

"We hit something," someone said.

"Who's driving this thing?" a random voice demanded.

"Oh, my God!" a man cried out. "Are we sinking?"

Addison turned to the woman next to her. "Did we hit the shore?"

"I don't know," she answered. "But I wonder if my baby is okay. The dogs probably got quite a fright up there."

Addison tuned into the sounds outside of the chaotic lobby. She couldn't hear any barking, just the captain arguing with someone from his wheel-house on the top deck.

"Felix!" a female voice called out.

Addison recognized Charlotte's voice and turned to find her pushing her way through the crowd. Along the way, Charlotte got a few nasty looks and a "Hey, watch it!" She didn't seem to care.

By the time she reached Addison and Felix, she was huffing, her cheeks flushed pink. "Felix. Here you are. I've been looking everywhere for you."

"What's wrong?" Felix glanced behind her. "Where's Naia?"

She shook her head, her chin quivering slightly. "I'm so sorry. I've looked everywhere for her. I thought maybe she'd found you somehow."

"You mean you don't know where she is?" His voice was loud, even among the excited chatter around them. He took a deep breath through his nose before continuing. "All right, when did you last see her?"

"Fifteen minutes ago, maybe. I-I don't know what happened. She was with me the whole time. I only turned my back for like a second, I swear. When I turned around, she was gone."

Felix laid a hand on her arm and spoke calmly to her. "Don't worry. I'm sure she's still up there somewhere, or maybe she snuck away to the dessert bar. We'll go up and look."

But when he turned back to the elevator, his actions were anything but calm. He jabbed the elevator button repeatedly until Addison thought it might break. Finally, the door slid open.

Before he got in, he looked over his shoulder. His face creased with fear, and his eyes filled with pleading. "Addison?" His voice cracked.

Felix didn't have to say any more. Addison squeezed her oversized dress inside to join them. "I'll help you find her."

His hand shook slightly as he reached out and hit the button for the third deck.

"Oh, Felix." Charlotte suddenly sobbed. "I'm so sorry. I swear I only looked away for a second."

"I know," he said. "We'll find her."

"But I've looked everywhere, and they had the doors closed and the gates in front of the stairs to keep the dogs from escaping. I don't think she could have gotten out that way. I just don't know where else she could be. And there are all those railings and she's so little. And what if—" She hiccupped. "What if …?" Charlotte broke down into full sobs, unable to say the words.

The color drained from Felix's face, and he didn't look like he wanted to hear any more.

"The fence is too tall," Addison cut in. "She couldn't have climbed over or squeezed through any of the gaps. They secured the entire deck for teacup dogs," she assured Felix. "Naia would have been fine."

Felix nodded, looking slightly relieved by the news. Charlotte was still crying. He reached out and rubbed her back as she wept against his chest.

"I'm so sorry Felix," she said, between gasps for air. "You trusted me with her and … I'm going to make such a terrible mother."

Addison's head whipped to Charlotte, her mouth dropping open, but neither she nor Felix seemed to notice. Addison glanced from the server to Felix and back again.

Mother? Charlotte didn't mean … Wasn't it a little too soon to be talking like that? They'd only just started dating.

But Addison couldn't ignore the ache in her chest, reminding her that Felix and Charlotte were close. They'd worked together for years. He always defended her, protected her, and, after what Addison had witnessed in Charlotte's home, there could be no doubt. Heck, it wasn't even like she knew a lot about Felix's past. Maybe they'd dated before.

Charlotte and Felix were obviously serious. Maybe it was just meant to be. Isn't that what Addison had told Felix when he'd asked about Philip? *When it's right, it's right.*

Addison stared down at the clipboard in her hands, unable to look at the two of them together anymore. She wondered if they were on the longest elevator ride in history. At least Addison had never lost Naia. Well, maybe she did, but only for a second, and she wasn't really missing. She was in Oliver's kennel the whole time.

Addison gasped. "That's it!"

Charlotte pulled away and wiped her face with the back of her hand. "What's it?"

"Naia must be in Oliver's kennel."

Felix seemed to exhale a thousand held breaths. "Of course. She was scared of coming on the boat. That's why she wanted to stay with Oliver on the sundeck, because she felt safer up there with him."

Charlotte just blinked. "I didn't even think to look."

"She does it all the time at home," he told her.

"It makes sense," Charlotte said. "I knew she couldn't have gotten off that floor."

The moment the doors opened, Felix ran for the stairs to the sundeck, taking two at a time.

Charlotte followed close behind, but Addison struggled to keep up with them in her high heels.

On her way to the stairs, she passed the captain and a few of the other staff heading to deal with whatever was going on below. They nodded their heads but otherwise took no note of her.

She leaned over the side rail to see what the holdup was. The *Belle* had collided with another smaller recreational vessel. The boater was busy arguing with the staff on the first deck even though it was clear he was the one who'd T-boned them.

Squeezing into the stairwell, Addison followed Charlotte and Felix to the top, hoping that she was right and Naia was safe in Oliver's kennel. But before she even got to the last steps, she felt something was off.

She would have expected, with all the commotion down below, that the dogs would be barking. But the only yapping and barking were coming from the human guests down on the first deck.

The bodice on Addison's dress seemed tighter than ever. She strained to hear any doglike noises coming from the top deck, but it was eerily silent. When she shot out the top of the staircase, she saw why.

The entire sundeck was deserted. All the dogs, all the kennels, and all the watchers were gone. Including Princess and Oliver. And Naia.

In the middle of the grass, Charlotte had sunk

to her knees. Her shoulders shook with silent tears. Felix stood off to the side, staring blankly into his hands.

The clipboard dropped from Addison's grip, clattering to the floor. Her legs moved toward him without even thinking about it. As she got closer, she realized Felix was holding something: Naia's stuffed bunny.

Addison's footsteps faltered at the sight of the stuffed animal in his hand, limp and bereft of its owner. Felix's fist clenched around the toy. He turned to face her.

"She's gone," he told her. "Naia's gone."

The deck swam before her eyes, and her stomach felt like it had turned inside out. The dognapper had struck again. Only now, they were also a kidnapper.

26

SEA DOGS

Felix stood in the middle of the sundeck's makeshift lawn, running one hand over his head, gripping his hair like he wanted to rip it out. The other clutched Naia's stuffed bunny. His mouth opened in a wordless scream before his chin dropped to his chest, and he closed his eyes.

Addison was afraid to touch him. He looked about ready to explode or maybe curl up into the fetal position and cry. She didn't know which one would be worse. All she knew was she wanted to hold him and tell him it would be all right.

But Charlotte was with him, murmuring that it would be okay, that his daughter was probably still on the ship somewhere. Addison turned away to give them privacy, but she doubted very much that Charlotte was right. By the look on Felix's face, so did he.

Addison wanted to search the sundeck, search the whole ship, the surrounding waters. All the show dogs disappearing at once could only mean one thing. The dognappers had gotten what they finally wanted, and then some.

Princess. A tear rolled down her cheek before she even knew she was crying. Addison felt both distraught and selfish at the same time. Felix was missing his daughter, his baby, and she was crying over her dog. But in a way, Princess was Addison's baby. If she wasn't, then why did it feel like someone had taken one of the silver spoons from the dining deck and hollowed out her insides?

She wished she had a DeLorean like in *Back to the Future* to go back in time. She would tell her past self not to bring Princess that night, to leave her at home. She'd tell Felix not to bring Naia. Heck, while she was at it, she'd kiss Felix on Philip's balcony rather than push him away.

Her head spun, caught in a useless cycle of regrets and random thoughts—fear for her precious Princess, guilt for worrying about Princess when Naia was missing too, pity for Felix. She glanced at him again, but he was holding Charlotte now, so she turned away and added self-loathing to the mix of emotions circulating through her.

Hugging herself, Addison shuffled to the back of the boat, heels sinking into the fresh sod. She leaned against the white picket fence and stared out into the night.

There was quiet splashing in the water below. Addison thought it came from the bow where the deckhands attempted to dislodge the small boat that crashed into the *Belle*. But then there was another splash close by. It was soft and rhythmic, coming from the stern.

She peered into the night. More fog had rolled in since she was last outside. Maybe that was why the recreational boat hadn't seen the *Belle*. However, she couldn't see how, since it was a three-hundred-foot-long floating torch made up of string lights.

The bay water reflected the boat's light like a halo around them before fading to black in the distance. She searched for the source of the splashing and saw a dark shape drifting against the sparkling ripples. It was a boat big enough for about ten people.

Oars dipped in and out of the water as it rowed away. In the glow of all the string lights, gold letters flashed along the side of its hull. *San Francisco Belle*. It was one of the *Belle*'s lifeboats. And inside the hull was a stack of boxes.

Addison's frantic brain finally caught up with the scene playing out before her. They weren't boxes. They were dog kennels.

The kennels. The dogs. Naia. Princess. Her knees buckled, and she gripped the railing for support.

The dognappers were right there, so close. Addison should have been able to hear the dogs' barking and whining echo across the water, but they were silent. Her mouth went dry as she considered why.

"Felix." Her voice was barely a whisper. She licked her lips and tried again. "Felix, look!"

It felt like a bad dream. Surely, this wasn't happening. She couldn't be the only one seeing this happen. But then again, at that very moment, all the guests and crew were distracted at the bow.

She suddenly saw the "accident" for what it was: a distraction. The smaller boat intentionally ran into them. But surely all the dog-watchers hired to watch over the show dogs hadn't run to gawk at the accident. Where were they?

Addison heard Felix's footsteps swish across the grass, but she didn't want to take her eyes away from the shape in case she blinked and lost it. She pointed straight out into the darkness. Felix's eyes followed her finger. She knew he saw it when his grip tightened around one of the fake fence posts, which broke off in his hand.

She blinked. The lifeboat disappeared from the *Belle*'s aura of light, blending into the foggy night.

Addison yelled, "Stop!" But her voice was drowned out by a long blast of the ship's horn.

The *Belle*'s engine whirred somewhere in its depths. The dark waters below churned around the stern of the boat until it looked like boiling water. The paddle wheel slowly began to turn. The *Belle* inched forward, in the opposite direction of the dogs.

Felix threw the piece of wood aside. "We have to go after them."

Charlotte started for the stairs. "I'll go talk to the captain."

He shook his head. "They'll be long gone by the time we dock."

Addison barely heard them. Her eyes scanned the crime scene, searching for a solution. She found it at the back of the boat.

"Maybe we don't have to wait," Addison told Felix, pointing to the other side of the ship. "Look. There's another lifeboat. They haven't gone far. We can follow them."

Felix tucked Naia's bunny into his jacket pocket, charging toward the spare lifeboat. Addison hurried after him, her heels digging into the grass like lawn darts, slowing her down.

By the time she reached the boat, Felix had already climbed inside. He grabbed the power controls to lower it into the water.

"Wait. Where are you going?" Charlotte asked him.

"To get my daughter back."

"We haven't even called nine-one-one yet," she said. "Why don't you wait for the police?"

"That will take too long. We haven't been able

385

to catch this guy yet. If we let him go now, we might not find Nai—" He couldn't finish the thought. He blinked, long and slow. "This could be my only chance."

Addison threw a leg into the boat. "You mean *our* only chance."

Felix held a hand up to stop her. "Where do you think you're going?"

"With you."

"No, you're not. It might be dangerous." He tried to push her out.

She swatted his hand away. "I'm going, and you can't stop me. I want to help you get Naia and Princess back. The longer we argue about it, we risk them getting away." She fixed him with a steady stare. "We're in this together, remember?"

Felix seemed to consider this a moment before helping Addison into the hull. Her poofy dress took up nearly the entire width of the boat. The moment her butt hit the bench across from him, he pressed the down button on the control switch.

The lifeboat jerked to life. Addison gripped the bench beneath her. With a whir of gears and pulleys, they descended to the water below.

"Charlotte!" Addison yelled over the rush from the paddle wheel. "Go find Zoe, the event coordinator of this party, and tell her everything that's happened!"

She saw Charlotte nod just before they hit the water. Addison squealed and shivered as the spray from the paddle wheel misted over them. Felix took off his jacket and tossed it to her.

"Thanks," she said, wrapping it around herself. She felt the bulge of Naia's stuffed bunny inside the pocket and swallowed hard.

"I can't move in the monkey suit, anyway," he said.

Felix reached down to pick up the oars resting next to their feet. He placed them in the oarlocks on either side and started rowing in the general direction the dognapper had gone.

Addison knew they needed to make up for lost time, so she spun around, her back to Felix. Setting her clutch down next to her, she grabbed another pair of oars and began to row. As they floated farther and farther away, the fog swallowed the *San Francisco Belle*.

Addison tried to keep the same pace as Felix, but she felt the powerful surge of their little boat with each one of his strokes, and she knew she wasn't helping much. Her oversized ball gown tangling in the oars didn't help either. And since there were two more sets of oarlocks, it wasn't meant to be a romantic, two-person rowboat. But every inch counted, every inch brought them closer to saving the day.

That's what Addison reminded herself when her back ached, when her muscles screamed as though the flesh was being torn from her bones, when her arms stiffened like drying concrete. But still she rowed. For Naia, for Princess, for all the dogs and their worried owners.

Felix's grunts grew louder with each stroke, but he never slowed for a second. Addison bit the inside of her cheek to keep from crying out each time she dipped the oars into the water and heaved. She didn't want to be the reason they lost the other boat.

The fog weighed on them, much thicker than before. Addison glanced behind her every couple of minutes, worried they could be ten feet from the other boat and never see it. But they slowly closed in on the bright glow breaking through the fog: the Financial District.

Soon, over Addison's own heavy breathing, Felix's grunting, and the splashing of their oars on the water, she heard something: rhythmic splashes. They were gaining on the dognapper.

Biting down so hard on her lip that she tasted blood, Addison worked through the pain. She knew Felix could hear the sound too, because their boat's momentum suddenly increased with a fresh burst of power. A last desperate effort.

The distant splashing suddenly stopped. Addison and Felix kept rowing. With each stroke, her heart quickened. What was going to happen when they caught up to the thief?

Someone yelled out, "Throw me the rope!"

Addison heard answering calls. Her eyes grew wide as she realized there was more than one dognapper. But of course, there was. To steal this many dogs, there'd have to be.

The voice reached their ears again. "Come on, hurry!"

Moments later, a loud roar echoed across the water, followed by the quiet purr of an engine.

Felix grunted. "They're going to get away."

His groan was guttural, visceral. Addison imagined him trying to go faster, but they'd been rowing so long; he was exhausted.

"Okay, go, go, go!" that mystery voice yelled over the engine.

The purr turned into a growl as the engine revved. It quickly faded into the distance until the only sound left was the splashing of Felix's and Addison's oars.

He stopped rowing. "Shh."

She turned around to see him holding up his hand, tilting his head to listen. But there was only silence.

In mere seconds, their lifeboat floated over white foam churned up by a motor. They'd been so close, but the boat, the dogs, and Naia were gone.

27

UP THE CREEK WITHOUT A DOGGY PADDLE

"Shit!" Felix hurled an oar into the water, spraying Addison. "We lost them. Dammit!"

He grabbed his other oar and flung it as hard as he could. It landed somewhere out in the fog with an unsatisfying splash.

His body tensed like he wanted to rage, to punch something, but they were stuck on the little lifeboat. So instead, he pressed his face into his hands and yelled into them until he turned red.

Addison's heart broke to see his pain. She couldn't help but reach out to him and hold his hand. He grabbed it and squeezed.

"We might still catch up to them," she said. "They still have to unload the kennels. That will take time. We're not too far from shore." The glow had, in fact, brightened. The angular outlines of the skyscrapers pierced the fog.

"They won't head back to the Embarcadero," he said bitterly. "Too many witnesses. They could be going anywhere." He kicked the hull of the boat, causing it to rock.

"Maybe Zoe's contacted the Coast Guard by now. Maybe they're already searching." Addison opened her clutch and dug through it to find her phone. "I'll just call her."

"Why bother? It's not like the police have been able to find any of the dogs since they first started to disappear." Felix's voice hitched, and Addison's heart lurched at the sound of it.

"But we can just call and see if—"

"What good will that do, Addison!?"

She flinched, startled by his anger. "I'm just trying to help. Yelling at me won't get them back. I lost my baby too, you know."

He laughed humorlessly. "It isn't the same."

Addison scowled. "It is to me."

"Princess is a dog. Not a child." His hands clenched like he was fighting himself. "I'm sorry. I didn't mean that. I know she's important to you. I'm just—"

"Scared," she said, reining in her flare of anger. "I know. I can't imagine how terrifying this is for you, but I'm worried too."

"You're right. I'm sorry."

She knew he was only lashing out because he was worried about Naia, but he'd accidentally hit a sore spot. She swallowed her indignation but hated it when her next words wavered. "Princess is as close as I'm ever going to get to having a child."

He lifted his gaze to look at her in question, but she couldn't meet his eyes.

"I can't have kids," she told him. "I had a hysterectomy when I was twenty-two. So, just don't pretend like I haven't lost anything today, okay? Because Princess is all I've got."

"I'm sorry," he repeated softly.

But now she was looking at her own feet, wishing she'd worn closed-toed shoes because the cold bay water was like a foot soak from hell.

When she didn't respond, she felt the boat shift as Felix came to sit next to her. He shoved her plentiful skirts aside to get close.

"I mean it," he said. "I'm sorry. Both for what I said, and for what happened to you. I guess there are a lot of things I don't know about you either."

Addison felt the sincerity behind those words, and she sank against him. Now that they'd stopped moving, she started to shiver, even with Felix's jacket on. He wrapped an arm around her and pulled her close.

In his arms was a nice place to be. It was so warm and comforting. Again, she felt the loss of something potentially amazing. She'd missed the boat that night. Now, both literally and figuratively.

They fell into an anxious silence. Felix fidgeted next to her, ready for action, but there was nothing they could do without knowing where the kidnappers went.

Waves lapped against the side of the boat, rocking them as they listened to the distant sounds of the city. As cold as it was getting in their damp formal wear, neither of them moved or suggested they head for shore, as though that would mean they'd given up. If they continued to float for eternity, then maybe they wouldn't have to admit they were up the river without a paddle, so to speak. If they never went to shore, they wouldn't have to face the truth or what came next.

They'd been so desperate to not only save the dogs but also their jobs, their reputations. Those things seemed so trivial now that a human life was on the line. And not just any human. The most precious little angel Addison had ever met.

She wondered if the thieves even knew Naia was in Oliver's kennel. What would they do when they discovered her?

Addison stopped that line of thinking, closing her mind to any possibility that meant they didn't find Naia first. Because Addison Turner didn't give up. She didn't give up when her business faced total ruin, and it was a thousand times more important that she not give up now.

Addison sat up straight in her seat. "There has to be something we can do. Maybe we can call Channel Five and have them fire up the chopper."

Felix snorted, despite the situation. Or maybe

because he looked like if he didn't laugh, he might throw himself overboard. "You forget, Holly Hart isn't exactly on your team right now."

"For the promise of a good story she might help," she said doubtfully.

"I shouldn't have brought Naia," Felix said. "I should have stayed home. I should have just given up on the reward money and the bar. It's all meaningless without her."

"This isn't your fault," she told him. "This party was supposed to be safe. Who knew they would go to such lengths to get to the dogs?"

"But I suspected they were going to try something or else I wouldn't have come. Charlotte was going to identify who's been stealing all the dogs."

Addison drew away from him. "Hold on ... What? How does Charlotte know who's behind it?"

Felix winced. "Well ... she might have had something to do with it." He spoke slowly, as though gauging Addison's expression with each word.

"Charlotte stole the dogs?" It came out in barely a whisper.

"She didn't steal them," he said. "She just helped. Sort of." He grimaced.

Addison's teeth clenched. "What do you mean, 'sort of'?"

"She had nothing to do with the cocktail mixer. But she might have, kind of, helped hide the dogs in the back of the van at Philip's fundraiser."

She gripped the oar next to her, ready to smash it over his head. "Then you sent her on her merry way out the front gates with them."

"It's not like I knew they were in there, did I?"

Addison could no longer feel the cold. All she could feel was hot anger flowing through her. "But you vouched for her. You promised that she had nothing to do with this. And this whole time, she knew who it was. She lied straight to our faces when we asked her about it."

She got to her feet, unable to stand being near him any longer. The boat rocked beneath her, and she nearly lost her balance. Felix pulled her back down.

"How long have you known?" she demanded.

He held up his hands. "I swear I had no idea until she told me Wednesday night."

"You mean when you went to her place?"

Felix did a double take. "How do you know about that?"

Addison's eyebrow rose stubbornly. "You have your secrets. I have mine. And you kept this from me." She didn't know if she was more angry or hurt.

He seemed to tuck that piece of information away for later. "Look, you don't know the whole story. Charlotte had no choice."

"Of course, you're still defending her." Addison moved across the boat to the other bench because that was as far away as she could get from him at the moment. When really, she wanted nothing more than to storm away from Felix, or rather swim away, and never see him again.

He opened his mouth to speak, but she held up a hand to stop him.

"You know what? I don't care anymore. It doesn't matter."

"You're right. What matters is finding Naia." He rubbed a hand through his hair, removing the last of the product until his locks flopped around his face as usual.

Addison found she preferred this Felix to the fashionable one. It was more natural, more him. It annoyed her all the more that she even noticed.

"Maybe I should have put a leash on Naia," he said. "Strapped her to my back and not let her out of my sight. Or at least surgically implanted a homing beacon like any reasonable parent would have done."

The words nudged something in the back of Addison's brain. Her heart skipped a beat. Or maybe it had stopped altogether. "What did you just say?"

Felix saw the shock on her face. "I was just kidding. Well, sort of."

"A homing beacon," she murmured quietly, lost in thought. "A tracking device."

"They don't work very well after the fact. You

kind of have to attach it before they disappear."

But Addison wasn't listening. "I dressed Princess in her morganite necklace tonight."

Felix sighed. "Look, I know you're worried about Princess. Maybe you're right. Maybe the Coast Guard has already intercepted them." He reached across the gap to place a hand over hers comfortingly.

But she wasn't upset. She was smiling.

He stared at her like she'd lost her mind. "Are you feeling okay?" He held a hand to her forehead and let it linger there, as though afraid she was coming down with something.

"Why didn't I think about it before now? I've wasted so much time." Addison dug through her clutch again, looking for her phone.

Felix reached down and picked up her oars. "We should get to shore. You'll catch a cold."

"Yes. Back to shore." She was practically vibrating in her seat. "We might catch up to them before they get away."

He began to row, slower and stiffer than before. "I think you've had too much excitement for one night."

She shook her head, trying to organize her thoughts. "No. Listen to me. The necklace that Princess is wearing is my own design. Inside every high-end outfit and accessory in the Fido Fashion line is a GPS tracking device to help find runaway pets."

Felix's arms froze, oars sticking out to the sides. "Princess is wearing one of them?"

"Yes."

"Does it work?"

Addison pulled out her phone. "The software designers developed an experimental app that I can track her with. It's still in the trial phase, but so far, it's been pretty reliable."

Felix didn't wait for her to say any more. He dipped both oars into the water and headed for the skyscrapers lighting up the night.

Addison's hands shook with cold and excitement as she tried to unlock her screen. She used both hands to hold it steady while Felix raced them to shore. It only took a moment for the app to open and a flashing pink dot to appear on a map of San Francisco.

"That's her." She pointed at the screen. "It's tracking Princess."

"Where are they?" he asked between strokes.

Addison zoomed in on the pink dot. She frowned. "They've already left the bay. But it's okay. The signal will remain strong in the city. As long as they don't remove the necklace, we can track them."

"Then we'll get to her before that." His expression was hard with grim determination. "And if we find Princess—"

"We find Naia."

28

SOLD A PUP

A half-mile row to shore, a ten-dollar taxi back to Addison's car, and a twenty-minute drive across the city on the trail of a flashing pink dot led Felix and Addison straight to the old-money neighborhood of Seacliff.

Felix studied Addison's phone while she drove. They approached the end of the street with the best and highest views in the city. Felix suddenly tapped the dash excitedly.

"This is it. This is the place." He pointed. "Pull up there, out of sight."

Addison swerved to the side of the road and slammed on the brakes in front of a sign that said Land's End. Felix lurched forward in his seat, bracing himself against the dash. He didn't even seem to notice, much less comment, on her Mad Max driving techniques.

The mansions had given way to trees. They'd parked at what appeared to be the head of the walking trail that skirted the cliffside.

"Looks like this is the end of the line," Addison said. She just hoped it wasn't the end for them. She shivered despite her car's heater cranked to overdrive.

She'd swapped her puffy Cinderella ball gown and heels for the hoodie, jeans, and Converse sneakers she kept in her trunk for fashion emergencies. She'd done it in anticipation of a ripped seam or an accidental stain. However, freezing to death after a boat ride in a tulle dress wasn't something she could have foreseen.

"Let's see the map," she said. "Can we tell which house it is?"

"Don't need it," Felix said. "I already know where we are. I served for a couple of house parties here before."

Addison's eyes grew wide. "For who?"

Felix frowned. "Alistair Yates."

"No," she breathed. "I don't believe it. I could have sworn he was innocent. Alistair seemed so devastated to lose Lily. Why would he steal his own dog that he meant to enter into the dog show?"

"I don't know. But now that we know he has a backup, maybe he never meant to show Lily at all." His forehead creased. "But why the head game? Did he want to lower everyone else's guard? Take them by surprise?"

"Philip mentioned something about it before." Addison didn't miss Felix's flinch when she mentioned Philip's name. "He said everyone knew that Lily wasn't the favorite to win. That she was past her prime."

Felix shrugged. "Maybe Alistair realized it too. But why go to such extremes to remove your dog from the show? Why not just withdraw?"

"Pride?" Addison suggested. "For some of these owners, when their dogs lose, they lose too. They take it personally. I just never expected that from Alistair."

Felix grabbed his suit jacket from the backseat. Reaching into the inside pocket, he pulled out Naia's bunny and held it in his hands. "Yeah, well, it got a little too personal for me."

Addison laid a hand on his shoulder. "Don't worry. You'll get Naia back."

He covered her hand with his, squeezing it. Picking up his jacket again, he slipped it on.

"What are you doing?" she asked.

"Covering up my white shirt. It'll be too easy to spot it in the dark."

"Spot you?"

He handed Addison her phone. "Call the cops. Wait for them here. I'm going to find a way around the back. There are probably cameras at the front entrance." Felix got out of her car, shutting the door quietly behind him.

Addison sat there for a moment in silence, her mouth hanging open. What was he going to do? Rambo his way in?

She grabbed her keys and scrambled out of the car. She took a moment to text Zoe their location to give to the cops before running after Felix. When she caught up, he was already marching for the trailhead. He quickly veered off, eyeing the thick pine trees and shrubs that clung to the cliffside.

Only a narrow animal trail traversed the steep, sloping land between them and Alistair's backyard. One wrong step would lead to a painful tumble down the ravine and into the cold bay waters far below.

Felix swung a leg over the low fence next to the trail. He tested his footing on the uneven ground.

Addison grabbed him by the jacket collar, dragging him back. "You can't go in alone."

"I'm not waiting out here when my daughter's in there." He pointed to the mansion.

"It's too dangerous. Something could happen to you." As the words spilled out, she realized how true it was and just how much she didn't want that to happen. "You don't know what's waiting in there."

He reached out and squeezed her shoulders

comfortingly. "You're safe out here. There are neighbors close by if you need to run somewhere and hide. Just lie low. You'll be okay."

His expression was so reassuring and soothing, so full of concern. And it pissed her off. He couldn't just charge in there, pretending to be some macho superhero, and leave her behind like a token damsel in distress.

She whacked him on the arm. "I'm not worried about me. I'm worried about you, you jerk."

Felix might not have been her man, but he was still a good man and a good father who only wanted what was best for Naia. The thought of Naia being rescued, only to have something happen to Felix, tore at Addison's raw insides.

"Stop being a hothead." Her grip on him tightened. "Please. For Naia's sake. Stay here. Wait for the police with me."

"It's for Naia's sake that I have to go in there."

Felix wrapped his big hands around hers and gently dislodged them from his jacket collar. She squeezed his hands, if only to hold him there longer.

"If it was a person you loved in there," he said, "I know you'd do the same thing. Because you're a beautiful person."

The comment startled a snort from her. Out of habit, she brought a hand up to fix her hair, which was damp and matted with seawater.

He smiled and chuckled lightly. "I don't mean

on the outside. That part is obvious."

Self-consciously, she tried to tuck in a stray lock. Felix reached up and pulled her fidgeting hand away. His bottom lip twitched, pulling into a sad smile. He ran a tender knuckle down her cheek.

"I mean you're a beautiful person on the inside. Philip is a lucky man."

Before she could move or blink or tell him she wasn't even interested in Philip, he bent down and kissed her. It was only a quick peck on the lips, but it was firm with passion and meaning. Maybe he worried it might be his last.

Addison reached up to keep him there, but he broke free of her arms and disappeared over the fence and into the night. She stumbled slightly, feeling unbalanced without him there beside her.

She listened to the rustling of the bushes as he forged a path through the thick underbrush to Alistair's home. It took only the briefest of moments for her to realize that Felix was right: she would go in there for the person she loved, because she was already chasing after him.

It wasn't just for Felix. Addison may not have known Naia for more than a few days, but how could anyone not love that little girl? Not want to protect her? Then there was her own baby, Princess. So, it was for Felix's sake, and Naia's, and Princess's, and all the other lost pups that Addison maneuvered her way along the steep slope.

It was slow going. Felix was long gone, but she pressed on. She fumbled for footholds in exposed tree roots and grasped wads of grass that tickled her arms like insects—or maybe they were insects. Swallowing her desire to scream each time, she moved along the land's mysterious terrain by touch. She was too busy holding on for dear life to use the light on her phone.

Finally, she reached Alistair's property. A tall wall rose out of the steep cliffs. The stones were smooth, and there was no way to gain leverage for a hand or foot. Inching around the wall, she searched for a way up: a notch in the stones, a magic ladder that would descend when she pressed on the right rock, a secret door, anything.

She was always a slippery misstep from a one-way ticket to the bottom of the ravine. Or worse, the bottom of the cliffs, to the rocky waters below. She could hear the crashing waves hissing, taunting her.

Addison's next footstep landed on the dewy grass clinging to the rough rock. Her foot slipped, and she fell on her stomach. Her breath escaped in a grunt. She slid down the damp slope, twigs poking and rocks scraping.

Her heart lurched as her flailing hands scrambled for purchase. Exposed roots brushed against her fingers. She grasped one. Wrenching to a stop, she cried out as her arm stretched back. The root creaked ominously, but it held.

Gritting her teeth, she pulled, tugged, and wormed her way back up until she was on firm ground again. Heart thumping in her throat, she laid her head on the ground, breathing in the scent of wildflowers and soil until she found the courage to move again.

When she neared the base of the house, the ground flattened out. She flopped down on the grass to catch her breath. Cold dew soaked through her pants.

She pulled out her phone and checked Princess's GPS location once again. This time, when the app opened, an error message flashed across the screen: *Signal cannot be acquired*. If something had happened to the tracking chip, then did that mean something happened to Princess?

But she didn't have time to dwell on that thought, to give into tears or pain. Who knew how much farther ahead Felix was?

Not wasting any more time, she scurried around the wall, searching for a way onto the forbidding property. She didn't find any hidden ladders or steps, but there was an old, gnarly tree. Its thick branches reached out beyond the walls high above her and into the backyard.

Grateful once again for her emergency clothes, Addison assessed the branches and rough bark, imagining her progress up the tree. In her mind, she visualized her body contorting and twisting, flinging from branch to branch before she swung out over the property and somersaulted into the backyard like a ninja.

No problem at all.

Instead, as she climbed, she hugged the tree for dear life, clinging to the bark with her freshly repaired gel nails, snapping one or two off. She hissed and stifled cries as multiple slivers pierced her, digging into her skin.

When she was high enough, she clamped her eyes shut, ignoring the drop below as she inched like a worm to the end of the longest limb. It shook and swayed beneath her weight until she slipped and fell like a rock into Alistair's backyard, very un-ninja-like.

Addison hit the ground hard, knocking the wind from her lungs and smacking the back of her head on the turf. A burst of light shot across her vision. She gasped and sputtered for air, staring up at the tree branch. It shook from the rebound as if it were laughing at her. She glared at it but remained still until her chest rose and fell normally and the stars finally disappeared.

Her back ached, her chest throbbed, and it hurt to breathe. Her legs and arms stung with countless scratches, and she was pretty sure she'd have a goose egg on the back of her head tomorrow. But she'd live. Painfully, she got to her feet.

She searched for signs of Felix. Lights shone from the windows of the imposing home, casting dark shadows over the landscaped yard. Her eyes followed the winding stone staircase that hugged the curves and swells of the yard to the house. When she saw no sign of him, she knew she'd have to sneak closer.

Crouching low, Addison kept to the thick garden plants, hiding behind shrubs and trees that reminded her of swirling ice cream cones. She moved as quickly and stealthily as she could—which mostly meant she tripped and stumbled her way across the property.

Her panicked gaze tried to take everything in at once, searching for infrared cameras or ex-Navy SEALs with night-vision goggles hired to patrol the grounds. But no nets fell on her head Indiana Jones–style. No one called "Get her!" And she didn't trip any invisible wires, because this wasn't an Arnold Schwarzenegger movie. This was reality. And she needed to stay in it if she was going to be prepared for whatever came next.

Where the garden ended, a huge stone patio began. In the center of it stood a three-tiered fountain. Otherwise, the area offered little cover. She was a sitting duck.

Addison's limbs froze as she psyched herself up to make a mad dash for the house. What came after that, she wasn't sure. But there was still no sign of Felix. She had to keep going.

She darted out of hiding and onto the open patio. Thankfully, the fountain's lively splashes muffled her footsteps and her panicked breathing.

Unfortunately, it was also why she didn't hear anyone come up behind her until a hand clamped over her mouth.

She cried out, but the hand pressed tighter. As they dragged her into the bushes, she bucked and flailed, thinking heels would have been a better idea than sneakers; she could have used them as weapons. Still, she kicked at bony shins and jabbed her elbow against ribs.

There were grunts of pain in response, but the person continued to hold her tightly until they were out of sight. Unable to do anything else, she turned her head and bit the hand covering her mouth.

"Ouch. Dammit, Addy. It's me," Felix's voice hissed in her ear.

She immediately stopped fighting. The moment he released her, she spun around, hugging him out of relief before slapping him.

"Ouch," he hissed. "What was that for?"

"You scared the crap out of me. Why did you do that?"

He pointed at a second-story window. Addison glanced up to see a dark shadow move behind a curtain. She supposed she could have been a little stealthier, but no one was yelling or flicking on lights, so she relaxed.

"What are you doing here?" he asked. "I told you to stay."

"I'm not a dog," she whispered back. "I told

you I wasn't going to let you go in alone."

"Look, I know you're worried about Princess, but—"

"Don't be stupid. She's not the only reason I'm here right now." She bit her lip before she said any more. It wasn't the time or the place for a confession. "Safety in numbers, right? You need someone to watch your back. You helped me. Now, I'm going to help you get Naia back."

Felix frowned. "But—"

"No buts. The longer you argue with me, the better our chances are of getting busted."

"You're the last person I want to argue with." A shadow of a smirk tugged at his lips. "And sometimes the first person."

Addison stared at him, wondering what that meant. Her pulse, which had finally started to slow, now thudded so hard she feared even Felix could hear her heartbeat.

He held a finger to his lips. "Shh. Did you hear that?"

"What?" Addison froze, wondering if he really did hear her heart.

He ducked his head. For a second, she thought he was about to lay his head against her chest, but then he knelt on the ground by her feet. He leaned close to a metal pipe sticking out of the house's brick facade. Addison crouched next to him, and they brought their heads closer to listen.

Beneath the soft tinkle of the fountain, the

breeze rustling the pink and orange zinnias, and Addison's heartbeat in her ears, she could just make it out. The sound was quiet and tinny after echoing its way up the pipe, but there was no doubt about it.

"Barking," she breathed.

Felix's eyes ran up the side of the wall, as though he had X-ray vision. "But where is it coming from?"

"Alistair wouldn't have all the dogs just running loose inside the house," she said.

"No. My guess is the basement."

Addison's eyes widened as she recalled Philip's comment on their date. "Or Alistair's famous wine cellar." She suddenly realized Princess might be all right after all, and her body sagged with relief. "That's why I lost Princess's signal not too long ago. She must be too far underground."

"Come on." He grabbed her hand. "There's got to be a way in."

"Wait. Over there." She pointed to the flowerbed at the base of the house. Hidden behind the colorful zinnias was a low window just above ground level.

Felix wasted no time tearing out the flowers by the roots to expose the window. The remaining orange and pink heads flattened under his weight as he knelt down to peer through the dirty glass.

Addison looked over his shoulder. "I can't see a thing."

"We'll have to find another way in. This window's too small to climb through."

"For you, maybe." She checked to see if the window was locked.

He grabbed her wrists. "Now who's being a hothead?"

"We're in this together, remember?" she said. "Let me help."

But he didn't let go. "Then we'll find another way in. Together."

"How?" She waved a hand at the house. "Are we just going to waltz through the front door?"

"I don't know. We'll think of something," he said, not backing down.

They were nose to nose, bickering as usual. Only this time, when it boiled Addison's blood, it wasn't in a way that made her want to shove the crushed zinnias in his mouth. She wanted to shove her tongue in his mouth instead.

She ached to grab him and kiss him one last time before something happened and it all went horribly wrong. Or maybe before everything went right and they parted ways and never saw each other again.

"May I help you?" a female voice asked from behind them.

Felix tensed. Addison jumped, her stomach somersaulting. When they turned around, they were staring up at Penny Peacock. And, more importantly, the barrel of her gun.

29

DOG MEAT

Addison was staring right down the barrel of a gun. And it wasn't a 3D movie. It was real. Too real. She wasn't a ninja, or Arnold Schwarzenegger, or Lara Croft. It wouldn't be a blank shot at her heart, or red paint that stained her sweatshirt, or fake brains that splattered the walls. It was going to be her blood and brains that splattered the bottles of expensive wine.

Penny's gun hadn't wavered since she'd taken their phones and Addison's keys. It had remained targeted on their backs as Penny marched them into the mansion, into Alistair's study, through the hidden door behind his bookcase, and down the long wooden stairway into the wine cellar.

Princess's sparkling necklace jingled as she pawed at Addison's leg. Her big brown eyes pleaded for attention. She whined, begging to be picked up, to be comforted by her best friend.

Addison's fingers itched to reach out to her beloved doxie, to scratch her behind the ears and give her a million kisses. But she fought her instincts. She kept her hands in the air where Penny could see them, while her brain groped for a way out.

She assessed the dim room. It was illuminated by a single flickering light bulb above them and a few wall sconces. Floor-to-ceiling racks filled with wine bottles formed the walls. Some bottles were probably so expensive, they weren't meant to be consumed.

A stack of wooden barrels sat beneath the small window. If Addison had the chance, she could climb them and escape into the yard, but that would leave Felix to fend for himself. Her eyes shifted to the stairs behind Penny, to the only way out of the tiny, cold cellar for both of them.

The gun flinched.

"Don't even think about it," Penny said. "Cozy little place down here, isn't it?" She spoke like she was thinking of redecorating it.

Addison thought she could start with some new hardwood flooring. The current one was coated in sticky urine puddles—and worse—from the thirty-five or more anxious dogs pacing the congested room.

A mop and bucket stood in a corner, so Penny

must have been cleaning up after them, but the smell lingered, absorbed by the wood planks. Addison's nose stung from the harsh ammonia smell, and her eyes watered.

"Nobody even comes down here anymore," Penny said. "Not since Alistair's heart attack. It was the perfect place to keep the dogs. It's nearly soundproof down here." Her eyes widened with glee. "No one can hear you scream."

Addison gasped. This time she risked bending down to pick up Princess. The doxie scrambled into her arms and kissed every square inch of her neck as Addison held her protectively.

"Oh no, don't misunderstand." Penny's expression transformed to one of innocence. She held a hand over her heart. "I'd never hurt the dogs. You, on the other hand ..." She waved the gun casually between Addison and Felix. "What am I going to do with you?"

Felix shrugged with his hands still in the air. "Let us go?"

Penny laughed. "And let you run to the authorities? I don't think so."

The handler had gone through both their phone histories to see if they called the police. But of course, they hadn't. Addison had sent Zoe a text instead.

She wondered what Penny would do if she knew she'd sent the text. If it would prevent her from killing the two of them. It wasn't like she would get away with it if someone knew of their whereabouts, right? Then again, if Penny knew the police were on the way, she might kill them sooner.

Straining her ears, Addison listened for sirens. Charlotte *should* have told Zoe what happened when they left on the lifeboat. Zoe *should* have gotten her text about their exact location. The police *should* be on their way. Was that too many shoulds for Addison to rely on?

"We won't tell anyone," Addison said. "I promise."

Felix took a half step forward. "I just want my daughter back. Let me take her, and we'll be on our way."

Though he said it like it was a simple business transaction, Addison could hear the desperation in his voice.

Penny tapped her chin. "Yes, your mischievous daughter was an unfortunate complication."

"Was?" Felix's voice grated like he'd swallowed sand.

"Don't worry," Penny told him. "She's still alive. I haven't decided on what to do with her. Maybe I'll let her go. Kids' memories are never reliable. But you, you ..." She waggled her gun at them again before turning to the swarm of dogs circling her legs. "What should I do, little ones? I can't very well let them go."

She altered her voice, pretending to be a dog

herself—if dogs could talk. *A little like Scooby-Doo*, Addison thought. Penny ignored Felix and Addison to confer with the show dogs, as though they were coconspirators in her master plan.

Penny seemed to trust the opinion of one dog more than she did the others: Kingy. The Pekingese still sported Addison's stylish smoking jacket and ascot from the night of the cocktail mixer and looked princely compared to the other dogs.

Thanks to her investigation, Addison could name almost every pet, or at least their owners. There was Baxter, Lily, Elvis, Precious, Rosie, and a handful of others whose owners had pointed fingers at her at one time or another.

Colin and Sophie padded over to Addison like it was a regular social call, and Oliver rubbed against Felix's leg. They acted like it was playtime. The dogs that had been there longer, however, knew the score. They skulked around, shiftily assessing the newcomers.

Addison was so relieved to find all the dogs safe and healthy, if in need of a little grooming. Their owners would be overwhelmed to see them. But it wouldn't do anyone any good if Addison and Felix didn't get through the ordeal to tell anyone.

Penny looked so put together on the outside, which was completely at odds with whatever was going on inside. She'd changed since the gala into a daffodil yellow pantsuit. Too bright and cheerful an outfit for such a maniacal evildoer.

"What was that, Kingy?" Penny asked. She listened for a moment, nodding in all the right places and making noises of affirmation.

"Bark," he told her. "Bark, bark."

"Yes, I think you're right."

While Penny was distracted, deep in her consultation, Felix tilted his head closer to Addison.

"Keep her talking," he whispered. "Ask her questions."

She wrinkled her nose. "What's the point? I don't think we're going to find a compromise."

"She's a total egomaniac. She thinks she's smarter than everyone else to have pulled this off. Just look at her." He nodded toward Penny. "She's gloating, but there's no one around for her to gloat to. She wants to tell someone. Anyone. For someone to know how clever—"

"Hey!" Penny screamed. "I didn't say you could talk."

Marching across the wood floor, she pressed the gun against Felix's cheek. Her mouth screwed up as she dug it in. His skin puckered under the pressure, and the metal scraped against his stubble.

A noise escaped Addison, but it was incoherent. It took her a few seconds of stuttering to get something, anything to come out. "W-We were just saying how ... how clever you were to keep the dogs down here. I mean, who would even think to suspect Alistair when his dog was one of the first to go missing?"

She didn't know if Felix's plan would work, but she trusted his judgment of people. And what else could they do? They needed to stall for time before the police got there.

"Alistair Yates." Penny said the name like it was a swear word. "All I wanted to do was win. In all my career as a handler, no one has ever defeated me. My dogs always win." Her eyes widened as though it were a promise—or a threat.

Addison pitied Penny's rivals. She was probably the type of person Kitty Carlisle had been afraid of at competitions.

Penny pulled the gun away from Felix's face. Addison's body relaxed until she thought she would melt into a puddle on the floor. She hadn't realized she'd been holding her breath until her lungs ached with the sweet—if a little smelly— oxygen that rushed in and out of them again.

"But it was an impossible win this time," Penny continued. "Alistair was going to destroy my perfect record. All because he couldn't let go of Lily's glory days."

Penny wheeled on Alistair's beagle cowering among the furry group. She glared at the dog as though everything was her fault.

"You're old," she told Lily. "You should have retired two years ago, for God's sake. You were lucky to win last year. But Fancy ..." She sighed. "Now there is a star. She has a bright future in the circuit. But could I convince Alistair she was ready? No!"

Felix was nodding along. He wore his sympathetic bartender expression. He'd probably used it a thousand times while listening to strange stories from people like Penny.

"Of course." There wasn't a trace of sarcasm in his voice. "It makes sense why you had to take Lily out of the running yourself. Alistair just wouldn't listen."

"Exactly." Penny said. "I would never do anything to hurt Lily, so stealing her was my only option."

It was just like the bad guys in cheesy eighties movies, Addison thought. *Penny is revealing her evil plan, convinced that she's already won. But the good guys always get away in the end.* Addison had to remind herself that this wasn't a movie, though, and in real life, the good guys sometimes die.

"But why not take just Lily?" Addison asked. "Why did you take all the other dogs?"

"Fancy wasn't a sure thing," Penny said. "She's untested. A virgin to the ring. All those lights, cameras, people. It can be a lot for a first-timer. There was no way to know for sure if she'd win, especially with so little time left to train before the big show."

"So, you took out all the competition," Addison said airily, trying to imitate Felix's nonjudg-mental tone.

Penny gestured to the collection of dogs. "I took out all the major players, but I didn't want to be too obvious about it, so I also took a mix of red, yellow, and white ribbons to throw off the cops' scent. I even ended up with this thing." She gestured to Oliver.

Oliver whined like he knew he was being insulted.

Addison nodded. "And by kidnapping Lily, it took the suspicion away from both you and Alistair."

Penny waved a hand, the one that held the gun. "Alistair will get over it. Lily was past her prime. I did him a favor."

Somehow Addison doubted he would see it the same way.

Penny grinned at Felix and Addison like they were good dogs. "And you two were the perfect fall guys. So naive. You were in the right place at the right time. For me, anyway." She laughed. "It was easy enough to sneak the dogs out of the cocktail mixer through the hidden trapdoors in the stage floor. Once I got your incompetent as-sistant out of the way, that is," she told Addison. "I barely even tried to insult the girl and her grooming abilities before she ran out the back door crying."

"And Charlotte helped you load up the dogs at Philip's party," Felix coaxed her.

"Your boss was very helpful too," she told him. "He closed up the bar and hid them in there for us until nightfall. Then I shipped them over here to Alistair's."

"How did you get him to agree to it?" Felix demanded, his sympathetic demeanor slipping.

"The same way I convinced the *Belle*'s dog-watchers to help me out. Everyone has their price. Your boss didn't seem to mind turning a blind eye for a few bucks. Apparently, he's built up quite the gambling debt."

Felix's teeth clenched with a squeak. "Joe knew. He knew I wasn't guilty, and yet he had no problem pinning it on me. As long as he kept the heat off himself."

Addison jumped in before he lost his cool. "But what are you going to do with the dogs?"

Penny considered the odd mix around her. "Find them good homes out of state. Maybe I'll even breed them myself. I mean, just look at all of them." She spread her arms, waving the gun again. "The ultimate examples of each kind. I would have a monopoly of blue-ribbon winners. I could breed nothing but superior dogs. No one would ever beat me again."

"I suppose that's why you've been sleeping with Judge Walter Boyd," Addison said. "To ensure Fancy had his vote. Is he somehow involved too?" She figured if by some miracle they escaped, it would be good to know all the details, everyone involved.

Penny spun to face her, her left eye twitching. "How did you know about Wally?"

Addison just shrugged. But the mere mention of her robust boyfriend seemed to shake Penny. She swallowed hard, the gun dropping to her side.

"Wally and I share a passion. Our love of dogs, of perfection, connects us." The fire left her eyes, and her expression softened like a schoolgirl in love. "We're kindred spirits."

"Does he know what you've done?"

"Of course not. And he can't ever find out. He'd be furious." She gripped her head like the voices inside of it were arguing. "But it's not like I'm hurting the dogs. They're well cared for." Her eyes filled with pleading, as though she were preparing an explanation for him. Or maybe just convincing herself. "They're okay. See?"

Sure, the dogs appeared to be healthy, but they seemed skittish, starved for the love that they were so used to getting. The normally well-behaved animals paced anxiously, growling at Penny, at other dogs, at nothing in particular.

Addison was surprised no fights had broken out among them yet. But then again, even during their abductions, they'd never barked or put up a fight. There were never any signs of a struggle. They always disappeared so quickly and quietly, and now it made sense. As devious as she was, Penny was one of the best dog handlers there were. She could get a dog to do anything.

Penny shook her head like a dog after a bath. When she looked back at Addison and Felix, her face was unreadable again.

"No. Wally can't find out," she said firmly. "Ever. I can't risk you telling anyone."

Penny raised the gun and pointed it at Addison and Felix. Before, she'd held it nonchalantly, like a martini glass, as if she pointed one at people every day. But now, her muscles tightened with intent, and her eyes narrowed with focus. This time, she meant it.

Addison set Princess down on the ground and pushed her away to safety. Princess just came right back, leaning against her leg. *We're in this together.*

Penny glanced between the two of them, trying to decide which one to do in first. Addison could feel Felix's muscles tense beside her. Her senses hummed with the awareness of his body, his presence, his held breath.

She wanted to move closer, to wrap her arms around him or simply reach out and grab his hand. She wanted to feel connected to him, to feel his solidity and dependability, to absorb his comfort like a sedative. To get through whatever was about to happen together. But her body felt frozen with terror.

In the electric silence that followed, the faint

wail of sirens snuck into the wine cellar. Penny must have heard it too because her head whipped to the window.

The pane glowed red and blue. The police had made it. *Thank you, Zoe.*

But was it in time? Would Penny still shoot before they got to the cellar? Time seemed to drag, like someone hit the slow-mo button.

The wine bottles behind Addison clinked softly. Already on edge, she spun in time to see Felix bring his arm back. A flash of glass in his hand—a bottle.

While Penny was distracted, he whipped it across the room. It flew cork over bottom, straight for her. But at the last second, she turned around.

It glanced off her shoulder. She grunted and stumbled back.

Bang, the gun went off.

Felix dove for Addison, blocking her with his body. They went down together. She hit the floor hard, and pain exploded in her shoulder and hip. Felix grunted next to her.

The dogs went wild. But their barking sounded muted compared to the high-pitched ringing in Addison's ears.

She blinked, a little dazed. Her head throbbed. Maybe she'd hit it again.

There was one bark that stood out from the rest, like a voice she'd recognize in a crowd.

Princess's deep bark was close by, an insistent command. *Get up! Get up!*

Addison struggled to stand. Penny collected herself first. With a hoarse scream, the dog handler whipped the gun around, advancing on Addison and Felix for a close-range shot. A vein throbbed in Penny's forehead and her hooked nose flared with fury, revealing the hairs in her nostrils.

The dogs barked around her ankles, their growls fierce. Maybe from the gunshot. Maybe from the excitement. It seemed something had snapped inside of them; Penny's magic hold on them had worn off.

Princess planted herself protectively in front of Addison, hackles raised beneath her morganite necklace. Lips curling back in a snarl, the doxie tensed and bared her teeth.

Addison felt the same tension in her own body. The instinct to fight back was at odds with the gun pointed at her; it wasn't exactly a fair fight.

Penny's finger wrapped around the trigger. Addison braced herself. Suddenly, Princess lunged at Penny.

Her sharp little teeth sank into the handler's calf. Penny screamed. The gun went off. Addison recoiled, expecting an explosion of pain in her chest. But the bullet went wide.

Penny tried to kick Princess free from her leg, but the doxie clung on. Her little furry body flung back and forth as the handler whipped around wildly, tripping over other dogs. Then Lily dove for Penny's other leg, and she dropped the gun in surprise. Together, they tag-teamed the handler over and over again, each bite drawing blood through her yellow pantsuit.

Soon, the other dogs joined in. They converged on Penny like a pack of wild wolves, barking, biting, chewing, ripping, until they'd formed a writhing, snarling ball of fur. Those that couldn't find a limb to gnaw on cheered from the sidelines. *Fight! Fight! Fight!*

Kingy nipped at Penny's ankles, proving he hadn't been on her side at all. But once Oliver and Baxter leaped into the fray, Penny went down with a guttural shriek.

Scrambling to her feet, Addison raced for the gun. She reached into the mass of fur. When her hand felt cold metal, she picked it up and held it at the ready. But Penny didn't look like she was going to get up anytime soon.

Addison set down the gun; she wouldn't need it. *Then again*, she thought, *the bad guy always comes back for a second round.* She picked it back up, just in case.

Princess had ahold of Penny's arm now, gnawing on it like it was a chew toy. Blood tinged her blonde fur pink. Oliver drew away and found a new purchase on Penny's neck.

Addison wanted to look away but found she

couldn't. She watched in horror. The sounds of chewing and licking filled her ears until she couldn't hear anything else. Bile rose in her throat. Penny had had enough.

"Hey!" Addison yelled. She stomped her feet on the wooden floor to scare off the dogs; she didn't want to come between them in case they mistook Addison as the aggressor.

A few skittered away, but not all of them were ready to give up on their revenge. Raising the gun toward the top corner of the room, she cringed and pulled the trigger.

The gun recoiled. Her wrist shot back with a sharp twist. She hissed at the pain and cursed Hollywood, which made shooting a gun look so easy.

Most of the dogs seemed to come to their senses and backed off as though in a daze. Baxter, however, she had to pull off by force. She coaxed the beast with soothing words and gentle strokes down his hackles while steadily tugging him away.

Eventually, Penny stopped fighting back altogether. The danger gone, the dogs finally retreated to lick their bloody chops as if nothing had happened.

Penny lay still and pale on the dirty floor. Dark liquid seeped through the fabric of her shredded pantsuit, but Addison could see her chest rise and fall. She was still alive.

Addison finally dragged her shocked gaze

away from the sight of Penny's body. Dropping the gun, she searched the room for Felix among the excited dogs. She found him slumped against a wine rack, where he'd pushed her out of the way when the gun had gone off. He wasn't moving.

Beneath his suit coat, deep red stains seeped through his white dress shirt, spreading across his chest. Felix had been shot.

30

PLAY DEAD

Addison fell to her knees beside Felix. His bloody shirt clung to his skin. He blinked slowly, just coming around. Or maybe she was already losing him.

"Oh God," she said.

Her limbs went numb as shock kicked in, and her body focused its energy on pumping blood to her vital organs, her heart, her brain. Her stupid, stupid brain. The brain that thought it knew better.

Her brain had ignored her heart's desires, and now it was her heart that was suffering for it. It ached. Oh, how it ached, like Baxter was making a snack out of it. Yet, somehow it kept pumping, and aching, and pumping, and aching.

"Hold on, Felix." Addison sobbed. "The police are almost here. We'll get you an ambulance."

Where are the damn cops, anyway?

Oliver wandered over. With a whine, he laid his head down on his master's lap. Felix finally roused, automatically giving Oliver a pat. The look on the wounded man's face was dazed as his half-lidded eyes met Addison's.

There was so much blood everywhere, spreading over his shirt, pooling beneath him. She imagined if her nose wasn't so full of the caustic mixture of wine and dogs, she'd even be able to smell it.

She had to stop the bleeding somehow. She wished Piper were there; she'd know what to do. Addison's sluggish brain groped through the catalog of medical dramas she'd watched over the years … Pressure. *That's it!* She had to apply pressure to the wound.

"You're an angel," Felix said.

Addison's eyes went wide. "Oh no. You're hallucinating." It didn't take a doctor to know that was a bad sign.

Gripping his shirt, she tore it open. Buttons flew everywhere. She lifted his undershirt and ran her hands over his bare chest, searching for the source of the bleeding. All she found was his six-pack and a firm set of pecs. She wished she had more than flickering light bulbs to see by.

She groped him frantically, dragging his jacket off to have a closer look. That's when he winced, hissing in pain.

"Where does it hurt?"

He blinked lazily. "If you wanted to get me naked, all you had to do was ask."

"What? This isn't the time to joke." Tears filled her eyes until she could barely see Felix, much less the entry wound. "You've been shot. You need to conserve your energy."

"Addy, it's okay." He reached for her hands. "I'm okay."

"Your hands feel so cold," she said, finding it difficult to breathe through the oncoming sobs.

The chilly floor stung her legs. It would be warmer upstairs, but there was no way she could drag him up there.

"I need to keep you warm." She tucked herself beside him to share body heat.

Princess and Oliver snuggled in close, making a human/dog pile, as if they understood what she was trying to do. Or maybe they just wanted attention after their traumatic evening. Colin and Sophie soon joined, also seeking potential petters.

There was so much to say to Felix, so much she wanted to tell him. She wanted to confess her feelings, to apologize for the things she'd said to him. She worried there wasn't enough time left.

"Addy," Felix said. "It's just a flesh wound."

Her chest shuddered as she bit back another sob. "You don't have to be brave with me."

"No. I'm serious." He took her tear-stained

face in his big hands. "The bullet just grazed my arm."

"What?"

Reaching for his shirtsleeve, he showed her a tear in the material. Bright red blood seeped through the fabric around the hole.

She touched the stains covering the rest of his shirt, much darker in color. "But all the blood ..."

"It's not blood. It's wine. The first bullet grazed my arm as I pushed you out of the way. When I fell, I hit my head pretty hard." He rubbed the back of his head and checked his hand as though expecting to see blood. "I think I blacked out for a few seconds, or minutes, maybe. The second bullet hit the wine rack." He pointed above their heads.

Frowning, Addison looked up. Wine dripped from a broken bottle. She hadn't smelled it over all the other scents saturating the small space. When she looked back at him, he had an annoying smirk on his face.

"Were you worried about me?" he asked.

"Worried" didn't begin to cover it. Sure, he'd moved on to Charlotte. He was never going to be Addison's. But she still couldn't imagine a world without him. His belly laugh, his messy hair, and his rumpled band T-shirts. Or a world in which his daughter had to grow up without a father.

After what had just gone down, Addison wanted to tell him that, and to tell him how she really felt. She had fallen for him. Not because she was desperate for any man at all, like Felix thought. She was just desperate for *him*.

But he was going to be okay. He wasn't dying on her. In fact, his chest shook with chuckles. He was laughing at her!

Speechless, Addison wound up and punched him in his uninjured arm. "Jerk."

He winced but gave a weak snicker. Blinking, he scanned their surroundings. His eyes flitted from the bloody dogs to Penny's body. He pulled a face and looked away.

His glazed eyes seemed to sharpen suddenly. "Naia. I need to find her."

"The police must be coming through the gates by now," Addison said.

"I'm not waiting for them."

He held out a hand, and she helped him to his feet. His face screwed up from the effort. Flesh wound or not, Addison imagined a bullet hurt.

"This place is huge," she said. "Where do we start? Naia could be anywhere on the grounds." She glanced over at Penny's motionless body. "And I don't think asking Penny is an option right now."

"We'll split up." He lurched for the staircase, gripping his head.

As though sensing an impending prison break, the dogs rushed to follow him. Addison nearly fell over as the pack of purebreds brushed up against her legs in their excitement to be free. Something small and brown skittered over her foot. She shrieked and backpedaled until she realized it wasn't a rat but a tiny hairless dog. A Chinese crested.

Once the herd cleared, Princess was still there by Addison's side. She scooped her up and cradled her in her arms. She held Princess close, letting the doxie kiss her despite the gruesome red stains around her snout. Princess had saved their lives. She was so getting treats when they got home.

"My hero," she told Princess.

In the wake of the fur tsunami, Addison climbed the stairs after Felix. The moment she walked through the hidden door and into Alistair's office, she breathed a sigh of relief—and clean air. She was glad to be free of the tiny, smelly dungeon.

"Come on," she told Princess. "Where's Naia? Let's go find her." Her legs froze and she blinked, a plan coming to her. She ran into the hall. "Felix!"

A second later, he came running out of a room. "What is it?"

"I have an idea. Do you still have Naia's bunny on you?"

"Yeah." He frowned in confusion as he dug into his jacket pocket.

Addison took the bunny and held it in front of Princess's nose. "What's this? Whose is this? Is this

Naia's?" she asked in her excited "You wanna play?" voice.

Princess sniffed it, snorting as the fuzzy tail tickled her nose.

"Where's Naia, Princess? Where is she?"

The doxie's ears perked up, and her tail whipped back and forth. She could tell by Addison's voice that this was a game. And oh, she remembered this game from the park. She liked this one.

Addison set Princess down on the hardwood floor. "Where's Naia? Go find Naia."

Princess took off, barrel chest quivering as she sniffed rapidly, following the stuffed bunny's scent down the hall. She circled the Persian rug twice and then ran off into the dining room.

Addison and Felix continued to follow Princess into a modern stainless steel and marble kitchen. The dachshund glanced back at Addison, needing encouragement that the game was still on.

"Come on," she said. "Where's Naia? Go find her."

Addison tried to infuse her voice with cheer, but it shook with anxiety and adrenaline. She hoped her plan worked, that doxies' noses were as strong as they were famed to be.

Princess limped up a set of stairs with her one short leg, chasing an invisible trail through the mansion. She followed it up to the second floor, then up to the third, down a long hallway, and right to the base of a door. Princess scratched and whined at it, determined to win the game.

Felix grabbed the door handle and pushed, but it wouldn't budge. "It's locked. Stand back."

Addison snatched Princess up and scrambled out of the way. She watched as he took a few steps back. Using his uninjured side, he rushed forward and threw his weight against the door.

Crack!

Felix grunted and held his breath, grimacing. He took a few moments to work through the pain. It wasn't for nothing, because Addison pointed to a crack up the side of the doorframe.

"Look. It's working."

Bracing himself, he tried once more. This time, the door flew open.

He charged inside, and Addison ran in after him. She didn't know what she expected to find, but whatever it was, it wasn't the scene before her.

Naia sat in the middle of a striped settee with a bowl of chips in her lap and cookies on a gold filigree plate on the table. *Toy Story* played on a big screen TV in front of her.

Startled by the noise, Naia stared wide-eyed at the door. As soon as she saw who it was, she cried out, "Daddy!"

If Felix was surprised by how Penny had treated Naia, he didn't show it. Without faltering, he ran to his daughter and plucked her off the cushion. He crushed her against his chest. "Peanut. Oh, peanut, I thought I'd lost you."

She laughed. "I was in Oliver's house the whole time. I was playing hide-and-seek with Charlotte. She never found me." Naia beamed with pride. The fact that she'd won the game seemed to overshadow everything else.

Penny might have been as twisted as the Joker in *The Dark Knight*, but it was clear she'd treated the child well. Addison leaned against the busted doorframe and sunk to the floor in relief and fatigue. The fight was over.

"Well, we found you now." Felix held Naia tight and kissed her hair. "We found you."

31

PUBLICITY HOUND

Addison stepped out of Alistair's Seacliff mansion and allowed the cool night air to soothe her frazzled nerves. She shivered slightly from the dewy chill, but she made no move to reenter the house; she was done with answering questions that night. But neither did she head back to her car. She wasn't about to leave until she talked to Felix and Naia again.

Seconds after they'd found Naia, the place was suddenly bursting with cops. Shortly after that, the EMTs arrived, followed by investigators, an identification unit, and animal control. The huge mansion was quickly flooded with people and noises and so many questions. At some point, the frenzy had swallowed up Felix and Naia. Addison hadn't seen them since.

Drawing up the hood on her sweatshirt, she

snuggled Princess's warm little body to her. Together, they watched animal control workers reunite the rescued dogs with their owners at the property gates.

Word had spread quickly around the *Belle*. The moment it'd docked and the initial questions had been asked, all the guests had rushed to Alistair's home, led by none other than Holly Hart.

Addison wondered who her sources were since Zoe wouldn't have given the reporter the scoop. Maybe she had an insider at the precinct.

As EMTs guided a stretcher out the front door and down the sweeping stone stairs, Addison stepped out of the way. She watched it roll past. The supine figure beneath the blanket shifted, and a head rolled to face her. It was Penny.

The famous dog whisperer's hair was matted with her own blood. Claw scratches marred her face, neck, shoulders, and probably everywhere else. She was a mess.

Penny's eyes widened when she saw Addison. "Tell them." Her hoarse voice sounded hollow beneath the oxygen mask. "I wasn't going to hurt the girl. Really. Tell them."

As she was wheeled past, she held out a hand. Addison stepped away from her in disgust, holding Princess closer as if the woman might do something to her even now.

Penny's reach came up short. She looked

down and seemed to notice for the first time that she was handcuffed to the stretcher.

The handler was clearly getting locked up, hopefully for a very, very long time. No hot-tubbing with Judge Walter Boyd, no more dog shows for her. No dogs at all. After what she'd done, she didn't deserve them.

Addison turned away, scanning the crowd of personnel coming and going from the mansion. She and Felix had saved the day—well, it had mostly been Princess. They'd cleared their names, and the missing dogs had been returned to their owners. But all she could think of was finding Felix and Naia to see that they were okay.

A police officer walked out of the front door and down the steps. As he passed beneath the lights, Addison noticed Naia's stuffed bunny in his hands.

She grabbed his sleeve. "Excuse me. Have you seen Felix Vaughn and his daughter?"

He shook his head. "Not for a while. I think someone called them a taxi. They might still be here." He pointed to the crowd of well-dressed lookie-loos clustered outside the wrought-iron gates.

"Thanks. Do you mind if I return that to his daughter?" She indicated the stuffed animal.

"Of course not." He handed it over.

Princess sniffed eagerly at the bunny, but Addison tucked it under her other arm for safekeeping. "Playtime is over, Princess. You did good. You deserve a treat."

Princess barked happily. *It's about time.*

Addison headed for the property gates. Over the excited chatter, she recognized a high-pitched voice arguing with the officers standing guard. At the front of the crowd, practically trying to squeeze through the bars, was *the* Holly Hart.

When one of the officers moved to let Addison out, Holly spotted her.

"Addison! Addison!" She furiously waved her microphone—as if anyone could miss her. In her other hand, she held the Chinese crested Addison had mistaken for a rat in Alistair's cellar. Holly hadn't been lying; she really did own a dog.

The cops unlocked the gate and cracked it open to let Addison squeeze through. Once she was on the other side, Holly practically tackled her. She winced as the reporter bumped her sore shoulder.

Princess grumbled at Holly in warning. The reporter backed off, holding up her microphone and hairless dog in surrender.

"I'm so glad you're all right," Holly breathed.

Addison gaped at her in surprise. She could hear the sheer relief in the reporter's voice and see the worry in her Botox-stiffened face. Addison was touched. "Holly, I—"

"I was so worried I wouldn't be able to get the exclusive." Holly flashed her bleached teeth.

Addison let out a grunt and rolled her eyes. That figured. She wanted to tell Holly to … well, to do a lot of things she normally wouldn't say. But as tired as she was right then, she said, "All right. I'll give you an exclusive."

Holly's eyes widened in shock and then settled into their normal conniving slits. "Great. Let's get started."

Addison held up a finger. "But it's not for you. It's for me. You got that?"

Holly was only half listening as she snapped her fingers in the air. "Of course. Of course."

A second later, Hey You materialized with his camera. As though reading Holly's mind, he placed it on his shoulder and held his eye to the viewer.

The reporter held her microphone in one hand and her Chinese crested in the other. By the way she cradled the dog, Addison thought Holly might have actually grown attached to the thing. And here she'd thought Holly was heartless.

As Hey You counted down on his fingers, Addison tried to rub away the blood on Princess's face. Princess wasn't exactly camera-ready. Neither of them were, really, but Addison just couldn't seem to care at the moment; her hair was the last thing on her mind.

Hey You's fingers counted down to "one." Holly beamed, radiant in her evening gown. "This is Holly Hart for Channel Five News, reporting live from an undisclosed Seacliff mansion for a dramatic show dog showdown," she said, like it was the latest gossip and not a life-threatening event.

"The San Francisco dognappings came to a head tonight on the eve of the Western Dog Show, when the infamous puppy pincher struck again. This time, they plucked the pups right off the *San Francisco Belle*, the beloved local paddle wheel boat, while it was cruising the bay. What was worse, they took my own precious Jasmine." Holly kissed her dog's bald, shaking head.

"Thankfully, a dog lover and local Fido Fashionista was on the exclusive guest list, along with yours truly, and saw the crime in progress. Addison Turner, how were you involved in tonight's events?"

Addison spoke into the mic. "I was attending the gala on the *Belle* when Felix Vaughn and I discovered the dogs were being stolen."

"My sources tell me there was also a little girl taken."

Addison thought it best not to mention Naia's name or the fact that she was Felix's daughter. "The girl was playing hide-and-seek in one of the dog kennels at the time of the theft. All the dogs were locked in the kennels and loaded onto a lifeboat to get away from the party unseen."

"And you were the only ones who witnessed it?" Holly asked.

"Yes, everyone else was distracted by another boat we'd collided with."

"Coincidence? I think not." Holly cocked an over-plucked eyebrow at the camera. "What did you do then?"

When Holly leaned toward her eagerly, Addison realized she probably didn't know. This was the first time Holly was hearing this part of the story.

"We knew that if we waited for the police, they would get away, so we followed them using a tracking device."

"A tracking device? Did you anticipate this happening?"

"My dog, Princess, was wearing a valuable necklace that I've created especially for my Fido Fashion line. Some of the more expensive designs have GPS locators inserted into them, including this one." She held Princess higher so Hey You could zoom in on the morganite collar.

"You're kidding? That's amazing." Holly actually seemed impressed. Real drama that she didn't have to invent. "So, you tracked them down across the city to this Seacliff home using fashion. And they say you have to choose between fashion and function." She gave the camera a cheesy wink.

"When we got here," Addison continued, "we found all the dogs that had disappeared over the last couple of weeks. They were being held in the cellar. Before we could free them, however, we were held at gunpoint."

"That must have been frightening. Was anyone hurt? How did you get away?"

"My ... friend was injured." It hurt to use the word, but that's all Felix was. All he'd ever be. "But the dogs protected us by attacking the dognapper."

"So, the dogs are safe, the child was rescued, and the dog show is still on, all thanks to Addison Turner of Pampered Puppies." Holly summed up with a dazzling smile. "Make sure to come out and watch the Western Dog Show championships this weekend."

Addison grabbed the mic, resisting Holly's tugs to take it back. "And don't miss the launch of my Fido Fashion line on Sunday after the Best in Show is announced."

Holly pulled back the mic, smiling into the lens. "This is Holly Hart, reporting for Channel Five News."

Hey You lowered the camera. He opened his mouth to say something, but Holly snapped her fingers, and he shut it again.

"Get some shots of the house through the gate and get a close-up of the owners being reunited with their dogs. Some sweet, tear-jerking crap. Got it?"

Addison could practically hear Hey You's teeth clench. How he put up with Holly, she'd

446

never understand. Rolling his eyes, he trudged off to do her bidding.

Holly turned back to Addison. "Thanks for the interview."

Addison's fake TV smile vanished, and she glared at the reporter. "Trust me, it wasn't for you. You owed me some positive promotion after the damage you did to my reputation."

Holly gasped as she held a scandalized hand to her chest. "It's my duty to report the news, and you were a suspect."

"Not the only one by far."

Holly held her hands out like "oh well." "But it all turned out for the best. Good guys win, bad guys lose. Your name has been cleared. It's the perfect story. I couldn't have written it better my-self." Her mouth puckered as she reconsidered that. "Well, the ratings might have been better if you'd been maimed or killed. But better luck next time, I suppose," she said cheerily.

Addison crossed her arms. "You'd better hope people show up for my fashion show on Sunday. Or I'll be calling your producer. I'm guessing this isn't the first story you've em-bellished."

She turned away, letting the threat hang in the air.

Holly gripped her arm. "Hold on. Hold on." The reporter laughed, light and clear.

Addison imagined she could be quite

charming—if she didn't know what Holly was really like.

Holly chummily slid her arm through Addison's. "Well, as a favor to my favorite dog stylist, I will personally host your fashion show. We can call it *Holly Hart's Hounds presents Fido Fashion.*" She waved a palm through the air like she could see the sign now.

Addison yanked her arm away. "How about *Addison Turner presents Fido Fashion, hosted by Holly Hart?*"

Her lips pursed. "It doesn't sound as catchy, but I'll do it."

Addison suspected the offer was most likely so Holly could boost her ratings on the heels of the breaking story. However, she thought having a local sort-of celeb host the fashion show could garner a bit of attention.

"Thanks," Addison said.

Something over her shoulder caught Holly's attention. "Oh, there's the detective. I'd better go get an official statement." She waved her microphone. "Yoo-hoo! Detective!?"

Addison watched Holly chase her story through the crowd of onlookers dressed in their tuxes and ball gowns. Above their heads she could see a mop of ebony hair bob along. She recognized those thick locks instantly.

Her heart clenched at the sight of Felix, and her legs automatically moved toward him. She weaved through bodies, both human and furry. When she broke through to the other side of the congregation, she saw Felix headed for a cab parked between a BMW and a Bentley.

One arm rested in a sling while the other held Naia. She sagged over his good shoulder, passed out after her long evening. It was way past her bedtime. Heck, it felt past Addison's bedtime.

She raised her arm to get his attention, but then she spotted Charlotte following close behind. The server must have come to meet them. She hovered close to Felix, checking on Naia, fussing over her in a motherly way.

Addison shrank back into the crowd. Ever since the police had arrived, she'd thought of nothing but finding Felix. However, seeing him and Naia with Charlotte, a little reunited family, she suddenly realized that maybe he didn't want to see her. That she might be intruding.

As Felix turned to say something to Charlotte, his focus locked on Addison like he'd somehow sensed she was there.

Addison waved awkwardly, trying to communicate "Hey, we nearly died together, but, yay, we're still alive. And thanks for saving my life, BTW."

The hand peeking out of the sling moved in a half wave, but then it froze. His face suddenly fell. A second later, a hand landed on Addison's shoulder.

She jumped and spun, her body geared up from all the action that night. Princess growled, on edge too.

"Philip," Addison said in surprise. Not surprised to see him there; he'd come for Baxter, after all. She was surprised because she'd nearly forgotten about him in the last few hours.

"Addison, hi."

"Hello," she said distractedly. She glanced back to the road to catch Felix's eye again, just in time to see the taxi drive off.

"I'm glad to see you're all right," Philip was saying. "I just wanted to thank you for rescuing Baxter."

Addison watched the taxi disappear down the road and sighed. She finally looked back at Philip. "What? Oh … yeah. You're welcome." She bent down and gave Baxter a pat on the head. "I'm glad he's all right."

"I became worried when I couldn't find you on the *Belle* after we ran into that boat."

Addison rubbed a hand over her face. Right. The gala. Her date with Philip. Had that been the same night? "I'm so sorry. There was no time to explain."

Philip held up a hand. "Don't apologize. Maybe you can tell me all about it tomorrow over dinner."

Addison's mouth turned down.

"Coffee then?"

But she shook her head, mostly at herself. Philip was honestly a great catch. And hooray, he wasn't the dognapper—always a bonus. But he just wasn't the guy for her.

"Sorry." She pulled a face. "It's a busy weekend and all. I had a great time getting to know you."

He nodded, his perfect lips curling into a sad smile as he took the hint. "Me too."

"Good luck with the conformation tomorrow."

"And good luck with your fashion show." He drew her hand toward his lips and kissed the back of it. "Goodbye, Addison."

As she watched the second guy walk away from her that night, another hand landed on her shoulder. She squealed in surprise and spun around again. Princess growled before she saw the friendly faces of Zoe, Piper, and Aiden.

Zoe threw her hands up in surrender. "Whoa. Are you two jumpy or what?"

Addison rubbed Princess's raised hackles comfortingly. "Sorry. It's been that kind of night."

"I can only imagine." Zoe leaned in for a hug. "Are you okay?"

Piper grabbed Addison the moment she was free and embraced her too, sandwiching Colin and Princess between them. "Zoe said you stole a life raft from the *Belle* and chased after the dogs."

"What's going on?" Zoe asked. "That

brunette, Charlotte, I think her name was, said they'd taken Naia."

Addison opened her mouth to explain, but she shut it again. "Everything's okay now. But it's a long story. I'll tell you guys all about it later."

Aiden laid a hand on her shoulder. "Sounds like you've been through enough already tonight. We'll save the third degree for later."

"Ice cream sleepover?" Piper asked with a grin.

Addison batted her eyelashes. "You know the way to my heart."

A wall of snow-white hair bobbed above the crowd, headed in their direction. Kitty Carlisle emerged and came at Addison with a wild look in her bulging eyes. Nestled in her arms, Elvis mirrored her dark, unreadable look.

Addison automatically backed away, but Kitty grabbed her. Turning her body to shield Princess, Addison tensed for the worst. But she was unprepared for what came next.

Kitty wrapped her thin arms around Addison and hugged her. "Thank you. Thank you for finding my Elvis."

Julia was right behind her, pushing her way past Piper and Zoe. "Yes. Thank you for what you did for my Precious. I thought I'd lost him forever." She bent down to be closer to her cocker spaniel, her midnight blue ball gown trailing in the dirt. "Now that's what I call good service, right, Precious?"

"Above and beyond," Kitty agreed.

Other dog show owners gathered behind them, protectively carrying or leading their pets. Their faces, which had been tainted with suspicion and allegation for the past two weeks, were now smiling, filled with appreciation and humility.

Rex Harrison clung to his pinscher's leash like it was a lifeline. "I'm so sorry I accused you. Thank you for saving Rosie."

Kayleigh, the woman who had supported Penny's story about her and Felix being partners in crime, surged forward. "Yes, thank you so much. How can we ever repay you?"

Addison stood there, shocked by the overwhelming support. "It wasn't just me," she said when she'd found her voice. "Felix Vaughn and I worked together."

"I heard he was shot," Julia said with more excitement than concern.

Piper, Aiden, and Zoe all turned to her in varying degrees of shock and horror.

"You were shot at?" Piper asked, or rather, nearly screamed.

"Yes, Felix was shot, but he's okay. And I'm okay," she assured her friends. "I'll tell you all about it later."

"I'm just so happy to have Precious back,"

Julia said. "And in time for the competition tomorrow."

"I don't think Gumball will be ready," the man in the toupee from Philip's fundraiser said. He rubbed at his dog's snout. "Is this blood?"

"I don't think any of the dogs will be ready in time," Kitty said, assessing the group with a practiced eye. "So much for this year's conformation. All the likely candidates have been ousted before it has even begun."

Addison took in the competitors as well. Compared to Kitty's taste for perfection, her eye for potential saw things a little differently. "Not necessarily."

"I don't see how they can compete," Kitty said. "They look like a pack of wild animals." Her nose turned up slightly at the sight of her bichon frise's red-stained fur.

Addison laughed humorlessly, shuddering as she recalled the gory scene in the cellar. Kitty didn't know how close to the truth she was. "Well, I just happen to know of a dog spa well-versed in specific breed styling for show dogs. And I think the owner might be willing to help out a few special new customers."

"Yes!" Julia shouted. "Absolutely! Can you schedule Precious in?" She hoisted her cocker spaniel in the air, practically thrusting him at Addison to be first in line.

A debate over who should go first rose among

the crowd. Some argued their dogs had better chances of winning. Others cried that it was first come, first served. A chorus of eager requests were hurled at Addison.

She held up her hands, shouting over the din. "Don't worry! I'll fit everyone in. Pampered Puppies will work through the night if need be."

"But how can you manage all on your own?" Rex asked. "Who gets to go first?"

There must have been fifteen or more owners wanting her services. A single dog could take hours. It wasn't possible to get them all done by the time the show began first thing in the morning.

She scanned the crowd in front of her. "Are there any handlers here with grooming talents?" she called out.

A couple of hands shot up.

"Okay, great. Owners, you'll have to get your hands dirty tonight. We'll need all the help we can get."

Taking out her phone to text Melody, she turned to Piper and Zoe. "We'll have to take a rain check on that ice cream. Feel like getting dirty tonight?"

Zoe gave her a saccharine look, full of promise. "You know I like it dirty."

32

EVERY DOG HAS ITS DAY

Addison sat in her car, staring up at Felix's front door. Her chest tightened like her bra was too snug. She wanted to see him, and yet, she didn't. Maybe he wouldn't even answer the door. Or worse: Charlotte could answer, if she wasn't in jail, that is. Or maybe she was keeping him too busy to even come to the door. It was late, almost ten o'clock. Maybe they were already in bed.

But she didn't want to think about that. She'd tortured herself enough over him. Maybe it was best to just slip Naia's stuffed bunny into the mailbox, where Felix would find it the next day.

Don't be silly, she told herself. It was just a stuffed animal. She'd hand it over, see they were both okay, and then move on with her life. A life that had felt so perfect only two weeks before. Like a blockbuster movie. But now it seemed like the

crappier sequel banged out on the heels of success, with none of the original cast. It had lost its
magic. Its heart. And she knew it was because her
heart belonged to Felix.

Her perfect life now seemed empty. Maybe it
always had been. Nothing had changed after all.
Except she'd received a preview, however small, of
how full it could be with Felix and Naia in it.

Addison sighed. She knew Naia would want
her bunny, so she got out of her car. With heavy
feet, she climbed the steps to the front door.

She would have returned the stuffed animal
earlier, but cleaning up the dogs had taken all
night with the help of her friends, the dog owners,
and a few handlers. Bleary-eyed and exhausted,
they'd driven the dogs straight to the competition
early that morning. Before heading to the precinct
to answer a few more questions, Addison had
helped those customers without handlers primp
and preen the competitors throughout the
morning.

Customers. She liked the sound of that. Something she thought she'd never see again. Now, she
had some of the most loyal customers a business
owner could ask for. She'd certainly risked enough
to get them—as in her life.

Addison's finger hovered over the doorbell,
shaking slightly in anticipation. Before she could
chicken out, she pushed it.

Inside, a muffled ding rang out, followed by

shuffling. Her stomach clenched with nerves. Her heart thudded so fast that it felt like a hundred bouncy balls careening around inside her chest. If she opened her mouth to speak, one might come flying out. She regretted not going for the mailbox option.

The door squeaked open, and Felix was standing on the other side. At least it wasn't Charlotte.

The moment he saw her, his dark eyebrows shot up, and a breathtaking smile stretched across his face. "Hi."

She gave an awkward little wave. "Hi."

"What are you doing here?" He almost sounded ... hopeful.

"Sorry to bug you. I just thought Naia might be missing this." Addison practically threw the bunny at him. "But I'm sure you're busy, so I won't keep you." She took a step back from the door, already fishing her keys out of her purse.

"Don't go." He opened the door wider. "Please, come in."

"Really?" She poked her head inside, checking for signs of Charlotte—a pair of shoes, a coat. "Are you sure?"

Felix stepped aside and tilted his head in invitation. She swallowed a bouncy ball and stepped onto the welcome mat, staring at her shoes while he closed the door.

"How is Naia?" she asked.

"Good. She finally went to sleep. She kept asking for Bunny." He jiggled the stuffed animal. "I'm really glad you found it. Thanks."

Felix was acting so hesitant, like they hadn't faced death together just the night before. Hadn't spent the last two weeks fighting their attraction. Hadn't ever kissed. Like he didn't know how to make her body, and her heart, sing. Then again, maybe it was because Addison hadn't looked him in the eye since she'd arrived.

Forcing her eyes to meet his, she noticed he wasn't wearing his sling anymore. "How's your arm?"

"A bit sore but not bad." He rolled his shoulder freely, wincing only slightly. "How are you after everything?"

"I'm fine. A little tired." She leaned back against the front door because "a little" was an understatement.

"I'm sorry I didn't say goodbye last night," Felix said. "Or thank you, if that even covers going through something like that with someone." He ran a hand through his curly hair. "You helped me save my daughter. You helped me clear my name. I couldn't have done it without you."

"Same here," she said. "Now maybe you'll start getting gigs again. It might be too late for your friend's Irish pub, but there will be another bar, I'm sure."

"Actually. There already is." His face lit up.

"Turns out my boss is looking at jail time for his involvement with the dognappings. With all that gambling debt Penny mentioned, he's selling the bar to pay it off, so no one will be hired to shiv him in jail." He grinned, like the threat of a good shivving was the best possible news. "The bar is up for sale."

"That's great." She gave a small fist pump. "Yay for shivving."

"And with forty percent of Alistair's reward money for finding Lily, I'll have more than enough for the down payment."

"Make that fifty percent." Addison smiled. "And that's great news. I'm really happy for you."

"Thanks. But what about you? You can use the reward money to keep your business afloat for a little longer."

As their natural connection flowed again, she forgot her shyness. It felt so easy to be around him. So instinctual.

"Actually, thanks to our solving the case, business is looking up," Addison said. "The fashion show, on the other hand, might still be a bust." She dreaded finally facing Aiden and telling him his sure-thing investment had become a bottomless money pit. But at least now, she could recover in time.

Felix pulled a sympathetic face. "Still no reservations?"

"No." She shook her head. "But it's not until

tomorrow afternoon. Still a few more hours yet. Things might pick up."

He chuckled, mahogany eyes sparkling down at her. It made her tingle inside and then hurt all over again at the loss.

"Ever the optimist. There's the Addy I know and …" He petered off. His Adam's apple bobbed as he swallowed. "But I'm sure Philip will be there. Maybe he has a few rich friends he can invite."

"Philip?" Addison's forehead wrinkled. "I don't think he'll be coming."

Felix gave her a questioning look. That's when she realized he still thought she was interested in Philip. Dating him seemed so out of the question to her now, but she'd never actually had the chance to tell Felix, what with the dogs and Naia being stolen from the boat and being held at gunpoint and all.

"I'm not with Philip." She wrinkled her nose. "I realized he wasn't for me."

Felix drew back, his expression unreadable. His eyes narrowed. "What happened? I thought he was Mr. Perfect."

"He is. He's just not perfect for me." She shrugged. "Anyway, I'm sure Charlotte is happy you're going to buy the bar."

He blinked, frowning at the change in subject. "She'll definitely have a better boss to work for."

"Well, you'll be more than a boss." Addison laughed, but it almost sounded like a sob.

"What do you mean?"

"I just mean …" Addison's throat felt tight. She swallowed. "I'm happy for the two of you."

"For me and Charlotte?"

"Believe it or not, I just want to see you happy."

He stared at her with a confused, lopsided grin. She was so tired, and her thoughts were difficult to put into words. Maybe she just wasn't making sense.

She rambled on. "Well, since you were at the gala together, I just assumed … And then Charlotte said she was going to make a terrible mother."

Felix nodded slowly, a curious look on his face. "Of course. Charlotte's pregnant."

Oh God! They were having a baby together. That explained the rush for getting serious so fast. Maybe they'd even get hitched soon.

Addison's brain, which had been struggling to keep up with only two hours' sleep, suddenly failed her. She took a step back like the news just blew her away.

"Pregnant." The word came out in a rush of breath. "That's … great." She tried to sound enthusiastic, truly she did, but it was hard to smile with the tears building in her eyes.

"Our boss found out she was expecting. Joe's

notorious for laying off women when they're pregnant so he doesn't have to pay them maternity leave."

Addison scowled, trying to pull herself together. "He can't do that. There are laws to protect her."

"Joe's done it before. He builds up files on everyone, a list of probationary stuff, discipline letters. It's all total made-up garbage, but whenever he decides he wants to get rid of someone, he has enough to make it look legit." His jaw tensed, the muscles in his cheeks working. "It's not fair. But it's a dive bar. It's not exactly like we have a union."

"That's terrible," she said.

"He's a cheap bastard. She worked for him for five years, had earned maternity leave." Felix crossed his arms. "When he found out she was expecting, he blackmailed her into helping load up the dogs into the van at Philip's fundraiser. He needed someone on the inside. He said if she didn't do it, he'd suddenly run out of work in the next few months and lay her off."

Addison's shoulders slumped. "So that's why she helped steal the dogs."

"She didn't think anything bad would happen to them." He rolled his eyes to the ceiling. "I know that's no excuse, but with a baby on the way and her man recently laid off from his job, I don't envy the position she was in."

Addison noted how casually he called himself "her man." She wanted to condemn Charlotte, but then she thought about what she'd been willing to do to save her own business. And it was just her and Princess. She couldn't imagine the pressure Charlotte had been under to keep her job.

"Well, congratulations," Addison said at last, valiantly trying for an earnest smile. "I hope you and Charlotte will be very happy together." But those tears were building again, and the last thing on earth she wanted to do was cry in front of him. She reached for the door handle behind her, ready to leave.

A line formed on Felix's brow. "Wait … What?"

He opened his mouth, his kissable mouth, and closed it again. He rubbed a hand over his face and considered Addison for a moment. Finally, he gripped her by the shoulders.

"Addy. Listen to me. Charlotte is pregnant, but not with my baby. It's her boyfriend's."

She blinked. "Boyfriend?"

"Yes. Boy-who-is-not-me boyfriend." He spoke slowly and clearly.

"Not you?" The cogs in her brain began to turn. "You're not pregnant? You're not marrying Charlotte?"

"What? No!" He laughed his rich belly laugh. "Where is this coming from? I told you we're just friends."

"B-But the flirting," she stuttered. "And you seemed so close at the gala. And ..." She didn't know why she was arguing, like she was trying to convince him he was really dating Charlotte, whether he knew it or not. She couldn't wrap her head around it. Not after everything she'd seen.

"What about the night you went to her house?" she asked.

Felix's hands dropped from her shoulders. Addison bit her lip. She hadn't considered how he'd react to the news before it flew out of her mouth. She'd glazed over that tidbit of information on the *Belle*. Now that she'd reminded him, his gaze narrowed.

"You were following me?"

She raised her hands, holding off his anger. "I had no idea you'd be there. I know that you insisted Charlotte was innocent, but I just didn't trust her. I felt there was more going on."

Felix seemed to think for a moment. "Well, I can't blame you. You were right." He sighed. "She'd called me over there and confessed everything about her involvement. She was so upset."

Addison's hand still clenched the door handle, mostly so she didn't fall over with fatigue or shock. He laid his hands on the door on either side of her like he was worried she was going to walk out. But she didn't think she had the energy to move.

"I've never been interested in Charlotte," he said. "Ever."

Felix's entryway grew quiet then, and Addison mentally pieced things together. All the looks she'd imagined between Felix and Charlotte, all the times she'd assumed they were flirting. All the misjudgments. Meanwhile, she'd been ignoring something real growing between Felix and herself this whole time.

"Why did you let me think you and Charlotte were at the gala together?" Addison asked. "Why didn't you tell me it wasn't a date?"

"Why should I have? You were on a date yourself. And, if I'm honest," his voice softened, "maybe it was because I wanted you to be a little jealous. I know I was." His Adam's apple bobbed again.

"There was no reason for you to be jealous. I left Philip's house that night, just after you did. You were right. It wasn't real. I was hung up on some childish fantasy." She held his eyes steadily. "But I don't want a fantasy. I want something … more." She repeated his words, hoping they meant the same to him as they did to her.

She craved his usual touch: firm, sure, and greedy. She gave him an inviting look that made sure he knew she meant she wanted more with *him*.

A glint in his eye, a flash of teeth; the animal was back. Suddenly, he pounced, dragging her into his arms and kissing her like they were back on the cliffs and this could be their last chance. She gripped his band T-shirt and held him closer, taking him all in.

Too soon, Felix pulled away. With a softer look than she'd ever seen in his eyes, he held her face tenderly. "I may not have come through for you at the start, and I regret that. But from this moment on, I'm here for you, for better or worse. You know that, right?"

Unable to resist, Addison brought up a hand to explore his sweet expression with her fingers, this new, unguarded way that he looked at her. "I know. You've already proven that during the last couple of weeks."

"And you've been there for me. And Naia." He flinched. Maybe he was remembering how he'd almost lost her.

While Addison had been worried about finding a guy who would stick around through thick and thin, she suddenly realized that he probably worried about the same thing. Hadn't he experienced his own sense of loss, of abandonment by Naia's mother? And like Addison needed him to be there for her, she wanted to be there for him.

"And I always will be," she said.

When Felix kissed her once more, it was like they'd said all they could with words. It was up to their bodies now. He explored her mouth, her tongue, slowly, confidently. There was no rush;

Addison wasn't going anywhere. She knew why she was there this time. It wasn't lust, or curiosity, or temporary insanity. She was there because she chose to be. Her heart and her brain had finally agreed that Felix was *The One*.

Felix swept aside her golden curls, forging a trail of kisses down her neck. "You must feel exhausted after the last twenty-four hours," he mumbled against her shoulder.

The vibration of his words against her skin made her lower half clench with anticipation, proving that she wasn't that tired.

"I suppose it is way past my bedtime," she teased.

"You do seem tired," he said with mock seriousness. "Maybe too tired to drive all the way home."

"You're right. It might not be safe." She tried to act cool, but her voice shook, revealing her excitement.

"I couldn't live with myself if I sent you on your way and something happened to you." All trace of humor was gone. His eyes flickered, and his breath hitched like he'd never meant anything more in his life.

"I couldn't live with it if you sent me on my way either," she said softly.

"Maybe you should stay here. I could tuck you in." He reached around her, grabbing her butt with a mischievous grin.

She arched against him in surprise. "Tuck away."

Bending down, Felix swept her into his arms, wincing a little because of his shoulder.

As he carried her to his room, for once in her life her mind didn't wander. It didn't transport her to fantasies of their future, all the adventures they could have, imagining them as different characters in new settings. She remained in the moment because she could think of no better place to be. Besides, who wanted to settle for PG-rated fairy tales when she could have R-rated?

And that was clearly what Felix had in mind as he impatiently booted his door open. In the glow from his bedside table lamp, she could see the desire in his expression. With a boyish grin, he suddenly let her go and dropped her on his bed. She squealed before she hit the comforter.

After locking his bedroom door, he peeled off his shirt. The light caught his tanned skin, highlighting every hard dip and swell of his muscles. Holding her gaze, he unfastened his worn jeans. They crumpled to the floor. He didn't hesitate before reaching for the waistband of his boxers and tugging them down too.

She gasped as Felix's entire body was revealed; he was obviously ready for her. A shudder of anticipation coursed through her at the sight of him exposed so unceremoniously, so confidently.

Diving onto the bed, he pounced on her. Addison's hands came up automatically, impatient to explore. But as hasty as he'd been preparing himself for her, he slowed down to remove her clothes.

He reverently slid each piece of clothing off her body like he was finally opening that Tiffany's box. Her anticipation built with each button he slipped free, each sock he tugged off like it was sexy lingerie.

When he dragged her pants down over her hips, kissing her legs as he went, she suddenly gasped.

"What's wrong?" he asked.

She pressed her lips together. "I, umm, forgot to shave my legs. I didn't expect this."

Felix laughed, his breath tickling her thighs. "Addy, I don't care. I don't care about the shaving, or the makeup, or the hair, or the clothes. I prefer you without all of it." He nibbled on her inner thigh, making her squeak. "Especially without the clothes."

As though to prove his point, he tugged her pants the rest of the way off and rubbed his face up her bare legs, his own stubble scratching her skin deliciously. She giggled and pulled her legs away, but he grasped her ankles and held them apart. His hands were firm and unyielding as his jaw rubbed higher and higher.

Addison shivered and squirmed until his stubble tickled between her thighs, the sensation at odds with his soothing kisses, his wet tongue, his probing fingers. Forget R-rated. This was XXX.

As her body warmed with each caress, each lick, she struggled to keep quiet. She grunted and gripped the sheets beneath her, twisting them in her hands. When her body began to shake and twitch with pleasure, she pressed her face against a pillow to muffle her cry.

Vibrating with pleasure, Addison sprawled out on the bed as she came down from her high. She hadn't noticed Felix put on a condom until he lowered his body on top of hers. He took a moment to study her flushed face and smiled down at her.

She felt his weight and presence secure her, ground her. It was as though without him she'd float away like a hot air balloon, drifting aimlessly without direction or purpose for the rest of her life. Doomed to look down at the people below, never attached or truly connected to anything.

Felix and Naia could be that connection. They could keep her grounded. Anchor her to reality.

Addison laid her palms against Felix's chest. She enjoyed the sensation as she dragged them down his torso, his abs, his hips, enjoying the security that came with how real he felt, how solid, how firm. Very, *very* firm.

Felix moaned as her fingers curled around that firmness and guided him inside of her, filling her up like he filled that last remaining part in her life.

He filled her again and again and again until she was stifling her cries of pleasure against his shoulder and he was groaning into her hair.

Addison knew in her heart that Felix was the one. He might not have been Prince Charming, and it might not have been fairy tale perfect. It was better. Felix was real. What they had was real. It wasn't someone else's story, but her own. The start of her happily ever after.

EVERYBODY AND THEIR DOG

Twenty minutes remained before curtain call. The tutus had been fluffed, the fur combed, the jewelry polished, and the lapels pressed. Addison was ready to start the fashion show. Only, was it still a show if there was no one there to *show*?

She peeked through the gap in the curtains for the hundredth time. She hoped all the seats had filled since she'd last looked thirty seconds before. But all she saw was Holly snapping her fingers at Hey You on the catwalk while her dad and Dora watched from the front row.

At least the reporter had followed through on her promise to host the show. Addison just hoped Hey You could angle the camera shots to avoid all the empty seats.

The air shifted behind her before two muscular arms wrapped around her waist.

473

"Don't worry," Felix whispered in her ear. "There's still time for people to show up."

Addison couldn't imagine ever being able to worry while in his arms. She spun to face him. "Thanks for helping today."

"I don't mind," he said. "Naia's having fun playing dress-up with all the dogs. And I've never seen Oliver look so dashing."

She followed his gaze. Naia was arranging a bow tie above Oliver's knitted sweater vest for the casual dress portion of the show.

Addison sighed, trying to look on the bright side of things. "If nothing else, at least Holly Hart's segment will get the show some coverage."

"And no matter what happens," Felix said, "you should be proud of yourself. You've worked hard to get here." His arms squeezed around her.

She stood on her tiptoes and kissed him. He was right; things had turned out better than they might have. Besides, out of all the drama, she'd gotten Felix and Naia.

Piper finished zipping up a camouflage jacket on Colin. "What do you think? He looks pretty cool, right?"

Addison squatted down next to him and popped the collar like the Fonz. "Very cool."

"Yeah, and I love this leather getup," Zoe said, holding up a chocolate dachshund named Peanut. "Do you have it in my size?"

Addison laughed when she saw the spicy

leather number on the dog. The vest and studded hat bordered on male stripper or S&M.

"You probably already have something just like it," Addison told her.

Zoe grinned devilishly. "You can never have too much leather."

It was at times like this that Addison could see Zoe missed her old doxie, Buddy. She'd lost him to old age only six months earlier. Of course, she put on a brave face, but they'd known each other too long for Addison not to notice. There was a sad crinkle next to Zoe's eyes as she looked sort of wistfully at all of her friends with their own dogs.

Marilyn crossed the stage, calling Picasso to come. He rolled over in his blinged-out ride, sparkling beneath the spotlights. Addison had be-dazzled the wheels and spokes of his wheelchair. They glistened as they rolled to a stop in front of her. He looked cool in his casual jean jacket, sleeves pushed up above his little dog elbows.

Melody came over and set a pair of tiny sun-glasses on top of his head to finish the look. "I was always a sucker for the bad boy."

Addison assessed the results of all their efforts and took a deep breath. "It's almost time!" she called out.

Everyone gathered around. Aiden carried So-phie, who was wearing her off-the-shoulder sweater over a flared jean skirt. Bob brought Princess over in her tutu. Since Addison and Melody would be scrambling behind the stage with wardrobe changes, he'd volunteered to walk Princess down the catwalk.

Naia dragged a reluctant Oliver over to the group. He waddled a little oddly, not used to wearing clothes—or being groomed, for that matter.

Felix glanced around at the other dogs, which all happened to be doxies. "Looks like you're the odd dog out, Oliver. Gives a whole new meaning to the term 'sausage party.'"

Both Aiden and Bob chuckled at that. But Addison took in the models with a frown. She'd hoped for a wider variety of volunteers. She had planned an array of outfits, different sizes and shapes for various breeds to show off the versatility of her line. Her "every dog" message wasn't all that effective when the only dogs she had were dachshunds and Oliver—whatever he was.

The show must go on, she reminded herself.

"I want to thank you all for being here today," Addison began. "And for all you've done to help me this weekend. I couldn't have groomed so many dogs in a single night without you slaving away alongside me. Aiden, thanks for believing in my dream and supporting me. I wouldn't be here today without your generosity. And Felix." She turned to her boyfriend, unable to keep the giddy smile off her face. "If not for you, I might not have been here at all."

Felix gave her a look that let her know he'd do it all over again. She allowed that look to fill her with love and support as she found the courage to say the next words. To explain that no one was coming to see the show except for her dad and Dora.

"Unfortunately," she began, "I have to warn you before you go out there that—"

"Wait! Wait!" a woman cried out.

Addison turned to the backstage door. Julia Edwards swept across the stage. Precious loped next to her, lengthy fur swishing around his legs like flowing skirts. And they weren't alone. Filtering in after them was a long line of purebreds and their owners. It was a parade of fur, blazers, knee-length skirts, and sensible shoes.

Julia rushed to Addison, a hand clamped over her chest as she caught her breath. Her wide eyes moved over the dogs in their outfits. "Are we too late to model?"

The newcomers drew close, staring at Addison in expectation. All the dogs and owners she'd helped that weekend had come. In fact, nearly all the rescued dogs had showed up.

Tears sprang to Addison's disbelieving eyes. She dabbed at them, grateful she'd worn waterproof mascara. It took her a few seconds to find her voice.

"Er, no. No, of course not. Please, come this

way." She gestured to the rack of carefully labeled outfits.

Melody was already flicking through sizes. "I was thinking the gym vest and shorts combo for Precious."

"Sounds perfect." Addison redirected owners to various racks.

Zoe, Marilyn, and Piper rushed to help— mostly because the three men couldn't tell the difference between chiffon and organza. Addison was swept up in the rush of getting everyone organized while Princess supervised with a critical eye, barking orders at anyone who would listen.

Snouts up, models! she ordered. *Tails perked! You over there, stop scratching!*

While Addison was doing a head count, she saw Kitty Carlisle's white beehive jostling through the crowd. When Kitty saw her, her eyes bulged, and she hurried over.

"There you are," Kitty said. "Sorry we're late."

"That's okay. I'm so glad you could make it."

"It was my fault. After it came out that Walter Boyd had …" She glanced around and spoke quietly behind her hand. "Had an inappropriate relationship with *you know who*, the association asked me to be the Best in Show judge this year. Big responsibility, you know. I just couldn't decide, so I asked for a few extra turns from the contestants."

"That's great," Addison said, already sorting

through the beachwear for Elvis. "Congratulations on the new position. Who won?"

"Precious did," Julia sang. She arranged the blue exercise headband on Precious to match the wristbands. "Didn't you, Precious? Yes, you're such a good boy, aren't you?"

"That's fantastic." Addison felt a bubble of pride that her longtime customer had won.

Rex Harrison sashayed through the door with Rosie trotting by his side. "Any room for us?"

"Absolutely," Addison said. "Rosie would be great to start the evening-wear portion." She pointed to the rack on the side. "Oh, and Melody? Can you get Kingy set up with the construction uniform?"

Someone tapped Addison's shoulder. She turned to find Kayleigh grinning at her.

She gave Addison a friendly half-hug. "We were so pleased with the work you did on such short notice. Lionel and I would love to help you out. Ooh, is this cashmere?" She reached out to rub a dress shirt between her fingers.

"Yes. I have it in Lionel's size." Addison plucked it from the rack and handed it over.

She could barely catch her breath between surprises. Her heart swelled at the sight of everyone bustling backstage.

Alistair Yates emerged from the crowd, Lily following obediently on her leash. As he approached, he leaned heavily on his cane. Addison imagined it had been a rough couple of days for him. Or weeks, rather.

"I wanted to thank you for saving Lily," he said. "I'm very sorry for the grief I have caused you."

By the number of extra winkles creasing his face, she knew he meant it. He wasn't a bad man. He'd just been taken in by the wrong person. It's not like Addison didn't have her own fair share of experiences with liars and deceivers—men she'd dated, mostly.

"I appreciate that," she finally said. "You've had a lot to deal with yourself."

"I'm happy that it's you I get to give the reward money to. You and your friend. I hope it begins to repair the damage I've done to your business." He studied the surrounding chaos. "And if you'll have us, we'd like to volunteer for your fashion show. I know Lily would enjoy it. Today is her last big hurrah, after all."

"You still showed Lily and not Fancy in the end?" She struggled to hide her surprise.

Alistair rubbed the back of his hand. "I knew Lily had no chance of winning, especially after the stress of the last couple of weeks. Maybe she wouldn't have had a chance even if things had gone smoothly. But I just wanted one more year with her. I wasn't ready to let go yet. We've been through a lot together."

Addison's heart practically melted. "Well,

since it's Lily's big day, I'm sure we can find something special for her."

"Thank you."

The backstage was a whirlwind of activity, silk, rhinestones, and ribbon. Ten minutes later, the perfect mix of breeds lined up, waiting for their big moment on stage. Tails whipped back and forth in anticipation.

It was just how Addison imagined it would be. Not a fashion line just for the elite and rich but for the everyday dog. Because every dog, from Precious to Oliver, deserved pampering, deserved to feel loved like they loved their owners and showed it every day.

Holly's head suddenly popped between the break in the curtains. "Are we all ready?"

Addison took a deep breath and cast a final glance at the lineup. "I think so." She handed Holly the cue cards with additional notes scribbled on them. "There have been some changes."

Holly took in the new arrivals. "Good, because we have a full house out there."

"What? Really?" Addison stuck her head out of the curtains.

Holly was right. Practically every seat in the house was filled. She recognized other contestants and even some judges from the dog show. Seated in the front rows, studious spectators held notebooks and cameras at the ready.

Addison nodded to them. "Who are they?"

"Oh, them? I called a few of my media friends." Holly waved a nonchalant hand, but her self-important smile gave her away.

Addison was touched that the reporter had gone above and beyond to make the fashion show special. "Thank you."

"Exclusives are only good if everyone wants a piece of the action. I couldn't very well host something no one's even heard of. It would be a waste of a PR opportunity."

Addison's smile faded slightly. "Oh … Well, thank you anyway."

Holly caught sight of Aiden and gasped. "Mr. Caldwell, I didn't know you'd be modeling today." Her breath hitched and released in a sort of shiver.

Apparently, Holly's obsession with the CEO was still going strong. Even though she worked for Channel Five News now, she'd spent years hounding him when she worked at *The Gate,* San Francisco's leading gossip magazine.

Aiden stiffened beneath her undressing eyes and held up his long-haired red dachshund. "Sophie is the model. I'm just helping out."

"But you are model material with that body and bone structure." Holly bit her lip as her gaze ran down his figure.

Addison clapped her hands to end the awkwardness. "Okay, time to go."

Holly waggled her manicured fingers at

Aiden. Addison shut the curtains on her before there could be any more delays. She heard a small huff, but then a moment later, Holly's professional reporter voice boomed from the speakers.

"Welcome dog and fashion lovers. I'm Holly Hart. You might recognize me from Channel Five News. I'm your host for the show, because I too am a fashion lover, and my dates say I can be quite the hound dog." She chuckled at her own joke.

Addison turned to the group behind her. "Everyone ready?"

She got a few thumbs up and some barks.

"Are *you* ready?" Felix asked her.

Her chest rose and her shoulders pulled back. "More than you know."

Outside, the music amped up, and Holly's voice joined it. "Let's have a look at the latest in doggy duds."

"Okay Piper, you're up," Addison said. "Good luck."

Piper gave her an excited grin and stepped up. Addison whisked to the side of the stage to peer through the curtain and watch.

As Piper and Colin walked out, Holly narrated. "First down the catwalk—or should I say dogwalk—is Colin. He's wearing a camouflage jacket that appeals to both the hunter and the city dweller with its hip, urban crossover feel."

The crowd clapped as Piper and Colin took a

turn around the catwalk.

"Next up is Sophie," Holly announced. "She's wearing a beautiful baby alpaca cable-knit sweater paired with a denim skirt. The flared skirt allows for easy movement to play in the park while being flirty enough to catch the eye of that poodle you've been after."

Aiden turned around at the end of the stage, and Holly gave him a wink.

"And of course, there's her owner Aiden Caldwell of Caldwell and Son Investments wearing …" She paused for effect. "Well, I'd prefer it if he were wearing nothing at all."

This got a few titters from the ladies in the crowd and a few of the gentlemen. Addison rolled her eyes, but she had to admit that Holly was doing a great job. She knew what the public wanted.

Marilyn and Picasso rolled out on stage to big cheers. Naia was also a big hit when she pranced out with Oliver. She got a few "aw"s and claps, which made her twirl and show off with a cheesy grin. Felix trailed behind, mostly for moral support and to make sure Oliver didn't get overexcited by the crowd. Of course, the dog of the hour, Precious, received extra cheers from the dog show fans.

There were more than enough models that most dogs only had to make two changes. When Princess came out at the end wearing a tiara and a pink ball gown with a train of real flowers, Addison was walking proudly next to her star.

She gave a gracious bow for everyone who came that day and a special wave for Dora and her dad, who wore proud smiles just for her. She might have imagined it, but it seemed like Princess gave a magnanimous bow of her blonde head, accepting the praise of her loyal subjects.

Addison turned and waved at the other participants to join her on the catwalk. One by one, they exited with their owners in tow. She held out her hands for Felix and Naia to stand with her front and center. She beamed at them in silent thanks since she wouldn't have been heard over the cheers from the crowd.

Felix returned her look, his handsome face filled with love and pride. He was proud of her, of who she was. Just the way she was. She knew in that moment that he'd always be there for her, through thick and thin. The three of them would be a family.

Everything was perfect. Exactly how she'd imagined it would be. No. It was better because she wasn't living in a fantasy world anymore. This was real life, a life that she'd built herself. As Felix took one of Addison's hands and Naia took her other for a final bow, she knew she'd finally found her happily ever after.

～

GET YOUR FREE SHORT STORY

He's a man controlled by rules. She loves to break them. She's just what he needs to find a new leash on life, but is he barking up the wrong tree?

Read the adorable meet-cute from *Paws off the Boss* through Aiden's eyes. Sign up for Casey Griffin's newsletter and receive your free short story now!

Get your FREE short story at: CaseyGriffin.com

THANK YOU FOR READING

I hope you enjoyed reading *Falling for the Underdog*. If you have a moment, I would be so grateful if you could leave an honest review online at your retailer of choice. Reviews are crucial for any author, and even just a line or two can make a huge difference. I genuinely appreciate your time and support.

Thanks!
Casey

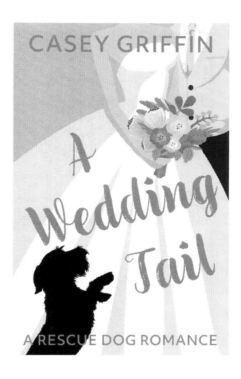

ACKNOWLEDGMENTS

I began writing *Falling for the Underdog* at a time when the changes happening in my reality coincidentally paralleled the stories happening within my writing. While this novel is purely fictional, I owe the passion and inspiration found in its pages to my partner, Devin, for simply coming into my world and giving me the life I never knew I truly needed. Thank you for the love, the support, and the wieners. You had me at "*Firefly*."

To Rose Hilliard, my biggest cheerleader and the top dog of editors, thank you for believing in me. You were always there with the best advice and puns. You had me at "wieners."

A big thank you to Dayna Reidenouer, Jennifer Herrington, and Susan Keillor who helped me get this puppy cleaned up. A special thanks to

Pat Esden and my amazing agent at the time, Pooja Menon, for helping me make this wiener rock solid before I put it into the hands of the magicians at St. Martin's Press, the most incredible team I could have asked for.

ABOUT THE AUTHOR

Casey Griffin spent her childhood dreaming up elaborate worlds and characters. Now she writes those stories down. As a jack of all trades, her resumé boasts registered nurse, heavy equipment operator, English teacher, photographer, and pizza delivery driver. She's a world traveler and has a passion for anything geeky. With a wide variety of life experiences to draw from, she loves to write stories that transport readers and make them smile. Casey lives in Southern Alberta with her family, and when she's not traveling, attending comic conventions, or watching Star Wars, she's writing every moment she can.

CASEYGRIFFIN.COM

Made in United States
Orlando, FL
22 June 2022

19038042R00276